AMBITION

CWC Collaborative Fiction Novel
Written by 26 International Authors

Copyright © 2015 CW Publishing House

All rights reserved.

ISBN: 0-9863159-3-1
ISBN-13: 978-0-9863159-3-0

ABOUT CWC

Collaborative Writing Challenge is aptly named to describe what we do. We bring aspiring writers together from all over the world to collaborate on a full-length fiction novel. We accept writers of all ages with varying degrees of experience, as we believe everyone has something to offer.

Each chapter is written by two or three different writers, and each week one is selected to form part of the ongoing novel. The experience is challenging and unique, as the writers never meet or discuss their visions for the story.

The book is guided by a story coordinator, who checks names, facts, and integrity, and who works with each chapter writer to get the best results. This story has been kissed by many hands who have yet to read the completed novel.

We also introduced a new element to CWC, a short story competition, to give our writers a chance to submit a stand-alone story to be published in the novel of the same genre. At the end of this book, you will find 'Noir Extra Dark' by **Jason Pere**. His story was selected as the winner. Our close runner-up was written by **Crystal M M Burton**, titled 'Embellished with Roses'. You can find Crystal's story on the CWC website. Congratulations to both Jason and Crystal.

For more information, please visit:
www.collaborativewritingchallenge.com

IBBY

As this is CWC's second project, 10% of profits from the sales of this book will be donated to the charity IBBY. This is a wonderful organization, dedicated to providing children from all over the world access to books.

We will be donating to the specific project called the **IBBY Fund for Children in Crisis,** which provides support for children whose lives have been disrupted through war, civil disorder, or natural disaster. The two main activities that will be supported by the Fund are the therapeutic use of books and storytelling in the form of Bibliotherapy, and the creation or replacement of selected book collections appropriate to each situation.

Please see further details about this charity by accessing their website: **www.ibby.org**

DEDICATION

This book is dedicated to all the writers who dared to get involved in a CWC collaboration. The interest in each new project is phenominal, giving the writers an opportunity to choose a prefered genre. This has resulted in an even better quality of submissions, giving the story the best chance possibe at being sucessful.

I would also like to mention my online writing friends who have brought so much fun and inspiration into my life. This encourages me to continue doing CWC and bringing people from all walks of life together!

Laura Callender - CWC Founder

THE WRITERS

We had over 39 writers involved in this project, twenty six of which had chapters selected for AMBITION. The authors came from 5 different countries.

Rather than fill these pages with details about our authors, all their pictures and bios can be found on the CWC Website. Please do stop by and learn more about our talented contributing authors. Some have very little writing experience, and some have reels of accomplishments under their belts. I think you would be hard-pressed to identify their individual chapters, and it's just possible that your favorite chapter could have been written by a fresh-faced, up-and-coming writer. There are certainly a few names that I will be looking out for in the future.

With this project it is inevitable that some writers will have their chapters rejected. We had some incredible submissions that we just couldn't use. These chapters were integral to shaping the story, as the variety in chapters gave me the chance to find the best fit. These writers are as much part of the team work that brought this project to completion so to those who go unnamed: Thank you for your wonderful contributions!

ACKNOWLEDGMENTS

This project has brought together so many talented people. Firstly I would like to thank **Moya Rooke**, who had her starter chapter AMBITION selected by her fellow writers from 8 submissions.

Our chief editor **Kathrin Hutson** has done an outstanding job getting AMBITION ready for publication. I don't know what I would do without her!

I also had the help of two assistant story coordinators. **L Vancelli** helped with the first fifteen chapters, then **Charlotte Rose Lange** assisted me from there. We also had a mid point review of this complex story, and the very talented **A J Millen** kindly volunteered her editing services to help us refine the story so far.

My biggest thanks must go to **all of our writers** who agreed to participate in this project, your imagination and dedication has made this story truly extrodiany. Every story written is unique to some degree, but with AMBITION, you would be hard pressed to find a more dynamic story that is so gripping, and it's thanks to you *all*.

Thank You!

A NOTE FROM THE STORY COORDINATOR

AMBITION is only CWC's second project, but the duration of any project lasts over 8 months. When the starter chapter was selected, I had an idea how the story may progress, but as always the writers surprised me and I very quickly became concerned. The characters and topic warranted information from the past, present and future. The complexity of keeping a multi author story on track without these challenges was mind blowing. It really took a lot of work and a sharp eye to keep it all flowing, resulting in 3 different sets of reference notes, and sometimes stricter guidance for the writers.

Despite my reservations, we managed to not only keep the story flowing, but the 3 periods covered in the story add so much depth to the characters, its hard not to fall in love with them. Also despite the variation in ages, occupations, experience, and locations of our writers, everyone still managed to find the voice of the characters and bring them forward with each chapter.

There were of course many challenges. We had weeks when no one submitted, and I called for backup writers to produce a chapter in under forty-eight hours. Some of the best chapters were written at these times. There were also weeks when I just couldn't choose between two chapters, as the writers had picked up different periods of the story that worked so wonderfully together. I frequently decided to keep both chapters which helped bring the word count up whilst also giving each separate period the focus it needed to ensure the story wasn't rushed. It truly amazes me when it all starts to come together in the final chapters. Every chapter received a minor touch up. As the coordinator is the only person to read every full chapter, the coordinators had an insight into the story that no one else did. Changes were always received well by the writers, and the chapters went on to get a full consistency edit once the story was completed.

The most challenging aspect of coordinating any story is being unable to write the next chapter yourself. I always imagine what would happen next, and I can honestly say that it never works out that way. It's very humbling to accept the fact that I don't guide or control the content of the story, but that I simply have to make the writers' visions work within the context of what had been previously written.

The coordinators collectively wrote over 17,000 words in Chapter Summaries, which the writers used as a quick reference guide to previous chapters, and I sent over 1,000 emails throughout the duration of the project . At the end of the book I have included the first chapter of CWC's third collaboration: ARK, which is also our first So-Fi collaboration. This story will be published early 2016, and is shaping up to be another wonderful example of how our unique method of collaborating is bringing to life some incredible novels. I hope you enjoy reading this book as much as I have enjoyed my part in bringing this story to life.

Laura Callender -
CWC Founder & Story Coordinator of AMBITION

CONTENTS

CHAPTER 1 - London, 1927

"So, why have you come to me?" said Delores Du Pre.

She sat at the desk in her office, which looked out over the embankment towards County Hall. The long, slender fingers of her left hand held a cigarette holder, complete with smoking cigarette, from which every so often she blew smoke rings at the young, nervous-looking girl standing the other side of her desk. She did not invite the girl to sit; the girl reminded Delores of how far she herself had come in the world. It was now 1922, and it hadn't been that long since she rose from workhouse girl to respected literary agent. It gave her a certain sense of superiority, reflecting on the fruits of her own hard-working hands.

She herself had once been a scruffy, nervous young girl, but she'd been taken in by a generous benefactor, as the man had liked to call himself. But there was very little 'prebenefitting' going on while she lived there. She was hardly ever off her knees, seeming always to be scrubbing floors. Then, a visitor who had designs on her had taught her to read, and that set her on the path that led to her current position. She could forget her origins; she wanted no one to know she'd been born in a workhouse to a gin-sodden mother and a violent father. But it was always there, under the surface, although she maintained a veneer of respectability that she never allowed slip. She had made certain assurances against anyone discovering her real origins.

The girl answered in a halting, nervous little whisper. "Because...because...I know you are the best literary agent in London."

"That much is true," Dolores crooned. "But what makes you think I would put you, an unpublished writer, on my books?"

The girl's shoulders drooped and she bowed her head in disappointment. It only contributed to the expression of a whipped puppy, but she gave no answer.

Delores enjoyed this. It was something she could share with the ladies tonight at Jemima's dinner party. "Well, are you going to answer?"

"I thought if you read my story, you might think it was good enough to publish. Then you would be prepared to put me on your books." The girl's voice was a nervous whisper.

"I am not in the habit of putting unknown writers on my books," Delores said. She knew she sounded cold. "Why on earth should I? There is little chance that I will earn any commission myself, so why bother?"

"I've come all the way from Essex in the hopes you would read this," her guest pleaded. "But I'm sorry, I seem to have wasted your time." With that, the girl turned and made quickly for the door.

Delores had enjoyed the little exchange immensely, and she could hardly wait until that evening when she could relate it, in detail, to the others over dinner. Of course, she would embellish the story. No point in surrounding herself with writers if she didn't learn a trick or two. She blew smoke in little rings as she stared out over the Embankment and thought about her rise up the social ladder. By the time she had left the big house, where she had learned to read, she had acquired other gifts as well. First and foremost came her unfaltering ambition, and after that, a readiness to claw her way to the top. If she was going to leave her poverty firmly behind, she had to be prepared to do anything. She had been at the time, and still was.

She finished her cigarette and stood to look out of what she called her 'window on the world'. She gave herself a few minutes to watch the boats in the harbor, the hustle and bustle of people going about their business. When she returned to her desk, she saw it. A paper bag lying propped up against the leg of her desk.

Oh, the silly girl has left her pile of rubbish. She tut-tutted with irritation and bent to pick it up. The idea of taking the time to look at some scruffy manuscript, brought to her in a dirty and even scruffier bag, made her laugh. The bag felt damp as well as soiled, and Delores felt her nostrils flaring as she made the unwilling effort to put it in the waste bin. She recoiled from the feel of the damp bag that, without warning, split open and scattered pages all over the floor.

Angry now, she collected the loose paper and threw it all into the bin. *Who on earth brings a dirty manuscript to a well-known literary agent without even binding it?* She glanced at one of the pages and noticed there were no contact details; the girl was an amateur. Then a phrase caught her eye. She wasn't quite sure why, but it compelled her read a few more pages. She very soon realized that this scruffy manuscript was of a quality not passed under her scrutinizing glance before.

She quickly retrieved the pages from the floor and rescued those she had thrown in the bin, some of which were crumpled and slightly damp. Carefully, she laid these out on her desk and did her best to smooth them into some semblance of neatness. The foolish girl had at least numbered the pages. It was a painstaking process to get them back into proper numerical order, but it was done. Sitting down, she lit another cigarette and started to read. She didn't reply, didn't even notice, when her staff called out goodnight. They knew better than to expect a response; the Do Not Disturb sign had been hanging from the outer handle of her door since before sat down to read.

Once she started, she couldn't put it down. Big Ben struck five, six, seven o'clock before she picked up the telephone.

"Hello, Jemima. I'm so sorry. I'm afraid something's come up that needs my urgent attention, so I won't be able to make it. Yes, I'm sorry, too. I was looking forward to it. Yes, I know it disrupts your table arrangements, but there's nothing I can do. Yes, darling, of course I will try, but don't hold out much hope. Kissee-kissee to you, too."

She slammed the phone back onto the receiver and hungrily picked up the manuscript. Her eyes sped over the dirty pages as she all but devoured the words, reading so fast her eyes watered. It surprised her when she realized suddenly read now in semi-darkness and had failed completely to notice the passage of time.

This manuscript, this dirty, unkempt manuscript, if handled correctly could make her a fortune—not as an agent for this girl, but as the writer herself! Delores' plan formed rapidly, but before she could truly act on it, she had to wait for the following morning to see if her receptionist had taken the girl's name.

It was a quarter to three in the morning before Delores finished; she had noted any edits she thought might improve what was already the best piece of fiction she had ever read. She was far too tired to return home to her flat, so she made an unheard of choice for someone who enjoyed her level of comfort. She slept on the couch in her office.

The next morning, when her staff came in, one of the young typists was astonished to find her employer quickly washing herself from the wash basin in the ladies' room.

"What are you staring at?" Delores asked, her voice heavy with fatigue. "Haven't you ever seen a woman having a strip-wash before?"

The young typist's thoughts were that she never had. Indeed, she had never seen her boss in her underwear, one foot high up in the wash basin, but she declined to comment truthfully. Instead she muttered, "I'm sorry. I didn't mean to stare. You just took me by surprise."

"Well, here's another one for you. I want you to go to Cresta Gowns and buy me some underwear."

"Do they sell underwear?" the girl inquired timidly.

"Would I be sending you there if they did not?" The agent's sarcasm was thick with annoyance.

The girl thought better than to argue. "When do you want me to go?"

"Next week." The girl nodded, and Delores rolled her eyes, flinging a hand toward the door. "Now, of course, you imbecile. Can't you see my predicament?"

"I'll go right away." The young girl moved towards the door.

"Come back, you stupid child. You need money. Cresta Gowns is not some philanthropic organization devoted to the supply of free underwear for business moguls who have spent the night on the office couch." The girl's face flushed as she stood waiting for Delores to find her purse and pluck the money she needed from within. "And mind you're quick about it." Fortunately, the girl correctly took Delores' statement as the final dismissal.

Delores quickly finished her ablutions, though she didn't like keeping on the underwear she had worn all the previous day and through the night. Despite her almost thorough wash, she did not feel clean, and her mouth was interminably sour. Her mind raced around the manuscript, and the foulest mood that gripped her was most probably due to her uncomfortable night on the couch. When she walked out into the general office room where most of the work took place, she caught two girls chatting in the corner and pounced on them.

"If you want to remain in my employ, I suggest you get on with the work I pay you to do. If not, the soup kitchens will be blessed with your appearance before close of business. Is that understood?"

"Yes, Ms. Du Pre," the girls chorused, immediately turning their attention to their typewriters.

Delores carried on through the office and out to the front desk, where her receptionist spoke on the telephone. "Put that thing down, right now," she said. Heather didn't respond quickly enough, and Delores snatched the phone from her hand and replaced it on the receiver. "I need to ask you about the girl that came to see me yesterday. Did you take her contact details?"

"Hm, no. I thought you would do that."

"Oh, did you now? Heather, I can't be expected to do everything in this damn place. That's why I employ people, mostly useless people, to share the workload. But today, that seems to be too much to ask. Have you no information on the girl at all, not even a name?"

"No, I'm sorry."

Delores turned quickly on her heel and marched back to her office. A dark smile spread slowly across her flushed face. She had heard what she wanted to hear. This was going to be easier than she thought.\l

Reaching her office, she once again put up the Do Not Disturb sign, then locked the door and pulled out the manuscript. She didn't want any witnesses to what she was about to do, and she settled herself into the most comfortable position for typing. It had been some time since she had done any typing herself, having left it mostly to her secretary, but her fingers hadn't forgotten the memory of it. The manuscript was typed, and easy enough to read, yet Delores resigned herself to the arduous task of transcribing.

She had already selected the publishers she intended to use, knowing them as quick and efficient professionals. It would be several weeks before the manuscript would be ready, and she wanted this book out and available as soon as possible. She wasn't at all concerned that the girl might see what had happened and blow the whistle. It wouldn't matter, anyway; Delores had changed the title, and when the book finally reached the shelves, its cover would give no hint of its previous provenance. Of course, Delores also had a *nom de plume*. Besides, if it came to a court of law, what chance would the girl have against her, a notorious and well-respected literary agent? The girl was a nobody. Who would listen to her?

She told her secretary to hold all non-urgent calls from the open of business each morning to three o'clock in the afternoon. After that time, she dealt with the day-to-day routine until five-thirty, and after a bite to eat she would resume typing the manuscript until she could type no more. It usually meant that she stopped around eight o'clock, because by then her head ached and her eyes refused to focus.

Eventually, the manuscript was ready to go to the publishers, even a little earlier than she had anticipated. This was an occasion to celebrate. She wanted to have a dinner party on the release day for her new book. It was a cold January morning in 1928 that finally saw '*My Death, Your Greatest Masterpiece*' released onto the bookshelves.

CHAPTER 2

"Dee-Lores, Duh-Loo-res." It had not occurred to her that she spoke aloud. It was not until the fourth odd look from Beth did she consider keeping her thoughts to herself. Angelina spent the entire morning attempting to sound like Ms. Du Pre; sultry, confident, and intriguing. After their first meeting, she knew she wanted to be like the woman. She wanted to absorb her entire being. Everything from her prim posture, leering eyes, and talon-sharp nails Angelina coveted. Above all, she wanted nothing more than to finally shed her humble beginnings.

She had bitten her nails anxiously as she made her way back down to the lobby, hoping her well-used satchel would not be discarded like old trash. She would become famous, and her stories would matter. She would travel the world and mingle with aristocrats. She would look down on the women of Essex and laugh at how foolish they were to live in such a place.

She could tell, through that entirely tough exterior, that Ms. Du Pre had once been like her. Back home, Angelina saw many variations of young girls dreaming of their chance at something more, but they always came up short. Ms. Du Pre was a rare breed, and Angelina understood that the brash demeanor was an earned characteristic of a survivor. Her thoughts went

21

back to the time she spent working for Madame Lockridge. In fact, she felt lucky to have been in her presence, in the service of such wealth. Angelina used to get lost in her tasks, imaging what would happen if the place were hers. Although it wasn't, her imagination entertained her. She was content.

She only wished she had tried harder to get Ms. Du Pre to read her story. If her had father taught her nothing else, it was that persistence paid off. She had already decided she would stay in London regardless, while she figured out how to contact her mother.

The money Madame Lockridge had given her to help her on her quest hadn't gone far. True to Madame's word, her nephew had taken Angelina in, and even provided her with work so she could earn her keep. She knew that once Ms. Du Pre came around, everything else would fall into place.

Angelina had purposely left the paper bag containing the manuscript where Ms. Du Pre would find it.

She had taken a job typing with her sister-in-law. It had not been what she expected, and once she finished typing up the manuscript she was relieved to put the cover on the typewriter for some time. She should have known her typing skills would be her strongest asset until she made a name for herself. She was grateful, though, and she always found some good in the worst situations. Madame Lockridge had prepared her well.

Angelina found herself enjoying her time in London. She started to understand how the city worked. She had only been there once before as a child and had instantaneously been enamored. The city was a burst of excitement in her mainly humdrum life, and Angelina realized she had to change. She could not survive as the meek girl from Essex.

"Time to go!" Beth sang from the corridor. It was still early, but the morning walk to work would help wake her up. She retrieved her handbag and coat off of the chair and followed Beth into the cool morning air.

"What are you waiting for?" Beth turned to her and asked.

Angelina had stopped, looking off into another direction. "If it's all the same to you, I'll meet you there," she told Beth. She thought of another route she had overhead two gentile ladies discussing, one with expensive boutiques and hat shops lining the streets. She wanted to take that walk to work, to familiarize herself with the things she would be able to buy once she became a best-selling author.

"So be it. But please don't be late."

Angelina walked a few blocks, trying to remember the directions the ladies had recounted, when she realized this was not the route she imagined. She thought, by now, finding her way around London would be second-nature, but she was painstakingly wrong. She backtracked a few blocks, but found an antique goods storefront unfamiliar. She tried turning down another path, but that was not quite right, either. She had just about given up when a man approached her. He seemed to have been watching her every move.

"I don't think that's the way. I remember you coming from that direction." He pointed just behind him. Angelina shook her head. She was suddenly frightened. As if sensing her fear, the man lowered his eyes and let out a smile. "I'm sorry. I thought you might have needed a bit of help. I thought you were lost."

Angelina looked at him, unsure if she should trust him. "You don't look like you're from here," she said.

As if noting her fear, he attempted a different approach. "Kent." Angelina only stared. "It's not polite to stare. I could be royalty!"

"Are you?" Angelina quipped, surprising herself.

Kent smiled. "I am royalty. I'm the king of...I am the king of this path." He bowed, then pointed in the same direction to which he had gestured earlier.

Angelina felt annoyed by the intrusion into her little journey, but she was quite sure the man was right. She remembered the lamppost almost hidden behind that tree.

"I can walk you to your destination, if you like," Kent said. She turned without a word, making her way past him and toward the lamppost. The man did not wait for a response, but quickened his pace to match Angelina's. The walk seemed longer with him beside her as he volleyed question after question.

Angelina of Essex would have been wooed by Kent with his tall frame, rugged face, and the body of an athlete. Just above his chin was a jagged scar and his eyes drooped just a little too low, but she allowed herself to laugh at a joke or two. The new Angelina found his line of questioning quite rude. The new Angelina also saw men like Kent as beneath her station. He did not say as much, but she could tell from his attempt at chivalry that he was nothing more than a well-dressed hoodlum. Her responses were terse and without affect.

"Why did you leave Essex?" he asked.

Angelina came to a sudden stop and turned to look directly into Kent's eyes. "I am a writer, and I came here to publish my book."

"A writer? You mean like Emily Bronte?" His eyebrows went up in mock surprise.

"Better." Angelina snorted, and the man chuckled. "Why is that funny?" She felt her face getting hot, most likely flushing bright red, and she suddenly wanted to wipe that smirk from the man's face. "I asked you a question."

Kent held his breath for a few seconds, and his smile faded a little. "Do you think me incapable of writing about passion and violence?" Angelina's stomach turned. She suddenly wished the man would disappear. He seemed to read that thought in her expression. "It's not funny, Angelina. I'm sorry. It's just that I think…well, I'm sure you are a great writer."

She shot him an icy glare. "Delores Du Pre also happens to be my agent."

Kent blinked a few times before responding, his humor replaced with unease. "You're serious." It was more of a statement than a question.

Angelina walked angrily toward the large white building finally within her sights. With a good number of women still trickling through the door, she was relived not to be late.

Kent grabbed her arm for a moment more of her time. ,Wait," he said softly. "I heard she has a new book."

This made Angelina turn around. "Who?" She pursed her lips, unable to decide if she wanted to continue speaking with him at all.

"Delores Du Pre. I've also heard it's very good." He lips pouted out at her, searching for face for whatever reaction it was he seemed to want. "I actually haven't read her work. I've just heard good things."

"Do you know the name of this book?" Angelina asked. She hadn't known Delores released a new book. She had written a few letters since their last meeting and had tried to visit, but Ms. Du Pre's assistant only told her Ms. Du Pre was traveling, and suggested she come back later. She had made seven trips in total.

"I'm not quite sure," Kent answered. "Something dark, I think. I can get it for you." She could feel how hard he tried to win at least an ounce of her interest, and she raised a brow in question. "I'll bring it to you. Wait right here." Then he hurried off.

She hadn't noticed before then that he walked with an awkward limp. It looked somewhat painful. Angelina glanced around at the slowly busying streets. It was a chilly morning, and she certainly couldn't be late, but nevertheless she silently consented to wait as Kent disappeared down the path. Once she lost sight of him, she made her way to the white building and opened the heavy wooden door. That Kent fellow must have been a fool if he thought she would truly wait for him. When she entered the building, she was greeted by a frustrated Beth.

"You just made it, Angelina. I think your explorations should wait until your day off next time. I don't want you tarnishing my reputation here."

"I'm sorry, Beth," she replied. "You know how grateful I am for this job."

The room in which they worked consisted of large wooden tables, each holding up four heavy typewriters. Angelina sat with Beth, Grace, and Anne. Each woman tended to her task with vigor. They worked with a tight deadline; Mr. Gregory was to return at half past four, and everything was to be finished by then.

Angelina found it difficult to focus with Ms. Du Pre on her mind. It unsettled her to think that maybe Ms. Du Pre had been too saddled with working on her own novel to acknowledge Angelina's. The thought then crossed her mind that perhaps Ms. Du Pre had in fact read her story, only to find it terrible. She tried to think more positively, but she could not shake the dreadful image of Ms. Du Pre burning the pages of her manuscript. She imagined the woman's face twisted in disgust, laughing at the foolish girl from Essex. Suddenly, Angelina found herself crying, and just couldn't stop.

CHAPTER 3 – Lockridge Estate, 1926

Angelina found herself doing the same tasks today she did most every day. This included the ironing and the dusting, turning down the beds, helping the cook with dinner—the regular sort of domesticity, as well as the more extreme. Her eyes were constantly on the lookout for a stray thread, wrinkle in the curtains, or possible crumb on the tablecloth. She trained herself to find flaws everywhere. The crescent-shaped crack on the ceiling above her bed, the crookedness of a painting in the living room—she noticed any slight acute angle the frame made with the trim on the floor. But Angelina's main fixation was the large ornate rug sitting in the center of the living room.

She and the rug knew each other very well at this point, for she found herself inspecting it at least five times a day on Madame's request. Its intricacy was burned into her memory, and she often saw it at night when she closed her eyes. This did not bother her, however. She thought the rug beautiful, and often imagined herself melting into the design and becoming part of some greater and fantastical story. Her eyes roamed across the different shapes, tracing the floral patterns as Madame would chastise her. Of course, she would need to reply a few obligatory "Yes, Madame"s and "No, Madame"s every time she heard the questioning intonation in her employer's voice. Madame did not particularly like to be ignored.

'Immaculate' was Madame's favorite word, and she did not hesitate to incorporate it heavily in her vocabulary. "One's home is the greatest reflection of one's soul," she would say, "and I like to think my soul is a clean, pure, and masterful piece of art that does not include any of your stringy black hairs, Angelina. We must keep this home immaculate." Madame would always put a dramatic emphasis on the second syllable. Angelina anticipated it every time; it had sort of a musical sound to it.

Angelina did her best to make sure Madame's home was a clean, pure, masterful piece of art, to the greatest extent that would not compromise her sanity. She put up with all Madame's strange philosophies and musings on art, music, and such. Listening to her rants, Angelina sensed how lonely Madame was and how she enjoyed being heard. Angelina loved the dramatizations and learning new things, even if most of it wasn't completely related to her duties. During the designated reading time Madame assigned to all her servants, Angelina would quell any skepticism she acquired from Madame's "wisdom". Angelina saw that, most definitely, Madame's sanity was compromised, but it would be inhumane for her not to at least try to indulge the crazy woman's obsessive perfectionism.

Besides desiring to be a well-mannered and kind-hearted person, Angelina just really needed to do a great job. She was surprised to be pulled out of school and thrust into a career as a housemaid. After her mother left, her father had no clue what to do with her, and was relieved when a young woman, visiting on behalf of Madame Lockridge, showed up on their doorstep. She had been sent to fetch Angelina for a swift interview the estate, Madame having heard about their unfortunate situation. Of course, Angelina had no idea how this woman could possibly have known that her mother had left, but she didn't mind. The prospect of becoming her father's aide had worried her.

After an interview that was seemingly more like an interrogation, and somewhat rigorous physical testing, Angelina always felt she would need to be particularly careful in order to keep her job, and was used to being on her toes all the time. She used the phrase literally, as well, for she quite liked to imagine herself a ballerina when she performs her everyday tasks.

Madame made it very clear that, while Angelina was only fifteen, her schooling would not stop. The woman wanted her to learn the skills of a typist, which at first Angelina found very intriguing. She felt fortunate to live in a nice house, with friendly staff that were kind to her. She worked hard at her duties and her studies, always eager to impress Madame's keen eye. She always felt Madam kept a particularly close watch on her, but never really thought too much of it.

A few months after her acceptance into the Lockridge household, Angelina adopted a more lax attitude, knowing the general perception of Madame Lockridge among the townspeople. Those previously employed by the woman had no sympathy for her quirks and, while understandably quitting, used Madame's antics and personality as the butt of jokes. The woman seemed to have become a character in stories to teach children how not to behave in social settings. Because of this, Madame did not technically have the number of servants the grand house warranted. But since she was the only person living there, and visitors where rarer than a raspberry jam stain on her skirt from her morning crumpet, the staff was sufficient. She made it a point to personally correct and speak to the servants. Madame seemed to want to *understand* them, wanting to know why they thought it was okay to polish the sculpture in that absurd pattern, or some such thing. Her "lessons" and demands to know everyone's motives were attributed partly to her loneliness and partly to her ego. Angelina didn't mind the lack of professional boundary. It just meant greater job security at the cost of being a bit more uncomfortable.

And she really did feel sorry for Madame. Today, however, Madame seemed more exuberant than ever. She pranced down the grand staircase to see Angelina dusting the entry table.

"You've missed a spot, my darling."

"Well, of course I have. I just began dusting, so most of the table would be the 'spot', now, wouldn't it?" Angelina replied playfully, still careful to watch her tone. She looked up and gasped as she took in Madame's appearance.

The woman wasn't listening, and instead remained busy admiring herself in the large, gold-trimmed mirror in the foyer. Madame kept mirrors everywhere, no matter the function of the room, for she believed it prudent one knew what one looked like while they performed any task. It was an important part of becoming self-aware. "You are all my little works of art. It's only natural that you are displayed on the walls, too!" Madame would remind her servants of this once in a while.

The work of art in the mirror opposite Madame was an explosion of color that one might say rivaled the eccentricity, as well as bizarreness, of a surrealist painting. She'd placed a hat on her head, complete with what seemed to be the feathers of a tropical bird. The colors ranged from a deep violet, to a shocking green, to an orange as vibrant as the most intense of sunsets. Her dress didn't seem to have any communion with her hat, and looked to be from another era. It was powder blue with copious amounts of ruffles—one had trouble distinguishing where parts of the satin fabric began and ended. The collar of the dress had some sort of rubies sewn into it, and while the dress itself looked a bit faded, in another time it may have been considered beautiful. She'd finished off the look with dark blue velvet heels with a pink rose embroidered on the side. Madame was surely a most interesting sight to be seen.

"It's all quite lovely, isn't it? You've probably never seen a person so finely dressed, Angelina. Drink it in, my dear, for it isn't every day I look this beautiful," Madame sang as she spun around. Her dress made quite a wonderful, whooshing sound.

"Yes, Madame. You look quite wonderful indeed! May I ask, though, what the occasion is?"

Madame stopped spinning. "Occasion? Does one need an occasion just to express life and beauty in the form of fabrics and gemstones and shoes? Does one need an occasion to breathe? If I recognized the confines of the necessity of 'occasions' to merit permission to randomly turn myself into the beautiful vision that stands before you, I would not want to live in a world as sad as that."

Angelina stood up on her toes. "I only meant—"

"That being true and said, coincidentally, there *is* an occasion today, my angel. We are going into town!"

Angelina breathed a sigh of relief and resumed dusting. "Oh, is that so? Well, I guess I better go clean up then, haven't I?"

Angelina knew Madame hadn't left the estate in over twenty years. When Ruth, the cook, told this to her, she obviously had her doubts. She thought it some playful joke that the staff told the newcomers. Ruth always joked about like that, teasing everyone. Her wit was as sharp as the paring knife she kept nestled in her hair bun.

"So I don't keep losing the bloomin' thing," she would say to any inquirer.

As time went on, though, Angelina began to see how

31

Madame was exactly the kind of person to never leave the house. And she could relate, for the most part. Angelina enjoyed staying on the property. It had everything she needed, and she was comfortable there. More comfortable than at home on the farm. Though she enjoyed the occasional outing into town, after a while, she just wanted to get back to her bed or the library room.

Angelina had been working at Lockridge household for almost a year now. Once every couple of months, Madame planned and arranged for a dinner party, whose guests were always no-shows. The excuses Madame told after these failed attempts rivaled something straight out of a novel.

"Amazingly enough, the Edwards' home burned down, so they've got to be dealing with that, and at the same time the Fletchers' little boy has come down with tuberculosis. So, of course, they're dealing with that! Rubbish how people can't commit to plans these days."

All the staff would just nod and agree with how inconsiderate her 'guests' had been. Then Madame would retire to her room, allowing the servants to throw their own little dinner party. The imaginary guests were never mentioned again.

Madame had proclaimed only one other time during Angelina's stay that she would be going out. It was while Angelina hung the laundry to dry. Madame had come out with flowers stuck all over her hair. She danced and exclaimed how the day was going to be wonderful, and how Angelina needed to get ready.

Of course, it ended the way Angelina expected it to also end today. Madame would wait for Angelina to clean up and change, and then inform her that, unfortunately, she'd come down with a head cold and that she must rest.

"It would be utterly disappointing to you and myself if we went whilst I'm in a bad humor. My health comes first, love.

Don't be so selfish."

After Madame would retire to her room, Angelina would spend the rest of the day reading or singing in the fields. She knew Madame wouldn't be returning downstairs for a while.

Angelina fully expected the same ending today, but, to everyone's surprise, Madame had the stable boy get the carriage ready. The poor boy was but eleven years old, but also assumed the job of the driver. This was to be expected from the Lockridge household, so the townspeople didn't give a second glance when he came riding into town. He was actually quite good at his job, although he couldn't quite yet be bothered to put shoes on.

"I have something special in mind for us, Angelina. Today is the beginning of a new era! We are getting a typewriter. And with that typewriter, you will write the story of my life."

Angelina suddenly found herself a tad worried, and realized she had started to sweat.

As they rode away from the house, Angelina watched everything grow smaller in the distance. She looked at the passing trees, then down to the dirt road. She liked the way things whizzed past her eyes. No one enjoyed a carriage ride more than her. Angelina sometimes wondered if maybe she wasn't rocked enough as a baby, and that was why she loved the motion of the carriage so. She didn't wonder about it too much, though.

Angelina glanced at Madame on the carriage seat across from her. The woman expressed an indeterminable expression; her mind must have been somewhere else. Her lips looked relaxed and slightly upturned, but her eyes reflected something else entirely. Madame stared out the window, but Angelina didn't think the woman actually focused on admiring the trees or the ground. She thought Madame was remembering something. Angelina saw hope in her eyes, and something sad. But most of all, she saw fear.

"Yes, my dear angel. Today is the day I finally tell someone my story. The story of why I had to murder my husband. My dear, dear Jonathan."

CHAPTER 4

What did she just say? Angelina blinked in rapid succession at Madame, suddenly at a loss for more than just her words, but for breathe itself. She attempted to swallow, hoping she could digest the words just spoken and deposit them into the part of her brain that discards all the insignificant details of her day-to-day life. Suddenly realizing she still gazed at Madame with a cold, blank stare of absolute confusion, she forced her eyes downward to her petite hands. As she examined her hands in hopes of mentally retreating from what Madame had just said, she noticed how cracked and horribly dry they were. Nothing but stubs existed where long, strong nails had once appeared attractively. What if Madame really had just shared that horrific detail with her? What if she hadn't just heard incorrectly? Would she be able to sit there, obediently listening to the details of a murder?

Angelina debated all this in the pits of her mind while staring down at her hands, which now rested on her legs that had turned to gelatin. She attempted to calm her erratic and trembling legs, as if to keep from revealing the wave of fear now drowning her serenity. She pressed down lightly on her legs, abruptly noticing that her hands were far stronger than she realized. Pressing her hands further onto her thighs, she felt the firmness of her arms—a power that had not been there before entering Madame's employ.

Working for Madame was a pleasure Angelina had only dreamed about as a young girl. She had expected to follow in the footsteps of her mother, whose life had been solely dedicated to the maintenance of the home. Angelina had watched her broad-shouldered, tough-as-nails father go off to work at the mines every week, and anxiously awaited his return on Fridays. However, she could never remember a time in which her mother would leave the house for any other reason than to visit the market for vegetables, when those in her beloved garden had not quite matured yet. Angelina recalled a time in her blurry childhood when she had accompanied her young mother, Elizabeth, to the farmer's market near their home. It was the first pleasant day they had experienced since the end of a brutally cold winter, and her mother had frolicked in the midst of beautifully ripe and delicious fruits and vegetables. Her mother's favorite stand of all, however, was the jam table. She visited once a week, and told Angelina that she saved up every penny Angelina's father had given her in order to restock the delectable strawberry jam she adored.

Angelina, in all her childhood mischief, had normally scampered around all the poorly made booths, tugging annoyingly at every tablecloth. But for some reason, on this particular day she decided to stay at her mother's side. As her mother inspected the stand for her strawberry jam, Angelina could not help but admire how beautiful her mother was. The midday sunlight beamed gloriously through the tree branches above them, hitting the fruit-filled jars perfectly so they reflected a rainbow, illuminating her mother's face. Her hair, dark as night, contrasted dramatically with her pale skin, which consequently made everything about her face stand out. Her lips were plump, but not too full as to distract one's attention away from her bright auburn eyes and perky nose.

Looking up at her mother, Angelina had not been able to help but wonder why her ravishingly beautiful mother condemned herself to staying home every day when she could be out exploring the world and having other naturally colorful patterns reflected upon her beauty. Then, day after day, she'd watched her mother's soul grow weary and dark. She'd listened to her mother moping about the small, shack-like structure that was their home, waiting anxiously, as each day passed, for Angelina's father to return home. Upon his arrival, the two would only end up arguing violently about money or his unexplained tardiness. Elizabeth had nothing to fill up her days but her daughter, and the hope that she would one day wake up and have something to do that made getting out of bed worthwhile. Angelina had watched her mother's soul deteriorate until, one day when she was fifteen, she awoke to a handwritten letter on her makeshift bedside table:

Angelina,

I'm sorry I cannot be the ray of sunshine a child like you deserves of her mother. It's not that I don't want you, because you are the biggest part of me, the best part of me. I simply cannot continue to keep living the way I have. This life suffocates me, and I need to run away from it before I come to any harm. I'm doing you a favor, my angel. I am merely discovering what it's like outside these walls. I am tired, my angel, of having nothing to wake to but an empty bed and no one to lay down with at night but an unhappy husband. I'm not sure when I will be back. I may return when I find something out there in this wide world that I can do for work while also making sure you are safe. For now, however, I have to take this first step, and I hope you never have to be pushed to the limits I've experienced myself. Do not waste your time on men, my beautiful angel. Do not submit yourself to the act of having to beg your own husband for a penny or two. Instead, learn to support yourself. Distract yourself, explore, and listen widely to all the stories you are offered, for there are people in this world like me who have many tales to tell. Until we meet again, my love.

Those were the last of Elizabeth's thoughts, and the last piece of her mother to which Angelina had grasped a hold for the rest of her young adulthood. She would often recite the letter she knew by heart whilst she busied herself working. She'd searched for a clue amongst the beautifully handwritten letters decorating the worn sheet of paper.

Madame had given Angelina the chance she needed to avoid falling into her mother's small footsteps, and for that she was eternally grateful. The memory of her mother's advice before she'd left indefinitely flooded back to her. She realized it had been Madame who had gifted her the opportunity to honor her mother's words, and she knew it was important for her to hear every word Madame had to say. Angelina snapped back to reality.

She lifted her head for the first time in what seemed like hours; her anxious gaze locked with Madame's. At that moment, Angelina realized she owed it to this woman to listen to whatever brutality existed behind her wicked story. Before she could inquire further about the events leading to Jonathan's murder, the carriage stopped with a quick and violent jolt.

Distracted by Madame's revelation, Angelina had not even realized they had not only already arrived in town, but they had now stopped directly outside the Stanley Brothers Typewriters and Amenities store.

Madame, unfazed by the fact that she had finally released her secret to someone, quickly stepped out of the carriage. She darted for the entrance of the store, and Angelina followed in her wake. Inside, they found the space cramped with everything one might need, ranging from a row of delectable-looking chocolate bars to knit scarves, and, of course, typewriters. The walls had been painted a soft vanilla-white, although hardly more than a sliver of any wall could be seen behind the dozens of typewriters stacked upon the shelves. Madame rushed through her purchase, selecting the first typewriter the blonde-haired boy behind the counter suggested. She moved excitedly, both from the exhilaration of finally sharing her life story in ink and the anxious gnawing in her subconscious, begging her to get home as soon as possible.

Once back in her luxurious home abode of comfort, Madame immediately put Angelina's typing skills to the test. "I'm going to need you to be able to type as quickly and as coherently as you possibly can, Angelina, because once I get started on this story, I don't wish to stop until it is complete. Do you think you can handle that?'' Madame asked in her most understanding tone.

"Of course I can, Madame. I will type both as fast as I possibly can while watching my grammar," Angelina replied respectfully, now realizing that her fear has been replaced with the curiosity of her six-year-old self. At that, Madame retold the events leading to what she called 'the last of her life', as Angelina typed furiously in the corner of the maroon-walled study.

"I loved Jonathan with every part of my soul. He was this blazing star that spread across my dimly lit sky, and I could not imagine a night without his glow," Madame began. There was a sparkle in her eyes as she spoke, a sparkle one could only find in the eyes of someone reminiscing about a lost love. A sparkle with both undeniable love and sorrow in its grasp.

CWC – Ambition

CHAPTER 5

Madame Lockridge had barely begun when she was interrupted by a sigh and moan from Angelina. She ruffled her velvet overcoat and shuffled in her chaise lounge in an attempt to patiently berate Angelina for the distraction.

"I just need to insert another page of paper. One moment." Angelina was flustered.

"You almost look as though you've never used one of these before, but we both know that's not true. What has gotten into you, my dear?"

"I think every machine is different, Madame. While I love this brand new model, I think I'm used to the old typewriter I've used to practice."

"Well, you better get used to this one quickly. This story deserves to be typed on the best typewriter there is, not some old piece of forgotten junk that prints a substandard 'J' every time. Honestly."

Angelina was surprised that Madame had noticed that slight alignment problem, which meant the woman had obviously been reading her work. She felt quite pleased about that, and wondered if Madame had enjoyed any of her typed stories.

"I'm ready when you are," Angelina announced,

straightening her posture in the high-backed chair.

"As I was saying, I met Jonathan on 23rd November, 1864. I remember the date well, because it was the year my friends and I all turned twenty. I'd had my birthday earlier on in the year, in February, but this was Josephine's birthday and the last we'd be celebrating that year. We had gone to so many soirées. Each had to be bigger and more expensive than the last, and for this, I must say, my father was quite glad I had been born in February. My birthday was the twenty-ninth of February, and this was a leap year, so I didn't get a big party like everyone else. Instead, I had a dinner party thrown for me with all my father's colleagues. You'd think it was his birthday we were celebrating. Josephine's event, however, was a party to remember.

"Champagne flowed and musicians played popular numbers. I always loved 'Silver Threads Among the Gold', sung by Elsie Baker. She did such a wonderful job of it that night. Jonathon approached me without me even knowing I had been approached. His wispy, tall figure allowed him to move across a room like a ghost. His facial hair reached down the sides of his face and below his chin, but remained separate from his narrow mustache, which he wore curled upwards. He kept his hair longer on top, but styled with a side-parting to the right. It was a very dapper style at the time, accentuated by his frilled shirt and cravat. He carried his top hat in his hand, though. He certainly didn't need it, as others did, to add to the illusion of height."

"Madame, please forgive me interrupting. I can't type at the speed of your story. I'm afraid I'll have to write notes while you speak and type it up later, if that suits you." Angelina hands were already sore from the very first part of this story. She noticed how dry they were from the day before, and berated herself silently for not moisturizing with the hand cream Madame had given her at Christmas.

"Angelina, I'm making an admission no one else has ever heard. It's important that it's presented as fiction and never read otherwise."

"I apologize, Madame, but I really want to make sure I don't leave anything out."

"Well then." Madame sighed "If this is how it is to be, I must insist the whole handwritten copy is burned, bit by bit in the fire, after you've typed it."

"Absolutely, Madame. I'd have it no other way. Please continue."

"As I said, Jonathan was quite suave. He reached for my hand and kissed the back of it. I never blushed so much before in my life. I remember not knowing where to look, but as my eyes darted about in my timidity, I noticed our encounter had caught the attention of many people in the room. I'm sure this made me all the more rouge. My father also saw this take place, and positioned himself closer in a very Victorian way.

"Jonathan introduced himself and mentioned he had heard about me through an acquaintance. I couldn't tell you who that was, because I barely remember him saying it myself. I was too mesmerized by this handsome young man, taking in all the little details about him. I didn't want to forget how much of a gentleman he was.

"He asked if I wanted to go somewhere quieter to talk, and it suddenly became obvious to me how close we stood to both the band and my father's ever-curious ear. He held my elbow and led me towards the large, open bay window, where I was finally able to catch my breath.

"We spoke for almost two hours that night about our favorite music and the books we had read, stories of hunting trips and rumors we had heard of mutual friends. We had so many similar interests, and we talked as if we had known one another before. He again mentioned our mutual acquaintance, but I only vaguely knew of whom he spoke. Some old school friend of his who worked with my father, but he certainly knew a lot about me.

"The former Lady Lockridge, Jonathan's mother, strode over to us with impeccable confidence. She was the epitome of Victorian elegance, slim in a beautiful silk dress, gloves of lace, and a well-matched but subtle tiara. Without even acknowledging me, she stood directly in front of Jonathon and bossed him around as though he were no different than her beloved King Charles spaniel.

"She excitedly told Jonathan that Miss Heathburn had arrived, and ushered him to the door to greet her. He was very polite and excused himself, then discreetly rolled his eyes with a smile on his face as he stepped back and glided across the room.

"I watched him from behind a pillar. Beside him, his mother bounced on her toes, eagerly trying to get a better look down the hall as they awaited the arrival of this so-called Miss Heathburn. Jonathan looked up and around the room. I think he was looking for me, but of course, I can't be sure. I watched his fussy mother interrupt him again as she clearly tutted, insisting he tidy his cravat.

"Valerie, my childhood friend, skirted up to me and followed my lingering gaze on Jonathon, saying I should forget about him altogether. She told me, as the rumor went, that he would soon be engaged to Miss Heathburn. My heart shattered right there, but Valerie continued to say they would be married week's end if his mother had anything to do with it. Apparently, she had been pushing him in the woman's direction for over a month.

"I surprised myself when I bitterly asked who that

Heathburn girl was. Valerie looked at me, puzzled that I could be so interested. I had never shown any interest in other men my age before, and I knew she could tell Jonathan had gotten to me. She reluctantly confided that Miss Heathburn had recently moved from Cornwall. Her father had died suddenly while out on his horse, and her mother had died young years before. The girl's aunt, who lived somewhere nearby us, had taken her in. I feigned sympathy for this Miss Heathburn, but jealousy overcame me. To make it worse, Valerie then went on to tell me that Heathburn was the sole heir to her father's fortune and was certainly not poor by any means.

"As the girl entered, every mother and her eligible son gradually filled the lobby to surround her. She had the pick of every eligible bachelor present, and I was sure she would go after the one man who had ever caught my eye.

"I suddenly felt quite unwell, so I made my excuses and left. My father certainly didn't mind, so long as I took my mother with me as my chaperone. Holding back the tears was all I could do during the journey home, but crying into my pillow without making a sound was even harder."

Madame Lockridge sighed heavily. "Goodness, is that the time? How it slips away from you. I think that is enough for today, my dear. I'm feeling quite weary."

"Very good, Madame. We made a good start."

"I think I'll have supper in my room, tonight. Please let Ruth know." Madame Lockridge looked for her walking stick, which Angelina quickly reached for and handed to her.

"Of course, Madame. I'll get right to it."

Angelina looked at the clock and was surprised to find how quickly the afternoon had vanished. She placed the cover over the temporarily discarded typewriter, longing to start typing up her notes before the job became too daunting. She was simply too tired to do anything now. Writing for a long period like this had awakened her more redundant muscles. Her body ached, and she stretched in response.

She walked back to her quarters via the kitchen to relay Madame's request to Ruth, deep in thought about the task at hand. Angelina knew this story would take up more of her time than she would have liked, but she now realized she had been groomed for this purpose. So far, the story intrigued her, and she knew the best was yet to come.

"What on earth have I gotten myself into?"

CHAPTER 6

Angelina's attempts to live up to her mother's wishes had become stagnant. Although she was independent, she had yet to see anything beyond Madame's walls. Transcribing Madame's memoirs might provide her with a new way to view the world through the past.

Once back in her quarters, Angelina thought about her own life. What did she have worth telling? So far, she had no answers, but she was determined to find them. Perhaps Madame's story was the way. Angelina herself had dabbled with fiction before, having been pushed by Madame to spend time on the typewriter. Her imagination was quite something, but she felt held back by the lack of inspiration she received from real experiences. She fell asleep thinking of what might come of all this.

***

"Angelina. For goodness' sake, girl, get up!" Madame yelled at her from the foot of her bed. Normally, Angelina wouldn't be caught dead in the servant's quarters, but then again, nothing had been the same of late. "This is no time to dilly dally!

Jonathan has been haunting me all night. I haven't slept a wink."
Madame was a sight to see in her silk evening dress, pacing back
and forth, her cane knocking about the floor.

"What time is it?" Angelina muttered as she looked
towards the clock. Her small quarters had a tiny window facing
the estate's stables. It was three in the morning, completely dark
outside, and she wouldn't normally be up for another two hours.

"Make it quick, darling!"

With that, Angelina hopped out of bed. Madame didn't
even let her change from her nightgown and insisted they
continue right there in her room. Angelina took out her notes
from the evening prior, not wanting to disturb anyone else at this
unfavorable hour to fetch the typewriter. Through half-open eyes,
she watched Madame pace impatiently. The sleepy fog had
barely lifted, but she sucked in a breath of air and hoped Madame
wouldn't dictate too quickly. She had never seen this sort of
fervor in the woman before and wondered what had changed.

"Now, where was I? Ah yes, the tears. At such a young
age, everything seems like it's much bigger than it actually is,
and I was sure my romance was over even before it had begun.
Tears shed for a man are tears wasted, but I suppose that comes
later on in the story.

"The next day, Valerie came to pay me a visit. I tried to
turn her away, but she insisted it was urgent. She was always the
first to know everything. How she came about the knowledge
was sometimes beyond me. She had noticed my interest the night
prior, and today's gossip was about Jonathan. Apparently, after I
had left, Miss Heathburn snuck away from the party. Naturally,
being the snoop she was, Valerie followed her into the ladies'
room in which she found her hunched over the toilet, vomiting.
The little rich girl was pregnant. As it turns out, her aunt just also
happened to be a midwife. It was all very convenient for her. It

was absolutely impossible that Jonathan's mother would push for a marriage once news of this got out. Oh, I was elated at the news. I made it my mission to expose her as the unfit lady she was.

"This is where it all began. It was the first time I ever got my hands dirty, and there really is no turning back once you do.

"Valerie and I began scheming a plan to ruin Miss Heathburn's reputation. Well, she had naturally done most of the work herself. To think, unwed and pregnant. The poor thing. I do have some sympathy for her, looking back at it now. "

Angelina nodded politely. Her eyelids felt heavy and her scribbling, although legible, wasn't quite as neat as before.

"There was a benefit tea to be held the next day at the Lockridge residence. Lady Lockridge was a very charitable woman, always hosting a benefit for this or that. My mother was scheduled to attend, and it took no convincing at all to secure myself a seat at the table. After all, now that I was a woman of twenty, it was my duty to be charitable as well. Miss Heathburn was bound to be there, with Lady Lockridge taking her under her wing in attempts to mold her into the perfect daughter-in-law. Sure enough, there she sat, to the right of Lady Lockridge. She looked stunning. I suppose what I felt was jealous. How odd, to be jealous of someone I had yet to really know. I suppose love really does drive one mad. I still remember Lady Lockridge's face when she found out. She almost choked on her tea—a priceless moment.

"However, it didn't exactly put me in Lady Lockridge's good graces. My gossiping made me appear unrefined. Me. Unrefined! But after that night, Jonathan and I began seeing each other in secret. Having spared him from the fate of taking Miss Heathburn as his wife, Jonathan became spellbound by me, intensifying the passion that had already sparked between us at

Josephine's soiree. Our bond grew immensely over the next few months. I suppose the same could be said for Miss Heathburn." Madame snickered at her own wit.

"The time came when Jonathan was to be married. He had a legacy to uphold, and I was afraid I would not fit into that legacy. After all, a man puts nothing in front of his legacy, and until then I had merely been a well-kept secret. A secret is no place for a woman. Without Lady Lockridge's approval, I feared the love I shared with Jonathon would not be enough for him to choose me. I would have done anything for the man, but would he do the same for me? In fact, it is the answer to that same question that later caused his death. Are you listening, dear?"

Angelina had stopped writing. "Oh, yes, every word." She attempted to conceal a slight yawn, then met Madame's gaze with a sheepish look of apology. "I apologize. It's quite early for me."

"I suppose that is enough for now. You have your regular duties to attend to this morning. Please have the kitchen hold my breakfast. I do believe I will sleep in," Madame said as she walked purposefully towards the door.

Angelina followed close behind. "Whatever became of Miss Heathburn?" The words escaped Angelina's mouth before she could stop them.

Madame turned around with a smile. She looked at Angelina with a glimmer of fondness in her eye. "Why, you know her. Miss Heathburn's first name is Elizabeth."

Madame left Angelina then, but her words lingered in the room. Angelina's thoughts flashed to the letter she kept beneath her pillow and the life she had lived in order to fulfill its wishes. Could it have been a coincidence that she ended up on Madame's doorstep that day, looking for a job? Or had she been hired out of pity?

The latter seemed infinitely more possible with the sobering revelation that Miss Heathburn was Angelina's mother.

CHAPTER 7 – London, 1928

"Angelina. Angelina!" Beth stood, waving her hands in front of Angelina's face and trying to get her attention.

"Oh. I'm sorry Beth. I...I was just thinking again. You know how I get lost in my daydreams sometimes. I was thinking about Madame Lockridge, about my time working for her. That's all." Angelina stood from her stool and walked to the large window on the second floor of the White Building. She loved gazing outside, especially during the warm seasons, when daylight lasted a bit longer. The sun would settle, often spreading streams of peach, gold, and lavender across the sky. Angelina loved those days. She'd look out at the beauty of the sunset and feel a moment of hope, a sigh of relief, from all the duties and the worries somehow always placed upon her.

At least at this job, she was lucky enough to have a view, which afforded her the luxury to daydream. The management were very nice, and as long as the work was done, they were pretty much left to it. Angelina had become a very fast typist indeed, and she found the work to be more than manageable. She prided herself on her speed paired with her accuracy, unlike her time spent with Madame Lockridge, reverting to taking notes.

Because she worked so fast, she was often sent on errands

to deliver documents around the building. She liked the quiet dominating the mostly empty hallways, and she would often get lost in her thoughts. Madame Lockridge came to mind often, as well as Delores Du Pre and the manuscript. But on really rough days, she thought about her mother. She wondered where she was, what she was doing. Was her mother seeing the world? Did she think of her still? Miss her even? Would she ever make it to London, and if she did, where would she go? Those days when she envisioned her mother's beautiful face and their days at the market were just dreadful. But lately the most dreadful days involved something else altogether. Her most horrible days spent meandering around the offices occurred whenever she thought of *him.*

"Angelina, is something wrong? Are you feeling well?" Beth had just returned from a tea break, and caught Angelina looking dazed.

"No, I'm not, but...but..."

"Do you want to talk about it?"

Beth knew how difficult Angelina had found it to adjust. She'd come off the coach from Essex with a strange mixture of excitement and trepidation. Beth had only met Madame Lockridge once, just before her wedding to Eugene. They visited Eugene's aunt, knowing she wasn't going to make it to the wedding. She remembered Madame being an unusual woman, and often wondered how Angelina's life had been in that household. She didn't know the details of why Angelina had come to stay, and the only thing Madame Lockridge had said was that Angelina had hoped to find her mother. Madame had been kind to them over the years, and they didn't hesitate to take Angelina in when she'd come to town.

Angelina and Beth had become quite close lately. Beth had a way about her, a way of making everyone feel safe. She was bold, brave, and brash, according to some. Angelina wanted to tell Beth how she felt, but was too afraid, too timid. Their personalities were complete opposites.

Angelina turned her face away, trying to hide the tear she couldn't prevent from rolling down her face.

"I can see you crying. Please sit for a moment. I don't think it's wise to go back into the workroom in this state. You know how the women like to talk."

"I'm afraid, Beth."

Beth took Angelina's hands and whispered back, "Don't be silly."

Angelina looked at Beth for a moment, with her big, brown, almond-shaped eyes and her golden hair, cut into the latest short hair style. Beth wasn't afraid of anything, at least she didn't seem to be. Like the haircut. Many men and society women thought this new look a disgrace. People thought a woman had no right wearing short hair, revealing their necks, in this new style they called a 'bob'.

But Eugene didn't think that way, and neither did Beth. Together the couple often went to their friends' apartments to listen to a new style of music called Jazz, and they smoked cigarettes, and talked about the artists and writers in Paris. They danced in a manner that caused ladies of an older age, those of the Victorian era, to shake their heads and sigh with disgusted disapproval.

Beth had also bought a copy of the scandalous book 'Women In Love' by D. H. Lawrence, as soon as it had finally been allowed to go to publication in London, just the year before in 1921. She'd had to go to the East End section of the city, the only part of London where a woman could buy such a novel. She had lent the book to Angelina as soon as she finished reading, and Angelina read a couple pages every night. It was an arduous task for her, as she would frequently pause to imagine her own story in print, wishing she would hear from Du Pre at some point.

Surely I should be able to tell her, Angelina thought after that memory. *'Surely she would understand.* But she had to say something. "I'm afraid to tell you what's bothering me today, Beth, and it's nothing like what I've spoken with you before about my mother."

Beth brushed back a piece of Angelina's long wavy hair from her face. "You can tell me anything, anything at all," she whispered. She pulled Angelina into a side room used as an additional stock area for supplies. She directed Angelina to sit on a large wooden crate while she positioned a smaller one for herself just next to it. "Now, go ahead. Tell me everything."

Angelina looked down at her feet, still not able to speak. Then she took a deep breath. "Well, it has to do with, with Henry."

Beth leaned closer and whispered, "Who's Henry?"

"Have you seen the man who sometimes comes into the typing room from the offices upstairs? He's brought work directly to me a few times. He's very professional and polite."

"Yes, of course. Everyone knows he prefers to give his work to you. He's usually only here for a few minutes, though." Beth stood and crossed her arms, saying in a louder voice, "Why? Did he say something to you? He didn't hurt you or anything? And how do you know his name?"

Angelina felt her face flush with a shy warmth, but suddenly it all came out. It flowed from inside the depths of her heart, and she spoke almost without even taking a breath. "Oh, no, no, Beth. Not at all. It's just, well...I think...I think I like him. No. Actually, I think I love him. No, actually, I do love him. I do. I think of him all the time. I think about his dark hair, his handsome face. His eyes—they aren't squinty. They're round and soft, and his face is, well, it's so kind. I often think what it would be like if he could be my husband one day. I see myself in a beautiful pink dress, dancing with him at some fancy party. I'm looking up at him and he looks at me and we're both smiling. I always think of how he's taller than me, that he has broad shoulders and looks so strong. I love how he holds his pencil over his ear, how he walks, how he carries his papers, how he smiles." Angelina took an exasperated breath, and chanced a glance up at Beth, who only smiled.

"Whenever I go up there to return his work, he always greets me so warmly. I really feel there's a connection between us. Then, just the other day, I saw a letter on his desk, addressed to him. It said, 'Dear Henry Parker,' but I didn't read any more of it. I promise. Oh, but I wanted to read the letter so much. I couldn't. Of course, I'm in love with him. I'm so in love, I've never felt this way before. My heart flutters when I see him. And…and I think about Madame Lockridge and how she spoke about her husband Jonathan when I worked for her, and how in love they were.

"I think about you and Eugene. It's lovely that you have a husband to go home to, just as Grace and Anne do. I'm the only one and, well, it's just hard for a woman to be getting a certain age and still not be married. Besides being in love with Henry, it's so hard not having a husband. Will I ever find one? Will I ever get to have those things I daydream about? Or will I…will I just become an old maid, a spinster, lonely, always and forever sad and afraid?" Angelina buried her face in her hands and sobbed.

"Oh, Angelina. I'm so glad you told me. I had no idea you were even interested in looking for a husband. I thought you were so focused on your writing. But if that's what you want, then of course you will find it." Beth stood and hugged Angelina as she sat and cried this time in Beth's arms. "It will happen for you. It will. I know it will. You have nothing to be afraid of. Nothing to be afraid of at all."

***

Beth held her, and the rain fell in a rage outside. Someone stood outside in the courtyard, directly across from the building where Angelina worked, waiting patiently for her. He had been watching for some time, knew when she arrived at work, and the time she usually departed. Always, he hovered within the shadows of the buildings dotting the street, always free from view. Even when Angelina stood and gazed out of the large second-floor window of the White Building, he stole another glance and always remained unseen.

But it was easy, so easy to go unnoticed when no one knew they were being watched.

It was easy to wait, to watch and learn. Angelina was afraid of so many things, but she couldn't be afraid of what she didn't know existed. Soon, very soon, his presence would be revealed.

CHAPTER 8

Angelina left work a little earlier, hoping to avoid Beth. She was still slightly embarrassed by her earlier revelation, and wanted to think about anything other than those heart-wrenching feelings.

Focusing on the destination ahead, Angelina elegantly weaved in and out of people as she walked home. There was a certain beauty in the dance pedestrians took part in as they avoided bumping into each other on their own individual routes. While no one chose to acknowledge another, each person was aware of everyone else so much so that he or she put the effort into not acknowledging every passing body. There were times, especially during the nostalgia of autumn, when she wished others would take a moment out of their busy days and make small talk, but not today. It had been a long day at work, and her disobedient mind filled with constant wonders as to who the mysterious sender of Henry's letter had been. With penmanship as fluid as that, it must have been a woman.

It was not as though she had made any claim on the man (or as though he had made any claim on her). The lack of clarity in the situation drove her crazy. She never thought herself obsessive or of the jealous nature, but when she thought about the letter that laying just perfectly on his desk in all its sentimental

58

glory, she was unable to think rationally. Beth was correct—she was of marrying age, if not starting to pass it.

She had never been one for jumping into relationships for the fun of it; she was much too proud for that. There was also the fact that there was not much time to date outside of her job and writing. What she knew about finding a good match, or even just tolerating someone to help sustain her, was minimal.

At this point, Henry was more a far-away dream than a missed chance in reality. Even so, it was not so easy to shake the attraction she had for him. Emotions were much easier to write about than experience firsthand.

Turning a corner, Angelina was shaken from her thoughts as she collided with another. Quickly taking a step back to apologize, she was surprised when her eyes fell on a familiar scar on the man's chin.

"It's fine." Kent brushed off his jacket. Before Angelina could politely excuse herself, he continued. "You left before I could give you the copy of Delores Du Pre's new book, or, well, the book for which she was the publishing agent, at least. I told you before that rumors say she actually wrote it, didn't I?"

"You said something along those lines, I think. Yes." Glancing beyond him, Angelina yearned to walk the familiar street home. She was so close to curling into bed with a cup of tea; all that stood in her way was the rather large man in front of her.

Nodding at her answer, Kent dug through his beat-up bag before revealing a clean and new copy of Delores Du Pre's novel. The cover, while immediately catching her attention with the title printed largely across the top, seemed insignificant in comparison with her desire to be home. Her head and heart hurt, and she was not looking for any pleasure reading.

"For you," he said as he handed her the book.

Accepting it as gratefully as she could, Angelina gave him a tight smile. She wondered how rude he would think her if she were to cut their meeting short. It was not as though she was ungrateful for the gift—not that she was quite sure why the man, who was practically a stranger, went to such lengths to retrieve it for her—but there were other things on her mind. "Thank you."

"You're very welcome." Scratching the back of his head, he gave her a look, which she could only interpret as concern. "I'm going to tell you something. I was walking this way the other day and saw you. I didn't have the book on me, so I didn't approach you, but there was a woman following behind you. At first, I thought she was with you and that you just got separated in the bustle of the time, but I don't think you knew she was there. She looked average, not too indecent, but I saw something was off. It's in the eyes. You should take care. Someone following you like that doesn't happen randomly."

Tipping his old hat her way, he walked past her and entered the dance of the main street. She watched him disappear before putting the book in her bag and continuing on her way, a nervous feeling building in her chest. She could feel her legs moving quicker than normal, but she tried her best to appear at ease.

Recently, it seemed as though every mystery, every part of the past she had wanted to forget had come right into the spotlight. With the published book of the woman who crushed her dreams in tow, it was nearly impossible not to think of all the hours she spent in front of the typewriter. That, of course, led her to remember her time with Madam Lockridge. The woman, despite her many quirks, was someone with whom Angelina cherished her time.

That was, until she told her about Miss Heathburn. Her mother.

All the stories Madame Lockridge had recounted were fascinating and beautifully tragic, but nothing stuck with Angelina more than the fact that she had a half-sibling somewhere. It was not fair that things like this—things that held her forever in the abyss of uncertainty and puzzles—kept holding onto her.

Madame had also entrusted Angelina with the knowledge of her husband's death. While it was a surprise and an honor at the time, it was more of a burden now—a heavy secret meant to be kept in the years she served. She was not exactly sure as to why she felt that way about it, but something weighed on her shoulders. The spinning sensation consuming her head when all she had were tidbits of incomplete knowledge was not forgotten. In fact, walking home and suspicious of everyone behind her, only knowing that a woman could be there, gave her the same feeling.

But even with the unnerving knowledge of having an apparent stalker, Angelina could not help but return her thoughts to the pages of paper, bound by leather, weighing down her bag. She could not forget the hurt and embarrassment that gnawed at her as she'd left the office that fateful day, her manuscript sitting in the soiled brown bag. The time she'd invested into crafting each sentence, into choosing each word was immeasurable, yet Ms. Du Pre could not have been bothered to read it. Angelina liked to think that if the agent had just read one page, she would have reconsidered.

She did not expect to be praised to the end of the Earth, just to be told that her manuscript was worthy of having the name 'Delores Du Pre' associated with it.

Upon arriving home, she slouched against the wall, her exhaustion finally taking over. She had not thought about the manuscript, her mother, Madame Lockridge, and Henry all in one day and in such little time before. Closing her eyes, she released a breath. It frightened her how much simply thinking drained her.

What she needed was to freshen up. Dragging her body upwards until she stood erect, Angelina moved towards the washroom. Yes, this would be good for her. Turning the knobs of the water taps, she patiently filled the large wash bowl. Quickly stripping, she stepped inside the larger tub and sponged herself clean.

With the soothing sound of dripping water lulling her into a serene state, she felt more relaxed already. Still wet, she reached for the book Kent had given her, which she had teasingly left on the side.

"*My Death, Your Greatest Masterpiece*," she read aloud. Beneath it was a name she had not seen before: Helen Williams. Irritation rose at the memory of Du Pre saying she only took in writers with credibility, yet this Helen Williams was no one. Angelina spent months wandering the shelves of bookstores and libraries; she would recognize a name worthy of the Du Pre title.

It had to be a pseudonym.

Sighing, she rubbed her temples with one hand. She could not think about that right now; she was not in the right mind to be deciphering aliases. She placed the book back down and quickly dried off, deciding she would favor reading it in bed tonight over 'Under the Greenwood Tree' by Thomas Hardy.

As she sank under the covers, she flipped through the first few pages, choosing to ignore the first few crediting the publishers. With her mind focused, she set herself to reading. Letter by letter, she easily took in the first paragraph. It was strange, the sense of déjà vu she felt when reading the words. As she continued to the next paragraph, she dropped the book into her lap. She had seen these words before.

They belonged to her.

CHAPTER 9

Adrian Spatchet meticulously patted his wife's makeup on his swelling, bruised knuckles, careful not to let a single spec mark his finely tailored tuxedo. The flexing of his right hand sparked a rush of pain, which was but a mild inconvenience, a pittance of a price compared to the profits of a newly transformed testimony. The bathroom in which he sealed himself was one of three marvels of decadent craftsmanship in his recently renovated home. The other two were located on the lower levels, and were currently at the disposal of the finest unwelcome dinner guests in London. Adrian applied a new, flesh-colored coat of sophistication to his freshly swollen hands. The coloration, scrapes, cuts, and calluses he covered to hide the full story from even the most scrupulous observer. There was an abrupt knock on the door.

"Darling, are you quite through in there? Everyone's asking about you," said Charlotte, clutching her third wine glass as she delicately leaned into the door. She was Adrian's compassionate wife, and easily his most sacred possession.

"I'll be there momentarily. I'm just finishing washing up," Adrian shouted while turning on the running water. He looked up into the mirror and smiled. Adrian often wondered what men thought when they saw his face. Did they see the charming, debonair grin of an aging man, or could they only see the monster underneath?

Adrian was a tall man in his early fifties, with a strong, barrel chest, which stood in contrast to his slender waist. His gristly physique was uncommon for men of his age and class. Most lawyers of his status were soft, letting their life of luxury slowly eat away at their masculine presence. As a barrister, Adrian had to work in both worlds. Any given day, he might find himself sipping the finest aged scotch in the smoking room of royalty, followed by a visit to the decaying slums of the city. He had to be feared by both classes of men; each class had their own measure of power. That was why his extraordinary, blacker-than-black suits were customized to never inhibit his fierce right hook, while at the same time complimenting his thick graying hair which he parted sharply to one side.

While his physical features spoke volumes about his character, no attribute described the true nature of the man quite like his handshake. He did not bother to overly grip or squeeze to create his sense of dominance. He merely held other men's hands in a firm grasp, creating a cage—never physically forcing his will upon them, but letting them know he was the new master of their universe. He, and only he, would decide when the moment ended. After one handshake from Adrian Spratchet, Esquire, no man would never doubt that he himself was no longer in control.

Tonight they threw a dinner party celebrating Adrian's selection into the General Council of the Bar, which was the main representative body of barristers in England. He had risen in the ranks to become the most highly sought-after defender, not because he was exceptional at practicing law, but because he was a man who helped people come to 'understand' what was best for the greater good.

Adrian believed that perception was more important than the truth, and would always be more powerful than reality. Civility, the ideas of right and wrong, were notions dictated by those in charge. The truth was something only weak men valued. It came from a misplaced sense of fairness in the world. The truth was irrelevant. A man may witness a crime honestly with his eyes, but he had to eventually call upon his words to tell the story, and men's words could always be twisted. A man's position could be easily swayed by drawing into comparison the things he loved most in the world against his falsely idealized sense of righteousness. The innate desire to believe one's own eyes would never outweigh his need to protect his family. Therefore, truth was one of eleven sad, easily replaceable pawns in the grand game of chess that was the law.

The reason Adrian was on top was undoubtedly due to his particular knack for being extremely persuasive. He was not a brute. The bruises on his hand were the result of his "charity work" for his country. A good, upstanding Englishman always made the extra effort to send a message to the heathen, Irish immigrants, reminding them of their position in this country. They wished to flood the courts with ideas of fairness, ideas not even worth discussing in the poorest grades of penny-dreadfuls. Other than that, Adrian never made a threat, nor did he ever lay a hand on anyone. He never took things from the victims tried to persuade. That would make him a criminal, a common thief. His methods were far more intricate. He preferred to back his target into a corner, make him do things he would never normally do, because now he had to. He wanted their consent, their willingness to surrender, and for them to always know the act he would have them commit was of their own choosing. The devil never pulled the trigger. He just put the gun in your hand and made men believe they had no choice.

Adrian wiped down the white marble ledge of the sink to conceal any trace of his unspoken activity. His pointer finger, wrapped in the towel, delivered one last circular swipe in the crevice of the drain to guarantee he would be met with no suspicion. Adrian folded the towel neatly and laid it upon the rail. His left hand reached for the door handle, he took a breath, sighed out a smile, lifted his chest, and opened the door.

Charlotte leaned against the post of their opulent bed, lost in thought and staring down at her half-empty glass. She was a radiant woman who had only grown finer with age. Adrian paused in the doorway to examine her disorienting beauty. He'd seen this dress on four other occasions, and each time it made him gasp for air. In his eyes, she was the complete and untainted essence of a woman—not in the way that might suggest she was of a delicate nature, but more because she embodied a grounded femininity. Charlotte glided like a butterfly across a ballroom floor, but when she paused, she stood firm, planting her roots into the floor. Most men of weaker stalk had found her intimidating, an attribute with which Adrian fell in love. A better pair of ferocious lions in the jungle of high society could not be found. He never would have met her had it not been for his mother. He considered this her only motherly act through the years, but the pain of his childhood made him less than grateful.

Charlotte hadn't even noticed Adrian stepping out of the bathroom until she felt his strong hand gently caress the inside of her palm. She was about to speak when Adrian placed his other hand on the back of her neck, his index fingers pushing into the base of her skull, lightly elevating her chin. They locked eyes, Adrian smirked a half-smile, and then he kissed her deeply. Their love remained strong over the many years, because Adrian knew the key to a successful relationship in his line of work. Women whom men took the time to kiss passionately never asked any questions. "You look stunning," Adrian whispered into Charlotte's ear as he drew his hands away from her face. "Shall we?" He raised his elbow, extending it out for Charlotte to grasp, and they walked out of the bedroom and down the stairs to the party.

As Adrian neared the bottom of the stairs, he caught his first glance at the room full of rigid black suits, standing amongst a flowing rainbow of sparkling gowns cascading throughout the dining room. He clutched Charlotte's hand, which rested on his right elbow. She would guide him through this, his most hated duty of this position. Dinner parties were fattening cakes, a self-indulgent treat of the elite, which they gobbled down in hordes. Adrian would much rather sharpen his teeth on the carcass of a freshly conquered case than listen to the onslaught of nonsensical concerns of his peers. The couple finally stepped into the dinner party, and all heads turned their way. A wave of plastered smiles splattered onto the faces of the two dozen guests in attendance.

Charlotte led Adrian through the gauntlet of well-wishers and laughable handshakes from the younger, eager men. Adrian, being a man of a more elevated position, expected now to be swarmed by these otherwise useless sons of wealthy gentlemen, hungry to apprentice under him in the hopes of reaching some level of respectable worth in their families. Adrian smiled through the pleasantries and stood firmly by Charlotte's side, for she was his anchor in this storm of flagrant admiration.

"Adrian, you remember Jemima," Charlotte said, nudging Adrian out of his world and into their conversation.

"Of course," he replied.

"Congratulations on joining the General Council! You must be so thrilled. And what a lovely party. I'm so glad I was able to attend," Jemima shouted over the crowd. She clearly had already indulged heavily in the champagne, striving to compete with the escalating volume of inebriated guests. Her blabbering continued. "Charlotte, have you told him about the book? I got her hooked on it. The story is absolutely wonderful. You'd love it. It's right up your alley. My dear friend Delores just published it and it is to die for! I don't know where she finds these masterpieces. This one is going to be big. You watch. I said it here, first. You watch!"

Charlotte chimed in, "It is very good. My poor dear hasn't been home, so I haven't had the chance to tell him."

Jemima lunged forward and grabbed Adrian's arm. "Oh, you simply must read it. It's so twisted."

"What's it about?" Adrian asked politely.

"It's about a murder!" Jemima replied with a giddy yelp followed by a hiccup. A number of people turned their heads towards her, scoffing at the gregarious behavior.

That was exactly what Adrian longed to avoid. "Well, I hear plenty of stories about that," he said.

Jemima fired back, "Oh, not like this one. This is a story full of such passion and corruption, such an enthralling web of detail you'd hardly believe it was real. The woman in the story is a lady of high society, who ultimately is backed into a corner when she learns of her husband's shady dealings and is left with no choice but to murder him."

"Sounds interesting..." Adrian said, now somewhat intrigued.

"I was telling Charlotte you should read it. You remind me so much of the Lockheart's lawyer, Malcolm!" Jemima shouted again.

Charlotte interjected, "She did write him as a devilishly handsome fellow. That I will agree. But, all that brutishness and black mail—it's rather unbelievable. My darling would be the first to see through this Malcolm's double-dealings and easily root him out." Charlotte grinned gleefully up at Adrian, who was now deeply wrapped up in Jemima's story.

"And you say this was a true story? Or is this a fiction piece?"

Jemima paused for a moment and then said, "I'm not quite sure. I'll have to ask Delores if she knows. I doubt it, though. It would be too scandalous if it were true. Surely, we would have seen such a calamity in the papers."

Adrian knew better than that. This story would never make it to the public, because the papers would never print it. The people in charge would never let them.

Adrian's curiosity ran rampant. Lockheart seemed like such a made-up and foolish surname for a book supposedly so well-written. Surely, an author who would take the painstaking labor to construct such an intricately detailed masterpiece would also put some thought into the names of the characters.

Adrian excused himself and stepped away from the party and hurried upstairs to the bedroom. On the nightstand next to the bed lay a few books, and from the one on top protruded a red ribbon. Adrian picked up the book titled '*My Death, Your Greatest Masterpiece.*' He opened the book and casually scrolled through the pages, reading sporadic lines of no importance. Then there, on page seventy-six, was a paragraph which stuck out at him and almost caused him to drop the book. The character of Malcolm the lawyer sat with Madame Lockheart, having tea in her study. The scene she described was too perfectly surreal—the cut of his suit, the calluses on his right hand, his hair sharply parted to one side.

Adrian slammed the book shut. "You clever bitch," he said under his breath. Adrian knew he would never forget that day. The image of Malcolm was forever etched in his mind. He had admired the man so much he'd modeled himself after him and became the man he was today.

Rushing over to the phone, he punched in the numbers. "James, I need you to contact my mother immediately. I don't care what time it is! Tell her I will be there in four hours." He slammed down the phone, his hair falling slightly into his face. With a very refined and precise gesture, he smoothed the straggling strands back into their rightful place. Then he paused, calmly opened the cover of the book, and looked inside. Grabbing a nearby pen, he wrote down every name on the inside cover page.

The phone rang and Adrian snatched it up. "Yes?"

"Sir, I have been informed that Madame Lockridge passed six months ago, but no one could find you to inform you. Her estate is in holdings, sir. I believe it will now be yours."

He spoke softly into the phone. "James, my mother has left me a bigger mess than the old estate. I need you to be here first thing in the morning. We have things to do."

Adrian replaced the receiver and held up the book, sighing heavily. *We need to burn this book.*

CHAPTER 10

"Angelina, good news!" Beth said, waving the crumpled envelope in her hands. She rushed over to the office window out of which Angelina had been staring for some time. Beth stopped and watched her for a moment, noticing that Angelina was off in her own world.

"I don't know how you get away with standing there. If it were me, I would be in serious trouble," Beth remarked.

Angelina attempted a half-smile. She just couldn't shake the thought of reading her words with someone else's name attached to them. Her words—the ones she spent hours typing while trying to keep up with Madame's storytelling. So much time wasted with no way of proving she was responsible.

"Angelina..." Beth reached out and snapped Angelina to attention with a subtle touch of her shoulder.

"Yes? Sorry, Beth," Angelina stammered, trying to decide if she should tell Beth of her book. She wanted to tell her. She wanted to tell everyone. She wanted to march right into Delores Du Pre's office and demand an explanation, but she knew no one will believe her.

"Did you hear what I said? I said I have good news."

"Yes. Go on."

"The envelope addressed to your dear Henry was nothing but a letter from his sister. You must go talk with him, now. That dream wedding may be possible after all." Beth tried to kid with Angelina, but to no avail.

Angelina's thoughts were buried deep in the pages she'd read, and even the good news about the letter couldn't shake her. "I'm sorry. I just have a lot on my mind." Angelina smiled weakly.

"I can tell. This is becoming a bit too much, Angelina. You must talk to him, before you get yourself fired."

"How did you learn that the letter was from his sister?" Angelina tried to push out the thoughts of her book and give focus to the only thing that may excite her. The sheer thought of a handsome lawyer giving her the time of day still seemed outlandish. "Did you rummage through his desk?"

"No, I would never!" retorted Beth. "I went to deliver some work for Mr. Grey, and I was instructed to leave it on Henry's desk if he wasn't there. I accidentally knocked over the garbage bin and it was lying on top. I simply couldn't ignore it as I gathered up the mess I had made. I quickly slipped it into my skirt. I did it for you."

"You shouldn't have, but thank you." Angelina tried to show a hint of a smirk with her newfound knowledge. Before the moment could last, she thought about marrying Henry, and how he'd accept her more if she was a well-known writer. Angelina set down at her desk and arranged some pages. After working for less than ten minutes, she blurted out, "Beth, she stole my book."

"What?"

"Delores Du Pre. My book. I brought it to her to be published. She stole it."

"How could she? How did she get it?"

Angelina told her about the last few days, about the way

she thought Delores must have thrown out her manuscript. She told Beth about the weird man who followed her and brought her a copy of the book, and about how she read her own words with the sickening lie of someone else's name on the cover. Angelina held back tears of anger and defeat as she told Beth every detail, except for what the book was about. Beth was, after all, Eugene's wife and Madame's niece by marriage. When she'd arrived in London, neither Beth nor Eugene mentioned the book. Angelina realized that, despite Madame having a close relationship with Eugene, she never revealed her plans to him.

She wondered if Eugene would even care. Madame was now gone; the story didn't really include him, but Angelina's instincts told her to hold her cards close to her chest.

"Can't you tell anyone? You need to go to a lawyer."

Angelina knew she didn't have a chance. She would be going up against the most renowned publisher in all of London, not to mention the name on the cover was clearly made up. Her manuscript was all she had, minus just a few hand-written pages from her meetings with Madame, which only she could decipher.

"Someone has got to be able to help, Angelina. Maybe someone in this office? Maybe if you talked to Henry—"

"Sure. The first time I ever talk to the man of my dreams, I will beg him for help as he laughs at me in disbelief. I'd rather not." Angelina scoffed at the idea. She ended the conversation, getting back to her work. She noticed Mr. Grey in the distance, regularly eying her table. The last thing she needed was trouble at work. She was grateful that typing somehow made the time pass quickly.

Before she knew it, the girls were ready for lunch. Sometimes they ate their sandwiches in the grassy park nearby. Angelina agreed to join them, but found herself pulling back from the group as the girls gossiped about the other women. Beth shuffled to her side and slipped an arm inside Angelina's to comfort her.

The last few sleepless nights had taken their toll; her hair was disheveled in an attempt to style it in a bun. Her makeup, now almost non-existent, showed faintly across her cheeks as evidence of constant wiping. The reflection in each and every window glass reminded her of this, as she tried her best to be presentable.

She couldn't stop thinking about the book and Beth's advice. She knew she had to talk to someone, even though she knew it would be a waste of time.

***

"Can I speak to Henry, please?" Angelina asked at the front desk. She had had numerous exchanges with the young, well-manicured girl, but this time Angelina hoped she'd go unnoticed.

"Henry?" the receptionist questioned. Angelina felt the blood rush to her cheeks, flushing away the tinge of makeup and replacing it with a rosy glow.

"I'm sorry," she said, embarrassed. "I mean—"

A booming male voice interrupted her. "Is it Thursday already? I could have sworn it was only Tuesday," Henry joked as he made his way out of his office, hearing Angelina's exchange with the receptionist. "Can I help you, miss?"

Angelina fluttered at the sound of his voice. She had always slipped in and out so quietly, while he was knee deep in work, but his voice and charming grin made him so much more lifelike. She couldn't help but focus on the fact that he knew when she usually frequented his floor.

"Hi, yes. Um, I need your help."

Henry invited Angelina into his office, his hand on her back, guiding her sending a chill up her spine. Even still, the gesture managed to calm her nerves for a moment. He closed the door behind her, offered her a glass of water, and pulled out her chair.

"I'm so sorry to bother you, but I don't know where else to go. You…you are a lawyer, correct?"

Henry let out a brief chuckle. "I'm hardly a lawyer, my dear. One day, I plan to be, just not quite yet. I am currently studying under Mr. Finley, one of the most influential lawyers around. I plan to be just like him one day, but for now, I am just his assistant."

Angelina first felt this trip to be a waste. She had hoped Henry would be able to give her sound advice as to how to handle her dilemma. She thought about apologizing for taking his time and then be on her way. Then, the romantic side of her reveled in the fact that Henry was not as far out of reach as she has once thought. He, too, was working his way through life, trying to make a name for himself. She immediately felt the potential bond they might share with one another.

"Oh, well, I'm not entirely sure that you can help me, then," she said, hoping for his assistance.

"I could at least try. Please, do tell me what you came for."

Angelina tried to contain her emotions as she told Henry what had happened. Her voice grew louder and faster as she couldn't keep up with the details. She wanted him to believe her, and she knew she couldn't leave out any detail, even if it made him see her differently. Between every sentence, Angelina swore the words were her own and hoped he believed her, even a little bit.

"Norman is going to love this…"

"Norman?"

"Sorry, Mr. Finley. My mentor."

Angelina couldn't help but worry that Mr. Finley would not take her case, especially since she didn't have much money to pay for a retainer.

"Well, Miss Angelina, I will surely have to talk to Mr. Finley about this. I'm actually to meet him in a bit to discuss some personal business. Once that is all handled, I will present him with your case and we can go from there."

"Do you think I have any chance? Do you even think he'd help?" Angelina asked nervously.

"I'm sure he'll at least point you in the right direction. Whatever he can't help with, I surely will. We will get this all sorted out, I hope. What this woman has done is quite unfair."

Angelina was relieved at the thought of any help with Delores Du Pre. She was even more optimistic that the help would come from the man of her dreams. Even if they did not fall in love and live happily ever after, she knew, for the time being, she would at least be in his company.

"Have a good day, Angelina. And, as always, I look forward to Thursday."

Angelina smiled, thanked him for his time, and turned towards the door. She felt the skin on her neck glowing from his comment. She tried to turn in time, but was sure Henry caught the flush of red blooming on her face. With one last goodbye, Angelina left Finley & Blackstone, hoping for the credit she deserved.

CHAPTER 11

Kent frowned and leaned back, examining the rough slashes of charcoal across the canvas sitting propped before him. Up close, the image was a jumbled, jagged mess. But from a slight distance, a clear image could be discerned. It was the rough facsimile of a woman's face, tender and soft despite the artist's inelegant medium. He stopped and considered each line, each blurred smudge, each crisp stroke that made up the whole.

Each part was so different, so unique. But it all came from the same source. Almost like…like a family. Kent gazed down at the small piece of charcoal nestled comfortably in his left hand. It was all just charcoal in the end—common charcoal. His eyes flickered back to the woman's face. Though beautiful, she looked haunted, insubstantial, somehow. So close, Kent thought, closing his eyes. The woman's face was still burned in his mind. Yet so far.

Kent let out a slow sigh, placing the charcoal down on the edge of the easel with a slight click. *It's not perfect*, he thought, considering the picture again. Suddenly, somehow, the picture seemed all wrong, the woman's face warped and alien. A stranger, when only moments before she had been like an old friend, or something more…

Something between a moan and a roar escaped him, and he knocked the easel to the floor with a loud clatter. He stood, his leg paining him, and shuffled toward the canvas. He bent down, averting his eyes from the woman's face, and picked up the drawing. He then walked across the disorganized, tiny work space and tossed the picture onto a pile of hundreds of others. They were nearly identical; all showed the same woman's face. Some in quiet repose, some with a bright smile playing on her lips, some of her asleep, her hair draped across her pillow. And all of them *wrong*.

It's not perfect, Kent thought again. *It's not the right time.* A terrible, gnawing emptiness overwhelmed him. He choked back a sob. *It's not time yet for us, Angelina.*

***

Broderick McMurray checked his pocket watch for the third time since setting out from his apartment. Half past eight o'clock. Right on time. He clapped the tiny silver circle shut, slipping it back into the breast pocket of his itchy tweed jacket. Just up ahead, he spotted light spilling from the window of his friend's modest townhouse. Broderick walked up the steps slowly, recalling all the times his life-long mate promised to spend a night on the town with him and the boys, only to beg off at the last minute. Half-expecting to walk to the pub alone, Broderick tapped the heavy metal knocker against the door.

Kent appeared a few moments later, his face intense and drawn. The scar above his chin had seemed to grow longer, exaggerated. It gave him a slightly demonic, frightening visage. His expression softened, however, when he saw his old friend.

"Broderick!" Kent chuckled softly. "You old Irish mutt. Why are you…" The mental gears seemed to turn in Kent's mind. "Oh," he stammered. "I'd…"

"Forgotten," Broderick finished for him. "Just like last time. And the time before that. *And* the time before that. The boys are really starting to miss you. *I'm* starting to miss you." Broderick shifted uncomfortably from one foot to the other. "I've *been* missing you, old boy. We're like brothers and we've hardly seen each other in, what, two years?"

"I know. I'm just always—"

"Busy." Broderick frowned. "Doing Lord only knows what. Please don't make me walk to the pub alone and tell all the boys you aren't coming. *Again.*"

Kent stood at the door, indecision wavering on his face. Finally, he took a breath and offered a resigned sigh. "I suppose a night out would do me some good."

"That it would, you churlish devil!" Broderick clapped his friend on the shoulder, practically dragging him out of the threshold. "Been too long, old friend. Too long by far!"

A short walk later, the two men entered One-Eyed Jake's Pub, so named for its owner and primary bartender. Stories varied depending on who one asked, but Jake either lost his eye in a war, a barroom brawl, or in a bet against a particularly vengeful leprechaun. The stories tended to get more fanciful as its teller got drunker.

"You again," Jake growled to Broderick. He stood polishing a glass at the nearly empty bar. "I'm guessing you're with them." He nodded towards a back corner, where a table full of rowdy men sat drinking, laughing, and accidentally spilling ale over each other in equal measure. One of the men turned in his chair and, spying Kent and Broderick, took on the appearance of a man seeing a ghost.

"Well, I'll be! Kenty-Boy is alive, after all." The proclamation brought a roar of excitement and approval from the other men seated at the table, all of whom jumped up and swarmed Kent and Broderick in fierce hugs.

Locally, they were known as the Whitfield Boys, so named for the Whitfield Home for Orphaned Boys—the place where they had all grown up. It had been a very long time since all the other orphans Broderick had grown up with had gathered in one place like this. They were all around the same age and had stuck together through thick and thin for their entire lives. Having Kent in present company made Broderick reflect back on his time at the home and, as he sat back, sipping his beer, he reminisced about his oldest friend.

Kent had been different in those days. Sunny, rambunctious, quick with a joke and a wicked, wolfish laugh. A gifted athlete, he had excelled at football and rugby. Despite his natural athleticism, which far surpassed the other boys', he was never showy or boastful. His behavior in school was rowdy without being too disruptive, and nearly every teacher had had a soft spot for him. He had been one of the most optimistic, energetic, happy people Broderick had ever known—until receiving the letter, anyway.

In his final year of schooling, and the final year of his residence at Whitfield Home along with it, Kent's prospects had been seemingly limitless. His rugby skills had caught the eye of every major talent scout in the country. It was highly unusual for an orphan to get such recognition, but his abilities were undeniable. With his added optimism and charm, there were no doors that couldn't be coaxed open for Broderick's old friend. Kent had even become something of a local celebrity, being interviewed by a newspaper about his meteoric rise to the top of youth rugby and his plans for the future. The article had featured several flattering pictures of Kent, both on the field and off.

Shortly after the article appeared in the paper, Kent had

gotten injured in a particularly vicious match. An accidental collision with an opposing player had sent him sprawling into the pitch, injuring his leg and creating the gash on his face. It was shortly after the injury that the *second* newspaper reporter had come to see him. Broderick could still remember the encounter, clear as day.

He and Kent had been sitting on one of the benches on the back lawn of the Whitfield Home. According to doctor's orders, Kent needed to stay in bed, but Broderick did his best to sneak his friend outside to get some much needed sunshine and conversation.

The headmistress of the house approached the boys, frowning when she spotted Kent. "I thought Broderick might've snuck you out here."

"I'm fine, Ma'am. Really, I am." Kent smiled, and even with the fresh scar on his face, he looked dashingly handsome— handsome enough to disarm the headmistress, anyway.

"Yes, well, another reporter is here to see you. She wants to write an updated story on you."

"Sure, send her out here," Kent said amiably. The headmistress glanced questioningly at Broderick. "He can stay," Kent said. "Brod might be able to add some details I've forgotten." With a nod, the headmistress, walked away, returning a short time later with a pretty woman approaching middle age. She didn't look like any reporter Kent had ever seen before. She didn't have the kind of no-nonsense swagger or direct bearing that a journalist should. If anything, she seemed slightly nervous.

She sat down on the bench across from Kent and Broderick. "Hello, Kent."

He nodded politely back at her. "Here for an update story? That's what the headmistress said. Guess the other reporter was busy or something? Catching a scoop—isn't that what you

81

call it?"

"Yes, that's right," the woman said. But there was an odd tone to her words. Something Kent couldn't quite place. As though just now realizing he was there, the woman inclined her head towards Broderick.

"Well, I don't have much to update you on as far as my playing goes." Kent chuckled, gesturing towards his leg, which was held straight by two wooden dowels wrapped tightly with white gauze. "I was injured a little while back."

"Not badly, I hope," the woman said, eyeing Kent up and down in a way that made him feel strange. "You'll recover, won't you? I know how important rugby is to your future."

"Oh, sure," Kent said with a wide smile. "It would take something more than a busted leg to keep me down. Besides, I've taken up drawing to pass the time. I'm going to be the next Monet, right Brod?" Broderick agreed, clapping his friend on the shoulder.

"So, you like it here?" The woman now glanced back and forth between Broderick and Kent, taking in their interaction with curious eyes. "You have friends here? You're happy?"

Kent's brow furrowed in confusion. "Well, sure. Me and the boys are like brothers. Why?"

"I wanted to ask you about your family. For the story I'm writing, I mean," she said quickly.

"There's not much to tell," Kent said. "My father left me here when I was just a lad. He lost his job and this was his only option. I don't blame him for that. It's a shame he never came back, though." Kent looked across the field, pain and wonder etched across his face.

"Well, because of the newspaper article, he might have seen you, might have seen your picture and your name. Couldn't that be? Perhaps your mother, too. You never said what became of her." The woman leaned forward now. "What would you do if, say, she tried to find you?"

Kent sat for a moment, collecting his thoughts. "I haven't thought about my mother, ma'am. My dad didn't mention her, other than to say she left us. I have only a very faint memory of her. If she saw it—if she's alive, even, I wouldn't want to meet her. She made her choice to abandon me, and that's something she should live with."

"Ah," the woman said, glancing down, suddenly preoccupied with her hands. "I wonder, too, are you curious if you have any siblings? What about them? Would you want to meet them?"

Kent blinked back tears, glancing at Broderick and then quickly away. "Now that," he said in a choked voice, "would be a different story. As much as we guys are like brothers, having a *real* brother or sister, your own flesh and blood...why, that would mean *everything* to me. Same for you, right, Brod?"

Broderick nodded in agreement, but he knew it was different with Kent. Though his friend didn't notice, Broderick had seen how he looked with terrible, hungry envy every time he saw a brother and sister walking down the street, every time a pair of giggling sisters skipped by, or a tussling trio of brothers kicked a football noisily down the street. Everyone had deep, secret needs—needs they never dared share with anyone else. And for Kent, his need was the kind of companionship, *true* companionship, he knew only a sibling could provide.

"I see," the woman said quietly. "But..." She stopped speaking for a moment before starting again, seemingly measuring the weight of her words in her mind. "Sometimes family can tie you down, make the things you dream about impossible. Who knows? If you reappeared in a long-lost sibling's life, who knows how that might interfere? Might ruin

83

carefully laid plans? Might shackle them down when really all they want is to be free of family—free of burden?"

"I suppose," Kent said. His face darkened, and for a moment Broderick was frightened by what he saw. "I would have to do it the right way, then. And maybe you're right. Maybe they would be better off not knowing I was their brother at all. Lord knows what having a...*bastard,*" his voice dripped venom at the word, "would do to their chances at improving their social standing. After all, personal ambition is all a person really has in this life, isn't it? And to Hell with the consequences."

The woman was very still and quiet for a long while. Finally, she stood and excused herself, walking stiffly back the way she had come.

"Funny lady, huh?" Broderick said, dumbfounded. "She didn't even ask you about rugby."

But Kent didn't hear. The darkness that had crossed his face earlier seemed to have sunken in, shaded the bright optimism his face normally wore. He got the letter a few months later. Broderick only knew about it from snatching glimpses of Kent reading it. When Kent saw Broderick watching him, he'd shove the letter back in his pocket without a word.

That was when Kent had changed. The shift wasn't gradual. It wasn't a matter of shades or degrees. It was drastic and immediate. The sunny, optimistic boy had become a sullen, limping man. Though the doctors had told Kent he would make a complete recovery, for reasons Broderick could never decipher, his leg injury never quite healed. He moved out of the boys' home and set up in a townhouse. No one knew how or why, or what Kent was even doing to earn a living, but they were his brothers and none of that mattered to them.

Brief flashes of Kent's old self sometimes shined through. His roguish charm and old laugh appeared from time to time, but the haunted, searching gaze never seemed to leave his eyes. To this day, Broderick only had two questions: searching for what, exactly? And what does it have to do with that letter from so many years ago?

Shaking himself out of reverie, Broderick drained his beer, wiped his mouth, and downed another, knowing he would have to be carried home tonight. Old memories could do that to a person.

CHAPTER 12 – Lockridge Estate, 1926

Angelina walked back to her bed, using the headboard to steady herself. She sat down slowly on the edge. Madame Lockridge's words rolled around her head. Had she really just heard the woman correctly? Elizabeth Heathburn was her mother? Tears filled her eyes as she tried to make sense of it all. Her mother had spoken very little of her own past. Angelina knew only that both her grandparents passed in a coach accident, leaving her mother to be raised by her aunt in a nearby hamlet. Whenever Angelina had raised the topic, her mother had shot a look of pain at her father, and he always nipped it in the bud. After a while, she knew it was just off limits to speak about it.

Angelina stood and made her way to the small window. She looked out past the stables and across the fields. Without a moment to spare, she stripped off her night attire and dressed quickly in her clothes from the previous day. She only had a small window of time before she was to start her duties. Careful not to wake the other sleeping staff, she snuck out the kitchen door, keeping to the small strip of grass beside the garden beds to avoid the graveled path. Reaching the stables, she slowly rolled open the door, careful not to startle the horses.

Four sets of eyes locked onto her, and the horses' nostrils

expanded, breathing in her aroma mixed with the cool air. The black Percheron horses had been specifically imported from France to pull Madame's carriage. Angelina smiled as she thought of another of Madame's quirks—her love for Roman history. She expressed this through naming her horses after strong roman characters: Octavia, Caesar, Augustus, and Marcus. Octavia was her favorite, though, maybe because she was the only mare of the group. They all quietly nuzzled the front of her coat, finding the carrots she had grabbed from the larder on her way out of the kitchen. Angelina took a bridle and placed it over Octavia's head, leading her out into the early dawn light. She stepped onto a log before whipping herself up and onto Octavia's warm back. No one at the house knew Angelina could ride bareback, as it was improper for a young lady unless riding side-saddle, but it was one of Angelina's best skills. Her mother had taught her before she'd left. Maybe that was why Angelina enjoyed it so much as she galloped towards the lake on the far end of the property.

She climbed off the horse and walked towards the edge of the water. The ripples lapped gently at the edge of the bank when she sat down and gazed into the reflection the water cast of the surrounding trees. Even after the ride, her heart was still heavy. Angelina wept softly; the earlier events of the morning took a toll on her already fragile mind and body. Her sobs turned into gulps when she was startled by a familiar voice calling her name. She turned to see Rupert, Madame's chauffeur, standing next to Octavia.

"What are you doing here?" She sniffed, scrunching her eyes together in confusion and finding it odd that he was here. He smiled weakly and nervously ran his fingers through his mop of curly black hair. About twenty years old and always smiling, he had a reserved confidence about him. With the build of a boxer, a strong jawline, and clean-cut features, he did not look like the typical Englishman.

"I always wake early enough to come here and read before starting my duties," he replied shyly, holding up his worn copy of *Tarzan of the Apes* by Edgar Rice Burroughs.

Angelina nodded, glancing away and unsure of what to say. A roadster bicycle was propped up on its stand next to Octavia, who grazed quietly as Rupert rubbed her side. Their silence hung in the air as the birds chirped in the trees and the comforting sounds of the water's gentle movement colored the early morning.

"Angelina, what's wrong? Why are you crying? Why are you out here by yourself so early?" Genuine concerned laced his voice.

She looked up into his warm, expectant eyes. Rupert had always been kind to Angelina. Even when taking Madame out, he would always give her a smile whenever she walked Madame to the car. On many occasions, when walking towards the servants' quarters while Rupert washed the car, she caught him stealing glances at her. She felt an unspoken trust between them, as if he had his own sad story.

Angelina took a deep breath and started from the beginning, explaining how she'd been writing Madam Lockridge's somewhat eccentric story about her past and her greatest love, Jonathan. Angelina did not mention the death; to be honest, she herself did not yet know whether it was true. They were not at that part of the memoir just yet.

"Before Madame left my room, I inquired as to what became of Miss Heathburn," Angelina said as she turned towards the lake. "Rupert, she said Miss Heathburn was my mother," she cried as the final word left her lips. "Please tell me she's delusional."

Rupert left Octavia and knelt beside Angelina. He put his arms tentatively around the sobbing woman. When she didn't pull away, he felt secure enough to pull her to him closely.

"No...no..." She hiccupped. "I don't think she's crazy. I think she's saner than even I am. I need the truth."

Rupert's strong arms held her until the sobs turned into sniffles. "I think you should keep writing Madame's memoirs. If she's opened up to you in this way, you should try to find out as much about your mother's past as you can," he said quietly.

Angelina glanced up into his face, noticing his warm, chocolate-brown eyes. She swallowed hard as she felt the heat creep up into her face. Rupert let her go as a warm smile spread across his face. "I've go-got to go." She stood up quickly, brushing the grass off her clothes. Rupert watched silently as she mounted Octavia and rode off without a goodbye.

She trotted back along the gravel road towards the estate before crossing into the field and breaking into a canter all the way back. Dismounting at the stables, she rubbed Octavia down before leading her back to the others. She gave them all one last carrot, then headed back into the house.

"Penny for your thoughts, My Lady," said Peter, the stable boy.

Angelina jumped three feet in the air with shock. She clamped her hand over her mouth to stifle the small scream, hoping to God no one else had heard. "Why would you sneak up on someone like that?" Angelina asked, panting.

Peter smirked a little; his freckles seemed darker today against his milky white skin, his gap-toothed smile now beaming at her. "You seem to have something heavy on your mind, that's all," he chirped. "Plus, I haven't seen you up this early before. Where have you been?"

Angelina crossed her arms, feeling irritated by Peter's

questions. "Never you mind, Peter. Is it a crime to get some fresh air before I start my day? Is there anything else you would like to know?"

"Nope," he chimed, and with that he spun on his heels, whistling a tune as he made his way down the driveway.

Breathing out slowly, she smoothed her hair back from her face and straightened her clothes. Angelina quietly hoped she would not encounter anyone else this morning. Opening the kitchen door slowly, she saw the light on in the pantry. Ruth was up. She heard the woman talking herself through the ingredients needed for the day's recipes as she tiptoed past. Feeling weary, she leaned against the grand stairwell. A memory flashed into her mind, one she had buried of the incident that had occurred about a week before her mother left.

On that particular morning, her mother had been in an unusually happy mood and promised she would pick Angelina up after school to take her for ice cream in the village. As Angelina waited outside her school, she'd noticed a man across the street sitting on a park bench and reading a newspaper. The more she observed him, the more she thought he stared over the paper, watching her. The angle of his newspaper had not been conducive to reading, and he hadn't turned any pages.

Angelina had taken a mental picture of him. He had round, framed, black glasses, and salt and pepper hair with a thick, matching mustache. He seemed well-dressed in a grey pinstriped suit and black overcoat.

"Mummy, Mummy," Angelina had exclaimed happily as her mother rushed towards her, looking flustered with cheeks flushed pink. As she went to hug her, Angelina had noticed her mother glance apprehensively across the street.

"Ready for ice-cream? Let's hurry. We need to be home before dark," her mother had stated, walking quickly.

Angelina noticed the man folding his paper before slowly standing and watching them leave. She'd hurried to catch up with her mother, and when she glanced back again, the man had gone. The following week, so had her mother; all that was left behind was the letter.

Rupert was right; she needed to help Madame Lockridge bring this tale of her past to light. She hoped it would give her some more clues as to her own mother's past, and why, really, she may have left. Pushing herself up, she went back to her room and gathered some fresh clothes before making her way down the hall to the communal bathroom. As Angelina wrung the washcloth in the warm water, she paused to look at her reflection in the mirror. She looked more and more like her mother every day, and if she noticed this herself, certainly Madame Lockridge did as well.

Is that why Madame hired me? she thought. Had seeing a ghost from her past brought Madame's memories to the surface, or was there so much guilt from what she may have done to Angelina's mother that the woman needed to rid herself of the burden?

She knew she'd find out soon enough Angelina scrambled to finish getting ready. Today would be a long day indeed.

CHAPTER 13

Angelina felt conflicted. Had she just left her previous life to come to the estate so Madame Lockridge could push her into her mother's past? Was that why Madame wanted her to write her story? Or was she playing some sort of sick game? Was she telling her because her mother had been involved? All these questions spiraled through Angelina's head for what seemed like hours, but she was just steps from her bedroom where Madame Lockridge waited.

Madame sat there, her eyes fixated on the exact spot where Angelina's face would appear, as if she had anticipated her arrival. "You're a tad late this morning," she said to Angelina, her eyes not wavering from the girl's face.

"My apologies. I went for a walk before it was time for my duties, and I just got a bit preoccupied out there," Angelina stammered, shuffling her feet nervously and trying to hold Madame's intense gaze. She hoped Madame did not know she'd used one of her prized horses for her little getaway.

"Preoccupied with what?" Madame asked in a measured tone, not blinking.

"Nothing in particular. Just the outside world. I never really noticed just how nice the grounds are towards the water."

"Yes, it's one of the many reasons Jonathan and I agreed to live in this place. He used to love it out there. He often talked about how he wanted to have fish brought in so he could put his rod to good use." Madame got up from the chair with the help of her cane and moved purposely towards the window, smiling. "I told him not to, because if he could fish out there, I'd never see him again." Angelina opened her mouth to respond but the words failed to come out.

"I guess while we're on that subject, we should pick up where we left off." Madame clapped her hands together as she moved towards the desk where a fresh stack of paper and pen sat for Angelina to begin her dictation.

"Right now? I haven't even started my duties for the day."

"Don't you worry about that. This is the only duty to concern yourself with at the moment. Have a seat." Madame waved her hand dismissively, ending any additional resistance.

Dropping her head in defeat, Angelina walked over to the desk and sat down. "Last we left off, you were talking about my mother," she said softly.

"Yes, we'll get back to her in due time. First, we have other matters to discuss," Madame said stoically, balancing her hands on the handle of her cane. Angelina swallowed hard as she picked up the pencil, bracing for the worst. "Now then, where did we leave off again?" Madame Lockridge added, feigning forgetfulness.

"You were talking about Jonathan and my mother," Angelina croaked. Her mouth felt as dry as a desert. Her nervousness over hearing the rest of Madame's story really took a toll on her state of mind.

"Oh, that's right. Well, after the party, I met up with Jonathan several more times. On second thought, that might not

93

be the right way to describe it. Whenever he was free, he came for me and whisked me away on whatever adventure he wanted to share with me that day," Madame said with a wistful expression on her face.

"Out in the city?" Angelina questioned as she wrote furiously.

"No, he was living in the city at the time. Between business meetings and being around his family, he always needed some fresh air." Madame paused thoughtfully before continuing. "Which was fine with me, because that was the type of environment I enjoyed."

Angelina frowned at her notes. Why didn't Madame tell her more about her mother? Was she simply drawing out the story to torture her? Or maybe she'd misunderstood the entire time, and she may never find out more about her mother. This was a story about Johathan's death, after all.

"Are you listening, darling?" Madame Lockridge asked, watching Angelina intently.

"Yes. You would meet outside the city because it was good for the both of you." Angelina shook her head as if removing cobwebs from her brain and finished writing down Madame's last memory.

"If that's the last you have, you are considerably behind. I know, you're just a bit nervous because I mentioned your mother, but I have faith in you. Perhaps I am rushing you slightly. If it makes you feel any better, you can tend to your duties now, and we can pick this back up later on." A stern frown crossed Madame's face.

"No. It's fine. Tell me more," Angelina said softly, feeling the heat creep into her face. She met her employer's eyes and gave a weak smile.

Madame ambled to the door, then turned towards the

desk. "In due time. You get to your duties. I have a few things to take care of on my own, anyway." Madame held up her head and walked out, leaving a pondering Angelina behind.

The thought of the connection between her mother and Madame Lockridge had dominated her thoughts of late. She could hardly wait until more was revealed to her.

"Well, first a trip to the lake and now sitting about? You must be getting accustomed to leisure."

Angelina looked up to see Rupert standing in the doorway grinning at her and wiggling his eyebrows. He was dressed in his uniform comprised of an English-cut coat with jodhpurs, a chauffeur's hat, and boots. Despite the confusion and restlessness within her core, she found herself returning his smile.

"I was just about to get started. Madame Lockridge apparently decided she did not want to continue her story just yet." Angelina arranged the paper and pencil neatly on the desk, then headed down the hallway to the closet beneath the grand stairwell. Rupert leaned against the wall and watched her silently while she found a broom to passively sweep the foyer. They quietly enjoyed each other's company until they heard footsteps on the top landing.

Madame Lockridge walked down the stairs in another one of her vivid dresses, her cane guiding each step. She walked confidently to the door, anticipating that Rupert would rush to open it. Angelina was surprised to see her going out again. Madame had a tendency to be reclusive and had surprised everyone the day they had picked up the typewriter.

"I am going into town. Try to finish your duties as soon as possible. Once I return, I want to continue my story," Madame said, putting on her riding gloves.

"As do I," Angelina responded, feeling a wave of relief washing over her. Madame nodded and disappeared out the door.

Rupert gave a small wave before closing the door behind him.

Angelina looked around to see if any of the other servants were in her immediate area. When she felt the coast was clear, she tossed the broom aside and ran up the stairs, taking two at a time. Madame's bedroom was her focus, and she knew she had to make most of the time she had. The tall, cherry wood dresser was her first stop. She tore through the drawers, looking for a diary, journal, anything that might provide a small piece of the puzzle.

She tucked a wayward hair behind her ear as she thought about where to look next. Her eyes were suddenly drawn to a jewelry box on a bedside table. Angelina ran over to it and ripped it open. Despite Madame Lockridge's extensive jewelry collection, this box only had three items within—jewelry pieces Angelina had never seen Madame Lockridge wear. Nestled in the middle of the box was a ring, one Angelina recognized; it had belonged to her mother.

She sank to the floor as she recalled the weeks before her mother's departure.

Her mother had always taken off the ring when she was upset and hurled it across the room. Elizabeth never failed to pick it up and put it back on soon after. Angelina had asked her mother about it when she walked into the room, catching her mother crying and sitting against the wall. Angelina had walked to the other side of the room, picked up the ring, and brought it back to her mother, who instantly slipped it back on her hand.

"Mommy, if you hate that ring that so much, why wear it?" Angelina sat down next to her mother, who hugged her close.

"It's a bit complicated, my dear. I don't hate the ring. It was given to me at a time when everything was beautiful, and still, this ring shines above all else. I wear it to remember those times, those feelings, and those relationships. They were great times." Elizabeth sniffed, wiping her eyes with the sleeve of her blouse.

"Is now not a great time?" Angelina questioned, her voice hopeful.

"Now is a great time, because I have you, Angelina. It was just different then. I was one among many, and while that was great, it's good to be just the two of us, too."

"So if you love it, why do you throw it?"

"Sometimes it's harder to remember those times. Sometimes, the only feelings I can remember from it are the sad ones, the empty ones. I don't want to see it when all it offers is bad things." Elizabeth spoke thoughtfully, glancing down at the ring now back on her hand.

"But you always taught me that we have to take the good things with the bad. You said that life wouldn't be as beautiful if it weren't so sad." Angelina nuzzled against her mother's arm.

"And that's why I keep the ring. We have to live with the bad things. We have to accept the bad things. But remember, we never have to be stuck with the bad things." A knock on the door broke the moment. Her mother had handed her the ring and headed to the door to answer it.

Angelina had held the ring, admiring it. It was too big for any of her fingers, but she put it on anyway, gazing at the three gemstones across a silver band. She held it tight, trying to understand the message her mother had given her.

The distinctive roar of the car engine interrupted her thoughts. She ran to the bedroom window and saw the Crossley making its way back up the driveway.

"Typical. She didn't leave after all. I should have known." Angelina chastised her optimism while glancing down at the ring. She noticed one of the gemstones was missing, and the piece was noticeably worn. Still, it was the exact same ring. She'd seen it for the last time the night before her mother had left, and she never found it in the house. She knew her mother would have taken it with her, and she even came to resent the ring, wondering how her mother could take that and not take her. *How does Madame Lockridge have it now?* she wondered.

Angelina heard the car doors slam. She slipped the ring on her finger and fled the room. Picking up the broom she had left at the doorway, she tried to look busy. Madame Lockridge entered with a disheveled look on her face. She walked up the stairs and noticed Angelina.

"Well, it is a shame to make it all the way to the end of driveway only to realize that I am indeed famished. I think a light brunch is in order. Would you care to join me, Angelina? You can't use the broom on the carpet, anyway."

Angelina's face burned red. Her attempt to be discreet had failed her. Unsure of what to say, she realized she had never eaten in Madame's company before. She felt a sense of panic, knowing her manners would be scrutinized, but Madame's tone made her feel obliged to say yes. "That sounds delightful, thank you."

"Can you please have Ruth prepare us something in the tea house? I will be there shortly." Madame walked up the stairs to her room with a slight smile playing on her lips. Angelina did as instructed and made her way to the kitchen.

***

Madame Lockridge shut the door to her room with a loud thud, then walked quickly over to the jewelry box. She picked it up and looked inside for the most important piece she owned. As she had hoped, the ring was gone, and she smiled at the revelation.

98

CHAPTER 14

Madame kept Angelina waiting for what seemed like an eternity. Her mother's ring burned a hole in her pocket, reminding her that this may be the last time her memories of her mother remained pure. She sat shyly with her notes, placing them on the table before folding her hands in her lap. She wasn't comfortable sharing a meal with her superior but knew it was inevitable as Madame made her way into the tea house.

"Ruth will bring out some tea and sandwiches shortly," Angelina said as she stood up to pull out Madame's chair. Madame had changed into a simple, comfortable skirt with a sailor blouse. The large-brimmed hat she wore made Angelina feel extremely underdressed.

"Wonderful. Let's not wait for her to begin. Now, where was I?" Madame sat down, settling into the chair.

"You were telling me about the times Jonathan took you away from the city." Angelina rushed to her chair and picked up her pencil, preparing herself to write.

"Why yes," she smiled reminiscently. "Jonathan was a wonderful polo player. He often taught me the game, when the weather would permit. I rode the horse with one leg on each side, however un-ladylike that may sound. We often picnicked by the lake, the very lake you took a walk to this morning. His mother had numerous properties, but she didn't frequent here so much, so we would meet here secretly, away from prying eyes of ground servants. Are you getting all of this?" Madame craned her neck to see how much Angelina had written.

"Yes, Madame." Angelina held the paper up. Madame nodded in approval and continued. "On one particular outing, we lay beneath the trees, talking for hours. We spoke of his being promised to Elizabeth, and the meaning behind their union. Both of us were relieved that particular problem was no more. It would have benefited his father's company greatly to be joined by the bonds of marriage to Mr. Hawthorne's. But Jonathan claimed to only have eyes for me since the day he met me at the ball. His parents quickly learned Elizabeth was no good for him after I exposed her pregnancy. We wed only six weeks later. Right here in the garden."

"But what about my mother? What happened to her child?" Angelina grew impatient as Madame filled the air with meaningless memories.

"Well, she was shunned by many after the truth came out, that it had all been a desperate attempt to get my poor Jonathan to marry her. She wasn't heard from for a long time. Others say she had the child at home, and her Aunt took it to the church at once to be put up for adoption. All just rumors, though." Madame fell silent as Ruth appeared with a silver tray, holding a steaming pot of tea.

"Tea?" Ruth inquired, hovering over the table with a steaming pot.

"Yes, of course. That's why we're here." The sound of Madame's stern response brought Angelina back from her daze. The seconds passed slowly as she waited for Ruth to leave before speaking.

Ruth went about filling up their cups and setting out their lunch plates, and Angelina found herself lost in her own thoughts. Once she finished, Madame dismissed Ruth with a nod. Not until she left did Angelina realize she'd been holding her breath.

"Oh." Angelina couldn't help but sound disappointed. "So, you have no idea what happened back then?"

"Well, no. Not until your mother and I became close friends did I discover the truth."

"What?" Angelina straightened in her chair, allowing her pencil to fall to the table.

"Keep writing," Madame scolded. "Elizabeth never loved Jonathan. She loved another, for a long time. It was his child she carried all those years ago. When she heard of mine and Jonathan's engagement, she sent me a beautiful letter, and I was quite surprised, to say the least. We had not been friends at the time, but she gave us her blessing, and her kind act bloomed into a wonderful friendship. We wrote each other frequently until we saw each other again, years later. Had I known she did not care to marry Jonathan, I may not have been so cruel exposing her the way I did, but fortunately she was grateful for my actions."

"Do you still have them?" Angelina held her breath.

"Have what, dear?" Madame absently took a sip of tea.

"The letters." She nearly jumped across the table.

"Yes, I believe I have them somewhere. I keep all of our correspondence."

Angelina's mind raced ferociously as Ruth reappeared with an assortment of finger sandwiches. *She's in contact with my mother? How could my mother keep in touch with this practical stranger, yet disappear from my life completely?*

"Can I read those letters? I can't believe you speak to my mother. I haven't heard from her in years. Did she tell you why she left? Why she abandoned me?" Heat rose to her cheeks as she felt tears form in her eyes. Her expression softened when she caught the inappropriateness of her outburst. She just couldn't understand why her mother would do this. Madame looked somewhat empathetic, and seemed to be softening to Angelina's vulnerability.

"Yes, all in good time, dear. Do you remember the day we met?"

Angelina nodded. "Vaguely."

"I'd sent Hollis, my old butler, looking for you, upon your mother's request. She'd asked me to take care of you before she left, and when I'd heard you were looking for employment, I thought it was the perfect opportunity. Of course, I had to put your skills to the test, ensuring you felt you earned your position here. I noticed immediately that you have Elizabeth's pointed nose, much like her first child." Madame paused to take a sip of tea. "Are you writing this all down? It's important you understand that your mother did not abandon you by choice. It's important you understand who she was as a person, not just a mother."

Angelina nodded, scribbling furiously. Her brows furrowed as she managed her pencil and her distracting thoughts at the same time.

"Elizabeth was a careless woman, as you can imagine. It wasn't long after your brother was born that her first husband grew rather exhausted of her spirited opinions and decided their son was to be best raised without her. He left without a trace, leaving Elizabeth behind in shambles. She tried for years to find them, but the odds were stacked against her. She was merely an abandoned woman, with nothing to offer her son even if she had found him. No one would side with her. She eventually met your father and started over." Madame took another sip of her tea.

"Now, let's take a break and eat some lunch. I'm famished."

I have a brother, Angelina thought, stunned, and reluctantly obeyed the woman's instructions. Madame Lockridge's vague and slow-paced storytelling left her feeling nauseous from frustration, but she nibbled on a sandwich regardless. They ate in silence, leaving Angelina's mind to wander. *Did she leave to find her son? Why didn't she ever come back? Ever visit? Ever write?* Angelina imagined the worst, a scenario where her mother had found her first husband and picked up where they had left off, preferring to be with them. Or worse, she imagined her mother had started over with a third husband, leaving her behind for good.

"Shall we go look for those letters now?" Madame asked after she'd finished her meal. Angelina nodded and hurriedly gathered up her work. As they headed towards Madame's bedroom, the woman paused at the entrance to the living room. "This is where it happened." She pointed with a long, elegant index finger. "I try to forget but, as you know, I'm drawn to this spot. I'm very particular about ensuring it is cleaned numerous times daily. I can still see his body sprawled across the rug as if it were part of the floral design."

Angelina noticed that Madame had gone into a daze as she reminisced about her husband's murder. She had initially been terrified of learning the awful truth, and the burden it would be, but compared to learning about her mother, the murder somehow seemed less important.

"Why don't you replace the rug?" she suggested.

"Oh, no." Madame shook her head violently. "I need to be reminded of why I've become this person. I know what people say about me. They laugh because I'm unlike them, but they never bother to ask why." She finally looked at Angelina. "Let's go find those letters."

CHAPTER 15

Madame watched the energy that had returned to Angelina after hearing of her mother's story with hooded eyes. She had promised Elizabeth that she would tell her daughter everything when she felt Angelina was ready. The careless socialite had learned something akin to wisdom with all her many mistakes, and caution was the greater part of wisdom. Madame slowed her steps and came to a stop just inside her bedroom. "I'll fetch the letters. Meet be back in the sitting room."

"But I—"

"Hush. You'll see them, and sitting to read them in a civilized manner is the least we can do to show your mother the respect she deserves." Madame looked at Angelina carefully. She had always been a good girl, her mother's beauty and charm seasoned ever so slightly with her father's more common and practical bloodline. Nevertheless, there was a flicker of will in there, a flicker of rebellion that made Madame choose to test Angelina, even just a little bit longer.

She smiled reassuringly, and after the slightest hesitation, Angelina returned the smile and left to do as she was bid. Madame didn't know what she would do if Angelina bucked her at this point. The girl already knew from her allusions what everyone had suspected, that Madame was culpable for her beloved husband's death. To Angelina, abandoned amidst mystery, this was about her and her story, and writing for Madame was merely a necessary price she had to pay to learn her own history. Elizabeth had told her not to bring Angelina into things unless she was certain the girl could be trusted, and now, Madame was unsettled about whether she had chosen correctly. She knew Elizabeth would not approve of her method, or her reasoning, but she had decided long ago that this was what she needed to do.

She gathered up all but four letters, which she slid deep into the lavender fragrance of her undergarment drawer. *They ought to be safe there*, she thought. *Nobody has wanted to go into that drawer for many years now.*

She laughed and quietly made her way down to the living room. Angelina was now accustomed to being kept waiting, but her inquisitiveness had grown overwhelming.

"Please, Madame, may I see the letters now?"

"Of course." Madame handed her the letters and settled back in her preferred chair. It took the better part of half an hour for the girl to read through the letters and then thoughtfully fold each back into their envelopes along the original lines. Madame saw Angelina's hands shaking, and she watched the girl surreptitiously wipe a tear from her eye more than once.

After she had read them all, she looked up, bewildered, as Madame had been certain she would be. "I don't understand! Those letters don't make any sense to me!"

"No, I don't suppose they would."

"Why is she talking like that? It's practically gibberish."

"It largely is. Your mother was very clever. She and I enjoyed riddling each other. We wrote entire letters in code, you know. It was a game we played together. It was also a way to ensure our adventures stayed private."

"You're playing with me! Why even show these to me if you knew I wouldn't understand them?" Angelina caught herself, eyeing her employer cautiously. It was obviously she feared being reprimanded for her outburst.

"Because you asked to see them, Angelina. I wouldn't withhold your mother's correspondence from you, not deliberately," Madame lied smoothly, without a trace of deception in her words or face.

Angelina took a deep breath and closed her eyes. "Please, tell me what she says in her letters. I need to know."

"And what will you do with this knowledge? What are you looking for? Do you want answers? Retribution? What will knowing serve you?"

"I don't know what I want. I just want to know. I've missed my mother, and often wonder about her. This is the closest I've ever gotten to filling the gaps my imagination has bridged."

Madame took great pleasure in hearing Angelina speak. "You have a beautiful way of putting things, my dear. I have great faith in your writing abilities. If you have Rupert fetch the typewriter and bring it in here, I will tell you the story behind the codes your mother used in the letters."

"I will be much quicker just taking notes to type up later."

"Yes, I know, but I think you're being lazy, and are more than capable of keeping up on that machine of yours." She watched the girl struggling to maintain a professional pace as she left the room, and very soon she returned, hands held stiffly at her side, with Rupert in tow. He had the typewriter set up for her on the small desk in no time.

When Angelina was settled Madame spoke. "Perhaps you should have asked yourself, 'Why does my mother need so much jam?'" She didn't wait for Angelina to answer. "It wasn't the jam she wanted in the farmer's market, you know. Your mother is a pool of deep, deep water, and the man who made the jam was only the tip of the iceberg. You see, my dear, some people are compasses, geniuses full of skills, spinning every which way until finally they find their true north and seize it. When that happens, no force exists that can stop them. Your mother was a compass, and when she found her 'true north' in 1913, she seized it."

"Am I a compass as well?" Angelina enquired, slightly confused by her own question.

Madame burst out in a laugh that mortified Angelina to the bone. "A compass? You, my dear? No, you are a leaf blowing with the wind. The only thing you can choose is which wind you favor. You will forever be the instrument of other peoples' stories, I'm afraid, and will likely never have one of your own. But, where was I? The Jam Man, yes, that's the best place to begin. Jam is a marvelous substance. You can hide a pill in it for a child to swallow with ease, you can spread it on your toast, and you can use it as a vehicle for you own ambition."

Angelina's typing was certainly improving. Her desire to hear the story fueled her to not only keep up, but be ready to take it all in.

"The Great War was a time of ambition for many women as well. Your mother, despite how you knew her in her lowly station as the wife to a low-born man, was a woman who knew the intoxicating taste of that spice. Once you've tasted ambition, it's impossible, no matter how good your intentions are, not to go back for more. Her unexpected pregnancy had soiled her prospects in the traditional way, but Elizabeth was not a woman to stand on tradition. Even while she was away, she busied herself making connections, and during the Great War, these connections blossomed into opportunities. I became involved with it, too. Filthy business, spying, but it was to protect Britain, and your mother cut a dashing figure with her intrigue, disguises, and how she had to hide so much from your father. She was romantic, and I admired her. I wanted to impress her, and so I became involved in MI6 business, in which I had no right to engage in the first place."

"My mother was a spy? But…she was always at home. It was my father who worked away from home. I'm sure I would have known!" Angelina protested.

"Are you?" Madame raised an eyebrow. "Perhaps you should tell the story, since you know it better than I do."

"I'm sorry," Angelina whispered. "I'm very surprised, shocked even. Of course I believe you, Madame. But my mother, a spy?"

"Someone had to be a spy. I didn't think what she did was very dangerous. Your father being away made it easier for her to navigate her contacts. She carried messages to and from various people, and the Jam Man was her handler. She reported to him and he gave her her assignments, most often concealed inside the lid of a jar of jam. She gossiped with me about it. We were like sisters then. In fact, we still are. I dare say I'm the only person in the world she truly trusts."

Angelina nodded grudgingly and stared at the teeth of the typewriter, but resumed typing. The excitement the girl had carried from the previous day's information seemed drawn out of her like bad blood, and Madame noticed the sorrowful slouch in her posture.

"Your mother was a star, and she shone brilliantly. It was part of her gravitation in which I became trapped, and that pull led to my beloved Jonathan's death. What I'm going to tell you next could land me in jail, or get a cyanide capsule put into my tea, if and when the intelligence community discovers I'm speaking to you now about their top-secret operations."

"Then why are you telling me? And more importantly, why ask me to write it all down for you?" Angelina asked with true curiosity.

"Because I'm unhappy. I'm getting older, my dear, and I don't want to meet my Jonathan without doing something to address the truth of what I've done. I'd probably end up a ghost if I didn't unburden it onto you or somebody else, and I would make a terribly cranky ghost, don't you think?"

Angelina ducked her head and avoided answering, but Madame saw the faint smile playing on the girl's lips as she chuckled inwardly. She liked Angelina, and often wished Elizabeth was around. Their similarities were striking.

"More and more often, Elizabeth asked me to do little favors for her. Hold onto a slip of paper, an item. Once, she asked me to get rid of a gun for her. I still don't know why she couldn't have done it herself, but I threw it into the lake as far as I could, and to my knowledge, it's never been found. In fact, make a note of that, Angelina, as a side note. I want to add it to my will that the lake should be dredged for that gun upon my death. It may help to prove my story."

She looked up at Angelina, who gave her a small frown and looked as though she was about to say something. But she shut her mouth, politely made the note on a scrap of paper, and Madame continued.

"I had a map and contact list I hid for your mother at the time, and then disaster struck. I knew this particular case was different. Elizabeth was scared this time, you see. She was also disheveled and, as I'm sure you recall, your mother was never messy unless she was sick to death's door or drastically distracted and upset. She was about to leave when Jonathan came into this very room without knocking or announcing himself in any way. Jonathan was very cross. He had his own suspicions about what Elizabeth was up to, and since she was here so often, I believe he saw more of her spy business than your own father ever did. Jonathan usually never made demands of me, but this case was different. He demanded the map. I refused. He insisted. Elizabeth was white as a sheet, terrified. He grabbed the map from me and unrolled it.

"Elizabeth ran at him. I knew she had learned tricks from her training as a spy, tricks that could hurt people. I cried out, 'Jonathan, no! Don't.'" Madame's voice sunk to a hoarse whisper as she invoked the very words she had said on that long-ago day. Her eyes were blank and dry as she stared at the fateful rug she refused to toss out. Shaking her head, she picked up the teacup Beth had discreetly delivered. She took a drink and paused before continuing. Angelina finished typing, 'don't' and looked up, waiting and expectant.

"Jonathan wasn't afraid of Elisabeth. He was scornful of her, a woman who had thrown everything away to become common, as he'd described her once to me. He lifted up his hand to strike her as she came at him with her fingers stretched out like claws. Without a thought, I picked up a marble bookend and struck him in the back of the head.

"He fell down to the ground, his head split open. I saw his mangled skull and his eye, his beautiful eye...it was barely in its socket anymore. He tried to call out to me, tried. I could see his lips moving—he was asking me why. I knew I could do nothing to save him. I knew it was possibly a long and painful death ahead of him, and so I struck him again, and again. Then he was gone.

"Your mother took the map and fled. She didn't ask for my help for quite some time after that, but of course, she did

111

eventually ask me for my assistance once more. I pulled over the bookcase that had held the bookend and wiped the bloody smears off the marble. I left it by my husband's battered head. When the bookcase fell, I pretended I had just walked in to see what the commotion was about. The servants were right behind me. I ran to Jonathan, which was easy to do, because it was what I had wanted to do right from the start. I held his head and I cried. I screamed at the servants to fetch the doctor. I had a motive outside of my love for Jonathan in my performance, which was to find a quick way to hide any smudges of blood on my person. By holding him in front of everyone, I succeeded in covering myself completely. No one would have been the wiser.

"Even with all my cleverness, the police questioned me. I inherited a sizeable fortune and, combined with my husband's violent and sudden death, they were right to do so, even though a great many people took offense on my behalf. Everyone knew we had loved each other, and so no one ever really questioned why, or even if, I would have killed him. It was for love that I did it, for love of your mother and for fear of my involvement.

"The war was at its height in 1916, and MI6 needed her help more than ever. She was told one day at the market that they needed her help overseas. Elizabeth was devastated by the news at first, and frightened by her mission. She survived it, however, as you can see by the dates on the letters, and then she absconded. Your mother was always busy making plans, tired of the shell of a life she led as a simple country wife. She had become tired of always being told what to do and where to go by not only her husband, but MI6 as well, and at this point they had knit her in with them. She was ready to burst out, and she had already used her considerable fortune to start the seeds of a life elsewhere."

"Where?" Angelina asked quickly, not even bothering to

finish typing the last sentence. Madame responded by sipping her tea.

"All in good time, my dear. Don't you want to know what happened to your mother's wealth and why you recall endless arguments about money? Strange, from a woman who could afford to keep trinkets and rings, that none of that money ever came home to roost, hmm?"

"I thought maybe she spent it all," Angelina confessed.

"No, she didn't. When she married your father, she thought she was in love. She liked the idea of eschewing all wealth and living 'the simple life'. The romance of peeling potatoes and wearing herself out scrubbing the floor soon wore thin. Your father ceased to be a romantic figure in her life and became an oppressive force, and for good reason. Your father had told her when they married that he didn't want to be beholden to his wife for money. Your mother lied and said she had given it all to an orphanage. In all actuality, she had only hidden it away from him. As the war tightened all our belts and good things could only be bought on the black market, your father grew angry that Elizabeth had 'squandered her money on widows and orphans', as he had been led to believe.

"Your mother knew how to look out for herself. She also knew that, especially for a spy during a war, it's very easy to get lost and start fresh. If there had been a way for her to take you with her, I think she would have. She did love you, Angelina, and I hope you can forgive her. She's your mother, but she's also a strong and passionate woman."

"Is she still alive, then? I want to see her."

"She is still alive, and I promise you that you will see her soon. She's coming to London, but I haven't received word yet of her arrival. We need to hurry so I can tell you the rest of my story, and then I will give you the names of some people you need to contact. It is crucial that this story be published. When you understand the rest of what your mother's letters have to say, you will understand why."

"We will get it published," Angelina reassured. "You can tell me what to do and I will help, whatever you need."

"You must promise me that if something happens to me, you will get it published, even if it means walking to London."

"I promise, Madame. Please, tell me where my mother has been."

CHAPTER 16 – London, 1928

Norman Finley, attorney at law, wished he had turned down Henry's pleas to meet with this Angelina, this nobody. Still, a good mentor ought to encourage his student taking an interest in a case.

Now that Norman saw the two of them sitting on the other side of his desk, he suspected Henry's interest was not lawyerly, but grossly romantic. Henry stared slothfully at where the girl's hair fell onto her shoulders. Angelina stared at something behind Norman.

"Is there a problem, my girl?" he asked.

"It's so cruel," Angelina said.

Norman turned in his chair and smiled when he saw the source of her discomfort—his prized, stuffed wolf head, mounted on the wall above him.

"The wolf is cruel." Norman bared his teeth in a false smile.

"The wolf didn't choose its nature," the girl countered with a small grin.

"Then life is cruel. Isn't that right, Henry?" Norman said, snapping his student out of his loving stare.

"Yes, sir. It is."

"One's home is a reflection of one's soul," Angelina added.

"Indeed it is." Norman paused to smile, but it didn't stick. "Now tell me, what evidence do you have?"

"I have these notes." The girl slapped the package to which she had so tightly clung down on his orderly desk. Scraps of handwritten notes and crumpled typewriter paper bulged out of the manila envelope.

"But you don't have the manuscript," said Norman.

Henry perked up. "Ms. Du Pre, the book's publisher, would have that," he said, and offered Angelina an encouraging smile. The girl only stared down into her lap.

"And how did Ms. Du Pre come to have your manuscript?" Norman asked as he rifled through the folder.

"I, um, left it at her office."

"You could have taken those notes after reading the book."

"But I didn't," Angelina said. She picked up her head and looked straight at Norman.

Norman ruffled through the scraps. "Are these interview notes?"

Angelina shifted in her seat.

"That means this is a true story, or at least based on a true story."

"I don't—"

"If you can prove that this is a true story, how you learned about it, and that Helen Williams had no way of discovering this same information for herself, then you have a chance."

Norman looked up to see the girl looking down at her hands again, and he smiled. She was the timid creature he first took her for, after all. The likes of her had no chance against the Delores Du Pres of this world.

"If you can't do that," Norman closed the envelope and tossed it into Angelina's lap, startling her, "then you have nothing."

"Thank you for your time, sir." Henry stood, the pride pouring off him. "We'll come back when we have more."

Norman watched Henry and Angelina leave. It sickened him to see Henry open the door to the stairwell for her. He snatched the phone up and dialed the numbers, his palms sweaty in anticipation.

"Hello. This is Ms. Du Pre's assistant, Heather. Who am I addressing?"

"This is Norman Finley, author of 'The Beast Within'."

"Mm-hm" says Heather. "Sir, Ms. Du Pre is very busy. I'm sure she'll read your manuscript soon."

"There's a different matter I need to discuss with her."

"What matter?"

"A private matter."

Heather paused. "Very well. I'll patch you through. Just a moment."

Norman straightened the pens that Angelina's evidence had pushed askew.

"Yes?"

"Is this Delores Du Pre?"

"Yes"

"This is Norman Finley, Attorney at Law."

"Yes?"

"I've just had a girl in my office who claims the book you've published, *My Death, Your Greatest Masterpiece*, was written by her and not Helen Williams. This is a ridiculous allegation, but I thought you ought to know."

"I don't recall owing you any favors, Mister..."

"Finley. Norman Finley, author of 'The Beast Within'.

On a different subject entirely, what do you think of my manuscript?"

"Why, Mr. Finley, it's on the top of my stack. I was just about to pick it up."

"Oh, wonderful. I look forward to hearing from you."

Norman set down the phone. The girl Angelina had no chance at legal victory. He may as well get something out of the situation himself. He turned his chair to face the snarling wolf, then grinned back at it, high on the success of his treachery.

***

Down on the street below, Henry smiled at Angelina again. This time she noticed and smiled back.

"May I walk you home?" asked Henry.

"I'd like that."

They walked a respectable distance apart. After two blocks of silence, Angelina spoke. "Thank you for helping me, Henry. I'm so sorry it was a waste."

"It wasn't a waste. Mr. Finley said all we have to do is—"

"I don't know how to prove the story is true now that Madame Lockridge has passed. I don't know if Madame even wanted people to know it was true." They walked the rest of the way in silence.

At Eugene's house, Angelina pulled away from him.

"I'll start by looking into Helen Williams," Henry called after her, then followed her up a few steps. "If we can show she had no connection to Lockridge—"

"Helen Williams is probably a pen-name." Angelina fumbled with the key.

"Then I've got my work cut out for me." Henry gave a quick bow and bounded down the steps.

Angelina opened the front door and returned the key to her pocket. "I'm sorry to put you to so much trouble," she said.

Henry turned, blew her a kiss, and said, "You, my angel, are worth it."

Angelina stood dumbfounded on the porch. Was that how he really felt about her? She thought it could only ever be a dream. Her heart wanted to chase after him, but her feet were too confused to know down from up. She would see him tomorrow. Perhaps he'd ask her out to lunch. With that happy thought lingering, she hung up her coat and didn't notice the man on the couch.

"Angelina," he said.

Her heart flinched. She turned to see him and offered a pained smile. "Rupert."

"It's been quite some time."

"Six months."

"Has it been that long since you ripped my heart out?"

Angelina turned away. "Where are Eugene and Beth?"

"Out," Rupert said. "I'll go, if you want. I know you can't stand what I am." He brushed past her and grabbed his coat.

"That wasn't why," Angelina blurted out. Rupert paused with his hand resting on the doorknob. "Madame said the reason my mother didn't marry Jonathan was that she was already pregnant with my half-brother. Madame hired me as a favor to our mother, same as you." Rupert's shoulders shook. "I think you're my half-brother." Angelina grabbed a stray thread off the coat in his arms.

Rupert threw his head back and laughed.

"I'm serious. We have the same hair and eye color, and our noses are similar. Madame never revealed more about who that person was. I wondered if she actually knew, or if she was trying to protect me."

"I swear to you I am not your brother."

"Half-brother," Angelina corrected.

"We look a little similar because your mother's father and my parents are Austrian."

"Then why did Madame hire you? How do you know anything about my mother?"

"Madame had a penchant for convincing people like your mother and me into living a normal life. She had me believing I could for a while, but then you showed me that wasn't true."

"And how do you know my mother?" Angelina asked, ignoring the hurt in his last words.

"You're so unlike her. Did you know you used to forget pages in the typewriter? I don't think Madame meant for me to know she was a murderer, but that did explain why my past never repulsed her."

"How do you know my mother?" Angelina pressed again.

"She's how I met Madame."

"But you came to work at Lockridge when you were ten —" Angelina cut herself off. Seeing Rupert, her brave, outspoken Rupert, looking down at the floor startled her.

"There was a time when I would have poured my heart out to you, Angelina. I did, once," Rupert said. His eyes glistened with memory.

"That night at the lake."

"When I told you what I am."

"What you were," Angelina said.

He shook his head. "What I am. Can't help my nature." Angelina gripped her own wrist, not knowing what to say. "You said you didn't love me. With you, I thought a normal life might have room for me. When I learned it couldn't, I—" Rupert let out a great sigh. "Like I said, there was a time I would have bared my soul to you." Rupert hung up his coat. "I could again, if you say

120

you love me."

Angelina twisted the thread from his coat around her finger. She felt ripped in two, torn between Rupert, the man she needn't have made herself stop loving, and Henry, the man whose love had freshly transformed from dream to reality.

"Do you love me, Angelina?" Rupert rested his hands on her shoulders.

She missed this, missed looking into his eyes and everything else falling away. The front door opened. Angelina and Rupert shuffled to the side to let Eugene and Beth in.

"Were you at the theatre?" Angelina asked before Beth could even take off her mink coat.

"Who's this?" Beth asked.

"Um," Angelina said.

"A colleague," Eugene offered quickly. "Shall we retire to my study?" Rupert followed him out of the room.

Angelina blinked. She'd assumed Rupert had come to see her. The pure coincidence of now learning it would be okay to love Rupert both amused and baffled her. Realizing Beth was speaking to her, she snapped out of her reverie.

"Sorry," she said, giving her friend an appropriate smile.

"What's wrong?"

"That was Rupert."

"Oh. The old love interest returns. You too sounded so cute together. Going on walks and reading to each other. Why aren't you happy he's here?"

"I'm confused. It turns out Henry does have some sort of feelings for me, and I thought I had stopped thinking about Rupert in that way. Now, maybe I still do. I don't know. It's happening too quickly."

Beth patted her on the back and nodded. "I'll do some laundry."

121

"Whatever for?"

"I've been asking Eugene for one of those fancy new electric washer and wringers, and he finally said yes. But boy, do they make a racket."

"How will a noisy machine cheer me up?" Angelina asked.

"Well, the hallway floor is creaky, so whenever I want to eavesdrop on Eugene, there needs to be other noises. The kettle used to be my go to, so he can't hear me coming."

"You think I should eavesdrop on Rupert and your husband?"

"Could be fun, and what if they're talking about you? What if you're the reason he's here?"

Angelina grinned. *I am like my mother, after all*, she thought. Beth left to start the washer. When a grating buzz filled the house, Angeline crept up the stairs and down the hall to the closed door of Eugene's study.

Angelina regretted the fact that her mother never taught her any nifty spy skills. She thought that would have been exciting, and in that scenario Angelina would have been allowed to know who her mother really was. But that wasn't the case. Angelina's mother's lifelong lies made her a stranger.

Angelina pressed her ear against the door.

"I stalled as long as I could, but Adrian knows," Rupert said.

"And Malcolm?" Eugene asked.

"I took care of it."

"Adrian doesn't deserve that inheritance," Eugene said. "He doesn't deserve the Lockridge name. He practically disowned himself, the coward. He wants to run away by becoming a Spratchet. Bah. It's me who's protected the Lockridge name, me! And I had damn well inherit something. No one can know that damned book is true. Of course Madame would go senile and publish our family's dirty laundry. Someone had to have helped the old bat, and I can't have that someone mucking around."

"I'll take care of it," Rupert said.

"Just to be sure, 'take care of' means kill, right? I want to know I'm getting my money's worth," Eugene said tersely.

Angelina prayed Rupert wouldn't say yes.

He didn't say anything. Angelina imagined Rupert shaking his head, but she knew he was probably nodding instead.

"I didn't believe Madame at first," continued Eugene. "I thought when she said you were a child assassin she'd taken in, she was delusional. But when I needed someone dead, I thought to check, and what do you know? You were indeed, and looking for work at that."

"If that's all," Rupert said.

Angelina stepped away from the door and scurried to the stairs. Rupert walked out of the study and saw her. He turned and stepped back into the study.

"Perhaps we ought to discuss this in greater detail," he said, closing the door behind him.

Angelina flew down the steps, hesitating at the front door. Rupert knew she was the one who typed the story for Madame, but he didn't tell Eugene. Is that because he was protecting her? Or was that because Rupert was going to "take care of her" without bothering Eugene with the details? Would Rupert do that? Would he be willing to kill her? She would like to think the answer was no, but what if a wolf couldn't change its nature?

If there was danger, where would Angelina even go?

She needed time to think, to stall, to wrap her head around the charming Henry, intense Rupert, and seemingly devious Eugene. "I'm stepping out for a minute," she called to

Beth.

"Are you sure?" Beth asked.

"Just for a minute. I'll be fine." Angelina opened the front door and breezed down the steps. She didn't stop at the curb. She needed more space, more time. A stray dog barked from across the street. The wet night air wrapped around her, luring her farther away from the confusion and fear. Angelina crossed the road and wandered, finding herself at the edge of a park.

She suddenly regretted coming out this far this late in the evening. No answers came to her, and now she was cold. She recalled telling Beth about her book at work and hoped her vagueness was enough to prevent Beth from telling Eugene about it.

Finally, Angelina settled on going back, or at least somewhere with better lighting, but stopped when she spied Kent sitting on another park bench. A woman was with him.

Her heart refused to clearly make decisions about either Rupert or Henry, but the strange and inappropriate behavior of Kent and this woman was something Angelina could solve right then.

Every muscle tense, she marched into the poorly lit park, right up to Kent and the woman, and only then found her courage failing her.

CHAPTER 17

"Kent, it's one thing to constantly bump into a woman. It's quite another to sit on a bench and watch her."

Angelina glanced at the woman on the bench, but she had had no context for her. Kent grinned at Angelina's brashness, forcing her to glance between the two faces in front of her, looking for an answer.

She hadn't recognized the before, between the bonnet-styled hat she wore, casting shadows on her features, and the new, dark hair color and severe makeup. She hardly looked like the inconspicuous housewife who had travelled to buy her devious jam.

"Mother?" Angelina asked, her voice quavering with hope.

Elizabeth nodded, tears in her familiar eyes. She stood up and reached out her arms, embracing Angelina.

Kent watched the two women smiling but still glanced around them nervously, looking for any witnesses to the scene. "We should get out of sight. We don't know who could be watching," he remarked with urgency. Elizabeth nodded, seemingly unable to take her eyes off her daughter.

"Kent, I suppose I should thank you for bringing my

mother to me." As Angelina spoke the words, she faltered in her own conviction. She couldn't fathom how he always seemed to pop up at strange times, and now this. "Actually, Kent, how *do* you know my mother?"

"I will tell you everything soon," Elizabeth said, "but right now, your brother is right. We need to move."

Angelina gasped, raising her hand to cover her gaping mouth with dignity. She could see it now, the familiarity to him that she hadn't even considered before. The news elated her, and her eyes sparkled with an intense amount of joy. She hadn't minded Kent, who just irritated her slightly, but knowing he was no threat to her and not interested in her as anything other than a sibling, she couldn't wait to get to know him better. Ever since the day Madame had told her he was out there somewhere, Angelina knew she would find him. She knew they would, someday, become great friends.

They quickly moved away from the open park, and after a short walk arrived at Kent's townhouse, which Elizabeth admitted she owned. Angelina was inwardly pleased to find that Kent, too, had only just met his mother in person. They had been corresponding by letter for some time, but finally Elizabeth wanted to bring her family back together. Kent appeared shy and awkward. It seemed as though Angelina was the one who took after her mother, and perhaps Kent was a little more reserved.

They had been talking avidly together for several minutes before a thought occurred to Angelina. Her mother had known Madame, and much of the story Madame had shared with her was also Elizabeth's story. Her mother could help her to prove that she had written the book, and that the woman they said had written it was a fake and a thief. She couldn't wait for a break in conversation to bring up the idea with her long-lost mother. It just came tumbling out.

126

"Mother, I don't know how to tell you this, but Madame, she said you knew she was going to tell me everything."

"Yes, I know. She said she'd thought you were ready. Now that I've met you, I agree."

"She didn't just want to tell me. She wanted me to write it all down."

Elizabeth's face paled. "I hadn't heard that part of it. What did you write down? Does this have to do with that manuscript I've watched you chase all over town?"

Angelina had the sinking feeling that she was in trouble. Her face flushed red, but she continued on. "Madame wanted it all written down, everything, because she felt guilty about her husband, I think."

"What exactly did you write down?" Elizabeth's voice was deceptively quiet and calm.

"I wrote down everything, about the jam, about your missions, about the murder... everything."

Elizabeth looked at Angelina, her eyes hard, and Angelina felt a moment of fear. "And this is the book that was stolen from you, the one about which you've been talking to lawyers and goodness knows who else?"

Angelina nodded. She began to see the edges of the sort of trouble she had started by knocking on Delores' door, and the chaos she had perpetrated by leaving her ragged manuscript at her doorstep.

"My cover could be blown. Angelina, you can't comprehend the enemies I've made, not just here but everywhere, all over the world. You've put my life in danger, and Kent's life. Perhaps your own as well."

Angelina thought of the conversation she had just overheard. She hadn't had a chance to tell her mother why she had fled Beth's house or about the threats she had overheard from Rupert. She had put all their lives in danger in her unthinking obedience to Madame.

Angelina couldn't just flee the way her mother had. To her, the manuscript was an investment, not only of her time but in how she had reformed her connection to her mother, her brother, and all that remained of her friendship with Madame. "I brought it up because I want you to help prove I'm the author. It was stolen from me."

Elizabeth looked at her daughter, aghast. "That is the last thing I would ever do. Leave it. Be glad that if it's out, someone other than you will get into the trouble it will bring down on them. Hope that their theft will buy us enough time to get out of London."

"Get out of London? But that manuscript, it's my only inheritance! I spent so much time on it. It may provide for my entire future."

Her mother's eyes were angry even though she controlled her voice. "That is the most foolish and simpleminded thing I have heard in some time. I'm quite disappointed that it's come out of my own daughter's mouth."

"What do you mean?" Angelina asked, hurt and bewildered.

"First of all, it was never your story. It was Madame's story, and it was *my* story. You didn't even write it in your own words, but merely took down Madame's dictation. It's not yours, and even if it was, it is a poisonous pill. Don't you see? Madame *used* you. Move on, Angelina. That story is stolen, and whoever claims to be the thief is in for a world of hurt."

Angelina saw everything she had fought so hard for, all her hopes for the future, dashed. She had had something of her own and she had lost it. But the small voice of her conscience piped up and agreed with what Elizabeth had told her. All she

128

had really been was a secretary, and she was no more the writer than the woman who had falsely published it under her name.

Elizabeth seemed quite aware that her daughter was hurt by the loss and by her own offensive but apt summation of the situation. She took a deep breath and tried to be softer and kinder. "My darling child, you're my little girl. My baby." She smoothed Angelina's hair and kissed her forehead. "Do you remember the note I left you? I know you read it."

"Yes. I remember every word."

"I told you to see the world, and I meant it. I'm glad you left Essex and came to London, and if it was for the manuscript, then I suppose it has served a good purpose. But now, I want you to come with me to Paris."

"To Paris?"

"Yes, for a time. I have a residence there and it's a safe place we can go to find out how badly this may turn out."

"I can't go to Paris!" Angelina protested.

"Why ever not?"

"I'm supposed to meet with Henry." Angelina's voice trailed off. She was living in a delusion, believing in the business of her mother being a spy with half of her brain, but not taking it seriously with the other half.

Elizabeth sighed and pinched the bridge of her nose. "You're trying my patience, Angelina. I want to help you, I want to make up for having left you, but if I can't do that, the very least I want to do is to save your life after the muddle in which Madame's conscience has left us."

"I'm sorry, Mother. I suppose you're right. It's hard to let all your hopes and dreams just fall through your fingertips and just walk away. I don't know how you did it."

"I found better dreams," Elizabeth snapped. Tears filled Angelina's eyes, and Elizabeth features folded into a wince of regret. "Now, Im sorry, Angelina. I didn't mean that. Please, come to Paris with us, even if it's only for a few weeks until we can find out if it's safe for you to come back."

"People will worry about me."

"Write them a letter. Tell them you received a telegram saying your father is ill and that you had to return to Essex."

Angelina was startled by how quickly the perfect lie had sprung to her mother's lips. Even with their strained relationship, she would run back to Essex if she knew her father had fallen ill. Nobody else maintained contact with him, so the story would go undetected.

Kent brought Angelina some paper and a pen and set it at the table for her. He smiled and watched her watching Elizabeth. She quickly wrote the letters and put them in neat envelopes for Kent. He gave her a teasing salute and left to deliver them.

Elizabeth had stepped out of the room, but returned only a few minutes later. "I've had the maid pack my traveling things. You're about my size, so I packed enough for two. You're going to have a wonderful time in Paris, a time like you've most likely never even dreamed of. I know some charming people who will be happy to meet you both."

It dawned on Angelina that she was about to be exposed to a whole new world, on the verge of glimpsing into the world of a spy, her mother's secret other life. Who would her mother introduce her as? She felt breathless; it was an adventure like she had only read about or imagined, an adventure nearly as marvelous as the one she had typed and had stolen from her. This story was different, though. This story would be her own, and she could do with it as she wished once she knew what happened on the next page.

"Don't say anything about Paris when the maid is in the room. Don't say anything at all. In fact, I'll tell you what to say when we're in the car." Elizabeth gave a small smile.

The maid came in at that moment with a heavy suitcase she could barely lug and a parcel tucked under her arm. "Mrs. Pentworth," she said, startling Angelina, who had never heard this alias of her mother's before. "There was a parcel at the door. Someone just left it on the front step. It's not addressed to anyone I know."

Elizabeth's eyes narrowed and she took the book-shaped parcel from the maid. Scrawled in ominous letters across the front it said, '*To Lady Elizabeth Heathburn. Don't you know, you can't ever go home? - Lord Pentworth*'

CHAPTER 18

"Thank you, Agnes. That will be all."

The maid bowed her head then turned and left the room. Angelina watched as her mother opened the package to reveal a book. Its cover was dark blue, plain, with no writing. Elizabeth opened to a certain page and retrieved a silver skeleton key tied to a red ribbon. "There's been a change of plans. I must leave now. Alone. Your train leaves tomorrow at eight in the morning, sharp."

Angelina's heart raced. "You mean, I…I have to go by myself?"

Elizabeth turned to face her daughter. "Don't worry. Kent will meet you there. You will both travel together to Dover, then take the ferry to Calais. From Calais, you will travel on the Blue Train to Paris. Kent will be with you for the entire journey.

With a sigh of relief Angelina thought, *The Blue Train? Does she mean* the *Blue Train?* She had to ask. "Mother, the train to Paris, do you mean the—"

Elizabeth smiled and hugged her daughter, cutting her off. "Yes, I mean that blue train. Or Le Train Bleu, as it's formally known." Elizabeth said the words "Le Train Bleu" with a perfect French accent.

"I've heard about it, how luxurious it is and how only the richest of the rich use it and—"

Elizabeth placed her hands on her daughter's shoulders, looked her straight in the eye, and interrupted Angelina with a warning. "Angelina, I know you're excited, but you must listen to me and listen well. You must do everything I say. It seems risky to even let you go home tonight, but I know from experience that if you can't move forward with your plans, you should fit back into normal life and act as though nothing has changed. Now go home, gather your necessities, and be sure to get to bed early. You must be on that morning train. Wear your finest, the navy skirt with the tan blazer will do, and please fasten your hair into a neat bun. Get everything ready tonight. You must be on that train, you must. Your life may be in very grave danger if you don't follow my orders without fail. Now go." Elizabeth planted a kiss on Angelina's forehead then showed her to the door.

On the walk home, her mind raced. *Danger? What kind of danger? How did my mother know what I had in my wardrobe? The blue train?* It elated her to finally have seen her mother after all this time. It struck her how youthful she was, at least compared to Madame, who was similar in age but had let the years wear her down much faster.

She couldn't believe that, in less than twenty-four hours, she would be riding along the rail that was used by noble aristocrats and royalty. She wondered what Madame would think of that as she fingered the ticket with caution.

"Hold onto you own ticket, Angelina. If anything should happen, it's imperative you are able to continue on alone, if need be. You must be ready for anything." Elizabeth's words echoed in her ears. She felt strong, not afraid. She knew she could handle this.

A few more blocks, and she was home. The lights were dim and she could hear Beth singing from inside her bedroom. "Beth?" Angelina entered her room to find Beth dancing around the bed. On top of the plain white bedspread, an arrangement of beautiful dresses were laid out.

"Oh, Angelina, you're just in time."

"For what?"

Beth beamed from ear to ear as she held up a light blue dress that sparkled with the finest material. "For the party. Or should I say *the* party! My friend from school, Eleanor, married a very wealthy barrister, Reginald Grant, and they're celebrating the purchase of their new home over in The Bolton's. And you're invited, too. Our invitation arrived very late, so I know it's all last minute, but…"

"But I can't go." Angelina felt a surge of disappointment for having to miss the event.

"Why ever not?"

Angelina scrambled for an answer. "I…I don't have anything to wear." She didn't like lying to her closest friend.

Beth pointed to the dresses on the bed and said, "Oh, yes you do. We both do, thanks to Eleanor. She sent along these dresses knowing we didn't have time to arrange something. See, she really wants us there."

Angelina shook her head. "I'm sorry, Beth, but I still can't go. I'm, uh…"

Beth stood and turned Angelina around to face the mirror. "And I'll fix your hair, too. You'll look beautiful. Don't worry. You know you worry a little too much, don't you? Now, you better go draw a bath. We don't have much time. Eugene will be back in an hour. One of Eleanor's drivers is picking us up."

Angelina couldn't think of any other excuse, so she fumbled along and went towards the bath. The warm water soothed her mind for a moment. As Angelina relaxed, a new, raw confidence seeped over her.

I should go to that party. I know what my mother said, but I never get to have any fun. It won't hurt if I go just for an hour or two. Then I can get a taxi back home and get my things ready for tomorrow. And Beth, she's right. I do worry too much. I do. Who knows if I'll ever be invited again to a party over in The Boltons? I can't miss this.

Angelina got out of the tub, dried herself off, and whispered, "I'm sorry, mother, but I *will* attend this party tonight."

With an unfamiliar stride, Angelina returned to her room, where Beth was still trying on different dresses. She stood straight and said, "I want you to cut my hair."

Beth turned away from the mirror. "Your hair? But it's so long and—"

"I know, and I want it short, like yours. I want to be in style like everyone else. So please, Beth, cut my hair."

Beth raised her eyebrows, surprised by Angelina's sudden, aggressive interruption. "I'll go fetch my shears."

Fifteen minutes later Angelina lifted her hand to the bottom of her new bob-style hair. "Oh, Beth. I love it."

Beth nodded with a grin. "It does look absolutely fabulous. Now, come. Let's see what to wear."

Angelina looked at the frocks, none of which she could ever afford. Light blue, dusty pink, gold, white, mint green, and lavender, each one with beads, a fringe, and sparkles—all so opulent. Angelina tried on the gold, then the white, then the dusty pink. "I think I like this the best."

"Yes, it's the best color on you. And now for the finishing touches." Beth went into her room, then returned with

135

three boxes. "Here are your shoes. I told her what size you are, and mine are in this other box. The third box has this." Beth opened the third box, which was full of rhinestone and ruby jewelry, a few strings of pearls, and two head wraps decorated with feathers.

Beth took a pink feather and fastened it with a white ribbon onto Angelina's new, stylish hair. Then she placed a long string of pearls around Angelina's neck, stained her lips ruby red, and drew black kohl eyeliner around her eyes. "Take a look."

Angelina turned towards her reflection. "Oh, Beth. I can't believe it. Thank you. Thank you so much."

They heard the front door close, and Eugene shouted, "I'm home. The car will be here at eight. That's five minutes from now, ladies. I hope you're ready."

As they walked out toward the car, Angelina smiled and thought, *So many things happen at eight, it seems.*

The car pulled up to a large white home with grand pillars on either side of a glossy, black door. A man in a tuxedo with long tails came down the front steps and opened their door. He bowed his head and said in a rather deep voice, "Welcome to the Grant residence. Follow me, please."

He opened the front door and Angelina almost fainted. The band playing sounded like an entire orchestra. A sweeping staircase with a railing that matched the front door opened before them, and black and white checkered marble floors greeted them at the door. The walls were all a deeply stained oak. Potted palms bordered each corner, and an enormous gold vase of white blooms rested on top of a circular mirrored table.

The man once more said, "Follow me," as he led them down towards the left and into the ballroom.

And what a sight. Men in tuxes and all but a few women

decked out in short, bright dresses, dangling with fringes and beads, filled the room. Angelina looked around, beaming with wide eyes. *It's a good thing Beth fixed me up. I fit right in. I can't believe it. I fit right in.*

At the back of the room, a tuxedo-clad orchestra played. Behind them, an entire wall of windowpanes revealed a patio and a lawn with a large willow tree. Several red velvet couches dotted the room, as well as round tables adorned with white and gold tablecloths. The floor was all white, all marble, and in the center of the floor, barely visible beneath the guests' feet, was a large black circle with a monogramed letter inside. Angelina took a step forward and almost bumped into one of the many waiters scurrying along with their silver trays full of champagne glasses.

"Pardon me, madame."

"Oh, I'm sorry."

"Would you care for some champagne?"

"Yes, thank you."

Angelina took a sip as she heard Beth say, "Go easy on that stuff. I know you're not used to drinking much."

"Don't worry, Beth. I'll be careful. Heavens, that's a change, me telling you not to worry." They both laughed and then Angelina turned her head towards the entryway of the ballroom. "Oh my God, Beth. It's Henry. What's he doing here?"

Beth put her arm around Angelina's back and said, "I invited him." Angelina watched as Henry waved at them and walked through the crowd in their direction. "Oh, I think I'll go look for Eleanor. Come on, Eugene." Beth took her husband by the hand and they walked away.

"Angelina, you look absolutely beautiful. May I be so bold as to even say the prettiest woman here?"

Angelina's face flushed, just as it always did whenever a blushing circumstance arose. Henry took her hand and kissed the top of it. Angelina's cheeks grew even hotter as she whispered her reply. "Well, thank you. Hardly the prettiest, but thank you. You look quite dapper yourself." The music stopped and everyone on the dancefloor clapped.

"Thank you, Angelina. And you *are* the prettiest girl in the room. You always are."

Angelina smiled, her heart raced, and she finished her champagne in one big gulp to calm her nerves. The orchestra started once more, this time playing 'Dizzy Fingers', and that was just how she felt—dizzy.

Another black-tailed, white-gloved waiter passed by, offering them champagne. Henry took two glasses for them and Angelina accepted the gesture. "I really like this champagne, Henry, and Heaven knows if or when I'll ever get to taste it again."

They most likely served this expensive stuff on The Blue Train, but she wasn't sure if they did, or if she would even be able to order it. One glass probably cost more than her entire week's pay.

"Yes, it's very good," Henry said. They stood and watched the crowd while sipping their drinks. "Would you care to dance?" He offered her his hand and a smile.

Angelina looked around the room, hoping to find Beth. "I, um, I don't know these new dances very well."

Henry placed his drink on top of the table beside them, took her by the hand, and headed towards the dance floor. "I'll show you. It's easy. Plus, I suspect you're not only the prettiest girl in the room, but also a very good dancer." With another big gulp, Angelina finished her second glass and then her third.

They moved through the kicking legs and twirling arms to

the center of the dance floor, right where the monogramed letters flourished on the sleek marble. Henry put his arm around her waist. "Just follow my lead. Put one foot in front and then in the back, like this." Angelina followed his lead, right on cue with the music. "That's it," Henry encouraged, grinning. "You've got it. You do. I knew you'd be a good dancer." The whole floor seemed to shake as they moved about.

People clapped and cheered. Champagne glasses clinked with toasts of happiness and trails of cigarette smoke lifted up in the air, looking almost giddy to be there themselves. Off to the left, a large buffet had been arranged with gourmet delights, and another very long table held every kind of desert she could imagine.

The music stopped, the crowd clapped, and then another tuxedo-tailed man stood up at the microphone to sing:

'I love you, I love you
Is all that I can say'

Henry took Angelina in both of his arms and they swayed. Angelina realized she did love Henry, without a doubt. Rupert had merely been a mild attraction, a glimmer of infatuation compared to how she felt now. Then the whole room stopped. Angelina looked into Henry's eyes, and everything else disappeared.

No more clinking glasses, no more trails of giddy smoke, no more laughter and voices ringing with joy. It was just her and Henry in the entire room, the entire world, even. Angelina forgot it all as she danced in the embrace of Henry's heart.

The song ended far too quickly for Angelina's liking. They clapped, and she worried if her makeup had at all smeared in the excitement. "Henry, will you excuse me please? I must visit the ladies' washroom."

"Of course. I'll wait for you right back there, at the table where we were standing earlier."

Angelina grabbed another drink on her way. Pleased with her appearance, she exited the ladies' room and thought, *I'm wearing a pink dress. A pink dress, and I'm dancing with Henry. This is just as I imagined, and it's happening. It's really happening.*

She rushed to return to the ballroom. There Henry stood, waiting for her, looking so handsome in his very own, fine black tuxedo. "Would you care to see the buffet?" he asked with such genuine care and affection. Angelina nodded, and Henry took her hand as they walked across the room.

The next few hours flew by. There was more dancing, more drinking, more drinking, and more dancing. A few minutes past midnight, Henry pointed towards the back wall and said, "Would you like to take a look at the garden with me?"

They strolled outside to find an empty patio and a stone bench beneath the weeping willow tree. Bushes of red and pink roses and white peonies bordered the cement patio. Henry bent down to pick up a white peony that had fallen to the ground, and he handed it to Angelina.

"I don't think anyone will mind, will they?" he said with a mischievous smile.

Angelina held the flower to her nose and smiled. "Thank you, Henry." They looked at the moonlight and the stars and the long stretch of manicured grass that went further than either could tell.

"Angelina, I was hoping you...you might like to accompany me to dinner tomorrow evening, maybe around eight?"

She started to say yes, only too happy to accept his

invitation, but then she remembered she would be gone. "I would love to," she told him. "There isn't anything else in the world that I would rather do. But, well, I…I have to leave town for a while. I can't tell you why. I'm sorry that I can't. It's a family matter, and I'm not at liberty to say, but I would very much like to write to you while I'm away. If I may? I'm…I'm so very sorry, Henry. I—"

Henry pressed his finger to her lips. "Shh. Don't worry, I understand. And of course, I would love the correspondence while you're gone. I just hope it won't be for too very long. I will miss you, Angelina. Deeply miss you."

"Me too," was all Angelina could mutter as she choked back the disappointment she felt. He leaned forward and kissed her, then kissed her again. And again, and again.

They were interrupted by Beth, who shouted from the door leading to the patio. "Come on, you two. They're about to do the Charleston. The entire party is about to be on the dance floor."

They laughed and held hands to return indoors. Angelina was practically floating on air with all the excitement as the crowd shouted their *woos* and whistled their *wees*. What followed was a blur—a big, boisterous blur of folly. And then sunlight came streaming through the large wall of windows.

Angelina jumped up. She had fallen asleep in Henry's arms on one of the red velvet couches. People slept on the other, curved, claw-footed couches, beside them on the floor, and a few slept with their heads on top of the tables. Confetti was strewn all over the place, along with empty champagne bottles, feathers, and one shoe. Somewhere, Angelina thought, there was a lady wearing only one of her black and white, ribbon-tied heels.

Then she realized it was morning, the next morning, and she was supposed to make the train at eight sharp, or her life could be in danger. She had nothing ready, and everything was a mess. She shook Henry's arm. "What time is it? Henry, what time is it?"

Henry rubbed his eyes, shocked by the urgency in her voice. He removed a gold pocket watch from his vest and opened it.

CHAPTER 19

Time seemed to slow as Angelina anxiously waited for the numbers to spill out of Henry's mouth. The time it took for Henry to read his pocket watch seemed infinite. The number rang in her ears as her current hangover became prevalent. The following moments seemed to go by very fast.

She picked herself up from the velvet couch, grasping at the feather and ribbon around her head, flung it onto the couch, and sprinted from the hall. There was no time for her things, no time for goodbyes. Her life depended on it, and so in her own, live Cinderella moment, she fled from the one she loved at the sound of a bell tolling for the time Henry had uttered—seven o' clock.

With but an hour to get to the station, she had to think fast. How would she get there? It was a peculiar thing, what lengths people would go to when they felt they had no choice. Her heels clicked through the estate as she scrambled to recall the location of the entrance. The sound echoing through the halls only further agitated her pounding head.

Once outside, she found a row of motor coaches, but she didn't know how to drive; not many women did. Angelina stopped to think. Her thoughts were interrupted by the neighing of Mr. Grant's horses. Of course, the barn! Angelina may not know how to drive, but she did know how to ride.

Mr. Grant's steed wasn't as poised as Octavia. It reminded her of her time at the Lockridge manor and how things had changed. How she had changed. Octavia was a lady's horse, one for show, not sport. But for this occasion, she needed strength and speed. Angelina ripped the sides of her dusty pink dress to free her legs, swung herself onto the horse, and bolted from the grounds. With the help of the rising sun, she knew what direction she traveled, but she had no clue how far away she was.

She rode back the way they had driven. If she could make her way back to something familiar, she would have a better chance at directing herself.

Passersby stopped to stare as she made her way through the town square, nearly causing a carriage accident as she changed her direction east. She could hear a train whistle in the distance and knew she was running out of time. She pressed the stirrups against the steed's ribs, urging him to go faster. Just a little bit faster.

Angelina pulled on the reigns and halted in front of the station. She climbed off, yelling at a pedestrian, "Please ensure this horse makes it back to Mr. Reginald Grant. He will surely be looking for it."

The man nodded and grabbed the reigns from her. She took off her shoes and ran into the station, heels in hand. She passed by a clock: 7:57am.

***

Kent stood on the platform, tapping his foot, torn whether to get on the train without Angelina or miss it himself. Elizabeth had stressed that they catch it, but she also made it a point that they stay together. He wasn't sure which of the two was the most important. The train blew its whistle, and Kent began to board when he heard a woman yelling.

"Wait! Wait!"

He turned to see a sparkly pink blur heading straight toward him, knocking them both onto the train. Angelina huffed and puffed, lying on the train floor for a minute. Kent picked himself up and offered his hand. Angelina gratefully accepted his offer in helping her up.

"Well, that's one way to catch a train." Kent found himself chuckling.

Angelina stood, looking embarrassed before him in a ripped dress, disheveled hair, smeared makeup, and smelling of hay. The furthest from elegant she had ever been. She brushed herself off, though it made little difference.

Kent helped her over to two nearby seats as the train slowly began its journey. Angelina gazed out the window, finally catching her breath.

"Angelina, where are your things?"

"Let's just say I didn't have much of any value, anyway."

One of the conductors entered the car to collect tickets. Angelina watched him walk off to the other end of the carriage before turning to Kent. "Kent, we have to move."

"I don't follow—"

"My ticket! In the course of everything…" Angelina pointed to her current disheveled state. "I forgot my ticket."

Kent's eyes widened. Sticking with Angelina had already started to prove more dramatic than his liking. It seemed to run in the women of the family. Thinking on his feet, he had an idea.

"Very well. If they stop us, follow my lead."

Angelina nodded. Kent took out a handkerchief and extended it towards her. She used her reflection in the mirror to wipe away any makeup that had run, and combed her fingers through her hair.

He stood and pulled her to his side, then walked towards the conductor, clutching her. "Excuse me, sir. My wife isn't feeling very well. She gets awful bouts of motion sickness if she sits in the front."

"Oh, of course. I'm sure a lovely couple will switch seats with you." The conductor stepped aside so that they could proceed to the back. "Can I see your tickets?" he asked.

Angelina put her hand up to her mouth, pretending to gag. She bent over, and Kent lowered himself to her side.

"All right, all right," the conductor said hastily. "I'll check back later. Take care, Miss."

Kent tipped his hat to him as they passed, and a couple, hearing the commotion, got up and offered their seats. They graciously accepted and sat down.

"That should buy us some time, but it seems we'll have to get off at the next stop." Kent didn't look too thrilled with her. They hadn't spent much time together at all, and they were already bordering on sibling rivalry.

***

Although she made it to the train, she had been anything but discreet. Who knew how many people had heard her mention Le Train Bleu last night in her intoxicated state?. Word must have gotten to Rupert, and now he was after her. She glanced across the aisle of the train, knowing she wasn't wrong. She chastised herself for being so careless.

"Kent." This time Angelina spoke with panic and tugged on the arm of his jacket.

"What now?" Kent scolded in as hushed a tone as he

146

could muster, but his eyes softened, and the agitated look on his faced disappeared.

"See that man in the brown hat and tan overcoat sitting over there?"

"Yes."

She took a deep breath. "Not to further dig myself into the damsel in distress category, but he's a trained assassin, and I believe I'm his current target."

"Hell, Angelina!"

"We can find a different way into Dover. As long as we catch our connection alive, it doesn't exactly matter how we do it...does it?"

"I don't know. Elizabeth was very specific."

"Alive, Kent. Alive!" In a matter of twenty-four hours, Angelina had transformed from worrisome and timid to fast-acting and thinking on her feet. "This time follow my lead." She smirked.

While the conductor was busy chatting with the passengers as he checked their tickets, they made their way to one of the empty compartment cars.

"Keep an eye out, will you?" Angelina rummaged through the luggage that had been placed overhead. Her new hairstyle would serve as perfect cover, but she needed to finish up her disguise. Rupert had once loved her; a mere change in hair would not be sufficient. How thin of a line it was between love and hate. "Aha, perfect."

Angelina came across a nun's habit. She quickly threw on the robe over her own clothing and tucked her hair into the headdress. Kent turned to her and his eyes grew wide. She took that as a good sign. Making sure no one had seem them, they walked out of the train compartment and headed towards the last train car. When they approached the dining car, she noticed

147

Rupert had closed the distance between them.

They tried to exit the dining car inconspicuously, but the train came to a sudden halt, just out from the next station. The sudden stop caused everyone and everything to be flung forward, including Angelina, who fell into one of the tables. In an attempt to right herself, part of Angelina's new robe caught on a piece of loose table edging. She struggled to tug it free, then, seeing that Kent had gone ahead, she glanced back to find Rupert only feet from her now. He set eyes on her as soon as he entered the carriage, smiling at her new hair and attire, then promptly reached inside his overcoat.

CHAPTER 20

The look in his eyes was a mixture of amusement and disgust, and Angelina did not want to believe it was all directed at her. She felt alarmed by the face she had known so well once upon a time, now a face that seemed to belong to a stranger. Rupert's hand froze inside the front pocket of his overcoat, and he only stared at her with that dark smile.

A compartment door to her left slid open, followed by the one behind it, and then all those who had enjoyed the train ride in far less suspense poked their heads out and into the aisle. The short-lived silence of the motionless train was replaced by murmurs of discontent among the other passengers. Rupert's gaze flicked quickly behind her, his brow twitched in and out of a frown, and Angelina knew she was safe. He couldn't do anything rash in front of so many witnesses. If that was even his plan.

He withdrew his hand briskly and shook out the folded handkerchief in it to give his nose an enthusiastic blow. A few of the other passengers spared him a glance at the noise, but most were focused toward the front of the train, waiting for information on their unplanned delay.

"My apologies, Sister," he said with a sheepish smile, then returned the handkerchief to his pocket. "The close quarters

149

of a train seem to have a rather strong effect on my sinuses."

Angelina swallowed, and only then remembered that she was dressed as a woman with religious dedication. Rupert's decision to play along with her hasty disguise confused her, was not what she expected, and she couldn't find her voice to respond. She only blinked rapidly in surprise.

"It would seem as though the conductor is having some difficulty," he continued, and glanced behind him quickly toward the front of the train. "I would recommend, Sister, that you return to your compartment to wait this out. There's nothing to fret over, I'm sure, and we'll be back on course in no time."

Angelina cleared her throat and nodded curtly. "Of course," she said, and a man from the compartment closest to them stepped into the aisle and clapped Rupert on the shoulder.

"You know anything about trains, old boy?" the man asked. Rupert slowly took his gaze off Angelina and turned to smile at the man.

"No more than the next gentlemen," he said congenially.

The man lowered his voice. "Well, my dear Janet is convinced that something is terribly wrong, and is likely to feint with worry if I don't find out what's happened." A woman's face, presumably the aforementioned Janet, hovered from behind the corner of the man's compartment, her eyes wide and cheeks flushed. "It's her first time, you know," he continued.

"Most likely a minor problem with the engine, or the tracks, I'm sure," Rupert said.

The man nodded. "That's what I've told her. But you know women. They tend to imagine the most preposterous things. Care to accompany me to the engine car, see if we can offer our help?" He extended his hand to Rupert and they shook.

Rupert nodded. "It's better than waiting," he agreed, and shot Angelina a sideways glance.

"That's the spirit," the man said with a grin, then clapped his hands in excitement. "Hear that, Janet? This gentleman and I are going to see if we can help. Don't strain yourself, dear. I'll return shortly, and we'll have this machine back on its way in no time."

Two more men from the adjacent compartments stepped out at the man's hollering to join them for the engine car, and Rupert gave her one last glance before following the man who introduced himself jovially as a Mr. Hammond Cartwell. One of the other men sidled past her and mumbled a quick, "Sister," nodding in acknowledgement.

Angelina felt her face flush hot, then glanced at the woman in the compartment beside her. Janet, she assumed, stared at her with the trembling attempts at a smile on her lips, wringing her hands in distress. Angelina tried to force a smile, and made her way again to the back of the train. *Where is Kent?*

She glanced up to try to catch sight of him, and found herself meeting the gaze of an older gentlemen in a black top hat, watching her intently from the doorway of his own compartment. His scowl went unmasked as he looked her over, even beneath his thickly oiled mustache, flecked with white. Angelina blinked back at him, feeling herself slow as she was hit with an unplaced recognition of the man. His eyes narrowed, and she clasped her hands demurely in front of her stolen costume and forced her gaze to the carpeted floor of the aisle. She had seen him before, but where?

"There you are," came the call, and she looked up quickly to find Kent leaning from a compartment doorway at the very back of the train car with a gentle wave. The familiar man still glared at her, and she almost tripped on the thick black dress in her hurry to pass him. "Come inside, Sister," Kent said when she neared, and placed a hand on her shoulder to guide her into the compartment. He slid the door closed with a click. "I thought you were right behind me," he said, taking a seat.

Angelina sat on the compartment bench opposite him and fiddled with the torn seam of the nun's dress. "I was just surprised when the train stopped, that's all," she told him, glancing out the window at the now still expanse outside. "A few people called me 'Sister'. I don't very much like being a nun."

Kent glanced at her, and she turned her head to meet his gaze. He looked her up and down in the black and white uniform, and a half smile creased the scar on his jaw. "I don't think even nuns enjoy being nuns, really," he said. She rolled her eyes at him but a quiet laugh still escaped. "We'll get you into something else soon enough. You've already been my bride, and now the bride of Christ—what's next for you?"

"I'm not trying to be anyone's bride just now." It came out more sharply than she'd intended, and she instantly scolded herself for the gruffness. Kent didn't seem to be offended by her tone, but he brushed some invisible hair off his pant leg and leaned back against the compartment seat. Hearing him bring up the subject of marriage, even in such a remote and jesting manner, made her think of Henry, and how badly she wanted to sit with a pen and write him as promised.

In the moment before Rupert had pulled out his handkerchief, she really had thought that he meant instead to withdraw a gun. She knew his feelings for her, feelings she once had returned, but she also knew what he was. What she didn't know was why he was on this train.

With all the correspondence her secretive half-brother had had with Elizabeth, it wouldn't have surprised Angelina if Rupert were a topic of that correspondence. But it was unlikely that Kent knew the man; he hadn't seemed to recognize him, or even catch sight of that violent ghost from her past. And Rupert hadn't actually done anything but scare her, and make her dangerously curious. As impossible a task as it seemed, right then she preferred to keep these men in her life, and what they represented, as separate from each other as she possibly could—for as long as she could.

It was almost another hour before they started moving again. Kent had expressed his confidence that the commotion had distracted the Conductor, enough so that he would most likely forget to come check their tickets. They agreed that remaining on the train was worth the risk after Angelina reassured him she could handle Rupert should the need arise.

The hum of the tracks beneath them and the gentle rocking of the car had an inevitable effect on her energy, and Angelina dozed off to the rhythm of it. She woke only after she heard the click of the compartment door sliding shut, and quickly blinked the sleep out of her eyes.

"I've found you someone else to be," Kent told her in a low voice. He opened his jacket to remove a bundle of chiffon he had hidden there.

Angelina stared up at him with a raised eyebrow. "You're joking."

"I don't quite like you as a nun, either," he said, and shook out the dress without ceremony. It was an afternoon dress of pastel jade green, with a hem and trim of purple satin.

"You can't be serious," Angelina whispered, and spared a glance at the frosted glass of the compartment door. "We've already rifled through luggage. Whoever that belongs to is bound to find it missing, or at the very least recognize it on me." She took in the airy elegance of the dress with wide eyes, realizing that she'd never stepped into anything as finely made, and had never imagined she would. "It looks expensive."

"That's why I thought it was perfect for you," Kent said

with a smile. "I believe it fits your measurements, or close to." He looked her over for a second from head to toe again. "Hard to be sure with you in that smock." Angelina only graced the comment with a frown. "Well, hurry up, then. We're almost to Dover Priory station. I think we can make it out the back carriage unnoticed if we're quick about it."

She stood and reached out to grab the shoulders of the afternoon dress from his hands. "A little privacy?"

"Nothing less," he replied, and gave her one last glance before he slipped quietly through the compartment door. She locked it behind him.

She felt a mixture of guilt and excitement when she looked at the dress, and she realized she had to change quickly so her now-clammy palms wouldn't stain the fabric. She stuffed the nun's habit under the compartment bench with a sigh of relief, and shrugged the new dress over her shoulders. It fit perfectly.

It was a little odd, she thought, just how perfectly. It felt like the dress had been tailored for her, the neckline cutting just below the first traces of her collarbone, the waist fitting to a perfect straight line before falling in an almost nonexistent rush of fabric to the middle of her calves.

The black shoes she'd taken with the last disguise worked fine, but she wished she had a pair of sheer stockings to complete the new ensemble, maybe a hat. She felt foolish in the borrowed dress and nothing else.

She reached up to smooth her newly fashioned hair, brushed off the shoulders of the cool chiffon, and slid her hands lightly down the dress to make sure everything was in order. Her fingers brushed the fabric just above her hips, and she heard a distinct crinkling that was not made by silk. She pressed harder and felt a lump which made the same noise. Curious, she felt the lump shift, and pulled on the hem of the dress to give it a little shake.

A small square of folded paper tumbled out to the carpet. Angelina glanced at the compartment door again, then bent to retrieve the surprise. *How had it not fallen out before?* She unfolded the scrap, expecting to see some form of hasty receipt, or a friendly note to or from the real owner of the dress. The writing was small and cramped, and not in English.

She froze, her fingers tingling as she scanned the note. It was written in the same code Elizabeth had used for her secret messages to Madame—there was no doubt. Madame had shown her those same letters, had one day even spent some time away from her desperate storytelling to share with Angelina some of the secrets of how to read them. She had been repeatedly assured that it was a style unique to the correspondence between Angelina's employer and her mother...so how did it get here? Kent had stolen the dress from another compartment, hadn't he?

A hot flush crept up her neck and she swallowed hard. She couldn't be sure, but she thought she knew what the note said.

The squeaking of brakes came faintly above the rush of the train, but detectable nonetheless. They were slowing down. A shadow formed through the frosted glass of the compartment door, and she hastily stuffed the note down the front of her dress and unlocked the door for Kent. He stepped in quickly and his ears turned a brighter shade of pink, stretching down the side of his face and causing his scar to stand out in stark contrast when he looked at her.

"That's lovely," he said softly. She tried to smile, but it felt like a grimace of discomfort. Kent cleared his throat. "We're coming up on the station." He moved quickly into the compartment and grabbed his suitcase from underneath the bench. "Ready?"

"Next stop, Dover Priory!" The voice came from the front of their car, but it carried over the squealing of the brakes. "Tickets out!"

Kent raised a questioning brow, and Angelina nodded. The train had slowed remarkably now, and the rising bustle of both passengers and the upcoming station replaced what had once been a relatively quiet compartment.

Angelina felt like her heart would burst from her chest, and could only give credit to her hopes that Rupert would not see them leave. She was already surprised he hadn't burst in on them during the rest of the journey and had seemingly vanished. But she conceded that could only be a good thing for her and Kent. It wouldn't make meeting up with Elizabeth any easier if he followed them.

The harsh scream of metal on metal drowned everything else out, and Kent grabbed her hand and led her hastily from the cabin door. The train hadn't yet stopped completely when they moved just a few feet further back and Kent opened the rear door to the car. She couldn't help herself—she looked back.

There was no sign of Rupert, fortunately, but then a man peered out from the doorway of his own compartment and looked back at them. He didn't even glance toward the front of the car first. The same man in the top hat who had watched her move down the aisle as a nun glared at her now with an icy resolve, shocking her into immobility. His overcoat had been removed, revealing the pressed white shirt he wore underneath. The man brought his hands in front of him to readjust his cufflinks with jerky movements, staring all the while, and Angelina saw a small crimson stain on his left sleeve at the wrist.

Kent pulled her again by the hand and out onto the small platform at the back of the car, and she stumbled forward. The train was only crawling now, barely moving at all, and Kent jumped down to the gravel beside the track, briefly set his suitcase down, and lifted Angelina down from the platform with a swirl of her skirts. He spared her a brief smile, and they headed out of the station.

The deafening hiss of a fully stopped train filled the air, followed by the harsh call of the conductor's whistle from the engine car. Angelina put a hand up to her bobbed hair and turned to look back at their car. The man had not followed them out.

Suddenly, she realized exactly why he had looked so familiar. She had seen that man watching her and her mother many years ago, but he had decided not to wear the thick, dark glasses today. The crimson stain of his sleeve played heavily in her mind; she couldn't help but wonder if the stranger was responsible for her having had no other sign of Rupert. Had it been Rupert's blood? Above all, Angelina couldn't figure out why both men had been on the train, nor just exactly how much it had to do with her.

CHAPTER 21 – Lockridge Estate, 1926

"When do I find out where my mother is? How can I reach her?"
Angelina was losing patience again.

"That is enough, Angelina." Madame threw down her
cane. "You have to let me complete the story in full. I need to say
it in detail so I leave nothing out! What I am about to tell you is
information I later found out from your mother. I persisted in
asking her because I needed the gaps filled."

"I know how that feels." Angelina sighed.

"Indeed you do, but patience is a virtue, Angelina."
Madame shuffled in her seat and then began. "I mentioned how
your mother and father argued a lot. This was only in the last
year or two before she left. You should know they were happy
for the majority of their marriage. People and circumstances
change, especially during wartime." Madame stared into the
distance, a reminiscent look on her face. "Jonathan and I
certainly understood that."

Silence permeated the room. Afraid to interrupt, Angelina
still felt the need to interrupt the awkward moment. "I remember.
They may have thought they were using hushed tones when
arguing, but they did nothing of the sort, I can assure you," she
said.

"So you remember what they argued about?" Madame quipped.

"Well, no..." Angelina searched for an answer.

"Then don't interrupt me, Angelina, and I shall tell you. They argued mostly about her money and where she had placed it, although other things came into it as where. Where her loyalties lay, how he sensed she was keeping something from him. Despite the distance between them, he was right to wonder such things. She spent more and more time away from the home, and the housework was piling up. She told him she didn't have the money anymore, and had donated it to widows and children of war at Chasiton Manor. If she wasn't doing what she did, he'd be justified in believing there was someone else involved in their marriage. I think Elizabeth didn't mind him thinking she had squandered all her money away to charity. Better he think that than know what she was really doing.

"The war was becoming expensive and everyday living costs had risen. Your father's measly income would mean they would struggle, and regardless of his not wanting to live on someone else's money, I think he saw what he thought your mother had given away as a safety net. Your mother, despite initially wanting to live a humble life, didn't know how to live by such a low income. The pressures of having very little money created cracks in their originally flawless marriage.

"The charity was only a half-truth, though. Despite being a shelter for the widows and offspring of the deceased soldiers, the basement of the manor kept soldiers of war. It was this cause toward which your mother's money was aimed. The WCW used the money to feed and shelter these soldiers."

"Why did the soldiers need to be hidden? Why couldn't they just return home?" Angelina questioned.

"This was one of the main tasks the intelligence

159

authorities gave to your mother. The men were more than soldiers. They were spies in the army. Their roles were to get to up-to-date information of enemy lines and pass the information back to government intelligence agencies. Making their way to your mother was a challenge halved, as she relayed the information back to London officials. It was one way the government controlled these spies.

"How she fell into the role is unknown to me. It may be something you wish to ask her. I fear the reason may not be particularly honorable. As I've told you, in return for the information they had, she would arrange meetings with family members for them. However, there was one such soldier who played a rather large role in Elizabeth's experience. Ordinarily, the soldiers were grateful and showed her a lot of respect. This particular soldier had no family or friends to meet him. When Elizabeth asked him what he wanted in return for his information, he said nothing. His name was Gerard. All of these soldiers had connections to either the French, Belgians, or German people. But their loyalties lay with Britain, mostly because they grew up here. Some had never set foot on foreign soil, but spoke the language growing up.

"Gerard reported on French activities, but it was only then that he would speak. The rest of the time, he just stared, frightened, into a dark corner. For a whole week he remained mute. This became increasingly stressful for Elizabeth. She plunged on, trying to find details about him so that she could offer some comfort somehow.

"After eight days, he eventually spoke to her. In an angry and frantic tone, he told her how it wasn't worthwhile for him to get to know her, that he wouldn't be alive much longer after he returned to the front line. His resolute acceptance of death chilled Elizabeth, but she didn't want to believe it. He warned her to get out of the situation of hiding informants, that it would only lead to her being uncovered, and that no one would thank her for it. He warned that it may even lead to imprisonment or death.

"She left the manor in tears and came here to me. That was when she told me about the whole operation. She had never shown any interest in politics or the state, so I wondered what had changed, but my thoughts didn't stay like this. I became more concerned for Elizabeth's wellbeing and future, but also, shamefully, I wished she had never told me. The responsibility of keeping it quiet was too much for me. I was afraid of keeping this secret from Jonathan. We never kept anything from each other.

"I formed a plan to create the code you've now seen in the letters. This way, your mother and I could converse about the whole situation without anyone ever understanding. I was right to do so. Jonathan thought nothing of the letters I received. He assumed it was from the women's institute, which is what I had told him, and he never even questioned it.

"A number of months later, Elizabeth appeared at the house, distraught and disheveled. That was the night Jonathan was killed. I needn't tell you again. I couldn't, even if you asked."

A tear rolled down Madame's face. Her shaky index finger wiped away the tear. Bravely she lifted her chin to continue on. "Prior to coming here, she had visited the manor. Gerard and the other spies had returned to the shelter with new information only days before. Elizabeth headed to the basement to discover the soldiers tucked up in their blankets in a neat row. Something didn't seem right to her, though. She told me they all had lain eerily still, in perfect alignment, with a single pillow positioned to the side. Elizabeth said she called out to the men, but there was no answer. When she'd slowly pulled the blankets back, one by one, she saw that each man had been smothered to death in his sleep. Elizabeth turned and was sick right there on

161

the floor.

"Gerard, supposedly, stood in the doorway to prevent her from leaving. You remember, I had in my possession a contact list and a map? Well, Elizabeth had given it to me a few days earlier. In one of the letters, written after the events, it explained how it had been given to Elizabeth to hand to one of the soldiers, Pierre, who now was dead.

"Gerard had overheard that conversation between Pierre and Elizabeth, and knowing she had the information he needed, he cornered her. Elizabeth described the conversation in one of her letters. The man was crazed, shaking like he hadn't slept for weeks. He revealed he knew about the contact list and map. She pretended she knew nothing of either. He grabbed her by the hair, dragged her across the room to a table, and insisted she give it to him. The man made certain advances toward her, but she fought him with all her might, pulling out tricks she had been trained to use. In hindsight, he probably knew the same tricks and anticipated her actions. He screamed, threatening to kill her then her own daughter, then one by one every friend and family member until she gave him what he wanted."

Angelina gasped at that revelation. Her life had been threatened and she'd had no idea.

"She agreed to fetch the items and bring them to him, but he insisted on going with her. That was when she appeared on my doorstep, looking quite terrible. After she left with the items, I have no idea what happened to them. She never mentioned them again. I believe Jonathan knew nothing about them, and that Elizabeth had known that if she couldn't retrieve these items from our household, we would all be Gerard's next victims. Instead, Jonathan became the sole victim."

Madame looked genuinely sad and confused. Angelina wondered if she somehow felt indebted to Jonathan for giving his life to save hers. Clearly, he'd had no say in the matter, but it was somewhat romantic nonetheless.

"Knowing this information," Madame continued, "I couldn't help but wonder how much impact the map and contact list had on the war. I pray no other souls were lost in the interception of those items. You may wonder how Elizabeth got away with allowing Gerard to get his hands on the items. Well, her only role was to get the information to Pierre. She lied to the agency, saying she had already given it to him. She managed to convince them that Gerard intercepted it from Pierre after killing him and the others. Genius. Your mother's mind truly is exquisite.

"The Mi6 became increasingly pleased with her results as a field agent. Her will to climb higher within intelligence and help win the war was matched by the despair of her married life. An opportunity arose for her to travel abroad and work on the front line. She would be one of many from the area willing to go and do what was needed. Your father saw this as an excellent opportunity to earn some more money, and encouraged her to go. I guess the strain on their marriage made it easier for both of them to accept. Lord only knows how it would have made me feel if Jonathan suggested I go. Fortunately, I didn't need to make that choice. Of course, the assignment was very different for Elizabeth. She had to report back to Mi6 on the condition in France and was rarely put in the face of action. She was a commodity, and a good one at that.

"Before she left, she said she would make contact as soon as she could, but in the meantime she asked me to watch over you and give you as many opportunities as possible."

Angelina cringed. She couldn't believe that working in Madame's household, cleaning her clothes and sewing buttons, was the best opportunity she could offer. Then she considered the fact that she had been given a good education and encouraged to learn typing. Perhaps her mother really had made the best possible choice.

"Leaving wasn't an easy decision for her. You were approaching your fifteenth birthday, so I offered you a role here and kept a keen eye on you. I couldn't quite understand why your father made it difficult for me to hire you, but now I think he was just afraid of losing you as well as your mother, even despite their difficult marriage. Loneliness is a person's biggest fear."

Angelina typed furiously while straining to hear every word. Her objective to write soothed her cascading emotions. She missed her father very much, and hearing that he missed her too was something new to her. She didn't know whether to be angry or proud of her mother. She considered that life would have been very hard back then, and her mother had made more than difficult choices. She had to believe it was all for the best.

"I didn't hear from your mother for two years. In her first letter, she had admitted that when she relocated to London in preparation for her drafting, she was persuaded to train as a nurse. As soon as she was qualified, she was sent to France to work on the front line, attending to wounded soldiers and the dead. She felt she had made a huge mistake. Life as a nurse was no elevation within the world of intelligence. The amount of blood she witnessed, the smell of death and infections of the wounded was unbearable. She wondered if they had in fact found out she had lied to them, and that this was her punishment.

"Her second letter was remarkably different, though. She no longer complained about the conditions, and mentioned a new role and how much she enjoyed it. I'd hoped she had been promoted to a matron nurse, overseeing things rather than having to get too involved, but she never did say. Four months went by before I heard from her again. The next time wasn't by letter but in person. I didn't recognize her at first. Her face was worn and her hair was fashioned into a black, stylish bob. She wore her nurse's uniform, which surprised me. Clearly, she hadn't been made a matron. She told me the war would soon be coming to an end. Everyone was always talking about the end of the war, but it was only from Elizabeth I truly believed the chatter was real.

"Overjoyed at seeing her, I couldn't help but relay everything I could about you. She delighted in hearing every insignificant detail. I suggested that, after the war, things might go back to normal. She could come home and live here with us. She turned down my idea and insisted that nothing must change. No one was to know she had a daughter, as it would only put your life in danger. She knew I didn't agree. But she made her excuses and left, with a promise to be in contact as soon as she was settled.

"The war finally ended, and a long time passed before she wrote to me in our code. It read that she was settled and living in Paris. She had a fiancé, and they planned to have a child together. She admitted her future was in Paris. Now that you were older, she felt returning home would be unfair to you. It was time for a new start and a new family. She said she hoped to be able to explain this to you and me both one day. It didn't seem right to me. I felt a bit as though she had abandoned me, too.

"She loved you, Angelina, like any mother loves her child. I couldn't believe she would willingly turning her back on you. Some years later, she did attempt to explain further. The explanation was insincere, though, and forgiving her is still something with which I struggle.

"When I received that last letter, I was so angry at her betrayal. I'd lost Jonathan for her, had kept you at arm's length for her sake, and she couldn't even give me what I desired most. The truth.

"Oh, for Heaven's sake, the time. Angelina, look at the time. We must end it there for now," Madame exclaimed.

"But there is still so much more to be told," Angelina pleaded.

"There is, and as I said earlier, patience is a virtue."

CHAPTER 22

Madame seemed tired after her recent outpouring of memories. She didn't emerge from her bedroom for two days. Angelina repeatedly asked Ruth if everything was okay, but Ruth never had much to say; she was as discreet as could be.

Having spent so much time with Madame lately, Angelina felt lost performing only her usual chores. She struggled most when working in the living room; she couldn't help but imagine Jonathan's body, lying there in the moments before death took him away from his pain.

Rupert had been rather sprightly recently. He seemed to pick up on Angelina's mood, and found ways to make her laugh. "Angelina, did you try Ruth's Shepard's pie today?" he asked with a grin.

Out of earshot of anyone else, Angelina knew a punchline was coming. "No, I haven't. Is it any good?" she asked dryly, knowing his question wasn't serious.

"Yes, in fact, it is," he added before disappearing in a flash.

To anyone else this wouldn't have been funny, but Angelina knew he was being daft, that he always tried to do the opposite of what she expected. It certainly worked; she never did

167

know what would fly out of his mouth next. Every once in a while her eyes lingered on his lips as he spoke to her. It seemed to happen more frequently now, and Angelina welcomed the exciting distraction.

When Madame did emerge from her quarters later that afternoon, she wore one of her most flattering outfits. Her makeup was flawless, and she seemed bright and alert. Angelina even considered the fact that she seemed happy, but was more than aware of Madame's many facades.

The fact that she hadn't seen Madame for a couple days filled Angelina with an awkward shyness, something she hadn't felt in a long time. The story had been a difficult one for Madame to tell, and Angelina did feel privileged that the woman seemed to trust her. She merely translated Madame's thoughts at the moment, but all the preparation Madame had given her would make her capable of writing a beautiful tale people would want to read. Aside from learning about her own family, Angelina couldn't wait to put the whole thing together and present it to Madame, knowing how proud she would be.

After a light snack, Madame requested Angelina's presence in the conservatory. The typewriter was already set up waiting for her, and Angelina knew not to wait for her instructions; she went straight to the machine and loaded a piece of paper. She sensed an aura of depression around Madame.

With her head bowed low, she slouched somewhat in her chair. "Today, Angelina, I came across a photograph of my son in my drawer, and I think it time I told you about him." Madame paused, looking down at the floor in a way that was so contrary to her usual, commanding manner.

Angelina had never heard Madame speak of her son. She brought her hands to the keys of the typewriter and glanced towards Madame.

"Adrian and I shared a very cold relationship. We had never been close. He spoke to his father, but not much. His childhood must have been very lonely." Madame relapsed into silence. Angelina looked down.

"His dislike for me became more apparent as he grew up. I don't even remember him much, even though we lived in the same house. Whenever we met in society, it was more as strangers than as mother and son. Everyone knew of our detachment, Angelina. If anyone is to blame, it's me, for I was far from a loving mother. He remained with his nanny and was sent to me for only half an hour after supper, although this arrangement was usually cancelled in favor of my parties.

"Adrian asked a lot of questions, and I had a lot to hide. Whenever he was sent to me for his half hour, his questions irked me and I kept him at arm's length. I remember one day, when he was much older, he asked me about Elizabeth's letters. I told him off rudely, saying he should mind his own business. He was already a young man of sixteen, and I should have known better than to speak to him like he was five. But to me, he still seemed impossibly young.

"He must have detested me even more after Jonathan's death, and I saw very little of him after that. Any chances of a relationship were already lost."

Angelina noticed the distant expression on Madame's face, and felt a sudden pity for the woman.

"All my relationships withered after Jonathan's death. I remember my lawyer Malcolm came for tea a few days later. He offered his condolences and we discussed the estate's legal matters for some time. Then he remarked that it was unfortunate for the bookshelf to have fallen like that. I replied that it was very unfortunate indeed, but I was very disturbed. My voice must have faltered, and even if it didn't, Malcolm was a very good lawyer and an expert at reading people. He continued on that topic until he left. I know he suspected me, but he had no proof. I hadn't disclosed anything. He came to the estate once more after that. It was a very formal visit, and I haven't seen him since.

"Adrian, though, was very fond of Malcolm. He went out a lot, I suspect, to meet with him. Once, I witnessed them talking outside, down in the driveway, involved in animated conversation. Whatever the topic, it seemed to be of great interest to them both.

"In the years that followed, there were times when Adrian would come home inebriated. It was nothing excessive for a young man, but I worried that if he socialized with Malcolm, perhaps under the influence of drink, my lawyer would convey his suspicions to my son. I tried to stop them from meeting, especially for drinks, but I was powerless at that point. Whether or not Malcolm actually divulged his thoughts around Jonathan's death, I will never know.

"A number of small things piled up, and different circumstances developed. It was natural for Adrian to leave, although what circumstance was the final straw, only Adrian could say. It would be very unfair of me to say that his departure was against my wishes, or that it was an inappropriate gesture. I could not have been of any use to him, and it was better for him to go."

Angelina heard the doubts in Madame's story. It was almost as though the woman wanted Angelina to agree with her. But of course, Angelina would never comment on such a private matter. She did have questions, though. "Couldn't your lawyer have told others about his suspicions if he'd wanted to?" she asked, hoping to divert Madame's attention from her son. The topic visibly upset her employer.

"He has no proof, Angelina, and even if he wanted to tell

others, his profession restricts him from doing so. Lawyers come across a lot of secrets in their work. It's important for them to maintain the image of trustworthiness, and if Malcolm ever decided to leak my secret, he would lose clients. The other families he represented would question his loyalty. No, Angelina, he can't take this risk after achieving so much. He's an ambitious man, zealous for success. Moreover, he appears to be a man of his word. Whether that was genuine, or simply part of his professional façade, I can't say for sure.

"He does know a lot of family secrets, and has a wealth of information about the estate and its affairs. If he ever wanted to defame the family, he could easily do so, sharing any of this other information. He would not risk his credibility by including a scandalous yet unproven claim along with it. He is too smart for that."

"Does he know about my mother?" Angelina asked.

"He is acquainted with her as Miss Heathburn, but does not know anything else. You came to stay with me around the time Adrian left, and no one else knows where you came from. As I told you, he is suspicious of me, but is not aware of the entire story behind Jonathan's death.

"Angelina, I have to admit that I've found this part of my story very taxing indeed. You will excuse me if I take your leave early today, my dear, won't you? I must lie down. Look at the clock. It's already early evening. Goodnight, Angelina." Madame got up and slowly exited.

Angelina sat for a while, thinking of all she'd heard today. Madame had been very out of character; Angelina had not written a lot, but Madame didn't scold her for being lazy today. Even though she didn't seem at all attached to Adrian, the woman got very upset when speaking of him. Maybe it was the fact that she had failed in her role as a mother that bothered her,

171

even though she didn't appear to have really loved the child, or even now the man. Angelina would have to tread carefully with this information and try to capture the truth with the required delicacy.

She went to the kitchen for some leftover pie. When she reached the kitchen door, she opened her mouth to speak, but then noticed Rupert deep in conversation with Ruth. She stood speechless for a moment, wondering if her ears had deceived her or if Rupert had mentioned her name.

He looked up at her and smiled awkwardly, then left. Angelina asked Ruth to send Madame's dinner up to her room, and resisted the urge to probe the girl about the encounter. Ruth prepared her a hearty plate of food, then left to cater to Madame. Angelina ate slowly while examining her own feelings. She was shocked by her interest in Rupert; she hadn't thought about how she would feel if she started to care for someone. The estate had almost guarded her from actually meeting anyone, let alone a man.

Just as she finished her plate, she felt a tap on her shoulder. Rupert had snuck back in, and politely offered her his hand. Jumping down from the bench stool, she took his hand and let him lead her outside. It was now dark, lending a mysterious air to their rendezvous. Angelina relished walking in the shadows, out of reach of the barn lights, scurrying around like naughty children. When they came to a quiet area behind a large oak tree, Rupert didn't hesitate to kiss her gently on the lips. She gasped but then smiled. She knew she had been hoping for that kiss, and wanted him to know she was completely comfortable with it. She was silently satisfied by his obvious relief. The thought that maybe she made a man nervous somehow excited her.

***

Madame Lockridge felt exceptionally emotional. She sat up with nothing but a small candle, trying to spread its light through the wide bedroom. It was dimly lit and failed to reflect the few tears escaping her eyes. She could usually mask her regrets of the past with her outlandishness and idiosyncrasies, but her past proved too much for her tonight. She wrapped her aged fingers around the framed picture of her son on the night table and gazed longingly at it. Her son's hard-edged ways and suspicions had drifted them apart, so she focused on the night her son had been the happiest with her.

It was shortly after Jonathan's untimely 'accident', when Madame's social life was still a little livelier. She had hosted a small soiree to wish her friend Elizabeth the best with her new work overseas. It was held on the estate, by the lake of which she and Jonathon had been so fond. It was a warm July night; white ribbons decorated every tree, long white tables set with champagne and snacks scattered throughout the grounds. Her servants wore white jackets with black bowties, serving trays of hors d'oeuvres and catering to her guests. All who had attended wore fine dresses and tailored suits, trying to out-do the rest of the company. It was a nearly perfect gathering.

Madame lounged under a tree with Elizabeth, discussing better times passed. They shared a knowing laugh, and when it died down, Elizabeth found it appropriate to show her gratitude. "Rose, I want to thank you for all you've done for me. I must be such a burden."

"Nonsense," Madame assured. "The moments we have shared together reveal to me those unbreakable bonds that have grown between us."

"But Jonathan..." Just the mention of his name cast a

somber silence on the pair. "You have given me more than should be asked of any woman."

"We must forget that now," said Madame, knowing the entire event was best buried, though her future concerns soon boiled to the surface. "What of the map and the list?"

"I must find my way across the map again someday, but I'm more concerned about the contact list. The people on it are good people, and I'm afraid Gerard will bring them harm."

Madame Lockridge smiled at Elizabeth. "So far, that does not seem to be the case."

A third woman approached them from the other side of the lake, and Madame whispered conspiratorially. "We can leave the rest of this talk for a more private time. Look who's coming to join us." She smiled at the woman and raised her voice to call across the lawn. "Adrian, my dear! Come over here, please!"

Her son grabbed another flute of champagne from the table before heading in their direction under the tree. "Coming, Mother," he replied dryly.

Madame smiled at the young woman who had joined them, a sweet thing with a family of good standing. She'd only met her twice before, but the dear had come of her own volition to present herself and say hello.

"I'd like you to meet someone, Adrian," she told her son. "This is Miss Charlotte Moore."

Charlotte turned around to meet Adrian face to face, and Madame's heart fluttered briefly when she caught the frozen expression of surprise on her son's face. He stared at Miss Moore for a few seconds, captivated and seemingly at a loss for words. It had been a long time since she'd seen anything other than apathy on his features.

"Charlotte, this is my son Adrian," she continued, pleased now with the introduction.

Miss Moore held out a dainty, gloved hand to the man before her, smiling wide. "A pleasure to meet you, Adrian."

Adrian was frozen for a second, then blinked quickly and gave the girl a dazzling smile. He gently took her hand and *kissed it. "The pleasure's mine."*

Madame glanced at Elizabeth, who shared with her a knowing smile. It was a bit of a foreign sensation for her, to feel such pride in her son's gentlemanly qualities, or even in the fact that he seemed to be quite smitten with Miss Moore. But it was a sensation she would not forget.

Madame Lockridge had known how passionate and brief Adrian's courtship had been with the woman whom he soon after made his wife. She fell asleep with the comforting knowledge that, at the very least, her son appreciated the small courtesy she'd given him that day so long ago.

CHAPTER 23 – Dover, 1928

"We need to get to Dover Marine, where our ship will depart," Kent said quietly.

Keeping a low profile just in case, they quickly made their way through the narrow cobbled back lanes running parallel to the main street.

"Kent, I need to stop and catch my breath. Just for a minute, please!" Angelina pleaded.

He slowed his pace while also loosening the grip on her hand.

Looking down at the single-strapped, black leather shoes, Angelina felt a blister forming on the back of her right heel. Each step she took rubbed away a little more of her tender skin until she started to limp every third step.

Kent stopped, pulling her around to face him. "What's wrong? Why are you limping? Have you hurt yourself? " he questioned, looking at her feet.

Angelina stepped up onto the sidewalk out of the sun and leaned against a cool brick wall. "It's just a blister. It's what I get for running so late and not having my own luggage or shoes," she added.

Emotions suddenly engulfing her, a single tear escaped

176

her eye. She turned her head so Kent would not see it. The stress of leaving Henry, getting to the train, the confrontation with Rupert, plus that strange man made Angelina question whether going to France was even a good idea. Everything just seemed to be spinning out of control.

"Here," Kent said. Angelina turned to find a white handkerchief being offered.

"Thanks," she whispered, taking it and gently patting her eyes.

Kent pulled a silver pocket watch from the left breast pocket of his charcoal blue, woolen, pinstriped suit. "We have an hour until the boat leaves," he declared, snapping the watch shut. Running his hand through his hair, he gazed down again at her shoes, lost in thought. "All right, we will have to be quick. Let's go."

He took her hand, pulling her up the lane and making a sharp right then left. Angelina could barely keep up, taking a set of steps two at a time. They reached the top and were suddenly thrust into crowds of happy people, clapping and cheering. Some waved British flags, others had American flags, and a brass band inched its way through the throngs of people playing Jazz. It seemed a celebration of something, but what? End of war celebrations had stopped long ago. *What could it be?* thought Angelina.

As they meandered through the crowd, Kent pulled Angelina into Peacocks Department Store. Pushing through the heavy, brass revolving door, Angelina took in the dark, wood-paneled walls, Art Deco lighting, and glass-topped counters displaying all manner of sparkly things.

"Ladies Department?" Kent enquired to the small, round, balding man who approached them.

"Up the escalator to the second floor, sir."

177

They stood in silence as the escalator lifted them up higher and higher until the ground floor disappeared, bringing them to the Men's Department first. They brushed between racks of suits and socks on sale until weaving around and up again.

Kent approached a middle-aged shop assistant, with black, round-rimmed glasses, her black hair scraped back into a neat bun at the base of her neck.

"Sorry to rush you, but we're in a bit of a hurry. My wife had her luggage stolen and we need to be on the boat to France soon. Could we have our purchases packed into a new suitcase from the ground floor?"

"Certainly, sir. I'll have Arthur bring one up straight away. Please take a seat over here, sir." She pointed to two black, over-stuffed club chairs.

"Madam, if you would kindly follow me, we can get what you need."

Angelina was whisked into the changing room and measured accordingly. Two day dresses, one skirt, one blazer, a white, long-sleeved shirt, a pair of button-up boots, undergarments, and three pairs of stockings. Angelina joined Kent in the waiting area and watched the assistant kindly pack the new suitcase. They were just about to close it up when Angelina noticed a mannequin holding a sign.

The 'Twelve Hour Dress' has come to Dover!

"Ah, I see you looking at the four-in-one dress by Carmel Myers," the shop assistant said proudly.

"Revolutionary," added Kent.

"You can make four completely different outfits by detaching various parts of the dress to reveal a different look. It's like being four different people. You could almost be a spy," she whispered, leaning further over the case as she said it. Kent and Angelina looked at each other, barely able to contain their smirks.

"We'll take one. I mean, who doesn't want to be a spy?" He laughed, pulling a crisp twenty-pound note from his money clip.

Running back down the escalators and out onto the street, it was much less crowded amidst the remnants of the prior chaos. They caught up with the crowd near the shipyard and fell into step, making their way down towards the pier. The atmosphere around them was electrifying. Angelina felt so alive, and she knew right then that she had to fulfill this trip, get back to Henry, and convince him to run away together and forget this whole debacle with Madam Lockridge's book. She felt for the first time there was hope at the end of the road.

Reaching the promenade, they struggled with their cases to get through the packed boardwalk. Angelina stood on tiptoes, trying to see over people's heads what was happening down on the pier. Smoothing down her hair and dress, she linked her arm in Kent's and they made their way down the last of the dock. A magnificent steam ship waited for them. Huge plumes of thick black smoke billowed from her two white stacks, the red lip of them barely visible through it all. To Angelina, it seemed as though the ship smoked a never-ending cigarette.

Victoria II was emblazoned across her side; she had recently been refurbished from World War I when all ferry crossing ships had been commandeered. She wore her name and battle scars with pride on her shiny metal hull.

They joined the last few people and stepped onto the gangway. The strong rope railing felt coarse in Angelina's hands as she pulled herself along, finally reaching the deck of the ship.

"Welcome aboard, Ma'am," chirped a young deckhand. "May I see your tickets?"

Kent pulled the tickets from his inside jacket pocket.

Angelina sighed with relief that they did not have to sneak onto this mode of transportation.

"Thank you, Mr. and Mrs. Pentworth. Have a lovely journey."

Angelina almost lost her balance as Kent gently nudged her past the deck hand from behind. "Why are we using that name?" she gasped.

"Well, technically, we're meeting our mother, Lady Pentworth. Seems fitting, don't you think?" He laughed.

It was good to see Kent smile. The adventurous morning could not have been easy for him, either.

Victoria II blew her final whistle as they entered the general lounge area on the main deck. The sea-blue carpet felt soft under Angelina's tired feet as she surveyed the room. Cherry red, oak booths with British racing-green cushions lined both sides of the main dining area. Each booth came with its own window for personal view. A circular restaurant dominated the center of the room. Here one could pick snacks while gently pushing a tray around on metal rails, eventually stopping at the cashier. Soft, brown leather couches filled the rest of the space as the ceiling fans tried in vain to push the hot, sticky air out of the open windows.

Kent waived her over to a spare booth. Angelina sat down with a thud; the day was really catching up with her. Seeing Angelina's fatigue, Kent offered to get some refreshments for them both.

She pulled Kent's white handkerchief from her bodice and proceeded to dab the small beads of sweat on her forehead. Laying it flat to refold it again, she noticed two small dots of blood in one of the corners. She held the handkerchief up to the window to get a better look. *Yes, it's definitely blood. Whose?*

"Everything all right?" Kent said as he placed the heaving

tray onto the table.

Pulling the handkerchief quickly down, she crumpled it up in her hand, placing it in her lap. "I'm just famished," she feigned.

Kent set a plate in front of her of two cucumber sandwiches and two of ham and chutney. "Now, if you finish these…." He hastily pulled a white paper napkin off the top of a third plate. "You may have desert."

Scones, clotted cream, and strawberry jam, with a handful of fresh strawberries. *Heaven,* thought Angelina.

"Tea, my dear?" Kent asked as he hovered the teapot above Angelina's cup.

"Please." She picked up her cup and saucer. They sat in silence, looking out into the vastness of the channel, enjoying the food and sipping tea. Angelina felt her shoulders relaxing and nestled her back against the cushion. She looked across at Kent's strong hands nursing his teacup.

"You missed some."

"Missed what?" Kent looked bemused.

Angelina touched the top of her left hand with her right. Kent lowered his eyes down to his own hands to see the graze Angelina had noticed there.

Angelina hesitated. "Would you tell me if I asked?"

"It's better you don't know," he said lazily, looking back out the window.

"You didn't kill anyone, did you?" Angelina spoke hurriedly but quietly, as though she had already decided the answer and judged him accordingly.

Kent whipped his head back to face her. "There are ears everywhere. You should really be careful what you say. It was just a slight altercation with the engine on the train, that's all," he shot back.

Changing the subject quickly, Angelina asked, "How long until we get to Calais?"

Kent shifted his weight from side to side. "It's twenty-seven nautical miles from Dover to France. If the seas behave, we should be there in another two hours.

"Is that how long it took last time?" Angelina couldn't help herself. She was desperate to know if Kent had ever met Elizabeth in Paris before.

Kent sighed as he eased himself out of the booth. "Angelina, I know this is a lot to take in, but like yourself, I have only just met our mother. But unlike yourself, we have been in contact for many years." He left his explanation there and headed towards the men's bathroom near the entrance.

Angelina stared into her teacup. Ever since she had moved to London to become a famous writer, her life had been one disappointment after another. She felt as though she had let Madame Lockridge down by literally giving away the piece on which she'd worked so hard. *When will I realize that everyone has their own agenda, except maybe Henry?* she thought. Angelina took a deep breath. She anticipated what she would next encounter once they got to Paris. Thoughts played heavy on her mind as she slowly exhaled.

Angelina felt a hand gently shake her shoulder, and Kent slid back into the booth. "We're just docking now. It's time to get off."

Angelina slowly sat upright, not realizing she had even dozed off. "How long was I asleep?" She yawned.

"A little while. I kept an eye on you from the deck outside. You obviously needed the rest."

Around them, parents organized their kids, uneaten food was wrapped up for later, and women adjusted hats and gloves. Kent pulled the suitcases from beneath the table. Angelina took the crook of his arm and slowly stood. She was as ready as she would ever be.

The blue sign with white writing told them they were at Gare Maritime Station as they disembarked the ship. Angelina couldn't believe she was finally in France, her stomach tied in excited knots.

A teenage boy appeared before them, holding a sign directing passengers to the train. His royal-blue uniform was perfectly complemented by gold piping down the outside seam of his trousers and around the collar and cuffs of his jacket. The whole look had been finished off with six gold buttons, spaced evenly down his chest, matching blue hat, and white gloves.

"Careful, now," winced Kent.

Angelina did not realize she'd dug her nails into his forearm as they moved steadily along the path towards 'Le Train Bleu.' Rounding the last corner, they heard a long hiss, followed by a huge billow of steam coming towards them. Angelina stopped, waiting for the steam to dissipate before raising her hand to her mouth and gasping. There it was, in all its glory—the royal-blue train with brass insignia.

Kent jolted her out of her dreamlike state. "You can stay here and admire it all day, if you want." He chuckled. "Or you could just get onboard."

Kent turned on his heel and made his way down towards the sleeper carriages. Two young French boys ran towards him, hastily taking the suitcases while the head conductor looked on.

The train hissed and rumbled again. It reminded Angelina of a racehorse just before it broke free from the starting gates. She hurried towards the carriage, catching up to Kent as he climbed the first brass step.

"Bonjour," shrilled the female carriage attendant as they stepped into the No4 Carriage. "I am Justine, and I will be

183

looking after you to Paris. Please follow me to your cabin."

Angelina was transfixed by her voice. *How do the French manage to make English sound so mesmerizing?* she wondered.

Justine lead them down the narrow corridor to Cabin 2 while Angelina studied her long, red, curly hair swept back loosely from her small face. Framed by piercing green eyes, it gave off a beautiful contrast with her blue uniform.

"If I can be of any assistance, please ring this bell." She motioned to a gold-plated button located beside the doorframe.

"Lunch followed by afternoon tea will be served from one-thirty in the dining car. We will arrive into Paris in approximately three hours."

"Excusez moi, excusez moi!" One of the young French boys was now behind Kent, dancing with the luggage. Kent stepped aside and the boy placed the suitcases upon small stands located at the foot of each of their hand-carved, canopied beds. Kent pulled a one-franc coin from his trouser pocket and, like magic, the boy had vanished again.

Justine started opening Kent's suitcase. He quickly placed both his hands over hers. "That will be all for now, Justine," he said, gently steering her hands away from the case.

"Oui, Monsieur. Madame." Justine dropped her head and backed out slowly from the room, sliding the door closed quietly behind her.

Angelina twirled around the room, taking in every detail: mahogany paneled walls with patterned inlays, midnight blue carpet, and luxurious blue bedding, finished with gold brocade. She ran her fingers along the bed then up to touch the matching canopy before moving towards the window to admire the handsome curtains framing it.

The conductor blew the final whistle. "All aboard," he cried.

Followed by Le Train Bleu giving off two long toots, before inching forward one step at a time, the mighty powerhouse finally broke free of its restraints.

"Shall we freshen up and go for lunch?" Kent asked, perched on the edge of the bed and having watched Angelina's performance in awe.

"Oh, yes, please. I can't wait to explore the rest of the train," she chimed.

Five minutes later, with her hair brushed and face washed, they made their way towards the dining car. Light piano music played softly as they approached the ornately decorated entrance. Sumptuous surroundings of Lalique glass paired with more intricately patterned paneled walls. Two crystal chandeliers dominated the ceiling, casting a warm sparkle over everything, all neatly tied together with the infamous gold and blue.

As they gazed out the window, they took in the landscape. Angelina couldn't believe the green farmland and forests could have once been a battlefield. It reminded her that danger had been, and still may be, all around them. A shiver went down her spine as the harsh reality of the reason why she was here, sitting in this luxurious dining cart, settled within her. For a moment, she had been so wrapped up in her excitement she had forgotten that, although the war may now be over. What remained was still so uncertain, and her mother Elizabeth was pulling her into a new, uncertain world.\l

"Well, I thought I recognized another English gentleman on this train," came a booming voice from across the carriage. Kent and Angelina slowly turned their heads in unison away from the window. Before them stood the familiar faces of a couple Angelina had seen on the train to Dover. "William Cartwell, and my wife, Janet." He reached out to shake Kent's hand. "Say, ol' chap, would you be headed to the French

Riviera?"

"Actually we're heading to—"

Kent touched her wrist, cutting Angelina off. "Yes, we're headed to Marseilles, actually," he interjected. "Pentworth," he said, giving the man their undercover surname.

"Oh, jolly good then," Mr. Cartwell added, ending their handshake.

Mrs. Cartwell had not taken her eyes off Angelina the whole time. "What a magnificent gown you have on there, my dear," Mrs. Cartwell declared.

It was the first time either of them had heard her voice. Angelina wondered if Mrs. Cartwell realized they had locked eyes before on the previous train.

Don't be stupid. You were dressed as a Nun. She couldn't remember that, Angelina thought.

"Please can you stand and show me the whole dress?" Angelina reluctantly did so. "Oh, how beautifully made. And the colors." Mrs. Cartwell touched the skirt fabric, studying the purple satin ribbon. "Oh, and let me see the back." She placed a hand on either side of Angelina's hips and spun her gently around before smoothing down the fabric again.

"Well, we must be off. A brief rest before we head into Paris I think, my dear," Mr.Cartwell said, turning to his wife.

"Sounds wonderful," she replied.

As Kent and Angelina watched them walk away, Angelina excused herself from the table. "Please order for me. I'm just going to use the powder room."

She strode quickly to the back of the dining car. She couldn't be sure, but she felt as though Mrs. Cartwell had been feeling for something in her dress, and Angelina knew exactly what that something was.

Closing the stall door to the ladies' room quietly,

Angelina pulled out the crumpled paper from her undergarment. She looked at the message written in code and tried harder to recall the lessons Madame had given her.

She gasped. This note was not intended for her, but for the true owner of the dress she still wore—the one Kent had acquired for her.

She was certain the deciphered note read: *Le Train Bleu, Danger, 15.30.*

Tearing the note into little pieces, she flushed them down the toilet, knowing she had to tell Kent what she had learned.

CHAPTER 24

"Where did you get this dress?" Angelina demanded with a blazing stare.

Kent returned her glare with his own, and he rose to grab her shoulder and shove her into the seat. "Might I remind you again, there are ears?"

"Mrs. Cartwell was looking for something in my dress," she hinted, rubbing the rising hairs on her arms as she remembered the contact, the woman's thin hands having sifted about like a spidery rodent in search of crumbs.

Kent leaned forward over the table as she sat down. He had finished his third course while she had one of hers waiting for her. Angelina folded her hands, barely noticing their trembling as she fought the urge to spit out the words in the note. They could be in danger, and they needed to get off the train if they didn't find out why. She considered the '15.30' at the end of the note, and started to open her mouth to speak. Kent needed to know.

"I didn't steal it from Mrs. Cartwell, if that's what's bothering you," he murmured. "And before you ask, no, she's not some kind of spy."

The thought hadn't necessarily occurred to her, but his

188

assuredness tossed her previous thought aside. "What makes you so sure?" she dared, hissing in a mocking undertone in an attempt to mirror his brusque whisper.

He threw her an almost baleful glare, his eyes taut above exhausted circles she just noticed. She held the stare down for a moment, but stopped when she realized he didn't plan on answering. *Ears everywhere,* she remembered as she sat impatiently against her seat. *But I have to tell him.*

It seemed unlikely for a high-class woman like Mrs. Cartwell, especially in her mature years, to be a spy. Kent was right, but he hadn't felt the cringing climb of lacey fingers along the jade fabric, like a gentle search for a possible treasure beneath the thread.

Angelina shuffled in her seat and glanced around for anyone who may be listening. The warm chandelier in the center of the cabin glowed a luminous gold that spread throughout the room as it shook ever so softly in the train's forward rush. Her eyes swayed around the cabin, taking in the aesthetics coincidentally proving to be quite calming. She was on Le Train Bleu, after all, but for the moment she felt like she was being interrogated in a spotlight under hundreds of eyes, watched by whoever threatened the train.

She stopped on a familiar, grey, pinstriped suit two tables behind her. He seemed to notice a gaze on him, for he looked up from reading and narrowed his eyes to meet Angelina's. She glanced down from his face as if to admire his uniform and continued to scan around the room, waiting for him to turn. His familiar scowl twisted her nerves into knots, and she fought the urge to look at him again. She smiled nervously, and Kent gave her a confronted look that implied she had done more than destroy their cover. He didn't say anything, though, and waited for her to speak with a cocked eyebrow.

189

"Have you seen that man?" she asked, flicking her eyes behind her.

Kent shook his head, and she almost accused him of not looking but thought twice about it. She sighed instead and asked again.

"No, my dear. Who, a friend of yours?" He tapped on the table like an awkward gentleman showing forced patience at her words. She waited for a 'tsk', though she knew he wouldn't be so brash.

Angelina turned to face the man, determined to make Kent look the fool for once. A ridiculous nun costume and blistered heels wouldn't make her the insolent woman she made herself out to be. She opened her mouth to speak, and her heart sank when the man's chair was empty. "Truly," she said, almost to herself. "He was there. I saw him."

"Did you?" Kent challenged. "Saw who?"

"I found a note," she said quickly, her heart racing now as her eyes darted across the room for the man. "I think it was meant for whomever owned this dress."

He rubbed his temple, as though drawing on a memory. "What exactly did the note say?"

"I believe it read 'Le Train Bleu—'"

Kent threw his hand up to stop her and tossed an empty glance around the room. He almost didn't turn his head, but she followed suit as they scanned the small cabin. No one seemed to be listening, though the people in the cabin had their own conversations to drown out anything she might have told him. "What time?" he mumbled.

"Fifteen-thirty."

Kent mouthed the words, and she watched as he pulled out his pocket watch and squinted at the time. "It's two-thirty," he said gravely. "Where did you find this note?"

190

"It was in the hem of this dress, written in Elizabeth's code."

Kent looked more shocked at the mention of the code than the note. "And you could read it?"

"Madame Lockridge taught me."

Kent looked furious. "We lost our mother to the war. You would think she'd have been a bit more careful with the knowledge she was afforded. That note was clearly meant for Elizabeth. Someone wanted to meet her."

"Madame told me the code was between her and Elizabeth only."

"Perhaps that's what Elizabeth told her, but that code is used for communication between informants all over the world. Like a universal in-between language. All I know is that can't be good news for us. Whoever wrote that note must be nearby. You're wearing your mother's dress. The person must have wanted to meet her. I hope he won't be too disappointed."

She searched for the man again, this time letting her eyes fall on the door at the end of the cabin.

"One moment. Stay here," Kent said. He pressed a firm hand to her shoulder and kissed the side of her head before walking swiftly to the other end of the cabin.

She didn't watch him go, but kept her eyes on the door through which the strange man must have disappeared. She knew him; she was sure. She saw him on the first train but didn't have the time to process who he may be. She thought back, and rose from the table without thinking as her memories all fell into line.

Angelina stole a sharp breath and chased her thoughts through the door, disturbing a few diners as they finished their meals. If the strange man was responsible for the note, he was expecting Elizabeth. Though he had seen Angelina wearing the dress, he must realize Elizabeth will not be here. *Maybe he would meet with me instead?* she pondered naively. She shoved through the door and ran about the next cabin, her eyes darting in every direction in search of the man without considering what she'd say if she found him.

The sleeping cabin jolted as Angelina moved through the doorway, nearly shoving her backward in surprise, but firm hands jerked her into the cabin and into an elegant bedroom. The door slammed shut behind her.

She barely found words as shock spread across her face. Rupert's harnessed snarl darkened his eyes where a cleaned gash lined the upper bridge of his nose. He stared with apparent disdain that soon dropped to concern. Angelina almost wanted to hit him, but he sighed and rubbed the side of his face, and she pitied him in return.

"So you *are* going to kill me?" she decided for him as he drew into his pocket.

Rupert gave her a tantalizing look and sighed, pulling out the gun. He chuckled softly, obviously noting the question before considering his reply. "Is that what you've been wondering throughout your trip?"

"I've wondered, yes, but I thought otherwise when you let me go."

"I could never kill a nun," he teased. "I'd go to hell." Rupert cocked a half-smile and waited for a response, but shrugged when he didn't receive one.

She only stared uneasily at the gun he caressed in his hand. She could die. She almost blurted her knowledge about the note but wondered, instead, if Kent had returned to the table with information. Telling Rupert of the coming danger would only speed up her death if he played with the idea now. It shouldn't matter what his feelings had been for her; assassins had to remain objective, she was sure. She still hadn't found the strange man, though if she died, it wouldn't matter who he was. Still she did want to protect Kent and her mother.

Rupert strayed to the bed and sat on it, eyeing his gun with sincere appreciation. He laughed airily at a silent joke he shared with himself and swiveled on the bed's corner to face her, rubbing the gun's trigger with a steady finger. "Might I say, you look ravishing? It was lucky your brother stowed such an item."

Angelina blushed at the mention of her in the dress but grew serious. "It's my mother's dress."

Rupert shrugged. "Kent collected it from the cleaners, so perhaps. Handy all the same. Now, my turn," he nudged. "I wondered how I'd get you alone, but what were you running from in such a beautiful gown?"

"Nothing of consequence," she sputtered, taken aback by the question. She quietly digested what Rupert had said about the cleaners. Her mother must have intentionally left that dress in order to throw anyone off her scent. Clever! She started to wonder if putting the darn dress on was a big mistake. She really had to find the man, or Kent, and figure this out. "Actually, I had wondered what happened to you."

He met her gaze for a moment before resting his hand on the wound above his nose. Angelina stepped in his direction but hesitated, unsure of what to do in her position. Positive she knew him, she wanted to take the gun and reassure him somehow that he didn't have to be an assassin. But his work was his life, and he had managed to hide it from her while saying he loved her, too.

"You have a guardian, it seems." Angelina pursed her lips to ask why, and Rupert beamed, pleased. "I don't know who. Older chap, grey pinstripe suit. He knew who I was, but he seemed to have bigger concerns since he only left me with a small token of warning. I also saw him outside the cleaners when I had followed Kent. He seems to have a particular interest in you both."

"Did he have glasses?" Now she was sure this man was somehow linked to her or her mother. Though she remembered seeing him once before, so many years ago, she needed to figure out if he was a threat in the present.

Rupert shrugged. "He isn't my concern." He paused, toying with the magazine as he clicked it around to place the next bullet parallel to the barrel.

"I have to know," Angelina said, trying to sound more innocently pleading than annoyed at his games.

Rupert's laugh caught her off guard. "You know," he started, "we could disappear."

Angelina walked toward the bed. She didn't understand what he suggested, but her eyes were on the small gun. *Less than an hour,* she reminded herself. "Disappear?"

Rupert nodded and tossed her a glistening smile like he'd given her when she worked for Madame Lockridge. Her heart leapt into her throat, and she saw the mischievously handsome man she once thought she'd love forever. He wanted to whisk her away, take her from the book and his threat to her life, but he didn't understand the full extent of the danger she was in at that moment.

She could leave with him. They could possibly find their way back to where they once had been, and maybe start a new life where lawyers, spies, and murder didn't challenge her normal life. She could write a new book, and it would be hers. She could write about the boy who charmed her out of her wits and drew her beneath an oak tree to steal a kiss. She could be the Angelina who temporarily became a spy upon her mother's reappearance and the revelation of her brother, saved by the same charming man who was hired to murder her but chose love instead. She could, but she thought of Henry.

She still loved him, and she planned on writing to him first the chance she had. Henry had stolen her heart by sight before he won her over, and she could only hope he ached for her as she did him. Even considering the idea made her feel as if she had betrayed him, and she couldn't stand for it. Her heart felt torn, not only between Rupert and Henry, but Kent and their mother as well. She steadied her breath and tested her lips, gambling as she glanced at Rupert's for possibly the last time.

"When I was a child, and your mother found me, I wasn't sure how to thank her," Rupert started. "I didn't think to, of course, but later I wanted to. I received a letter from her one day. I'm not quite sure how long ago." He cleared his throat, smiling a little. "Madame read it to me, actually, but in it your mother asked me to protect you if anything happened. If, in any case, something were to perhaps happen to her."

"So you have to choose between your word and the life you know?" she asked.

He smiled awkwardly but gave her a curt nod. "Your words speak truth but nothing more. My word to the devil or my life…" He trailed off, brushing his hand down her cheek with a gentleness that sent a shudder down into her stomach. "Life lasts longer than words, yes?" he whispered, giving her a questioning grin that presented her cue.

She chuckled softly, a tear breaking off her lashes and streaking down her face. She almost wanted him to kill her right then. She couldn't stand breaking his heart when, this time, she may have accepted him. May have, but still could not.

"Rupert…" she began, but he only nodded and squeezed her hand.

Then he rose, rubbing the butt of his gun with his thumb. "The first rejection wasn't enough, was it?"

Angelina's ears burned at the hurtful words. "It's not that.

195

I just can't…the train, it's—"

"Neither can I," he said desperately. His finger trembled over the trigger, and Angelina thought she saw his eyes glisten with forming tears. "I can't kill you, Angelina."

"I know," she tried, her hope rising as she instinctively reached for the gun. Rupert shook his head and motioned for her to stop. She did, but reached her arm out as if to ask for the gun, or at least his hand. She needed the reassurance.

"An assassin lives by a code, Angelina, and I cannot break it. I had hoped…" he said with a soft smile. "I can't." He lifted the gun and pointed it at his own head. He rendered a smile for her, but then closed his eyes and hesitated.

"No!" she screamed, and jumped over the bed. She crashed into him as the gunshot ran out in the small room. Then Kent burst through the door with blazing eyes. Angelina leaned toward Rupert in search of blood, but Kent crossed the room with quick steps and pulled her into his arms as three other men entered the room behind him.

He shoved Angelina to the side as one of the men struck him with the back of a walking cane. Kent couldn't prevent his head from slamming into the floor, and Angelina struggled to crawl toward him. The man grappled her between his arms and swung a bag over her head.

"Quickly," an older woman's voice said. Angelina thought it might have been Mrs. Cartwell, but she couldn't be sure.

She fought the man's grip on her, suddenly remembering the gunshot. "Rupert!" she squealed, muffled inside the bag.

The man pulled at her and she screamed again, feeling Kent's weak hand brush against her foot. He called for her, and she heard a tumble of feet. Her own foot struck the door, and she grabbed at the threshold.

She fell to the floor, and the man who had held her grunted in pain. Dark liquid spilled into the bag and Angelina screamed, twisting blindly across the floor in an attempt to escape. She scratched at the bag to find an edge, and finally ripped it from over her head. As a flash of light filled her eyes, a pinstriped suit dashed from the hallway and into another cabin.

Mrs. Cartwell was nowhere to be seen, but Mr. Cartwell lay on the floor next to Kent, who writhed in pain. Angelina looked after the door to the next cabin, sure the pinstripe-suited man had helped her. She started toward Kent to tend to him but, remembering her last moment with Rupert, Angelina's priorities shifted. She moved cautiously through the silence of the room and stumbled to the body that lay still beside a fallen chair. Blood drowned Rupert's hair, his skin pale; her love, dead.

CHAPTER 25

Adrian looked deep into the silver spoon he held in his hand. He examined all his slowly fading features—his sagging eyes, his graying hair, his deeper wrinkles. They were all dwindling. A scowl became his face as he internally critiqued and loathed every new crease forming in his rough skin. A voice then rang out, breaking Adrian's disgusted self-analysis.

"Now, if you'll sign this, it will finalize your claim to your mother's estate with the bank," Henry said as he slid Adrian's tea aside and placed a handful of documents in front of him.

"Yes, of course." Adrian hurried with a hint of his previous feeling still lingering about. He skimmed through the pages briefly before retrieving a pen from the inner hidden pocket of his black suit. After making sure all was in order, Adrian scrolled his name on the line.

Adrian had tea with the apprentice of his new lawyer, on matters of his mother's inheritance, in the fabulous Cafe de Paris in London. He knew that weasel Eugene had his sights on owning the estate, and it was time he put a stop to it. Even if he never saw eye-to-eye with his mother, she was still his mother, and he still had a right to claim her property.

His mentor and confidant Malcolm had vanished into thin air. Adrian thought his timing could not have been worse, so he reluctantly found another lawyer to handle his business. He was incredulous to think Mr. Finley was so busy he sent his assistant to see the great Adrian Spratchet. He made a mental note of that misdemeanor.

Adrian leaned back in his chair and pulled out a shiny cigarette case from yet another concealed pocket as he spoke. "Oh, yes, and I had arranged for the premises to be searched. Have they found any of the items I listed?"

Henry's satchel was open and he rummaged through it, spreading even more documents on his cluttered side of the table. "Yes," Henry stated but only to indicate he found the report from the search. "No items or signs of items specified found," Henry recited off the sheet of paper.

"Of course not," Adrian harked in disappointment, rolling his eyes. He anxiously leaned back in his chair and packed a single hand-rolled cigarette.

"Well, if I mail these to the bank tomorrow, your claim to the inheritance is all but assured," Henry pleasantly reported as he took only a few of his scattered pages and straightened them out.

"Great." The word instinctively rolled out of the distinguished man's mouth. He crimped the cigarette between his lips and lit it with a match. A smoke plume floated away as he added, "All this lets me know is that I'm soon to face Eugene's brown-nosing side."

"Excuse me a moment. I need to use the men's room," Henry said before heading to the bathroom.

As Henry headed away, a bored Adrian took another puff and gazed around, hoping to hurry along the proceedings. A passing glance to Henry's paperwork made him notice text that looked all too familiar. As his curiosity peeked, he rose from his chair a bit and leaned alongside Henry's half of the table.

Adrian whispered softly and slowly to himself as he read the writing. "*My Death...Your Greatest...Masterpiece.*" His eyes widened as a revelation came to him. He needed that case file. He gave a quick scan around to make sure Henry was nowhere to be seen, then snatched the paper from the small dining table. Adrian popped up from the table with such speed, he accidentally banged his leg against it, spilling tea on the nice white tablecloth. He charged for the door at an incredible walking pace and left Cafe de Paris.

Adrian had turned the first corner he came across in hopes of losing anyone who may follow. In the alleyway, he slowed down a bit and closely examined the document.

"Hey!" someone shouted out behind him. He looked back to see Henry at the other end of the alley. "I believe you have something of mine," Henry yelled as he assertively made his way towards Adrian.

"I'm sorry," Adrian apologized with a fake grin. "I thought this was something of mine."

Henry reached a forceful hand out to retrieve Angelina's claim. "It's from a different case entirely, it doesn't concern you."

"Oh, but I believe it does."

A tad surprised by his response, Henry asked. "How so?"

With the speed of a python, Adrian's right cross swung at Henry, bashing flush against his left cheek. The sucker punch struck Henry with such force that it nearly spun him completely around. In the daze, Adrian locked Henry's arms behind his back and pinned him face-first against the wall of the alley.

"Now, I'm going to tell you something, Mr. Parker. May I call you Mr. Parker?" Adrian only received grunts of frustration as Henry tried to wiggle free. "This book, *'My Death, Your*

Greatest Masterpiece', is in fact a memoir depicting the life of my mother."

"Your mother?" Henry questioned. He eased his struggling body as the new circumstances were brought to light. "So the book *is* real."

"Of course it's real!" Adrian shouted in his ear. "In this book, a man named Gerard McMurray retrieved a certain document from my mother's home, though his name is different. Most in the book are."

"So what?" Henry barked back.

"This document was a roster of MI6 spies the man wished to assassinate. One of those names on that list is my wife. Now, I love my wife, Mr. Parker. Do you have someone you love?"

"Yes," Henry answered, swallowing hard.

"Good. Then you know how far a man would go to protect who he loves. The closer I get to this Angelina, the more I know of this Gerard McMurray. So what do *you* know about her?" Adrian had shifted to a cold, stark demon in a mere instant, at the flip of a switch.

"I don't know anything," Henry yelled back.

Adrian shoved his arm deeper into Henry's back. "Her case was in your bag."

"I swear!" Henry blinked rapidly. "Norman met with her while I was out. He only asked me to file the paperwork. I forgot and placed it in my bag!"

"You better be telling me the truth."

"I swear."

"And as you're a representative of my attorney, I advise you to keep your mouth shut. Have a good day, sir." Adrian threw Henry to the floor before casually trotting out of the alley with the claim still crinkled in his hand.

Adrian then drove to the house of James Taylor, a tall,

thick man with red hair who had hard, rough skin like a rhino. Adrian would always contact James for his more dirty dealings. He was a man who seemed a definite match for Adrian in brute strength, but had none of the same craftiness or cunning. He kept James paid enough to live a fairly comfortable life for his shady services. He explained to James that they needed to visit his new lawyer, Norman Finley.

It was raining as Adrian pulled up to the small white building and stepped out onto the sidewalk. He wore a long black coat over his suit, not wanting anyone to recognize him. Adrian and James stood in front of Angelina's place of employment.

"This is the same place Eugene's wife works," Adrian noted. "Why do I feel that has something to do with this?"

"What about Eugene? You going to do something since he tried to swindle you out of your mother's money?" James inquired.

"Eugene is not the issue. He's just looking for money, and those kind of people can be bought. The real issue is that blasted book and the people behind it."

"Charlotte will be expecting you later for Delores Du Pre's latest shindig."

"This won't take long," Adrian assured.

They headed up to Blackstone & Finley and walked into Norman's office. A receptionist packed up her things, ready to call it a day, when they entered. "I'm sorry, our offices are actually closing—"

Adrian interrupted the lady. "We'll only be a moment. We're looking for Norman Finley."

"Finley? Well..." She then recognized the man who spoke to her. "Adrian Spratchet!" she squealed.

Norman came from his office, viewing the scene. "Adrian, nice to finally meet you." His tone then shifted to address the receptionist. "Thank you, Alice. That will be all."

"Goodnight, Mr. Finley," she said as she gathered her things. "Nice to meet you, Mr. Spratchet."

"Likewise," Adrian politely stated as the receptionist headed out.

They walked through the wooden door of Norman's office to see a sizable wooden table with two chairs. The office had a few plants, a single file cabinet, and numerous diplomas and plaques neatly placed on the walls to commemorate his reputable number of academic achievements.

As Adrian and James took seats in the two twin wooden chairs, Norman joked, "I was surprised to hear you required our services. I would have thought you could take care of real estate matters yourself."

"Well, as they say," Adrian bantered, "a man who is his own lawyer has a fool for a client."

"Of course, of course." Mr. Finley laughed as he sat behind his dark wooden desk. "So, what brings you here? Did Henry deliver those papers to you?"

"It's not about my private matters. My visit is about this book, *'My Death, Your Greatest Masterpiece'*. A woman came to see you recently, claiming she wrote the original to this book. It happens that some of the contents in this story might defame my character. I'm going to need to get in contact with this Angelina." Adrian hoped his new position might sway the lawyer.

Norman sunk back in his chair, and politely explained, "Well sir, I'm sure you are aware of attorney-client privileges—"

"I know about attorney-client privileges. That's how I know you're going to keep your trap shut."

James got up from his seat and locked the door to Norman's office, then the two visitors approached Mr. Finley from both sides. Once they stood next to him, they leaned in close, resting their strong arms on the armrests of Norman's chair.

"Allow me to reiterate so you understand the severity of the situation," Adrian rumbled. "If the truths of this novel were to become evident, it may cost me my job and status, so it's imperative I find her."

Norman seemed to look deep within himself as a man. His watery eyes looked up at Adrian, and he said, "I'm sorry. I'd like to help you, but that's something I can't tell you."

James grabbed the back of Mr. Finley's head and slammed it into his wooden desk, breaking the man's nose. They each held down one of Norman's arms to the desk while Adrian rummaged through the desk drawers with his free hand. A pool of blood formed on the desk, quickly running over the hands of the assailants. Adrian unsheathed from the table a pair of long, metal scissors.

"Give me his hand! Give me his hand!" Adrian shouted as he pinned the man down.

"No! Stop. Please Stop!" Norman pleaded as the violent intensity of the moment overwhelmed the poor lawyer.

Adrian raised the scissors high and swung them down to the desk. Norman screamed. Adrian plunged the scissors just a hair to the right of Norman's hand with such strength it stood firmly there on its own. Norman breathed heavily, his eyes glued to the scissors nearly impaling his hand.

"Tell me who she is," Adrian ordered.

"I don't know much about her. Henry brought her in one day."

"You see, he told me you found her. Now, you tell me he found her. It makes me think one of you is lying. Trust me, you don't want me to think you're lying."

"She works here. She's a typist downstairs." Norman

stuttered.

"Thank you for your time." Adrian and James released the lawyer and calmly exited his office, leaving Norman to sit there with gaping eyes, cupping his hands under his nose in a vain attempt to control the continual bleeding.

The violent duo waited outside as they formulated their next move. "You're not going to see where she works?" James asked.

"No, their offices are closed. Besides, my cousin's wife holds the same position here. I should ask her about Angelina, but that will need to wait for a later time. Tonight, we need to appear at Ms. Du Pre's newest act of debauchery." Adrian pulled a handkerchief from his front pocket, wiping the blood off his hand.

"Understood."

Adrian dropped James off and they planned to rendezvous at the party. He then headed back to his lavish home. Opening his front door, he silently stuck his head in, searching for any sign of his love. With vacant surroundings, Adrian headed into his grand main hall, attempting to be as quiet as a mouse as he closed the door behind him. Suddenly, one of their elderly maids named Esther walked up from down the hall.

"Mr. Spratchet," she called out. "Where have you been? Mrs. Spratchet has been looking all over for you."

"Forgive me, Esther. I have been running some last minute errands that had slipped my mind. Is Charlotte ready?"

"Almost sir," Esther informed as she took off Adrian's large coat.

"Esther! Is that Adrian?" Charlotte yelled from her room, hearing their muffled discussion.

Before Esther could reply, Charlotte appeared at the top of the stairs, clearly not fully prepared for the event. She wore a short, backless dress that ended just before the knee, with classy, intricate sewing and weaving patterns on her lovely figure. The dress ended in fine tassels, hanging a few inches below the dress. She also wore long, white silk gloves that stretched past her elbow. Her hair had been arranged in perfectly loose, shoulder-length curls, but she still appeared to be missing makeup and accessories. Obviously, none of that really mattered to a man like Adrian, but he found the fuss she made over such occasions adorable.

"Adrian," she said again as she sprinted down the steps. "Come now, you should have been here hours ago and we need to get going." She reached the bottom of the steps and approached the middle-aged man to further scold him. "What exactly have you been doing?"

"A few things," he retorted. "Are you ready?"

"Almost. If you make me wait, we're going to be late," she warned.

"You're not going to wait. I'll be ready in moments."

Charlotte then noticed Adrian's bruised right hand. She gasped. "Oh, dear, what happened?" She cradled Adrian's black and blue hand, taking a good look at it.

"Nothing, nothing."

"It's not nothing. It looks bruised. Tell me what happened," she insisted while further analyzing the hand.

"Nothing, I was hurrying out of a building and a door was closed on it," He nonchalantly claimed.

"It looks bad."

"It's fine. I can't even feel it anymore. I promise."

She placed the hand at eye level, then finally conceded. "Well, all right. We need to hurry."

"Yes, darling."

She scurried back upstairs to finish getting ready, and

Adrian soon followed. He went up and changed into an all-black suit with thin white, vertical pin stripes and a matching vest. Once they were both ready, they drove to the hall in which the soiree would be held. The entrance swarmed in waves of well-dressed socialites flocking to the door and waiting to get inside. Spinning spotlights cut through the night, calling forth the privileged few. They handed the valet their keys and walked to the door.

"I can't believe you wore that suit. You don't have anything white?" Charlotte probed, rustling in her small white handbag. Her makeup was fabulous and had on three oversized pearl necklaces dropping from her neck.

"I don't, as a matter of a fact," Adrian playfully yet firmly answered. "I feel uncomfortable in anything but black."

"Have it your way, then, but your bland fashion sense is going to make you stick out like a sore thumb tonight. I think you come off as a gangster."

"Adrian," James shouted by the entrance, flagging him down.

"Over here, James," Adrian commanded as they continued past the doormen without stopping.

Once James came up alongside the couple, he blended with their stride in greeting. "Mr. Spratchet, Mrs. Spratchet."

"Hello, James," Charlotte courteously replied.

Once they muscled to the front through the crowd, they came to a small man with thin, frail glasses, holding a list. "Good evening," the man said with a smile. "Name, please?"

"Adrian Spratchet and guests."

The man thumbed through his list, halting halfway through the second page. "Ah, here we are. Please head in, Mr. Spratchet."

The three walked in and were immediately blasted by the

sound of trumpets from the live band burning up the stage. A few people danced wildly to the lively, hip, jazzy music. The venue was massive, easily fitting the hundreds of people already inside, plus those still waiting to enter. Ladies in revealing white dresses danced gracefully on stages set throughout the hall, some gleefully swinging from giant swings hanging from the rafters of the high ceiling. Soap suds were everywhere, under the tables, in all the corners, and even creeping up to the stage. The floor was almost invisible beneath it all. White confetti fell in swarms and circulated the party. No expense was spared for the extravagant festivities.

The event had a very high-profile crowd. Politicians, artists, old money, new money—they were all in attendance. Even some stars of the silver screen like George Arliss and Marion Davies mingled their way through. The list formed a 'who's who' hierarchy between the powerfully wealthy and the privileged, carefree youth born with silver spoons. Most guests wore white in tandem with the 'bubble bath' theme of the party, but there were a few exceptions, like Adrian, who wouldn't be caught dead in that color.

"Oh, dear," Charlotte worried as they entered. "How do I look?"

Adrian stopped and took a good long look at his beloved wife, really soaking in the sight of her. "I'm with the most beautiful woman here."

Charlotte smiled sweetly, accompanied by a little blush. "Thank you, darling." She gave him a sweet and heartfelt kiss on the cheek, which he accepted lovingly.

Jemima appeared from the crowd, waving. She weaved through the masses toward them, holding a nearly empty glass of champagne. She had on a long, white, strapless dress, which confined her legs too close together, so she continued to stumble over to them.

"Charlotte! Adrian! Where have you been!?" Jemima wailed in glee. She leaned over to Charlotte and both of them shared a quick peck on the cheek.

"My apologies," said Charlotte. "We were running a tad late."

"Adrian," Jemima once again greeted, shifting her attention to him. "How dashing you look tonight."

"You flatter me," Adrian replied with a smirk. "This is my friend, James Taylor."

"Hello," the lug said.

"Jemima," she said, introducing herself. She eyed the man, and refrained from offering him her hand.

"Nice to meet you," James fired back.

"Charmed," she hummed, absolutely drenched in sarcasm. Her head twisted back to Charlotte. "Come with me, my dear. There's a couple here I'm just dying for you to meet."

"Very well, then. I'll see you later, darling," Charlotte stated as Jemima whisked her away.

"Of course," Adrian said, waving to her disappearing body. When she was gone, he took out his silver cigarette case and lit one. "I am already finding this tiring," he vented.

"I think it's fun," James commented.

Adrian suddenly heard his name being called out again. A good three times it was yelled, and he turned around to see Delores Du Pre sitting at a big round table filled with laughing, jubilant people. She rapidly waved him over.

"Do you see what I mean?" Adrian sighed. He plucked a glass of champagne off a passing platter and walked to Delores' table, plastering a fake smile on his face. James didn't follow. He just looked around, biding time.

Adrian neared the table as Delores scorned, "I have not

seen you or Charlotte all night. Where have you been hiding?"

"We just arrived," Adrian explained.

"He's not wasting any time there, then," a little man seated next to Ms. Du Pre joked, pointing at Adrian's glass.

"Oh, stop it, Nox," Delores said in an obviously more playful mood "This is Nox Harrington, the 'hard hitting' journalist," she introduced.

"Adrian Spratchet. Nice to meet you."

"Mr. Spratchet has recently been selected for the General Council of the Bar," Delores announced to the entire table. Nods of respectable acknowledgment greeted him all around.

"There wasn't much competition, I assure you," Adrian joked. The other guests let out a good laugh; Adrian could be charming when he chose to be.

"Congratulations then, my good fellow," Nox said, extending his hand.

Adrian shook it. "Much appreciated."

"Have you heard about the latest book I published?" Delores mentioned. "They say it's soon to be a best-seller."

"'*My Death, Your Greatest Masterpiece*'?" Adrian questioned, as if he wasn't familiar with the title. "Yes, I've heard many good things about it. The book haunts me."

"I should hope it would!" Delores exclaimed. "I'd love it to be the talk of London."

"I'm sure it will be." Adrian was dying for a reason to leave the table. "Now, if you'll excuse me, I need to find my wife. I believe Jemima abducted her."

Delores let out a giggle, then demanded, "Once you find her, you make sure she comes and sees me. We should have a drink together."

"Of course," Adrian claimed as he walked away from the table, taking a long-awaited puff from his cigarette. He made his way back to the patiently waiting James and cursed. "That bloody novel again."

"You know what I've been wondering?" James inquired. "You told that lawyer we roughed up that the book could defame your character. Is that true, or were you just blowing smoke?"

"It's true," Adrian revealed.

"What do you mean? I thought you just wanted to find that list."

"Think about it. A mother who killed his father, a wife who is a former government spy…I would definitely lose my seat on the bar if the truth became public. Not to mention the shame and humiliation my dear Charlotte would endure. It would bring her into the light, and as far as I'm concerned, that list exists for a reason. That's why it's imperative we not only find it but bury anyone who may know that book is real. This mysterious Gerard, this poor author Angelina..." Adrian formed his fingers into the shape of a gun. He slowly lifted his arm until he aimed it at the unsuspecting Delores. "...even Ms. Delores Du Pre." He pulled the trigger and shot his fake gun at Delore's laughing face. "Have you gotten any closer to finding out where Malcom is?"

James gave Adrian a pained look. "That line of enquiry is stone-cold, I'm afraid."

Adrain sighed. "Things are escalating, James. This is all too much of a coincidence. We need to be ready for anything, understand?"

CHAPTER 26 – France, 1916

Elizabeth had never seen so much blood before. She'd seen men shot and killed, but they were usually cleanly executed. War was not so clean. Men screamed, crying for their mothers, their lovers, and sometimes the words they screamed made no sense. Elizabeth despised it. She retired to the apartment she shared with the other nurses, so bone-tired she was sure she would make it to her bed. She didn't think she would last very long, and often she wondered if she hadn't made a mistake leaving the spy business.

Hours turned into days, and days into weeks. She developed a rapport with the soldiers, sometimes feeling as if she paid penance now for the awful things she had done. Her hands were healing, and her words offered them hope when they often had none. She grew and relished in her newfound profession.

Elizabeth would be lying if she didn't admit there was one particular reason she started to enjoy her work. His name was Charles Shepard, a Lieutenant Colonel in the First Army. He had wavy, dark brown hair, emerald eyes, and the tanned face of a man who spent plenty of time outdoors. When Elizabeth first came upon him, the dirt on his body was caked and thick like frosting. Weeks of stubble covered his face, and the left half of his body had been badly marred and burned by a grenade. He was lucky he hadn't lost more than just skin and some tissue.

There wasn't much they could do for him; they'd run out of painkillers. The doctors said he was in constant, excruciating pain, and he may have soft tissue damage for the rest of his life. They asked Elizabeth to sit with him, hold his hand, and keep him distracted while they worked on him. Elizabeth sat down next to him and pulled his hands into hers. They were warm, calloused, and felt strangely like home.

"My name is Elizabeth."

He smiled as his eyes made contact with hers, and he nodded. "Lieutenant Colonel Charles Shepard, ma'am. Pleased to meet you."

She found herself enjoying the way his face looked when his eyes crinkled. He winced as the doctors pulled on his skin, and Elizabeth noticed the gravel embedded into the side of his face. She squeezed his hand reassuringly. "Tell me where you're from, Lieutenant Colonel Shepard."

"Charlie," he corrected, speaking through gritted teeth. "I'm from London. Not the nice part, mind you. I joined the military when I was a kid to see the world." His laugh sounded bitter. "I saw something, all right." His eyes went darker then, and Elizabeth knew he had also done and seen some things that changed who he was.

"How much longer do you have in the military?" she asked.

"I have a feeling I may be done, now. Don't know if they'll want me back in this condition."

"What will you do if they won't have you?"

"I'd like to go to Paris," he replied. "Get a small apartment, explore the city. Stay in one place for some time. I think that might be nice."

"That sounds wonderful." The doctors told Elizabeth she could take her leave now as the worst was over.

"Will you come again?" Charles asked.

"I will."

"Will you come tomorrow, perhaps?"

"I will," she said again.

The man pressed his luck a little further. "Will you marry me?" A smile played on his lips. She smiled back and left before giving him an answer. She thought he couldn't possibly be serious.

She found herself making excuses to visit Charles. At first, they just sat and talked. Sometimes, Elizabeth was tasked with changing his dressings. She tried to imagine what his face must have looked like before the grenade went off. Somehow, the damage to his face made him look more rugged. Elizabeth was sure she preferred him this way. He often asked her where she came from, if she had family, and she made sure to avoid the subject and quickly change it to something else. Charles hadn't failed to notice that fact. He didn't press the subject; it was obvious her past held something darker. Instead, he tried to keep the tone light.

He asked her about her favorite flowers, how old she was when she received her first kiss. She found herself blushing when answering that question. Her eyes lingered on his lips a few moments too long as she thought about what it would be like to feel his lips on hers. Would his lips be soft and tender? Would they be rough and searching for answers? It had been so long since she had been kissed—and kissed well. She wondered how long it had been for him. She didn't imagine he'd seen much kissing on the battlefield.

Before she could stop herself, she leaned over and pressed

her lips to his. She'd startled him, and she quickly pulled away. "I'm sorry," she whispered. "I shouldn't have—" Before she could finish her sentence, his hand was on the back of her head and he crushed his lips to hers. When she pulled away a second time, she was breathless and her head swam.

"Marry me?" he asked again.

Elizabeth gave no reply.

When Charles got stronger, they went for walks around the grounds together, sometimes holding hands. Charles asked her to marry him every day, and every day Elizabeth refused to give him an answer. *What kind of crazy person proposes marriage the first time they meet someone?* Elizabeth had to admit that she hadn't felt this way about anyone in a very long time. Sometimes, she imagined she would tell him yes the next time he asked. She felt guilty for feeling as happy as she was when he was around. She had done so many terrible things, hurt so many people, even if it was for their own good. What right had she to happiness?

Charles noticed her dip in moods when they were together, and he finally approached her about it. He told her he knew something had happened in her past, that she didn't have to tell him what it was, but that he wanted to make sure she spent the rest of her life happy. Elizabeth broke down in tears and told Charles more than she had told anyone besides Madame Lockridge. When she finished spilling her secrets, she threw her hands to her lips. She hadn't meant to tell him, and now she was afraid he wouldn't look at her the same way.

He took her hands away from her mouth and kissed them softly. "Nothing you can say would ever change the way I feel about you." He pulled her to him and they sat on the bench while the sun went down. Elizabeth allowed herself to fall asleep in his arms.

She woke to the glaring light of the sun announcing its entrance. Charles escorted her to the apartments and kissed her once more before turning and taking off. Elizabeth called after him. He stood in front of her, hands in his pocket, a cocky smile curling at the sides of his mouth.

"Ask me again," she said. His smile widened, but he didn't say anything. "Ask me again." She laughed, tears playing at the corners of her eyes.

"Marry me," he said, slightly above a whisper.

"Yes." She nodded and wrapped herself around him.

They spent the next few weeks planning and mapping out what they would do. Elizabeth had quickly jumped on board with his plan to go to Paris. Charles had contacts there and was already promised work. It wasn't what he always dreamed of doing, but the tissue damage to the left side of his body would make it impossible for him to perform remedial manual labor for the rest of his life. He was sure the military would discharge him. What good would he be fighting the enemy when he wasn't the man he used to be? His skin was discolored down his arm, over his hip, and down his left leg. The doctors told him how lucky he was that it wasn't worse, and that he healed the way he did. He was lucky, and thankful. He was thankful he may never have to spend another day fighting in a war, watching his brothers die as evil men destroyed them. He would be thankful for a new start.

Two months after Elizabeth said yes, she found herself arriving in Paris with Charles. The military had honorably discharged him and he was now a free man. They were both free to start a new life together. They found a small apartment above a patisserie that sold fresh-baked breads and desserts. The smells wafting up to their apartment were indescribable. Elizabeth found herself working there part-time. It was a far cry from Mi6 and the constant dredge of wounded men, but she liked the continued work of using her hands. She liked the way the dough would knead under her fingers and the way a desert looked after she had spent hours working on it.

When they started to plan their wedding, Elizabeth realized it was going to be very one-sided. She had neither family nor friends who would attend on her behalf, and she wasn't about to risk the safety of her children. She had left them behind for a reason, had she not? The thought saddened her; she had missed so many things. She wondered if they knew she loved them, that she was only doing what was best. She had hoped that, one day, she would be able to explain to them.

After much thought, she brought up idea of children with Charles. This time would be different, she told herself. She wouldn't make the same mistakes, wouldn't put her children in constant danger, wouldn't make them a scandal. This was her chance to do things differently. Charles was overjoyed; he would bring life for the ones he had taken. Nothing could be better than that. They would be married in a week's time, and hopefully a child would follow soon after.

Elizabeth scoured the Paris shops for the perfect wedding items. Charles himself had never been married, so Elizabeth wanted it to be everything for him. The first item she wanted to cross off the list was flowers. She had a hard time deciding between lilies or tulips. When she found herself at the flower market, running her fingers over the soft petals, her mind wandered to what each would look like in a bouquet. Then she felt the strangest chill run up her back.

Her eyes opened quickly and her head turned in each direction. She was certain someone watched her. Her adrenaline kicked up as she made her way down the row of flowers. She was careful to pretend her attention focused on the arrangements when it couldn't have been further from the truth. She scanned each and every person, making sure she knew where the exits were located and what she could use as a weapon should the need arise. Elizabeth may have left MI6, but her training remained.

Elizabeth waited and waited, but nothing happened. Nobody jumped out at her; nobody so much as glanced her way in a threatening manner. She brushed the feeling off, convincing herself it was just a bad case of pre-wedding jitters. She wondered if she would always be waiting for the other shoe to drop.

"Elizabeth," a voice said from behind her.

Her blood went cold. She hadn't been expecting his voice, not at all. She should've secured the location and left post haste. It was her own fault for sticking around. She knew better than that. She spun around, meeting the icy-steal gaze before her.

"You are a hard woman to find." His accent was thick and heady, and it sent shivers up her spine. This man wasn't one with whom she could have used her training.

"Maybe I didn't want to be found," she replied.

He laughed. "We'll always find you, Elizabeth. No one stays hidden very long."

"I'm out. I've been out. I have a normal life now."

"You of all people should know you never get out. That's not an option for people like you. Pack up, girl. This is the big time."

"No. I won't," she said defiantly.

"You will," he growled, "once you see what's in this folder." He tossed it at her, and before she could catch it he was gone. She ripped open the folder, scanning the papers before her.

"No," she whispered. "This can't be happening."

CHAPTER 27 – Lockridge Estate, 1927

A week had passed without Madame sending for Angelina. She kept her door shut, and all was silent other than the occasional shuffle of her feet. Once, Angelina nearly knocked. Her knuckles braced themselves for the gesture as she strained to hear anything through the thick mahogany. Silence. Angelina glanced at the half-eaten toast left on a tray of empty dishes, thinking that if Madame was well enough to eat, she could surely continue the story. But she found herself unable to disturb Madame, and left quietly.

There was much to distract Angelina that week, as her and Rupert's flirtation developed into regular encounters. They met every evening beneath a large oak tree by the lake. It kept them away from prying eyes so they could laugh and kiss. This particular night, Rupert was convinced that Ruth had spotted Angelina walking towards the lake.

"I saw her. There, at that window." He pointed to one of the lower windows which looked into the dining room.

Angelina looked. "I don't see anything. You worry too much."

"No, I saw her. We have to go." He hurriedly grabbed his shoes, as he'd been there waiting since he'd finished his supper for Angelina to finish her work.

"We can talk to her. I'm sure she wouldn't speak of this to anyone." Angelina started to rush after him, but he turned abruptly and put his hand on her shoulder.

"No." His face was stern and somewhat older-looking. Angelina had never seen this side of him before. "No one must know of this. *Especially* Ruth, understand?" Angelina nodded, perplexed, as she watched Rupert storm off towards the house.

She hung back by the tree, curious about Rupert's reaction until he was out of sight and she felt it was safe to follow. As she found her way inside, she felt eyes on her. Angelina looked up to see Ruth moving slowly around the kitchen, refusing to meet Angelina's gaze. Angelina kept moving. She didn't want to see what was in Ruth's eyes. She didn't want to learn the truth, as she already feared what could be.

Angelina spent the rest of her evening sifting through the notes she had made during her time with Madame. The manuscript was nearly complete, but she still felt Madame was hiding something—something that brought upon her enough shame to lock herself in her room for days at a time.

***

Another day passed before Madame and Angelina sat down together.

"Bring me your notes," Madame demanded. She was in a sour mood, refusing to dress for the day before their meeting. Angelina cautiously handed Madame her manuscript, feeling uncomfortable to be meeting under such conditions. Madame wore only a nightgown, her hair tangled behind her ears. Without the usual facade of her makeup and silk scarves, Angelina hardly recognized her. Underneath it all, Madame was frail and sickly.

220

"This is unacceptable!" Madame burst, tossing the loose pages to the ground. "The truth needs to be told, by you and *only* you, and here you've written nothing but rubbish."

"I apologize, Madame," Angelina said quietly as she picked up her work, cursing herself for not numbering the pages. "It's still a work in progress. I'm waiting for the story to be complete before the editing is done."

"What do you mean when the story is *complete?*" Madame barked. "Do you think I killed my husband *twice*? The story is over!"

Angelina nodded, preparing to leave the room. "I'll start editing immediately then." She heard Madame muttering under her breath, pushing Angelina's frustrations over the edge. "Actually, Madame." She turned back towards the bed just before reaching the door. "I believe there's more to your story, and I refuse to complete this work until you tell me everything." Then she left.

Angelina's heart raced as she reached the hallway, shocked by her own actions. How dare she speak to Madame that way, after everything she'd done to help her? Shame washed over her and tears fought to stain her cheeks. She considered turning around to apologize, even taking a dozen or so steps in that direction. But the moment passed and she lost her opportunity. Madame called her to come back.

With her stomach in her throat, Angelina shuffled back to Madame's bedside with her eyes on the floor. She thought for sure she'd be fired, or worse, that Madame would put an end to their little side project. But neither occurred.

"Relax, child. You're right." Their eyes met, and Angelina felt it all coming to a close. She pulled up a chair and scribbled furiously as Madame began visualized her story, helping her tell it in a mesmerizing way.

"What happened then?" asked Angelina, her face lit up with excitement.

Madame, however, had started to fade nearly an hour before. Her breath caught and she struggled to sound like her usual, assertive self. Angelina had become accustomed to Madame's mood changes, but realized there was more to it.

"After that... Well, we're getting close to the end of my story. I still have a few surprises for you, and I still have a secret you don't know."

"Tell me." Angelina's fingers were dark with ink stains. She had traded the typewriter for pen and paper over the past few sessions entirely as the story had closed in on what followed Jonathon's murder. She had to settle for writing down notes as Madame's words tumbled from her pale, wrinkled lips, too quickly for Angelina to make sense of it with typing. Her typing had improved since she'd come to work for Madame, but not enough to keep up with the forthcoming deluge of information.

Madame drank the last of the tea from her cup and smiled tiredly. Her eyes were clouded. "It's just the last chapter left to write, now."

"But what about the secret?"

"The secret will have to keep until the morning. I'm so tired just now, my dear, so tired. I'm going to have to go to bed early."

Angelina glanced at the clock; it was only just after seven. She had to bite her lip not to implore further. Instead, she gathered up their things from tea on the tea trolley and helped Madame to her feet. Angelina was startled by the feeling of Madame's frail body, like old parchment, too light to be alive—more like an autumn leaf than a living, breathing woman. She heard a rattle in Madame's breathing and looked at her face with deep concern. She had always thought of Madame as incredibly

222

strong, so sure of herself, but the woman had withered of late and seemed to have aged in only a matter of weeks.

"Are you well, Madame? Should I call for someone?"

"No, I'm fine. These things happen when you don't get out much. One day, your parts run down and they don't give you replacements for them. Once they go, they just go."

"Madame, you speak as if you're a woman in her eighties, and I know you're much younger than that. Have you seen a doctor?"

Madame settled back into her chair and brushed off Angelina's fussing, "On second thought, I think I'd like to just sit here for a bit. I want to think about this next part, the last chapter. I need to get right with myself and God before I tell you."

Angelina was frustrated by Madame's lack of concern for her own health. She now had no choice but to address this with Ruth. Angelina wheeled out the tea trolley but turned just before she exited the room. She walked back to where Madame sat imperious, impenetrable, and seemingly immortal. On a whim, Angelina darted forward and kissed Madame's cheek; it felt like delicate a rose petal saved between the pages of an old book.

"You'll recover, Madame. Call if you need anything...or if you change your mind."

"Oh, shoo, you! Silly little thing. Secrets will keep."

***

The door closed softly behind the young girl and Madame closed her eyes. The only noise in the room was the sound of her breathing and the sound of the grandfather clock ticking. The truth that Angelina had sensed about her health was more real than Madame felt comfortable admitting. She sensed a veil had torn between her and the other place, the world of ghosts and death. Madame wasn't afraid of it, except for the trepidation that came with any new adventure and the fear that came with confronting any ghost.

She reached into the edge of her seat cushion and pulled out the four letters she had withheld from Angelina's prying gaze. She chuckled a little to herself. The girl, in many ways, reminded her more of herself than of Elizabeth. Angelina was full of the spirit of curiosity like Madame, rather than the spirit of adventure like Elizabeth. As the girl wrote her story, she felt herself growing almost motherly towards her, and Madame wondered if Angelina would still care for her the same way after the final chapter.

The four letters concerned the last big secret Madame had kept from everyone. Even Elizabeth only knew the edges of the story. She pulled one of the letters out of its sheath, and ancient lavender briefly scented the air.

My Dearest Love,

I had to write to you one last time, even though our love is as forbidden as the child of our union. I know I said you would never hear from me again, but I can no longer raise our son. I am sending him home to you with this letter. I know he won't open it. He is a good lad and he does not know you are his mother. I have instructed him to work for you, and he has been raised well to serve.

He spent time with your dear friend Elizabeth, and although he has never spoken to me about their encounters, he seems grown beyond his years. Elizabeth will bring Rupert to you with this letter in hand once I pass.

My love, I am dying. The doctors have told me it is tuberculosis and there is no cure. This is why our son must come home to you, even though no one may ever know our shame. I will try not to write again. It is best this way, my love. You are ever present in my thoughts and my last breath will be your name.

> *Loving you for eternity,*
> *Walter.*

Madame tried to imagine telling this part of the story, the last part, wrapped up with an inheritance she had held in trust and never given to the boy she had birthed but never mothered. Everything would go to him—the estate, her fortune, the rights to her manuscript that was the story of her life. All of it.

She still recalled those early years with Jonathan, and how she had shamed Elizabeth for her indiscretion, only to find herself in a similar predicament. Although she had been married, she knew it would have been unwise to pass the child off as Jonathan's. It had been easy for her to progress with the pregnancy but fiddle the dates. When she was due, Jonathan would believe she was only thirty weeks along, and losing a baby at birth was not unusual. Her doctors had been paid well to look after her and see the baby's father took the child. It was hard for her to watch Jonathan mourn the loss of what he thought to be his child, but Madame's love for Jonathan exceeded everything. She never had a chance to bond with her baby, and Walter had been a simple, foolish mistake. Fortunately, though, he'd had such strong feelings for Madame that his love allowed him to go along with her plan, preserving her life and status.

The other letter was from the hospital where Walter had died, and the other two were to Elizabeth with detailed instructions about how her Will should be dispersed. That was the only incomplete letter. She knew Elizabeth would not care for the story being published, and may even see it as an act of betrayal, but in many ways, that was the most pressing issue for Madame. Her wealth and her estate were not as important to her as the sanctity of her story.

Madame gripped her armrests and levered herself up. She was failing physically and she knew it, but her mind was still sharp. She hid the letters under the bust she had used to kill her husband. Nobody ever touched it—a superstitious fear kept the maids away except to give it the briefest of dustings. Nobody could see those letters. She would have destroyed them if they weren't integral to uncovering the entirety of her Will. She knew, or at least she thought she knew, that Angelina would check under the bust. Maybe not right away, but soon enough after her demise to protect her Will. Angelina knew the bust's significance, and she wouldn't be able to keep from touching it, snooping at it, when she wasn't afraid of Madame's eyes catching her at her macabre intrigues.

Satisfied, Madame stood back and checked that nothing showed of the letters. Would she be able to bring herself to tell Angelina the truth in the morning? She shook her head; she had to make herself speak the words. She bent down low for any sign of unevenness in the bust, and then she saw a bright light.

It flared across her left eye and brought a sharp pain searing into her brain, deeper than anything she'd ever felt before. She tried to call for help, but only a dull noise like the quiet caw of a crow came out of her throat.

Madame fell to the ground, her light body barely thudding with the impact. She scrabbled at her throat as though she was choking, even though the pain focused in her head. She tried to pull herself to her feet but only managed to tug a doily from the table. She slumped to the ground, resting her cheek against the carpet and wondering if this pain matched what her husband had felt when he died on this same spot.

Her thoughts were of her murdered husband, and her last breath was his name. "Jonathan," she murmured.

Then the light dulled down, and with it, the pain. Her vision faded as she stared at the pattern on the rug. Her gaze followed the pattern into eternity.

CHAPTER 28

Angelina awoke to the crash of porcelain and a shrill scream. She knew no one on the estate who had such a scream. She raced out of her room and followed two other maids and a butler whose name she'd never known, but they all called him 'Mustache'— not to his face, of course. They turned the corner and all joking vanished from Angelina's thoughts.

Ruth stood paralyzed at the door to the living room, shards of porcelain and toast at her tea-soaked feet. Angelina held back when the rest of the staff pushed forward. She already knew what had happened; it was the only thing that could happen on this estate to make Ruth so distraught. Madame had passed away.

Angelina had felt a strong bond with Madame. She was her mother, father, sister, grandmother, all in one. She had been the only person in Angelina's life to open up to her and trust her. That had made Angelina uncomfortable at first, and now she didn't know how to feel about Madame's passing. She wanted to grieve for her appropriately, and the best way she knew how was to finish the book.

Everyone on the estate was in mourning. No one wanted to talk to Angelina, let alone help her piece together the past—a past many of the staff had been a part of themselves. The content of the story so far was enthralling. Angelina knew it could be a fantastic book, but it still needed a great ending.

What would Madame have told me next? What could be the secret? she wondered.

Letters were written and sent with great haste to every relative and acquaintance whose address could be pilfered from Madame's correspondence. '*Madame Lockridge has passed. Funeral service this Sunday the 12*th.'

No one attended but the staff.

Weeks passed. No relatives or well-wishers arrived. Angelina did not speak to Rupert during this time. She had been playing with the idea of distancing herself from him, but she hadn't expected him to do so first. Time and again, chance gave her a glimpse of him coming and going from the woods. Perhaps he expected her to follow, but she did not.

The final chapter of Madame's life story haunted her. Day after day, Angelina shut herself away in the living room, which everyone now avoided. She wanted to skirt the awkward, casual mourning of the staff, and busy herself soaking up any lingering influence from Madame. Most hours, the bust held her attention. She recalled her innocence when she thought it to be nothing more than décor. Now, she stared at it, hoping for inspiration from a murder weapon.

Madame's last words to her wisped about the room, trailing every speck of dust and shadow. *Secrets will keep.* Madame's secrets were gone to her forever, now. Even so, the manuscript needed an ending. With every ounce of courage and craft instilled in her by Madame, Angelina selected a crisp new sheet of paper and began to write the ending. If the truth wouldn't come to her, she would create an embellished death, drawing on the irony of reality. She could only hope Madame would approve.

*On the 2*nd *of June, ten years to the day, her dear husband passed away. The cook—with toast in one hand and tea in the other—found the cold Madame Lockheart lying still on the same carpet where dear Jonathan had died. Every maid, stable boy, and rat on the estate heard the porcelain crash and the cook's shrill scream.*

A dark figure crossed the moonlit lawn, dressed in a tailored suit complete with a cloak and derby. Anyone who may have seen this shady figure slipping out undetected would have presumed it to be a man. Beneath the cloaked eyes and fake mustache, only Madame really knew the truth.

Evelyn had loose ends to tie up, and her loyalty to her country gave her the strength she needed to kill the one person whom she had always trusted. With Madame's death, her darkest secrets would also be buried. Or so she thought.

The mourning period was respected, as it should be, with all wearing black and in a somber mood. But what happened next is far more interesting. Inheritors, well-wishers, and devoted staff scrambled about, asking questions, unlocking chests, knocking holes in walls. Some continued the search for weeks, others for years. All tried to piece together the life and Will of Madame Lockheart, but no one came close to the truth.

If one sits quietly in the living room, a slave to time, it seems the ghost of Madame Lockheart creeps across the room to impart her final wisdom: "Secrets will keep."

As Angelina sat back, she hesitated before committing to her tale. She's just written her mother as Evelyn the murderer and, in this case, it was a complete lie. While her mother's true identity was protected, she felt a resounding doubt over whether or not she was doing the right thing. It certainly gave the story the dramatic ending it needed.

Will secrets keep? Angelina's worry cut into her. The

blossoming love she felt for Rupert may indeed have been filthy, incestuous sin. Why else did Rupert fear Ruth knowing of their love? Angelina had to know. This secret would not keep. She bundled the manuscript, tucked it away in her bed, and headed to the kitchen.

"Ruth?" she asked. Ruth continued chopping carrots, fresh tears coating her cheeks. "I was wondering something... about Rupert."

Ruth grunted, then stabbed the nearest loaf of bread with her knife. Angelina winced, but would not be so easily dissuaded. Ruth swept the carrot pennies into the pot and slammed an onion onto her cutting board.

Angelina tried again. "Rupert. Is he...related to—"

Ruth's knife pricked the onion. The golden outer shell cracked open. "What put that idea in your head, girl?" Ruth asked. Her knife slid into the onion, and the fumes stung Angelina's eyes. Ruth only stared down at her work.

"He's the right age. Why did Madame have him work here? There's a similarity in the eyes and—"

"You going to say anything?"

"Shouldn't I?"

"Can't you leave well enough alone, girl? Rupert's life is fine as it is. Don't go mucking about the place." Angelina glanced out the window and saw Rupert heading into the woods. "Besides," Ruth continued, "your carriage will arrive in a few hours."

"What?"

"Madame arranged for you to live with her nephew Eugene and his wife in London. She had always been clear about this, and you were to leave as soon as the book was completed. I presume it's done. You've hardly left the living room since... since...well, have you finished?"

"As it happens, I have. Why are you only just telling me this now?"

"What was the point of you knowing sooner? Go pack. You can have some pie when you're finished."

Angelina left the kitchen in a huff. It seemed everyone else was still making decisions for her, as though she were still a child.

It made sense that Madame would send her to London. The first step in publishing a manuscript was to find a publisher, and all the best were in London. But why had Madame instructed Ruth to pack her off so soon? Surely Madame had not anticipated passing before the manuscript was completed.

If she was leaving tonight, then she had to speak with Rupert. Ruth may not have seen the point, but Angelina couldn't leave Rupert without an explanation. She owed him, and their love, the truth. She owed him the truth because he was her blood. The paradox tore at her soul as she slipped into the woods.

Rupert stood by their oak tree, waiting for her as though he'd wanted her to follow him after all. "I've been wanting to tell you something," he said, never taking his eyes off the lake.

"I think I know."

Rupert laughed deeply and fully. It was the first laugh Angelina had heard since Madame passed. "I've never told anyone this before. I really don't know how to say it. So if you'd stay just there, I'd appreciate it."

"All right." Angelina sat down against the other side of their oak.

"Before I came here, I wasn't well-supervised."

Angelina had imagined Rupert's childhood had been this way. It matched his carefree nature and foolish jokes.

"I was quite clever," he continued. "Too clever, most likely. I fell in with some people who had vowed to make a

232

positive change in the world, and I wanted to be a part of it, too. I thought the rules were different for me—for us."

Angelina poked her fingers beneath the leaves, into the decaying earth.

"I thought a little sin didn't matter if I could just look toward the greater good, the lives saved, the secrets kept."

Is he justifying loving me even though I'm his sister? Angelina penetrated deeper into the muck, her knuckles trembling and twigs scratching her palm.

"But I couldn't live with the look in their eyes. Maybe it's because I was a child, maybe it's because I'm human, but when I had the opportunity to stop, I took it."

Angelina's fingertips brushed against something colder than dirt and stone, something unnaturally smooth. Something manmade.

"I haven't taken a single life since I came here, Angelina. I swear it to you. And if you can live with all the death in my past —if you can see me as myself and not some idealistic child killing for his country—will you run away with me?"

Yes! The word rushed to the tip of her tongue, but she cut it off. Nothing in Rupert's past could make her stop loving him. But that love disgusted her. He was her brother. This could never be.

She used her finger to outline the buried object, tracing its shape still deeply submerged. Her unfocused mind prevented her from paying any further attention to what could be there. *But— what if I do love him?* She wished she could justify it, but she couldn't. An instantaneous downpour snapped her out of her weakness.

"I can't love you," Angelina said quite abruptly. She sprinted away from Rupert—away from their oak, away from the truth. The rain drenched her dress and the ground beneath her,

233

weighing her down. Cloth and mud clung to her body, and she roughly breathed in the wet, betraying air.

She imagined Rupert running after her, grabbing her hand. She could feel the reassuring pressure of his hand around hers, like he held all the pieces together. But he wasn't, in fact, holding her hand, and he didn't follow her. There was nothing he could do to make this right. The imaginary hand slipped away.

"I don't love him. I don't love him. I can't." Angelina repeated the mantra with every step away from the man she could not love. Muddy footprints followed her to the servant's quarters. She'd made a muck of the place, just like Ruth had said she would. She heartlessly packed her belongings in a rucksack Ruth had left out for her. She owned nothing that mattered that much, except for the manuscript, and she placed that gently inside. The carriage, and London, were waiting for her.

CHAPTER 29 – London, 1928

Delores Du Pre removed her coat as she entered her lavish office adorned with her many awards. Beneath her own personal trophy case was a small bookcase, filled with the books she'd published in her successful career. She strutted toward her desk, sat down to turn on the small desk lamp, then reached for her phone.

"Heather, might I trouble you for a cup of tea?" Delores said with an almost eerie sense of joy.

"I just made a fresh pot. I'll be there in one moment, ma'am." True to her word, Heather walked in soon after Delores hung up the phone. "How has your night been, Ms. Du Pre?"

"Very well, Heather. It seems my book will be a real hit." Delores stretched out in her chair.

"That's lovely, ma'am. But…I mean, do you mind if I ask you a question?"

"Ask away, my dear."

"Aren't you worried at all about the allegations, Ms. Du Pre? I'm sorry. I don't want to disturb your mood, but I worry sometimes." Heather poured the cup of tea.

Delores put two sugar cubes into her cup and stirred it with a sterling silver spoon. "Not in the least. Do you know how many times some small time-lawyer has sauntered in here,

235

spouting that their client thinks I've wronged them?" Delores sipped her tea, shuddered, then added another cube of sugar.

"No, I don't, ma'am," Heather replied.

"Neither do I, dear. It's such a bother to keep track of after a while." Delores looked down at her desk, which had become inundated with paperwork, some of which had Henry's and Angelina's names on it.

"Why do they do it?" Heather asked.

"Because, my dear, everyone wants success, and it's often easier to leech off those who have it then to find it for yourself. Some people come here saying the deal I gave them isn't fair, though they had no complaints at the time we struck said deal. Some people come here saying I owe them something extra. I don't owe anyone for their own lack of foresight. Then there are the people who come to me saying I've stolen their ideas." Dolores opened a drawer and slid most of the loose clumps of allegations into it.

"What do you tell them, ma'am?"

"I rarely have to do much at that point. Their arguments fall apart on their own rather quickly. I just get to sit and watch." Delores finished her cup of tea and motioned for Heather to fill it up again.

Heather quickly moved to do so. "I will admit, this one has me a bit more nervous. I mean, you never work with authors who use a pseudonym. You always told me that if an author can't be honest with their names, you can't expect honesty in their story." Heather put three sugar cubes in Delores' tea and stirred it for her this time.

"Are you accusing me of stealing the book now, too?" Delores put a fourth sugar cube in her tea, just because she could, and took a sip.

"No, I would never—I'm sorry. I didn't mean to..."

Heather fumbled through her words after Delores' reversal of the accusation.

"It's fine, dear, perfectly fine to accuse me. I did steal the book."

"Ms. Du Pre! You stole it?"

"Can you blame me? Look how well it's doing."

"But what about the original author? You know I hold you in such high regard, but this could have been an author's big chance. You still would have received credit as an agent, but someone else's name would also be out there. You could have opened up a whole world for someone." Heather rarely spoke out against Ms. Du Pre, but apparently her opinions were too grand to keep to herself.

"At the cost of part of my own world," Dolores answered calmly. "Don't be fooled. I do feel some guilt for my actions. A writer with that talent will find her way up the ladder with very little issue. I need to make good on my opportunities while they're still on the table." Delores never talked about her future, and she noted Heather's wide, shocked eyes. She wished the girl would close her gaping mouth.

"I've never heard you speak like that," Heather almost whispered.

"Well, I've rarely felt this way. But every now and then, you have to show that you're still on top. This book does just that."

"What are you going to do about the author? If they press charges, they have legitimate claims."

"Like I said, many people come to see me here with disputes, and they all have one thing in common. They leave with nothing."

A knock on the door grabbed the attention of both women, and Adrian Spratchet entered. "Good evening, ladies. I

237

hope I'm not interrupting you two in the middle of something," he said.

"Be thankful you entered at the end. A few minutes earlier, and I'd have to kill you," Delores said. After a brief silence, she and Adrian broke into laughter.

"I almost wish I had been early. Getting the exclusive chance to see Ms. Du Pre's placid demeanor fade away for a moment would almost be worth it." Adrian walked to a chair in front of Delores' desk and sat down. He took the pot of tea from Heather's hand and poured himself a cup. They stared at one another, both harsh and unwavering as if they waged a bloody war shooting looks instead of bullets.

"Trust me, darling, it's not a sight you want to see." Delores ushered Heather away with her hand, and the girl quickly dashed from the room. Adrian remained silent, staring at Delores. His cold exterior seemed to affect the room around him, almost like a chill moving down the walls. "So, twice in one day," she continued. "I must have done something right to warrant this much attention from you, Adrian. Tell me what this is about." Delores crossed her legs and leaned forward in her chair.

Adrian sipped his tea. "Can't two friends just enjoy each other's company for a short while?"

"They can, but we are not friends."

Adrian stood, walking to one of Delores' bookshelves and looks through its contents. He grabbed her own copy of '*My Death, Your Greatest Masterpiece*', then returned to the desk to sit once more. He thumbed through the book and sipped his tea again.

"Are you really going to talk to your guest like that?" he started. "After he decided to take some time out of his very busy schedule to—"

"I have been friends with your wife for years. And in that

time, you have shown yourself to be callous, calculating, and cruel. You may truly care for your wife, but she is the only thing you cherish in this life other than yourself. So don't you dare come into my office and try to play me with this 'enjoy each other's company' foolishness when I know damn well you came here with a purpose. So what is it?"

Adrian slammed the book shut and tossed it onto the desk. "Wow, Delores. I'm hurt. I thought after you'd talked me up at your event earlier, maybe you and I might have acted more than just civil with one another."

"Why are you here?"

Adrian fixed her with a level glare, the humor gone from his face. "The book. What do you know about the woman who really wrote it?" He sat toward the edge of his seat now.

"You were never into literature, Adrian. Why the sudden interest?"

"You know damn well why."

"The story about an eccentric recluse, Madame Lockheart? I don't see how that concerns you. You were never close to anyone like that." Delores pushed aside her tea and sat back in her chair.

Adrian stood to walk around the desk, sitting on its edge right in front of Delores. "Tell me what you know."

"Unfortunately for you, nothing. Some nobody typist came to me with a book. It was great, so I took it. Her name escapes me. I hope that's enough information for you."

Adrian slapped Delores across the face. "I'm going to give you one chance to say something, anything, useful to me. You won't like what happens if you refuse."

Delores fixed her hair and smoothed out her dress, realizing that Adrian must be more desperate than she'd thought. He thought hitting her would assert himself as the dominant force in this discussion, but really all it did for Dolores was tip his hand. "It must be hard to have kept that side of you hidden from your wife for so long."

"I'm serious, Delores."

"I don't know anything about her. And even if I did, what good would it do you? If we played bridge every Tuesday at the club, would that change your situation? The book is out, Adrian, and the names are fake. You have nothing to fear."

"As long as there are people who know the real names, I have something to fear. People who can speak those names. All it takes is a little coercion or money, depending on how generous the person is. You stole a tell-all book from an innocent girl just for some money. How much more money could you get from your tell-all?"

"If you walk out the door this instant, without any further incident, I can assure you no force in Heaven or on earth would make me tell anyone. But if you don't leave, I will share with anyone and everyone I can find every detail I know about you. I don't care if you ruin me by telling them what I've done. I will drag you down with me. Is that understood?

Adrian stands up and walks to the door. "Yes, it's quite a shame. I thought this would go better. You would tell me something of use so I can track down this writer and I would've gotten here before you had told anyone else about the true story behind your novel."

Adrian opened the door to find a puddle of blood pooling just on the other side.

Delores' defenses dropped immediately. She had enjoyed verbally sparring with Adrian, but she had no idea he feared the book so much that he would result to these kinds of actions. She couldn't help the sinking pit in her stomach. What did Adrian have in store for her? "Adrian!" she shouted, eyeing the carnage on the other side of her office door. "I knew you were sick, but this is too damn far. She didn't know anything, and even if she did—"

"She knew enough, even if she had no idea what to do with the information. I can't take that chance." Adrian stepped over the pool of blood so as to not any of it on his shiny shoes.

"And is that what you plan to do with me as well? Kill me so I don't tell everyone about you? I never had any intentions of doing that, Adrian. You should know that. I just wanted to sell a book."

"I know you did, but don't be silly, Dolores. I'm not going to kill you. I try not to get directly involved in these things. I prefer to let accidents happen as they will." Adrian left, his presence in the room soon replaced by a man in a long, black overcoat. He pulled a gun from his pocket and shot Delores Du Pre.

CHAPTER 30 – France, 1928

The morning started much better than the last, as Angelina awoke to the sounds of a gentle voice. "Oh, my precious. There, there."

It was her mother, Elizabeth, whispering in her ear as the new day's sun peeked with glory through the large windows in a rather large bedroom.

Angelina lifted her head from the pillow, still damp from her night full of tears. From that horrible moment on the train, Angelina had spent the entire evening without speaking a single word. Not one. The shock of the image of Rupert and his blood-soaked hair, his eyes penetrating, wide and frozen. And the sounds. The scuffle and the moaning, then there'd been a thud and yet another. But the worst, the absolute worst noise in that carriage, had been the sound of the trigger. Click, click. It resonated, burned in her brain for hours and hours. Click, click. Hours passed and still she heard nothing more. Click, click. It was almost daylight by the time she fell asleep, and for a few hours Angelina was free from the burden of remembering it all.

Elizabeth hugged her daughter and rocked her in her arms. "Breakfast is ready, my dear. Please come to eat?"

Angelina shook her head, walked to the windows, and glanced outside. Down in the street, a woman carried a baby with a pale blue cap and blush-filled cheeks. Angelina could hear him laughing, his little baby giggle traveling all the way up to her room. The windows were almost as tall as the entire length of the wall, bordered with a thick gold trim at the top, and they opened with a twist of a golden handle.

Angelina opened one and listened to the sounds of the baby and the cars moving by. For a moment she stood and watched, listening to a man whistle as he walked, in harmony with the hymn of the leaves and the breeze. Somewhere, something smelled so good it was euphoric. Across the street a couple walked hand in hand, stopping momentarily to kiss. Angelina concluded they appeared to be about the same age as Henry and herself. *Oh, my dear Henry. I miss him so much*, she thought as she watched them move along.

"Angelina, dear, won't you please come down to breakfast?" Angelina turned and followed her mother, who had been watching her from the doorway.

As they walked down the hall, it was as if Angelina saw the place for the very first time. There hung a beautiful carved mirror that was larger than life and trimmed with thick gold. *Surely I must have noticed it the night before*, she thought. And most of the walls were adorned with expensive-looking paintings of lush landscapes or rather serious-looking men. They reached the parlor, where more paintings resided, and heavy, plush furniture sat beneath a crystal chandelier. Angelina saw Kent, lying across an arched-back sofa, all ivory and clean.

"Good morning," he said in a drained voice. Angelina knelt by his side, eyes wide with concern. "It's all right, Angelina. I'm fine. You do remember the doctor who came last night, don't you?"

Then it all rushed back with unbearable force—the events, the horror, the permanence of it all. Angelina whispered,

"Yes, I...I remember now. I'm so glad you're here, Kent. And thank you. Thank you for saving my life, for saving *our* lives last night."

Kent had been a real savior, a true hero. The order of it all came calling, and Angelina remembered everything. She owed it all to Kent.

There, through the agony of his pain, with blood oozing from the knife wound in his left side, Kent had stumbled to his feet and pulled Angelina away from Rupert's dead body. Through the unknowing terror flashing in his eyes, Kent led them down the train corridor, and moments later they disembarked at the first stop. Kent quickly flagged a taxi and effortlessly relayed an address to the driver. As their car sped through the dark streets of Paris, past statues and stone-made stairs, café tables were filled with consumers and their consumption. Lovers tucked themselves away, filling alleyways with the lust of their embraces. They all went about their business, coexisting under the protective eye of the Tower. Angelina knew it was all there, right outside the taxi—the one and only gay Paree', but she didn't see a thing. She couldn't shake that image of Rupert, lifeless and ashen, his body still there yet the man forever gone.

Soon after, the taxi had pulled up to a building. It was tall and wide, its tan exterior full of curves and carved stone, dotted with a few black, wrought-iron balconies. Through the open archway was a courtyard with a small patch of daffodils atop manicured grass, directly in the building's center.

A few steps beyond the daffodils a small, round fountain kept perfect rhythm and did its duty, moving the water where it was meant to move, and then a door opened—a door that led them to Elizabeth.

Angelina had collapsed in her mother's arms, full of fear and despair while others attended to Kent. Elizabeth took her straight to a bedroom, and after a time rivaling eternity, she succumbed to an exhausted slumber. Too soon had she been awakened by the sunlight of a new morning.

But now it was a new day, and Kent smiled and pinched Angelina's cheek. A uniformed butler with white gloves delivered a silver cart full of warm croissants, fresh butter, blackberry and strawberry jam, and little oval-shaped donuts. The sugar-laced dough burst with still-warm jelly. There was hot coffee, tea, and fresh cream. Angelina didn't hesitate to indulge after such a long, tiring journey. The sweetness of the fresh orange juice combined with the rich pasty made her feel slightly queasy. She unashamedly sat right there on the floor to eat next to Kent before collapsing into an oversized chair. Her mind was full of questions for Elizabeth.

"Is this your apartment here in Paris?"

"No, Angelina, this our apartment. Me, you, Kent, and a friend of mine, too. We can all call this place home. And of course our beloved butler and his wife, who is the maid, and another dearest friend who—well, let's just say he's a protector. Your protector. A protector for us all, really. He's a true guardian. So you're quite safe here in Paris, Angelina. But whenever you go out, whether it's for a short walk or a visit to a cafe, he will be there close behind, ensuring your absolute safety."

Angelina wondered if the man on the train in the pinstriped suit was another guardian, as Rupert had said. She wondered where this man had gone, and why he had disappeared from the train. Kent nodded along to Elizabeth's warning, and she realized he'd already been made aware of the many secrets she was just now learning herself.

"I have another question," she said. "It's…well, I'm not sure how to say it."

Elizabeth moved to sit next to Angelina. She placed her

hand on top of her daughter's. "What is it, Angelina? You can tell me. It's all right."

Angelina looked down at her mother's hand, petite and smooth, and reveled in the comfort of her mother's touch. How she'd longed for this for so many years. "I was wondering... surely you must have seen many terrible things, so much violence, and well, um, probably much death. And I need to know how...how can you forget? Am I ever going to forget what happened on the train? Are those sights and sounds and that smell...that smell of death I've never known before... Will my mind ever be free of it?"

Elizabeth poured a fresh cup of peppermint tea from the pot's white porcelain spout and dropped three sugar cubes into Angelina's cup. Peppermint tea had been Angelina's favorite; whenever she'd had a temperature or a cough as a child, her mother had prepared plain toast and peppermint tea. It was one of Angelina's best memories of her childhood in Essex.

"Drink some tea." Elizabeth stood and paced back and forth, her head bent and hands clasped behind her back. "It will take a while, but you must help it go away. The only way to do that is to give it time. During that time, you must do all the things you love, all the things that bring you happiness. I know daffodils are your favorite. That's why I had them planted out there in the courtyard. So many days I've stared at them and thought of the time I'd be with you once again. Oh, and music. You must listen to the music that makes you feel as if you're floating. Then there's sherry. A glass of sherry always seems to help me a bit, now and then. And you must fall in love. Fall so deeply in love that you'll never remember anything else, nothing else but his smile, the way he holds you, the way he keeps you safe in his arms. Angelina, you must start today. Not tomorrow or the next day or the next. Today."

Angelina knew exactly what she wanted to do to fill her heart with happiness. For the rest of the day, whenever that death and destruction and despair burst through the sanctuary of a moment's peace of mind, she picked up her page and continued her letter to Henry until she was content it was ready to send.

Dear Henry,

It's been three days since we kissed under that willow tree, and I miss you with all my heart. I do miss you so. I long for the days when I'll hear your voice, when I'll finally hear you call my name once more. If only you could come to Paris. Then, together we could see the Mona Lisa, listen to the accordion players along the river, and skip stones along the way. We could watch the people looking up at the tower of Notre Dame as we talk about life and love and everything in between. I want to stand way up top, at the very tip of the Eiffel Tower, and there I'll soar far into the clouds, all white and full of fluff, as you kiss me and kiss me yet again. I often close my eyes and imagine it all so clearly. Even though you're far, far away, you're always with me. Tomorrow I'll send this letter to you, Henry, and I hope your heart will skip a beat when it reaches you. The last few days have been dreadful—the most dreadful days I've ever known. But I'll think of you, of your smile and your eyes, and I'll imagine I'm wrapped in your arms, free from the harm of the world. Finally, in your embrace, I'll be home. Once more I'll find myself exactly where I belong.

Until then, Your Ever-Loving

Angelina

She placed the letter in an envelope, walked to her bedroom, and hid it in the top drawer of the white dresser already full of soft nightgowns her mother had bought for her arrival.

The memories of the day before kept coming back, firing like clockwork with a duty as faithful as an army of royal palace guards. Angelina knew she had to keep doing all the things she loved to prevent herself from getting sucked into the darkness.

Soon dusk arrived, and with her mother's approval and the hidden, watchful eye of her guardian, Angelina went across the street to her very first Parisian cafe. She intended on writing and eating dinner alone. The excitement of it made her heart race. She wasn't sure what she would write, or how she would know what to order, but she went along, armed with her velvet-tipped pen and a book of fresh, empty pages.

She ordered a glass of champagne and opened to the first page. Out of nowhere the words came.

\J

Secrets will keep. A blue book with a hidden silver key and red string. An alias, Mrs. Pentworth. Mr. and Mrs. Cartwell enemies? What or who were they after? The pinstripe-suited man—was he an ally as Rupert said, or an enemy? Blood stain on his sleeve. The war was over, so why was Elizabeth still in danger?

Angelina wrote in bullet points, surprised by the ease with which her concerns flowed onto the page. Her meal arrived, and while she ate and sipped the delicate drink, she made more notes.

Does Henry miss me as much as I miss him? Will he write back right away? What if he doesn't write back?

She realized her notes had transformed from inquisitive to frantic. First, she scribbled *Henry*, then *Mrs. Henry Parker*, then *Mr. and Mrs. Henry Parker*, then *Mrs. Angelina Parker*, then *Angelina Parker*. She eventually shut the notebook in frustration.

She decided to indulge in a selection of desserts. Cream puffs, tarts, and little meringue pies were delivered to the table, and she ate each one slowly and with care, taking in every smell and flavor, analyzing each bite the way any good writer would. She ate and then she wrote a beautiful poem about her first impressions of Paris. Once she finished, she smiled. She knew she loved Henry, but writing was always such a wonderful outlet.

Angelina toyed with her empty glass, wondering whether another would be too much. The decision was made for her when the waiter delivered an entire bottle nestled in its very own ice-filled bucket.

He leaned over and said, "Mademoiselle, compliments of the gentleman," in his thick French accent. Angelina turned to find a man bowing his head, wearing a mustache and a big smile.

He called out, "I see you've been writing. And I heard you say thank you. British. Well, you haven't stopped with that pen and paper. I'm also a writer. And that intent you possess did catch my attention. Would you care to join me? My friends will be here soon. Some fellow writers and artists. Oh, and one composer. He's quite possessed, too. All of us, possessed by the art we do breathe."

Angelina thought, *Who is this stranger? Is it safe to sit with him?*

Aware of her hesitation, the man added, "Don't worry. I don't bite, and neither do the rest yet to arrive. We smoke, we drink, we talk about love and war and the meaning of things. We drink some more and dance while our composer friend bangs out his madness on that piano over there in the corner."

Angelina rose and moved to the stranger's table, the waiter promptly appearing to move the champagne bucket to join them. They talked about great literature, writing, and D H Lawrence's new book *Women In Love*. He asked Angelina what had been the most recent, most exciting book she had read.

Angelina sighed, wishing she could talk about her own book, fast becoming a very popular read. But knowing how Elizabeth disapproved of her involvement, she thought better of it.

She enjoyed the freedom she felt with her new, eccentric friends, and could see why Elizabeth had chosen Paris as her home. It certainly held a charm Angelina had never experienced before.

CHAPTER 31

Henry's mind raced. He now knew Angelina's claims about the book were real. Adrian Spratchet was Madam's son, and had explicitly told Henry the book was based on her life and contained information that could damage Spratchet and his wife. Further, Spratchet made it clear he would do whatever he needed to protect his wife and his reputation. The first thing Henry knew he had to do was to find Angelina and warn her about Adrian. He realized he was in love with her and, just as Adrian would do whatever necessary to protect his wife, Henry would do the same to protect Angelina.

He thought about the last time he'd seen her and realized it was the morning after the Grants' housewarming party. Angelina had rushed off like a madwoman after she had realized it was seven in the morning. All he knew was that she had private family matters to attend to and would write to him soon. That was over a week ago, but just waiting to hear from her was no longer an option. In visible pain after Spratchet's beating, Henry pulled himself together and headed towards the office building where he and Angelina both worked.

Finding Beth, he asked her for a quiet word up in his office. "Beth, there's something I need to tell you, but you must promise to keep it to yourself." When she nodded, he continued in a serious tone. "My telling you this information could put your life at risk, as well as the lives of others should you repeat the tale. Do you understand the seriousness of what I'm saying? If you would rather I not tell you, that's fine, but I must ask you to tell me anything that might help me find Angelina."

Beth took a moment, then looked Henry straight in the eyes and replied in a strong, calm voice, "Henry, tell me everything that's happened. If Angelina needs my help, you must tell me the full story. As for the information and the risk it carries, I certainly will not repeat it, and I'm willing to take the risk of knowing what it is you have to tell me."

Henry was glad Beth wanted to share his knowledge and help him find Angelina. Although he was taken aback by her sudden directness, he secretly brimmed with pride. Beth certainly could get down to business when the circumstances called for it. He was confident he was doing the right thing in telling her about Adrian.

Henry began by telling Beth about his meeting with Adrian to sign the papers for his mother's estate. "I must admit, the man made me uneasy at the onset. I realize he's one of the top defenders and was just selected for the General Council of the Bar, but he has quite a sinister way about him. After Spratchet signed all the requisite papers, I excused myself to go to the men's room. I must have been in a rush to get through the meeting because I left all my paperwork on the table, including Angelina's case file and her claim that Dolores Du Pre stole her manuscript."

Henry knew Angelina had confided in Beth that Delores Du Pre's new book, *'My Death, Your Greatest Masterpiece'*, had been stolen from Angelina when she'd left it at the publisher's office. Beth listened intently when he continued. "When I returned to the table, Adrian was gone and it appeared all my papers had been moved about. It was then I noticed Angelina's file had disappeared."

It didn't take long for Beth to absorb the implications of this revelation. "Oh, Henry, what did you do? Don't tell me you chased after him."

Henry couldn't help the pride in his courage as he explained chasing Spratchet in the alley outside the café, demanding to have his file returned. He also described, with more than a hint of embarrassment, Spratchet punching him and pinning him against the wall of the alley.

Beth turned a stern gaze to the bruise on his left cheek. "Were you badly hurt?" she asked.

"I was more shocked than hurt. The man took me completely by surprise. He's certainly very cunning. I can imagine why he's such a good defender." Henry then looked Beth in the eyes and said, "This is why I believe Angelina's in danger." He leaned forward across his desk, speaking in a quieter tone, genuine concern spread across his face. "As he had me pinned against the wall, Spratchet explained that *'My Death, Your Greatest Masterpiece'* is actually the story of his mother's life. His mother is Madam Lockridge, otherwise known as Madam Lockheart in the book."

Beth seemed suddenly shaken. Henry could see she struggled to digest what he'd said, opting to avoid eye contact as she looked down at her shoes and gently toyed with her left earlobe.

"Beth, are you all right? Is this too much to take in?"

"I have been so stupid," she said with wide eyes. "I didn't even realize the magnitude of all this. I thought Angelina and I were best friends, but what kind of friend fails to ask the right questions?"

Henry was now lost, frustrated by Beth's apparent tangent about her own relationship with Angelina. "What does that matter? You're here now, aren't you? We can get her help."

"Henry, I knew about some book Angelina had written, but I didn't know it was that book. She never told me, and I didn't ask. My husband Eugene is Madame's nephew, and Adrian's cousin. If what you're saying is true, you're telling me members of my own family mean Angelina harm."

Henry sat back in his chair with the weight of her words thundering down on him. He rubbed his chin, realizing the mistake he may have made by telling Beth what he knew. "Does Eugene know about all this? Is he close to Adrian?"

"No, he's not. They don't get on at all. He's more like a distant acquaintance than a cousin. Eugene has never mentioned the book to me, and I have no idea if he knows about it. Perhaps I should contact him. Maybe he can help Angelina, too."

"No, don't do that. I haven't read the book, and neither have you. We don't even know what we're dealing with right now. Promise me, Beth. Promise me you'll keep this to yourself."

"Are you asking me not to confide in my husband?"

"I'm sorry, Beth. I really am, but just for now, yes. Let me do some digging, and maybe I can find out more about this situation. I'm sorry to involve you like this. I can see you care for Angelina, and had no idea I was putting you in a difficult situation."

"Do you really think Angelina is in danger?"

"As of now, Adrian doesn't know who Angelina is. It won't take him long to find out, but the less people involved, the better."

"Henry, there's one more thing I think you should know." Beth looked uncomfortable. "Angelina told me her book was a memoir but that she had to make up the ending herself, and it was very hard work. She said there was a big secret was never revealed to her, so she had to create a plausible ending. She felt like Ms. Du Pre had taken advantage of her creativity, and I got the impression Angelina was very proud of that book. Knowing what I do now, Angelina must have written the end of the book after Madame Lockridge died so suddenly. Eugene didn't care to go to the funeral in case Adrian would be there. It didn't really make any sense to me. I told him we should go, but he was adamant. Why didn't I see all this before? How could I have been so naive?"

Henry stood up swiftly and he searched around his desk, disorganizing what was a very organized workspace. He found a piece of paper with a phone number scribbled on it and held it up while, flicking the paper's edge in excitement.

"What's that?" Beth asked.

"When Norman gave me the task of dealing with Adrian, he gave me some contact details I didn't think I would need. Just basic case details, but I have an idea. It's early in the day. Let's go up to the Lockridge estate and do some snooping around. Presumably the staff there know you. You can help me do some digging. What do you say?"

Beth paced around the room. She had already been away from her own work for half an hour, and Henry watched the multiple expressions flittering across her face as she pondered his proposal. Finally, she looked up at him and nodded.

"I want to help you. Let's go."

***

When they arrived at the Lockridge estate, they were met at the door by Ruth, who looked visibly shaken. Beth had met her a few times before, and thankfully still recognized her. "Ruth, what on earth is wrong?" she asked.

The woman looked as if she'd seen a ghost, or worse. Ruth glanced at Beth and exclaimed, "Oh, Miss, it was awful. Mr. Spratchet was just here with his hoodlum friend, James. He said he was looking for something he needed. The two headed up to Madame's room, and I kindly asked them not to disturb Madame's things. That was when he turned on me and told me in a most awful tone that everything in this house was now his, and that he had every right to disturb what he wanted. He said if I knew what was good for me, I'd stay out of the way. They finally left, and I was on my way up to Madame's room to see what damage they caused when you both arrived. I'm sure they made a mess of everything." Ruth started crying, then looked at Henry and asked, "Is it true, sir? Is Mr. Spratchet the owner of Madam's estate? It's been seven months since Madame passed. Surely matters will be resolved soon?"

Henry gently replied, "Not yet, Ruth. At least, not until I file the papers."

They followed Ruth upstairs to Madame's bedroom. Upon seeing the condition of the room, Ruth cried out, "They've destroyed all her precious things." Beth looked on in disgust, wondering how a son could have such disregard for his mother's memory.

Henry walked around the room, then abruptly turned to Ruth and asked, "Ruth, where did Madame and Angelina sit to write her memoirs?"

Ruth was visibly taken aback by the question. "Well, everywhere, sir. They would write here, in the living room, in the conservatory."

"Thanks you." Henry placed a gentle hand on Ruth's arm, giving her a bit of much-needed compassion. "Why don't you go downstairs and make yourself a cup of tea? You've had quite a frightful day and could use a rest. Beth and I will clean up the broken glass, and then we can all try to figure out whatever it is Spratchet's taken." Ruth looked at Henry gratefully and quickly left the room.

After quickly cleaning up as best they could, they took a tour around the rooms Ruth had mentioned. Adrian had been looking for something and he may have found it, but Henry had a feeling there was something else waiting for him in the house.

"This room is...odd," Beth observed as they entered the living room where Madame had died. "Did you hear about Jonathan, Madame's husband? He died right here on the rug. I believe that's where Madame passed as well."

"Is that so?" said Henry, frustrated that he hadn't yet read the tell-all book of Madame's life. Scanning the room, he felt a chill go through him. He had to agree with Beth; beyond the room's macabre history, it definitely felt odd. As he stepped towards the rug, he tripped on the edge of it, which sent him propelling forward into the mantelpiece and knocking an ornamental bust with one hand. The weight of the bust prevented it from falling, but the slight wobble caught his attention from the floor. Crawling to his knees, he looked closer, then nudged the bust aside to reveal three well-concealed, hand-written letters.

CHAPTER 32

Angelina listened to the conversations bandying about her in the café. It was all so sophisticated and artsy. She felt naive and young in their presence, yet none of them treated her that way. They included her in their comments and questions. After her second glass of champagne, she felt a little lightheaded and decided to stop drinking. How embarrassed her mother would be if she had to be escorted home by her new friends in a drunken stupor! She smiled a little at the thought of the shock on Elizabeth's face. André, the stranger who had asked her to join them, noticed it.

"Such a roguish smile, ma petite. What are you thinking?"

"Oh, nothing really. Just a story I'm writing," she lied as she tapped the little notebook in which she'd been jotting down notes.

She didn't want to talk about her mother's probable reaction. She didn't want them to think of her as a little girl with an over protective mama. She had been through a great deal since Madame's death, but the experience didn't show outwardly. For all intents and purposes, she supposed she still appeared to outsiders as an unsophisticated innocent—which in fact she was, in spite of it all.

"Oh? What is it about?" André asked.

She made a noncommittal noise, realizing she had to think fast. She certainly couldn't tell anyone what she was really writing in her notebook. "It's a mystery…on a train."

"A murder mystery?"

"No. Well, not so far, anyway. It's a mystery about valuable jewelry…and silver that was stolen during the war and taken to Germany on the train. Now, my brave heroine must find the thief and make him return her family's heirlooms."

She could feel the flush on her face, appalled by how quickly and conveniently she managed to lie. Perhaps she'd inherited that trait from her mother, the international spy. She looked around her to see what her new friends thought of her false storyline. She was flattered to see they all nodded and smiled in encouragement. Perhaps she would write a real book of her own someday. She couldn't wait to tell Henry about it, thinking about the letter hidden in a drawer in her bedroom. If she left now, she could add to it and post it first thing in the morning.

Angelina stood from the table. "Thank you so much for your wonderful companionship, everyone. It's quite late, and I have had a very long day, so I must bid you all bonne nuit. Perhaps I'll see you again tomorrow," she said as she picked up her notebook and prepared to leave.

A wave of farewells and good wishes accompanied her to the door. She quickened her step across the street, eager to finish her letter to Henry.

When she walked through the door, Elizabeth greeted her with a smile. "You look much happier than when you left. Did you have a pleasant evening?"

"It was lovely, yes, and I met some new friends. I'll tell you all about it tomorrow. Goodnight, mother."

"Goodnight, dear." Elizabeth sighed with pleasure. It was the first time Angelina had called her 'Mother' since their reunion.

Angelina went straight to her dresser when she entered her room and took out the letter she'd started earlier. She sat at the little writing desk by the window and dipped her pen in the ink well.

"I have had the most wonderful evening. I just had to tell you about it before closing this letter. I wish you had been here to experience it with me."

She went on to tell Henry in the minutest detail about the café, her new friends, and the stimulating and interesting conversation. When she was finally finished, she signed her name again with a flourish. As she put it back in the envelope, she realized that her mother had been right—doing something she enjoyed had made her forget the horror of the last few days, if only temporarily.

Desperate to send the letter, Angelina checked the time. It had only been half an hour since she'd left the cafe. Knowing Elizabeth's guardian would be watching her, she formulated her own plan. She rushed out the door, catching Elizabeth by surprise, and darted across the street. Everyone was still there in the cafe. *Perfect,* she thought. Laughter erupted from the table, and André barely noticed when Angelina crept up behind him.

"My dear friend, I have a favor to ask," she whispered in his ear.

"Angelina, back so soon?"

She slipped the letter inside his jacket and sat down in the chair next to him. "Can I ask just one small favor, from one new friend to another?"

"Of course."

"Will you see to it that the letter I just slipped inside your jacket gets posted? It's somewhat private and, well, let's just say my family may not approve of me sending it."

"Oh, I see. It's a love letter. Well, young Angelina, you already know I am a sucker for a great romance. I will post it first thing."

Angelina left once again with a satisfied smile on her face. She returned to a flustered-looking Elizabeth. She pulled out the delicate scarf she had concealed as she'd left her room and claimed to have retrieved it from the cafe. With a little spring in her step and a grin of misinterpreted satisfaction, Angelina's mission was complete.

She grabbed her notebook from the dresser and brought it to the writing table to ponder the unsolved mysteries she'd noted earlier. Angelina absently underlined the words *'A hidden silver key'*. When the ink blotted on the page, she stared at what she had done. *A hidden silver key?* What was her subconscious trying to tell her?

A memory involving rain, a lake, and something shiny buried in the soil flashed across her mind in vivid color. Then she remembered the day Rupert had met her under the big tree by the lake. While there, he told her he had been a child assassin. It had rained hard that day, and the soil was soft. While she listened to Rupert's confession, her hands dug nervously in the soil. They had unearthed something shiny—a tin, perhaps. She closed her eyes and took a few deep breaths, trying to relax. Nothing. She couldn't coax the memory to return. It could have been a scrap of metal, she supposed, but if it was a container, could it hold an item such as the key that had been sent to Elizabeth inside a blue book? If it was, how did it get from there to here, now in

Elizabeth's possession?

She shook her head; she was getting nowhere, and her imagination was heightened after such a creative evening. She could go downstairs and ask her mother, but she knew she wouldn't get any answers from that source. Elizabeth had been incredibly secretive since she'd received that package at Kent's townhouse in London. Perhaps Elizabeth was still a spy, in which case she couldn't tell Angelina what was going on without putting her daughter in further danger.

Elizabeth knew Angelina had written the life's story of Madame Lockridge as a manuscript, but she didn't know Madame had given Angelina Elizabeth's correspondence. She hadn't mentioned those, in case her mother wanted them back, which was Elizabeth's right to ownership.

Angelina jumped to her feet. The letters! She ran to the two suitcases sitting by the door. Elizabeth had sent a telegram asking Eugene to prepare Angelina's things to be sent to a porter at the station. The two suitcases had already been in her room when Angelina arrived. She had no idea how her mother knew she had boarded the train in London without her luggage, but supposed Elizabeth still had a vast intelligence network to use when needed.

She opened the smaller suitcase and pulled out lingerie and personal toiletries. She took the letter opener from the desk and ripped open several delicate stitches in the heavy linen lining. The letters were still there. She heaved a sigh of relief, then dug a little deeper and pulled out Elizabeth's diamond and emerald ring she had taken from Madame Lockridge's jewelry box.

When she moved from the Lockridge estate to Eugene's house, she had sewn the stolen ring and the letters Madame had given her into the lining of her suitcase. They contained information that proved the story published by Madame Du Pre was actually written by Angelina. Madame had taught her the code the letters were written in, but she hadn't been able to decode them all before Madame died. She hoped she would be able to find some reference to Lord Pentworth, the blue book, or the silver key when she decoded the rest of them. That was going to take some time, though, and right now she was exhausted.

She put the letters aside for the time being and picked up the ring. Her mother had only worn it occasionally before she'd left Angelina for good, and Angelina hadn't had a chance to really look at it since then. It held a beautiful oval emerald surrounded by small, yellow teardrop diamonds. She remembered her mother telling her once that she kept it because it reminded her of happier times. This had confused Angelina then, because she thought their lives were already happy, and they didn't need to be reminded. Of course that was years before Elizabeth had thrown the ring on the floor during a temper tantrum just weeks before she left.

Angelina held the ring up to the lamp light and watched it sparkle. Elizabeth must have sent it to Madame, but why? Was it something complicated, like an identifier between spies, or was it just as simple as a thank you gift to Madame for everything she'd done for Elizabeth? She wondered if Madame had discovered it missing before she died. She shook her head with fatigue. There were far too many questions and hardly any answers. She decided to go to bed, and would delve into the mysteries of the letters and the ring in the morning. She put the lingerie and toiletries in a dresser drawer and decided to tackle the other suitcase in the morning.

Dragging the chair from her writing desk to the closet, she climbed onto it to retrieve a large hat box from the top shelf. She removed the old-fashioned millinery concoction of peacock feathers, satin, and lace, and hid the letters and ring beneath it among the hat's protective tissue paper. She returned the box to the top shelf, burying it under several spare blankets in the closet. She returned the chair to the desk and prepared for bed, worried that the confusing thoughts chasing their tails inside her head might keep her awake. Angelina feel asleep as soon as her head hit the pillow.

***

"Oh, dear God in heaven!" he gasped.

Alarmed by Henry's outburst, Beth joined him and quietly took the page he had pulled from one of the envelopes. Her face went pale, and her hand shook as she read it.

"This is Madame's handwriting, and it's dated the same day she died. It looks like it's some kind of an amendment to a previous Will. Rupert the chauffeur is named—I think. The writing is difficult to read near the bottom. Why on earth would she leave anything to Rupert? She signed it…but the sentence above was never finished. This must be the very last thing she wrote. She must have hid the letters just before she…"

Both Beth and Henry looked to the floor, shuddering at the memories of death in the very room in which they stood.

"We have to keep this from Adrian. It strongly suggests he was dropped out of the Will in Rupert's favor. Do you know if Eugene was expecting anything from his aunt?"

"He didn't say. He's been very quiet of late, and I thought he's been grieving. I wouldn't think inheritance matters to him, though. We're getting by just fine, all things considered." Beth seemed slightly embarrassed that she didn't have a better handle on her husband. *Could Eugene be expecting inheritance?* she pondered as Henry paced the room, waving the letters is silence.

He stopped, then paced again. One by one, he read the letters, each seeming to affect him for profoundly than the last.

"We have to get back to London and present this to Norman. We can ensure it's accepted as evidence. Meanwhile, we have to keep these letters safe."

Beth opened a compartment inside her large handbag, took the letters from Henry, and tucked them safely inside her now-closed purse. "They'll be safe in here for the time being. No one has any idea that I know anything. You might be searched by Adrian, and maybe even Eugene, but I won't."

"Excellent idea, Beth. I think these may be among the items Adrian ransacked the house to find. I wonder if he knows Rupert is his brother and listed as the sole benefactor."

"From what you've described, even if he does, he's unlikely to cooperate with us. Especially now."

"Yes, I suspect you're right."

***

On the way drive back to London, Henry brooded about Adrian's discovery of the manuscript and the fact that Angelina had written it for the man's mother. That alone put her in terrible danger, and she probably didn't know it, wherever she was. The things both he and Beth had read stunned them. When they asked Ruth to confirm the truth, she had burst into tears, perhaps after finally letting out a well-guarded secret or from possible guilt over thinking she had somehow betrayed Madame. Either way, she'd done the right thing, and Henry reassured her he would honor Madame's final wishes.

"Did Angelina give you any hint where she might be going when she returned to your house the morning after Grants' party?" Henry casually asked.

"No. I didn't even see her. I expected her to be at breakfast when I came downstairs at about eight, but she wasn't there. I asked Alice, our maid, about her absence. She told me my husband had received a telegram earlier saying Angelina had been called away to her father's sickbed. It asked that he have Angelina's belongings sent to the train station. Alice told me she'd packed the two suitcases lying open on Angelina's bed herself, then handed them to Eugene just as he headed off to work. I presume he did as the telegram asked, but I hadn't spoken to Eugene since the night before driving home from Eleanor's party. His workday often starts much earlier than mine. I've been hoping to get a letter from her."

Henry nodded but didn't say anything. Reassured that Beth, and therefore Eugene and potentially Adrian, couldn't possibly know Angelina's whereabouts, he doubted that Angelina had gone to her father's sick bed. He'd look into that immediately once returning to London.

Back at the office, he suggested Beth finish the late shift while he spoke with Norman. As normal, the man wasn't there, but Henry did notice a new bulk of mail on his desk and searched through it frantically. One letter stood out immediately.

It instantly felt familiar in his hands despite the address being typed with no visible return address. The post mark was a little town just outside Paris. Obviously, someone was trying to keep their identity secret from any casual observers, and he knew it was from Angelina; he could feel it. She had promised to write to him.

He ripped it open, rushing through her sweet words and unmasked feelings. He felt his heart race faster and faster, just imagining her and knowing she missed him. He sat back with a childish grin. The letter didn't help him find her, and he couldn't even reply, but he smiled.

He jumped up suddenly. "The letters," he shouted. Without a second thought, he ran out of Norman's office and down the stairs to the typists' room. Beth had left already, along with the four letters so discreetly hidden in her bag.

Henry slipped out a curse, annoyed by his own carelessness.

CHAPTER 33

Angelina scowled as light pierced the veil of her violet satin curtains and groaned softly. She stopped for a moment to listen and take stock of the morning, and she found that she could hear nothing. Angelina threw off her covers and slipped on a simple dress that had been folded neatly on her dresser, then ambled downstairs.

The clock read nine, almost on the dot. She noticed a note on the table next to a plate of eggs, bacon, and toast that read, '*Enjoy! We will be back from errands before lunch. – Elizabeth*'

Angelina frowned, finding it odd, given the circumstances, that they hadn't informed her beforehand of their foray into town. She couldn't help but wonder if they were actually running errands. She recognized her mother's handwriting, which allayed her unease somewhat.

Well, at least the food is still slightly warm, Angelina thought. *This is a perfect opportunity to finally finish translating those letters.*

She took her breakfast upstairs with her, her thoughts racing as she speculated about what she would find in the encoded letters. Angelina opened the curtains to let in the light

268

and left the door open so she would clearly hear the return of her mother and brother. Finally, she retrieved the letters from their box, along with the ring, and sat down with her notebook to begin translating.

Angelina had become adept over the past few months at interpreting the code, but it still took her a pause to get into the right mode of thinking. The rhythm of it up after a few sentences, and she scribbled down her mother's words to Madame. It began with a brief description of then-recent events, but these letters wasted few words, favoring brevity over loquacity. Her eyes widened as she recognized code for *'Lord Pentworth,'* then narrowed as she slowed to read carefully. To her surprise, another familiar name appeared as well: *'Lord Pentworth ordered the purge of Chasiton; Gerard had no hand in it.'*

Angelina's head spun as she kept reading.

Last week, I was on my way home late at night when I felt I was being followed. There was a man behind me, about fifty yards' distance. I ran, but the man's intent was clear as he matched my speed. I tired and he gained on me. I ducked into a narrow alley in hopes that my smaller stature would be an advantage, but realized too late that my pursuer had no difficulty fitting between these buildings. I turned to see him enter the alley and glimpsed another figure appear behind him with a flash of steel. It was Gerard, who covered my assailant's mouth with his hand, and a blade tip protruded from the stranger's chest. Gerard then removed his weapon and supported his victim gently to the ground. Then he looked at me, touched the brim of his hat, and was gone. I quickly searched the corpse afterwards, and in the inner jacket pocket I found a small, nondescript envelope. The note inside read, 'Finish cleaning house. – L.P' Damn that man. He may yet be our deaths.

***

Angelina still ate her food when she heard a key turn in the front door.

"We're home!" Elizabeth called out from the lower level.

Angelina came down to greet them. Kent made his way into the living room after removing his shoes, while Elizabeth removed hers. "Mother, may we speak after lunch?"

Elizabeth smiled again at hearing herself called mother. "Of course, Angelina. What would you like to talk about?"

"House cleaning." At that, Elizabeth straightened abruptly and affixed Angelina with a steady gaze. "Given the current situation," Angelina continued, "I deserve to know. Kent deserves to know, if he doesn't already."

Elizabeth could only exhale and nod. "Of course."

The meal itself was rather uneventful when the family reconvened at one o'clock for a late lunch, but also rather tense on Elizabeth's and Angelina's parts. Elizabeth suggested they all get settled in the living room. "Angelina, would you let Kent know why we are here?"

The words tumbled out of Angelina's mouth as quickly as she could form them. "We have been threatened and assaulted by people we don't even know, so we deserve to know these things. Who is Lord Pentworth to MI6, and why did he want to clean house? Why did Gerard help you? And—"

"One at a time, dear," Elizabeth interjected calmly. "One at a time. Lord Pentworth, as you might have guessed, is a codename for the man who was at the time head of our department. I was Lady Pentworth, because I worked so closely with him on our operations and became his deputy. I suspected, after Gerard proved an ally, that someone in the department must have known something about Lord Pentworth he didn't want known. Couldn't want known. I have been unable to learn just what that 'something' was, or is."

"And what of Gerard?"

"He was genuinely distressed when he demanded the contact list that night all those years ago. He didn't trust me then, but he didn't hurt me, either. He must have decided to trust me when he discovered I had lied to MI6. He probably did for all those operatives on that list what he's been doing for us. Come to think of it, I always felt there was more to him than met the eye..." Elizabeth trailed off in thought, staring out the window. She snapped back to the present when Angelina asked,

"How can we make contact with Gerard? He may know Lord Pentworth's secrets."

"We can leave Gerard a message, but whether or not he responds is out of our hands. He seems to know our every move, although we know nothing of his aims and methods. He was always the best spy of us all."

At this point, Kent spoke up after a long period of silence and deep thought. "You must have chosen this location for a reason, mother, and not for isolation alone."

"You're perceptive. Here, we sit near the heartbeat of a network, and we can read its pulse. Knowledge is power. Lost in a sea of people, we can catch our breath and possibly grasp the information we need to regain the initiative against Lord Pentworth."

"We can't have much time left," Kent mused, "after that incident on the train."

"I'm sorry, dears." Elizabeth sighed. "I had no idea they were so close."

Angeline's eyes brightened as she spoke with soft determination. "That's fine, mother. We can only look forward, now."

Elizabeth smiled. "You're quite right. There's no use in

271

dwelling on the past."

"Our first order of business is to attempt to contact Gerard," Kent thought aloud, "because he isn't trying to kill us and he's obviously nearby."

"Angelina and I will draft the message, then," Elizabeth replied. "We'll find drop locations tomorrow in the city proper."

***

They spent most of their time watching and waiting. The message they'd put out was meant for not only Gerard, but also any other of Elizabeth's old contacts. Picking up messages would be risky, as it was unknown who else would be watching. Their only shield was Gerard, who was also their best hope.

The three decided to take turns in making thirty-minute patrols of that day's selected park to check on drop locations there, while the other two sat at a roadside café, discreetly watching people while pretending to dine and lounge. If the one didn't come back within forty-five minutes, the other two would go look for him or her together. Every change of patrol, they chose a new rendezvous point, usually another restaurant.

Their first two days had produced no results. Elizabeth would go first today, and they had decided on the Parc Monceau. Angelina and Kent sat at a nearby bistro to enjoy the scenery. No sooner had they selected their seats than a voice called out from the next table over.

"No need to get comfortable, now. Come with me."

They looked over to see their guardian angel, with bowler hat and sunglasses, bring his right foot down from where it rested on his knee. Then the man stood. "Let's go fetch your mother."

Angelina could scarcely believe their luck, and Kent seemed similarly taken aback. She opened her mouth to speak,

272

but was promptly shushed.

"All will be explained in due course," Gerard said. "Follow me. If we hurry, we can catch her as she nears the Pyramid." His gait was characterized by economy of motion, his stride sure and swift. Kent kept up with no trouble, but Angelina found her heart rate rising as she had to move her limbs at a much quicker pace than her compatriots.

As they traversed the paved paths of the park, Angelina found herself wondering how much more she would have admired these gardens under less stressful circumstances. There were surprisingly few people within the garden's gates, and with gentle sunlight and a light breeze, only their presence disturbed the serenity.

Eventually, they spotted Elizabeth in the distance, about two hundred yards away, standing before the Pyramid. She seemed lost in thought, as if wondering why the curiosity was there. The group slowed as they drew closer.

Gerard cleared his throat. "Lady Pentworth." Elizabeth turned, startled. "That always was one of your weaknesses, Elizabeth—lack of complete focus."

Elizabeth smiled. "So it would seem. Where are we headed?"

"You'll see."

***

Gerard took them on twists and turns, through alleys and even buildings to ensure they weren't followed. Angelina had long since lost all sense of where they were in the city, and by the looks of it, so had her mother, despite having lived here. Finally, he led them to a nondescript door in a shaded alleyway. Gerard pulled out a key ring and carefully inserted each in particular order. The door unlocked, and he ushered them all inside.

"Make yourselves comfortable. I suspect we will be here a while."

The room was small, but cozy; sofas lined the walls, so the family took their seats as Gerard hung his hat and his jacket. When he finished, he turned and raised his arms. "Welcome to my safe house. This is not all I am, of course," he said simply, and bowed. "Gerard Fitzhugh, former Counterintelligence, at your service."

Neither Elizabeth nor her children knew what to say, so Gerard continued. "I would have never made contact with you unless things were serious, and I'm not talking about your safety, not primarily. Don't get me wrong, I care for you all, but my foremost concern remains my investigation of Pentworth. Late in the war, when the Russians fell out of it, things got pretty desperate for us until the Americans came. After it was clear we were going to win, we realized we needed to know what was happening on the ground in Russia. Efforts after the war to set up and maintain a network there failed, and conflicting information returned all the time about the Revolution and the struggle between the Reds and the Whites. You were there, Elizabeth."

Gerard then pulled out a bottle of brandy, along with a few glasses.

"That was after Chasiton?" she asked.

"Yes. Well, because of Chasiton, really. Before I came to this department, my previous department head had approached me, saying C wanted your unit investigated because of the poor recommendations produced there." Gerard swirled his glass thoughtfully and took a sip. "They suspected a mole and sent me to find it. There isn't a single report from field agents in Russia during that time that I haven't seen myself, and their information was consistent. Of course, it was too late by then to keep Russia out of Lenin's hands. My judgment of the operatives who reported to the unit and came through Chasiton was that they were all motivated, smart, and loyal, so it had to be one or both of you Pentworths. Unfortunately, I didn't know I'd aroused enough suspicion to initiate housecleaning."

Gerard took a gulp this time. "When Chasiton happened, I barely got out by jumping off the second story balcony into the bushes. Loyal, all of them. And all murdered because of it. I'd been watching when you arrived at the manor, then left again. I followed you, because I knew at least that you had a contact list. When I confronted you that night and you gave me the contact list, I realized you had no idea what was going on. That left that bastard Pentworth himself. The only problem was that I got framed for Chasiton. I warned the other operatives on the list that we'd all been burned, and we all went to ground." Gerard drained the rest of his glass.

"I don't mind the besmirching of my name, you know. But the names and faces of the men and women at Chasiton and abroad…they're still burned into my mind." Gerard shouted now through gritted teeth with his index finger pressed to his temple. It seemed he and Elizabeth both were on the verge of weeping.

"They did their part for king and country," he whispered. "I do my part for them. God, those beautiful spies."

Angelina and Kent could do no more than sit dumbly.

CHAPTER 34

Elizabeth and Gerard talked late into the night, a luxury Angelina had never associated with espionage. While initially intrigued, it hadn't taken long for her to fall behind in the conversation. She wished to know everything she could, not only about her mother's life, but also about their current predicament. However, she simply wasn't accustomed to the unique language her mother and Gerard used, full of meaningful nods, half-sentences, and knowing looks. The language of spies, she assumed. She turned towards Kent, who, like her, had been doing his best to process the information traded between the two veteran agents. She watched as he stifled a yawn, immediately feeling one of her own attempting to overtake her.

"Please, don't feel as if you have to follow along," Elizabeth suddenly announced, turning towards her children. They stiffened.

"If I'm already involved, I would at least like to know as much as I can about what it is I'm actually involved in," Angelina said, somewhat more harshly than she intended. Gerard raised a questioning eyebrow, but other than that showed no acknowledgement of her outburst. "I'm sorry," she added sheepishly.

"Don't be," her mother said easily. "You have every right to be frustrated. Unlike us," she added, motioning to herself and Gerard, "you never signed up for this life, and I'm sorry to have pulled you into it. Both of you."

Angelina and Kent traded awkward glances. She hadn't expected such an understanding response, but even though she heard the sincerity in her mother's voice, she couldn't help but feel a sliver of anger welling up inside her. Whether it was towards her spy mother, Madame, or even herself, she wasn't quite sure. All she knew right then was that her entire life seemed to be a product of other people's decisions. From her mother's work with MI6 and Madame having her write and publish her memoirs, to a half-brother she never knew she had, Angelina's life began to feel like a story written entirely by strangers.

"You can get some sleep, if you like," Gerard interrupted her thoughts. "Pentworth may be a tenacious bastard, but you don't have to worry so long as you're here. Though I wouldn't suggest staying anywhere for too long," he added to Elizabeth in a lower voice.

Angelina curled up near the end of the couch. It wasn't as if she could follow their conversation anyways. Instead, she turned her mind to happier thoughts—of Henry and what lay ahead in her future. Thoughts of a life writing her own stories, away from the listening walls and prying eyes of her mother's not-so-former life. Although, at the back of her mind—not that she would admit it—despite the terror and danger, a part of her found this life exciting. She could see why her mother had done the work she did. Angelina felt her eyes growing heavy as she drifted to sleep with dreams of dark-eyed men and foreign lands.

If a peaceful night's sleep even existed in the world, it was somewhere far from Angelina. Raised voices and shouts woke her in the early hours of the morning. Instantly, her mind went through countless scenarios of what had caused the commotion, not the least of which was a fear that, despite Gerard's assurances, they had in fact been found. She sat up to find Kent already standing, his fists clenched tightly at his sides. Elizabeth and Gerard stood mere inches from one another in the throes of a furious debate.

"….understand what you've done for me," her mother said, forcing herself to lower her voice and speak in a measured tone. "But I will not let my children be used."

"Kent, you understand what I'm trying to say, don't you?" Gerard huffed, clearly frustrated by Elizabeth's failure to see reason. "You can see how this is necessary."

Angelina watched Kent clench and unclench his hands over and over while he thought. He seemed torn between the two spies standing before him. "I…do understand," he said, but from where Angelina sat, the words seemed forced and almost painful. "But you can't just expect everyone to go along with it like there aren't any risks."

"Of course there are risks!" Gerard exploded. "Your mother has risked everything for years. I've risked everything, and there are plenty of other spies who risked and lost even more. Saying this can all end without taking a risk is impossible, but sitting here and doing nothing will only buy you a little more time before all of this catches back up with you."

"Angelina," her mother said, noticing for the first time that she had woken up. How they assumed she could sleep through the screaming, Angelina had no idea.

"What's going on?" Angelina asked, but no one seemed eager to answer. "What's all of this about?"

"It's nothing," Elizabeth said quickly. "Gerard and I were just having a difference of opinion," she finished pointedly, glaring daggers at the man who had saved both their lives.

"A difference of opinion?" Angelina stammered. "If something is happening, I want to know about it. I deserve to know about it," she finished adamantly.

Her mother groaned, pushing her fingers into her temples as she tried to massage away her obvious headache. "Angelina, this isn't something I want to involve you in anymore."

"I'm already involved...Elizabeth," she finished, fixing the woman with a hard stare. Angelina had no idea what she was getting herself into, but after all the lies and secrets in her life, she wanted to know as much as she could. For better or worse, she needed to know.

"Well, Angelina," Gerard began, turning towards her and extending a hand to help her off the couch, "I'm fully aware of how traumatic things have been for you, but like I was just telling your mother, I think I have a way to bring all of this to an end."

"You can?" Angelina asked, almost daring not to hope.

Gerard smiled, a cross between both concern and victory. "Would you like that, Angelina? Would you like to go back to your old life without having to spend your days looking over your shoulder?"

Angelina hesitated. It was like the man read her thoughts, but something about the way he led her along with her words brought an unbidden image of sheep being led to slaughter.

"That's enough," Elizabeth said firmly, but Gerard seemed to be past listening to her at this point.

"What I'm proposing is a way to free not only you and your brother from all this, but your mother and I as well. This has been going on for so long, and the end is finally in sight."

"That sounds like a good thing," Angelina spoke, feeling more defensive with every word the man uttered. "But what does this have to do with me, and what's the risk Kent mentioned?"

"Well," Gerard began as Kent and Elizabeth fidgeted in front of her. While her usually calm and collected mother seemed agitated, Kent, on the other hand, seemed distraught. The anguish on his face was that of someone truly torn. "Even after all this time, we still don't know what it is Pentworth's hiding, but we do know he's hell bent on *cleaning house*."

"Which is precisely why we should be going to ground and putting as much space between him and us as possible," Elizabeth interjected.

Gerard's face grew dark and he looked like he was about to shout at her, but just as quickly his muscles relaxed and he rubbed a slow hand down his cheek. "I'm tired, Elizabeth. I've been too tired for too long, trying to make things right."

"I know how you feel," Elizabeth agreed, but Gerard shook his head.

"Do you? Do you really?" he asked. "I don't know how much more of this I can take, and it's time you stop running."

Angelina took a cautious step backward, bumping the backs of her legs against the couch as Elizabeth and Gerard held each other's gaze in yet another nonverbal conversation. She turned towards Kent, hoping for a sign, a warning, really anything that would help make sense of what was happening in front of her.

"He wants to use you as bait," Kent blurted, seemingly no longer able to contain himself.

Angelina's jaw dropped as she watched the three people standing around her. Bait? How was she supposed to be bait? Why would that even work? Sure, she wrote a book over which people were obviously willing to kill, but that was something else entirely, wasn't it?

"Tactfully put," Gerard said in a dull voice. "But he's not entirely wrong. If we can draw Pentworth out, we can finally put an end to this."

"Still, that doesn't guarantee Pentworth will come himself. We would need to use something he couldn't afford to pass up," Elizabeth argued, moving to stand between Angelina and Gerard.

"That's exactly why I need your daughter," Gerard pressed. "I have something in mind that would get Pentworth to come running right for us."

Elizabeth shook her head, pointing a finger into Gerard's face, but at that moment, something in Angelina broke free.

"Stop, Mother," she said in a low, firm voice. Surprise filled the room. Did they really expect so little from her? "Tell me what you want, Gerard. I can't decide until after I know, but I won't have my decisions made for me anymore." Kent turned away from her, but Elizabeth's eyes never left Angelina's. Maybe she only imagined it, but behind the fear and anger, she thought she saw pride.

"Very well," Gerard said, taking hold of the conversation while he could. "The reason you're so deeply involved in this is because of late Madame Lockridge. She was never a spy, but was a trusted ally to many people, not just your mother. No one knew Madame had documented all the secrets passed before her until after she had you start her memoir. These secrets were kept in a sealed chest Madame had thrown in the lake just after the war ended."

"How do you know all this? She never mentioned the chest to me."

"Lord Pentworth had one of our team investigate her. We always knew what was going on. She was never a real threat, and we knew where the chest was. It turns out Madame's daughter-in-law Charlotte had the chest removed from the lake some years ago, possibly to ensure her own protection, but we don't know what she did with it. Lord Pentworth somehow retrieved the key, which he recently sent to Elizabeth. His message was clear. Find the chest or consider yourself marked."

Angelina gasped in horror. "So that's what the key is for."

"What do you know of the key, Angelina?"

"Only that those insane Cartwells on the train were looking for it. Everything finally makes sense. The book I wrote is damaging, but if anyone can produce the contents of that chest, it will back up every word I wrote."

Angelina couldn't help but feel a redundant sort of glee. How exciting to have written a tell-all that could go down in history as the greatest book ever written, only to accept that it placed her own family in the heart of all the danger.

"How do we fix this?"

"We send a copy of the book to Pentworth with a note written by you, claiming to know exactly where the chest is and thanking him for the key he sent your mother. This will infuriate him, because he won't know your priorities. He won't know if you dare to release the contents to the authorities at the risk of your mother's freedom."

"But of course I wouldn't. That's obvious."

"Not to him. Pentworth is devious but irrational. Things have never been so far out of his control before, and he won't take any risks now. Trust me, he will want to meet with you. That's where your mother and I come in. We each take a vantage point and one of us will take him out."

"Make that three vantage points," Kent chimed in. "I want a hand in this."

Everyone stood deadly silent. The plan was laid out bare, and the biggest risk was for Angelina. She looked at her Mother, Gerard, and lastly Kent, and she saw strength amongst them. She trusted these people despite everything, and felt that her only way home to Henry was the dangerous and bumpy road ahead.

CHAPTER 35

Beth felt for the three letters at the bottom of her purse. They were all there; strange, that such fragile paper contained the fortune of her family—whether that be in money or in name.

When Madame had last contacted her to request that Angelina stay with her and Eugene in London, Beth was at first reluctant. She knew an outsider might quickly notice the way her husband barely said hello to her, the way her husband only brushed against her by accident. Yet when Beth learned how close Madame and Angelina had become, she couldn't help but wonder if Angelina would open up and tell her something of importance one day.

For years, Eugene had been searching for something on the estate, like he believed there was a small fortune to be found. Beth found it odd but insignificant, and as far as she knew, Adrian didn't know about it. That man was always so consumed with Charlotte, who did nothing of any use except for indulging in frivolous things. Beth understood that was part of Charlotte's appeal; the woman was beautiful and light-hearted. She laughed frequently, and any irritation could be calmed by diamonds, love notes, or even petite fours. Beth, a typist herself, couldn't imagine that life, and often waited to see if Adrian would realize

284

there was someone better for him.

Still, Beth had climbed the social ladder with Eugene—awkward, over-analytical Eugene. It was her job to protect him now. It was her job to protect their fortune.

"Darling?" She let her voice echo throughout their home and arch its way back to her. *Good, he isn't home. No one is.* Beth made her way to the office and sat at Eugene's desk. She appreciated that it was always kept tidy, and quickly pulled out the letters from her bag. The first letter stated that Rupert inherited everything. Beth decided she could easily change that. His aunt's handwriting was easy to copy, and Beth was a quick study. She stretched out her cramped hands and practiced on an envelope until her handwriting matched that loopy, elegant scrawl. She found it hard to pen Madame's confessions, but if she wanted this plan to work, she knew she had to stick as closely to the original letter as possible.

For good measure, she would give Rupert a little bit of the fortune, knowing she couldn't falsify the hospital documents, but the rest she believed should be equally divided between her husband and Adrian. The original letter was now redundant. It was easy enough to destroy; she simply struck a match and watched the letter burn until it was no more. Beth knew Henry had seen the letter and would question this new version. But she was sure she could cloud him with enough doubt to believe his own eyes. Sweet, innocent Beth—why would he question her?

Beth couldn't imagine Angelina settling down with Henry. True, to a younger girl's eyes, Henry looked dashing and accomplished. He was handsome and had an interesting way of ending all of his sentences in a question mark. But his clothes were ratty; he spoke only of what he read in newspapers and the poetry he had memorized in school. His eyes were watery and his moustache not well-maintained.

"Oh, he's perfect," Angelina had said to her once over tea.

And Beth, always the perfect hostess, said, "Of course he is, Angelina. A girl would be lucky to end up with someone like him. Do you want more sugar with your tea? Milk?" Beth knew she could have served Angelina boiled water, and Angelina, in her haze, would not have noticed the difference.

Skipping past the second letter, which contained the hospital documents proving Rupert was Madame's son, she eyed the third letter curiously. The last letter was written in sloppier writing, as if Eugene's aunt had been nearer her deathbed when she wrote it. The letter was difficult to read. She held it up to the light, but that complicated the viewing. She concentrated so hard that her head ached. It was as if Madame had slipped in and out of some sort of code. She could make out some of it and make out an idea of what it said, but it was draining.

"I see you have a letter from my late aunt, there," Eugene said.

"What, dear? When did you get home? You startled me."

"Why, you were so concentrated on that note there, you didn't hear me come in. I mean, I could have been a stranger walking into our home, and you wouldn't have known. You need to be more careful, Beth. You didn't lock the door, either. I've told you to always lock the door. You know that."

"Of course, dear." Beth was now very confused. The plan wasn't for Eugene to see the letters but for Henry to ensure they were acknowledged in a bit to help Angelina. It was clear Henry didn't trust Eugene, but now that her husband had returned home, her options were slim. She could see the interest peak in her husband's demeanor, and she wondered how he would react to the news of the inheritance. She knew better than to talk of Angelina, though; she still very much cared about her friend's safety.

"Do these letters have something to do with her estate?" he asked.

"They were found under a bust in Madame's living room. It seems these are the last letters your aunt ever wrote before she tripped on the rug."

"Oh, yes, just like Uncle Jonathon. It is a cursed rug, no doubt. Look through our humble abode. Not one rug on any floor. Look."

"Yes, I know, Eugene. I've begged you for at least one. It gets so cold here during the winter."

"That's why we have tea, my dear. Besides, a rug is not a good thing. Just ask my uncle and aunt. Wait, you can't, because they're dead. Not to nail a point into the ground, but there you have it. Speaking of having it, why do you have these letters?" Eugene was very sharp and looked directly at his wife with severe scrutiny.

Beth fumbled for words, settling on a lie that would stroke her husband's ego. "Well, Henry found them when he visited the estate today. He gave them to me at work, as he wanted to ensure you received them, trusting you would see to it that Madame's wishes were carried out."

"Really? Hand them here." Eugene removed his glasses and set them on the table by Beth. He stood over her while he read. Beth was glad he didn't notice her holding her breath as he read the re-written letter. "Why, this handwriting is a little more elegant than I remember, but I suppose she was on her deathbed, and my memory is a little foggy. So, Rupert is her son."

"Doesn't that surprise you, Eugene? It's a bit of a scandal for the family, if you ask me."

"I suppose, but that boy always had a certain look about him. It was…it was the eyes. He looked a little like my aunt in

287

the eyes, and I never trusted him. He was strange and oddly possessive. Not a chap you would like to meet on a corner in a dark alley. I had wondered why she kept such a strange fellow, but he being her son, I suppose that all makes sense. Adrian won't be happy to hear he has a brother."

"I thought you and Rupert had become friends."

"Hardly. Besides, he's vanished into thin air. I haven't been able to reach him, and he proved to be somewhat of a disappointment."

"She wrote the three of you should share her inheritance."

"Yes, I just read that. It is awfully generous of her," he remarked with an edge of bitterness. "I don't remember her as a particularly generous woman, but you know, people change. It does sound like her. She was both direct and elusive." Eugene sat down and steadied his nerves with a neat brandy from the side unit.

As he looked across at Beth, he sighed deeply. "I struggled reading the last letter. Did you manage to make out what it said?"

"Yes, just about. Madame always used some silly code to converse with her friend Elizabeth. It seems in her last moments she'd lost touch with reality somewhat, but from what does make sense, it's easy to assume the rest."

"What does it say?"

"It says, *The silver key is beneath the tree, by the lake where the sun sets ever so gladly before the darkness takes it away. It is this key that will unlock many secrets, some so grand as to be catastrophic. I trust my son Rupert with this key, which will open the chest resting at the bottom of the lake.* It's quite cryptic. Do you think it's some sort of joke?"

"It so happens that Adrian found that chest many years ago. He never did find the key to open it, and I suspect he gave up. I have no idea if he even still has it."

"Do you think it would be unwise of us to tell him it contains some very delicate information?" she asked. "Perhaps it's wisest to let sleeping dogs lie."

"Or perhaps not. It's unlikely to have anything to do with us. Let's try to get that chest opened, and see what we find." Eugene smirked, surprising Beth.

She looked closely at her odd, analytical husband, the one who didn't exactly make her pulse race, and she wondered if she really knew him at all. Had she been living with a stranger this whole time? It seemed Eugene saw this as a last opportunity to spite his cousin, and now Rupert too, for the way they had betrayed him.

"But we don't have the key," she said.

"I will call the estate and have someone dig for it where Madame has written it's located. But I suppose we need to see if we have the chest first. What do you say? Shall we call my cousin?"

"I think it's better to call Charlotte," Beth added, eyeing her husband.

"Why's that?"

"Charlotte would never realize the importance of something like this. She would barely care. While she remembers some details, like how to match fabric to a suit, she doesn't pay attention to others. How else would you explain how she can live with a man like Adrian for so long without realizing what he does?"

Eugene nodded. "Let's call her, then. But Beth?"

"Yes, dear?"

"You better let me make the call. Darling, I love you, but you can't hide the contempt you feel for Charlotte in your voice. She may not catch on to some things, for whatever reason, but she will catch that. Angelina was your friend without asking. Charlotte has always wanted to be your friend, but you have denied it. I should wonder why, but I won't wonder too much. I'm not sure I want to know the answer."

"What do you mean, Eugene?"

"How long have you been in love with my cousin, Beth?"

CHAPTER 36

The plan was in motion. Angelina had given a copy of her book with the thank you note inside to Elizabeth. Being the only one who even knew Lord Pentworth's true identity, Elizabeth was the only one who could ensure he received the book. No one was sure if this plan would work, or if this was even the right thing to do, but it had been formed out of desperation, not intelligence.

Angelina sat in the café across from the apartment, thinking about everything that could happen next. She was to lure a man she didn't know into the line of fire. She would have to lower the guard of a leader of spies and assassins enough to walk him directly into a trap. Elizabeth and Kent would be too far away to get to her should something go wrong, and she wasn't sure Gerard would try to help her even if he had the opportunity. The more Angelina thought about the plan, the more she realized that the brunt of the risk fell upon her. She wasn't sure she could carry that weight.

Fortunately for her, Lord Pentworth gave her little time to second-guess their idea. Within three hours of sending him the book, the owner of the café, Clementine, handed her a letter. "A man told me to give you this, chérie," Clementine said.

"Did he say who he was?" Angelina tentatively grabbed

291

the letter and glanced over the exterior for a moment.

"Non, just said 'give this to her' and then left. He was young, but his eyes looked cold enough to freeze your coffee." Clementine shivered.

"Thank you. I'm sure this will say who it's from, anyway." Angelina laughed nervously. She thought again about how insane this whole thing was, and for her to be at the center of it.

"Not a problem. Enjoy your coffee." Clementine left with a smile.

Angelina ripped open the letter and quickly unfolded it. On the page was simply written, *Lockridge Estate. 5 pm tomorrow. Bring the key.* Angelina put the letter in her pocket and made a mad dash for her apartment. They had little time to spare.

***

Adrian Spratchet sat in an oversized leather chair in his study. Across from him, on the edge of a mahogany table, perched James, wearing his black trench coat.

"What's the plan, Adrian? You've just been sitting there grumbling and writing for the past two hours. I would think eventually you'd come up with something you wanted to use," James said with a half-smile.

"That's why I don't pay you to think, James. When I come up with something good, I'll say full words."

"What are you waiting for, anyway? The book's already out, people are reading it, they're enjoying it, and then they move on. I don't see why you're pulling your hair out on this one."

"Because not everyone will move on. Not when there's

292

someone out there who knows it's all true. Questions will be asked, and that author will sing. And then everyone will know the family they read about is my family. *My* family, James. Do you know how hard I've worked to make a name for myself? Become as successful as I am today without my family? I've spent years distancing myself from those people, their secrets and lies, because if I didn't, my family's past would have held me back. All I've done to get my head above ground is about to go out the window because my selfish mother had to offload before she died. Twenty years of digging my way out, only to be dragged back down." Adrian displayed real emotion, something James was not used to seeing from him.

"I didn't realize—"

"Don't."

Ester knocked on the door to the study before entering quietly. "Mr. Spratchet?"

Adrian quickly flipped on his 'everything is fine' switch and turned to face Ester with a smile. "Yes, Ester, what can I help you with?"

"You have a visitor. I tried to tell him to wait by the door until you allowed him in but—" Ester was cut off by the man opening the door and entering the study.

With ice-cold eyes, he almost glided across the floor as he walked. Despite his controlling presence, he moved as if he was barely in the room at all. He wore a jacket with the lapels up and a top hat. His manner of dress covered all but a glint of his facial hair.

"Sorry for the intrusion, but I'm a busy man." He positioned himself in the center of the room.

"As am I," Adrian responded. "So if this isn't important business, I'd like to get back to mine." He studied the somewhat familiar stranger but couldn't place him.

"You have concerns about a book, its author, and the evidence confirming your connection to the piece."

"How did you know that? And who are you, for that matter?" Adrian didn't like being out-witted by anyone. It killed him enough not knowing who the real author was, and now he had to deal with this man, who appeared to know everything when Adrian knew nothing of him.

"For now, call me Pentworth. But more importantly, I know where the author of that book will be tomorrow at five in the evening."

"Then the next thing out of your mouth better be to tell me where that is." Adrian hated being strung along. He knew this man held all the power in this situation. Adrian also had a hunch this stranger only told him these things because he was going to use him in this situation; even with that suspicion, Adrian had no choice but to play along. He had no answers. This man had all of them.

"Lockridge Estate. I'd like you to be there by three. Bring your friend as well. I imagine it might get a bit messy." Pentworth headed for the door.

"Why are you telling me this?" Adrian called. "Why is the author going to my mother's estate?" He ran to the door, but Pentworth had already left, almost vanished.

Adrian ran his hands through his hair, took a deep breath, then pointed to James. "Get Charlotte. Tell her we're going on a trip."

"You're actually going to go?" James wasn't the smartest guy in the world, but Adrian noticed the turn of the man's lip, as if he too smelled the stink of this whole mess.

"I have to."

***

"Wake up, Angelina." Elizabeth nudged her. She had slept the entire train ride back to England. After learning about their deadline, the group did not have the time for the same level of precaution as their trip to Paris, but they still managed to arrive with little incident.

"We there already?" Angelina tried to shake the sleep out of her eyes.

"Almost, but we don't have a single moment to waste when we get there. If Pentworth wants to see you at the estate at five, we need to be there and ready for him before then." Elizabeth held her daughter's hand tightly as she spoke.

"How do you know I'll be able to do this?" Angelina hoped her mother would provide her some much-needed strength, but the cold, white-knuckled grip on her hand did little to give her confidence.

"Because I believe in you, Angelina. You will simply meet him outside, then draw him inside. Kent, Gerard, and I will each be waiting. Keep a bit of distance between the two of you, and we'll take care of the rest."

"But this man is supposed to be, you know, high up. You make this sound so easy. Won't he be ready with extra precautions?"

"Possibly, yes. That's something we have considered. But the only way to counter that is to bring more people into the fold. Gerard and I know people, but if Pentworth gets a whiff of a large operation, he won't show, and we will always be looking over our shoulders." Angelina simply nodded.

The train slowed to a steady stop, and the cabin door opened to Gerard on the other side. "It's time to go," he said. Elizabeth nodded and helped Angelina up to exit the train.

Now, with just under two hours to spare, was the time for

caution. Elizabeth, Gerard, Kent, and Angelina made their way to the estate. They avoided main roads and tried to remain as out of sight as possible.

When they arrived, it was just past four. No lights shone out from the building; the staff must have been sent away. Gerard made a thorough inspection. "It doesn't appear anyone's inside. We can go."

Elizabeth hugged Angelina. "We're going inside, dear. This will all be over soon. I believe in you." She kissed Angelina on the forehead.

"I can do this." Angelina took her mother's hands off her, then gave it a little squeeze before turning around to wait for Pentworth in the driveway. Kent, Gerard, and Elizabeth enter the house and close the door behind them, leaving Angelina on her own.

Angelina sat on the front steps of the building in which she'd been employed for years. The place had a very different aura than she remembered. The classy, elegant, bright place of her memory was now drab and dour—a house of death. In the distance, Angelina could see the lake, covered by the shadows of the surrounding trees. Part of Angelina had been excited to return. The estate had been her home for so long, and she had fond memories of both Madame and Rupert here. But sitting there in the eerie silence, she counted down the minutes until they'd be able to leave. She could never come back here. Life had moved too far forward for that.

"Miss, I believe you have something that belongs to me."

Angelina looked up to see a man in front of her. "Lord Pentworth, I presume." Angelina stood and rounded back her petite shoulders, portraying courage and strength as she faced him.

"Correct. It's been quite some time since we've seen one

another."

"I don't believe it's ever happened." Angelina had to keep her mind on the task at hand and didn't want to be diverted by Pentworth's mind games.

"Trust me, my dear, we've met. But this isn't really about warm reunions or friendly chit-chats, is it?"

"No, I suppose not. You want something I have, and I want something you have." This wasn't part of the plan, but Angelina had seen a unique opportunity.

"What could I have that you want?"

"Answers. There's still so much I don't understand about you, my mother, or Madame Lockridge. I know you do understand these things, and if you want the chest, you're going to tell me everything you know." Angelina took a deep breath. She had never felt this rush of power before. She held the situation in her hand. Not her mother. Not Lord Pentworth. She did.

"And what makes you think I know anything?"

"You worked closely with my mother, and if you're this concerned about what's in that chest, you must know your fair share about Madame Lockridge as well." Angelina stood her ground as the man stepped closer. She wasn't going to be intimidated.

"Very inquisitive. It's only fair you receive answers. I'm surprised your mother held them from you. I can be a bit more agreeable than her, though. Let's discuss it inside."

Angelina panicked. If Lord Pentworth went inside, he would be dead and she would be back where she started. She ran to the door and pushed the door closed just as Lord Pentworth turned the knob. "There's a lot of bad memories in that house for me. Why don't we talk out here?"

"Don't be ridiculous, girl. It's freezing. I wouldn't want

you to catch pneumonia while I'm boring you with the truth." Lord Pentworth moved Angelina's hand, opened the door, and stepped inside. Angelina sighed and waited two seconds before following. Lord Pentworth walked toward the center of the room and turned back to look at her. "Isn't this better?"

A gunshot echoed through the house. Lord Pentworth was still standing, and a split-second later something fell from the second-floor balcony. It smashed through a glass table in the living room, and only a brief moment existed between the chaos and the realization that the man lying on the floor was Kent. She ran to him, then looked up to see a man standing on the balcony, smoke still rising out of the gun barrel.

Angelina screamed and Lord Pentworth grabbed her from behind, pulling her into the center of the room. Her violent jerking and kicking did nothing to loosen the man's grip. He pulled a gun from his pocket and placed it at Angelina's temple. "You might as well show yourself, Elizabeth."

"Mother, no. Get out of here!" Angelina cried.

Elizabeth appeared from her vantage point. "Don't you dare harm her."

"I'm changing our arrangement. Bring me the chest or your daughter dies. You have until dawn. I'm serious this time, Elizabeth. Just ask Gerard."

Gerard tumbled down the stairs, at the top of which stood Adrian. "Our deal still stands, Pentworth?"

"What benefits me, benefits you, Adrian. I guarantee it."

"James, you'll finish it?" Adrian looked to James.

"No need." Lord Pentworth swiftly removed the gun from Angelina's head and deftly pointed it at Gerard. Another shot rang out, and Gerard dropped to the floor before Pentworth returned the hot muzzle to Angelina's head. The gun barrel sizzled her skin, and Angelina's squirmed again in a futile attempt to escape. "If I don't have the chest by the time the sun rises tomorrow, you'll get to bury both of your children, Elizabeth." Lord Pentworth exited with Angelina gripped tightly in his arms, James and Adrian close behind. They left Elizabeth behind in the house of death.

CHAPTER 37

Nox Harrington slammed his fist down on his desk. He'd just gotten off the phone with the Chief of Police, who still declared they had no idea who killed his best friend, Delores Du Pre.

After twenty years of hard-hitting journalism, he knew one thing. Never trust what the police have to say. Grabbing his coat, he downed what was left of his stone-cold coffee and headed for the door to do his own investigating.

The night guard at Delores' office building unlocked the door for him. Having been to see Delores countless times before, he knew the man's face well.

"Just picking up some papers Delores left for me," he told the guard.

"Any idea what happened that night, sir?"

"Hopefully someone will come forward with information. I don't suppose you saw or heard anything? The guard's blank look was all the answer Nox needed. "I'll return shortly," he shouted, making his way to the lift.

The full moon shone brightly through the window as Nox opened the door to Delores' office. He could see why she never wanted to give it up. *That view is incredible,* he thought, staring out at the Thames to see the boats moving up and down.

Switching on her desk lamp, he searched for clues. He could tell the police had already been through the desk, but again, one could never completely trust the police. He smirked at the thought.

Searching the trash bin, he noticed, wedged in the corner, a piece of a telephone memo from Heather to Delores regarding Angelina. He left the office for Heather's desk, finding the telephone memo pad and grabbing a pencil. He softly shaded over several pages of the pad until he saw Angelina's name once more. The process continued until the message underneath revealed itself.

Norman Finley called regarding your new book. He has a possible claim against it by the real author, Angelina Waters. He's sure this is just nonsense, please call him back. Also, did you receive his manuscript?

Nox ripped off the note and stuffed it into his pocket. He returned to searching Delores' office, under the desk and in the drawers, finding nothing. Pushing back her chair, he lifted a corner of the fur rug to find that one of the carpet tiles had been cut. Grabbing a ruler off the desk, he thrust it into the crevice and slowly wiggled the tile free. There, underneath, was nestled a safe box.

The key, Delores. Where the hell is the key? Nox pulled himself up into Delores's chair. His eyes swept the office again, looking for any hint of the thing he needed. He picked up the only framed photograph on Delores's desk of a well-dressed, older gentleman, possibly her father. Delores had always kept her private life very private.

"Damn you and your secrets, Delores," he shouted, smashing the picture frame down on the desk.

Sighing, he grabbed the frame to throw it in the bin. A silver key fell into his lap.

"You've got to be joking. I knew you would help me, you sly fox." He winked at Delores' portrait hanging on the wall.

Opening the safe box, he pulled out a stack of papers and envelopes. He ripped apart what remained of the tatty brown envelope, revealing manuscript entitled, *My Loves, My Lies, Our Deaths.*

Nox flicked through the dirty pages, some torn and crumpled. He gulped. *Delores, what did you do?*

***

Henry hailed a taxi and headed to Eugene and Beth's house. He needed to retrieve the letters from her before anything happened to them and they fell into the wrong hands. Paying the driver, he walked briskly up their path, raising his hand to the door knocker. Yelling greeted him from the other side of the door. He decided instead to sneak around to the back of the house, then climbed through the kitchen window and tiptoed up the hallway.

"How dare you say I'm in love with Adrian?" yelled Beth.

"I've done everything I can for you, and it's never good enough," Eugene shouted back.

"Do you know how many people have died so I could get my aunt's money? After all the deaths, after I killed her, I still have to share it with a bastard brother I never knew Adrian had. Not to mention 'His Highness' Adrian himself, who never loved his mother as much as I did."

"What?" snapped a stunned Beth. "You never loved her, either, you filthy liar. You just wanted her money. I'm going straight to Adrian to tell him what you've done, and that I know where the key to the chest is. And yes, I lied! I *am* in love with

Adrian. He's the man I want in my life, not this weak excuse standing before me."

"Weak? Rupert is weak. I asked him to do one simple thing, kill Angelina, and he couldn't even get that right. They are the weak men, here."

As Beth ran for the front door, Eugene grabbed her from behind and dragged her back into the sitting room. He snatched the lamp from the side table and smashed it over her head. Beth fell to the floor, and the man's hands wrapped around her throat. Henry watched in horror as Eugene strangled his wife, Beth's eyes rolling back in her head as she gave very little struggle. Eugene stood, snatched the letters, and dashed out the front door to slam it shut behind him.

Henry ran into the room, kneeling by Beth to feel her barely perceptible pulse. He lifted her in his arms and carried her outside, frantically hailing a taxi to take them to the hospital.

Henry paced up and down the hallway outside Beth's hospital room. Having hardly slept in the last twenty-four hours, he used the solitude of the hospital to think about everything he'd just learned. He had no idea where Angelina could be, but he did know her life was now most definitely in danger. Henry was training to be a lawyer, nothing more. He knew he was no match for the likes of Eugene or Adrian.

"Sir, she's awake. Would you like to see her?" enquired the nurse.

Beth looked as white as the bedsheets, except for the purple welts around her neck. Henry had to look away. She pointed to the writing pad and pencil beside the bed, and when he handed them to her, she scribbled a few lines and turned the pad to face him.

Charlotte. Chest. Before Eugene. Quickly.

Henry looked into Beth's frightened eyes and nodded.

***

Charlotte wandered down the narrow, cobbled streets of the small village not far from Madam Lockridge's estate. Adrian had whisked her out of the city for a spur-of-the-moment, romantic weekend at the quaint hotel in which they always stayed. Even though her husband's relationship with his mother had been difficult, he still enjoyed visiting the place of his childhood. He had brought James along with them, whom Charlotte had never liked but was loyal to her husband and helped him 'carry out business' at the estate.

She paused outside an antiques shop and admired the pocket watches in the window, thinking they would make a fine present for her ever-doting husband. Then her eyes fell on something else. The small bells chimed as she opened the door. An elderly gentleman with small, round spectacles greeted her.

"May I help you?" he enquired.

"That silver key in the window. May I have a look at it?"

As the man retrieved the key, Charlotte admired the various ornaments, vases, and paintings around the shop. *I feel as though I've seen these before,* she pondered.

"Here we are, Madam. Antique late-1800's silver," he pronounced smugly.

Charlotte removed her gloves and rolled the key through her fingers, recognizing the engravings, identical to those on the silver chest Adrian had pulled from his mother's lake.

"May I ask how you came upon this?" she enquired politely.

"A young boy came in with a collection from the Lockridge estate. He told me he'd found it all while fishing in the

304

lake. I thought he may have worked for her when she was still alive," he replied cautiously.

Regaining her composure, Charlotte couldn't believe her luck. She offered the man twice what he wanted for it on the grounds he kept no transaction of the purchase.

Wrapped in brown paper and safely in her purse, Charlotte made her way back to the hotel. Retrieving her room key from the bellhop, she gasped. There on the front desk, in black and white: *London Agent, Delores Du Pre, Found Murdered!* Charlotte quickly grabbed the paper and rushed to their room. Closing the door behind her, she eagerly read the article. Du Pre's assistant had been found as well, both women having been shot in the head. "Oh, Adrian, you fool!" she whispered.

Waiting at the bay window of their third-floor suite, she could just make out in the distance the chimney stacks of the Lockridge estate. She recounted fondly that day, a few years back, when Adrian had taken her out rowing on the lake after a particularly stressful afternoon with his mother. As he'd pushed them out from the shore, his oar had hit something solid. Keen to investigate, Adrian had stripped down and jumped in, ever eager to impress her. The chest had been wrapped in animal skin and weighted down with rocks. They never told Madame Lockridge they had found it, and never knew for sure if it contained anything. Charlotte had overheard Adrian asking Henry to look for the key at the estates. *No wonder he never found it,* she thought. *And now that I have the key, Adrian will never know what truly lies inside.*

Charlotte did love Adrian; if she didn't, he would have died a long time ago. As a young woman who was bored with finishing school and longing for adventure, she had found that and more in the spy world. Then one single mission had changed her life, her orders given to kill Adrian Spratchet. After following Madame into the fabric shop in town, it hadn't taken long to charm Madame over and secure an introduction with Adrian, who'd been even easier to lure. When the time came to fulfill her orders, she realized she had fallen in love with the rogue and confessed to him her secret life. The only way she could save him was to marry him and keep watch over him, all the while looking for the chest and key. That was the deal she had brokered with the agency, for both their lives. With the key to the chest, she could now turn its contents over and finally live a normal life.

The sound of car doors slamming jolted Charlotte out of her daydream. She opened the window and watched James walk to the end of the lane, scanning the main street then glancing back to the car. Adrian waited for him at the trunk. Together, they lifted something out. Charlotte gasped; it appeared to be a women. The men walked her to the side-door of the hotel.

"What the…"

Knocking softly on the door in case Charlotte was napping, Adrian found her sitting on the edge of the bed, facing him.

"Charlotte, darling, I am so sorry to have kept you. Mother's was exhausting, as usual."

Pulling the newspaper from behind her back, she thrust it into Adrian's hands without a word.

"Charlotte, I'm as surprised as you are. What an awful thing to happen to them." He looked pleadingly into her eyes.

Charlotte walked to the window, keeping her back to him. "Adrian, after everything I've done for you, this is how you repay me. All we ever wanted was to keep the past buried, and now it's on the front page of every newspaper in the country. Did you not think people would just move on, forget about it? Your ego has always been your downfall, and now I have to help you clean up another mess."

Another knock at the door caused Charlotte to whisk around, her hand on her heart. Adrian took long strides across the room and opened the door to find the hotel-owner's wife on the other side.

"Sir, I have a telephone call for you downstairs. The woman says it's urgent."

Following the owner's wife and her husband down the three flights of stairs to the foyer, Charlotte eyed her husband with thinly set lips. She couldn't let show the waves of anxiety flooding through her.

"Hello?" Adrian said, answering the receiver. "Yes. Yes. What?" he shouted. "Stay there. I'm leaving now!"

***

Elizabeth ran down the stairs to Kent. After not finding a pulse, she cried out in pain, holding him to her chest. She should never have come back here to this house of horror. Dragging herself up, she stumbled toward Gerard, who she found fortunately still breathing. Ripping open his jacket and shirt, she inspected the gunshot wound in his chest. The bullet had gone clean through. She briskly tore her skirt into strips, padding both his chest and his back, then wrapped strips around his chest to hold it in place. She dragged him to the wall and propped him up against it. Then she ran to Madame's study to call for help, her hands trembling as she dialed the one number she never wanted to use.

***

Charlotte had no idea why her husband had to suddenly dash off back to their home with James in tow. "Some type of plumbing issue," he'd mumbled when he came back up to fetch his coat. Not expecting him back for a few hours, Charlotte decided to find out who that women was they'd deposited in James' room. Applying tactics she hadn't used for years, plus some rouge lipstick, Charlotte made her way down to reception.

Spinning a nice yarn to the young bellhop about how her husband had bought her a gift but the driver had accidently taken it to his room by mistake, coupled with some eyelash batting, she was soon on her way up to the third floor, James' room key in hand.

She listened at the door for a moment before sharply turning the key and entering the pitch-black room. Using the light from the hallway, she found the bedside lamp and turned it on. *His room is almost too neat,* she thought. Making her way towards the ornately carved wardrobe, she rattled both locked doors. Pulling a hairpin from her head, she proceeded to pick the locks, smiling as she heard the click. It had all come back so easily. Pulling both doors open, she found the woman inside, her hands and feet bound. Pulling the cloth bag from the woman's head, Charlotte turned the woman's head towards her by the chin and removed the gag.

"If you value your life, you will tell me exactly what you're doing in this cupboard," Charlotte whispered. The woman only stared back at her with curiosity. Charlotte's voice came out sharper the second time. "I suggest you start before they return."

She quickly poured a glass of water for the woman and held it to her mouth. She couldn't believe her husband would be so cruel, even if he was protecting her.

"Let's start with who you are. The truth."

"My name is Angelina. You need to get me out of here.

Please. I have to get back to my mother," Angelina begged.

"Back where?"

"To the Lockridge estate. Something awful has happened and I need to get back to my mother."

"What where you doing at the Lockridge estate?"

"Meeting some people. I used to work there, years ago, and they wanted something I hadn't returned."

"What did they want?"

"A key I had that opened a chest, and now they want both. I have no idea where to even start looking for this chest, but they will kill both my mother and me if I don't find it for them."

Charlotte decided to fish a little. "Sounds as though this chest contains something for which people are willing to die. Any idea what's in there?"

Angelina shrugged, looking at the floor. "Madame Lockridge liked to keep secrets. Secrets were her life. Then I came along, and for some reason she decided she could trust me. I believe the secrets were too much of a burden to take to the grave. I helped write her memoir, but it's been stolen."

Charlotte offered her more water "I see."

"You may have heard of it. *'My Death, Your Greatest Masterpiece.'*"

Charlotte was struck by a violent fit of coughing. "I don't think I have read that yet."

"Madame Lockridge was murdered before I could truly finish it. I will never find this chest or who really killed her. Please untie me, I beg you," Angelina whispered.

Charlotte paused, looking at Angelina's tear-streaked face. "I will try to help you, but for now I need to leave you in here. Just do whatever those men tell you to do."

She then closed the wardrobe door to a few shouts of objection, locking it behind her, and rushed up to her room to grab her coat and purse. Dropping James' key at reception, she hurried out of the hotel and hailed a taxi. She needed to be quick before Adrian returned.

***

Adrian and James walked in on Eugene as he ripped apart the bedroom mattress with a knife. "What the hell are you doing? Have you lost your mind, man?" Adrian screamed.

"Don't talk to me, you cuckold! I should have known all along you two would run off together." Eugene's words slurred.

"Are you drunk? What the hell are you talking about? Grab him, James."

James tackled Eugene, knocking the wind out of him, then dragged him off the bed and pinned him to the floor. Adrian grabbed the knife that had clattered to the floor and held it to Eugene's throat. "Now, start from the beginning. Don't leave anything out."

Eugene burst into sobs like a frightened child. "I deserved the money, not you or your bastard brother. I'm the one who took care of your mother. Isn't that what you always wanted, but were too gutless to do, Adrian? Don't worry, I made sure she felt exactly what it was like for her dear Jonathon."

"What brother?" Adrian spat.

Eugene laughed. "Yes, Adrian, you have a half-brother named Rupert. It's all here in the letters." Adrian searched Eugene's pockets, unfolding the crumpled letters which he read in silence. "Oh, and the best bit is," Eugene added, "your darling wife Charlotte has the chest with all the secrets. She took it from right under your nose, probably when you were too busy pandering to her every need. Maybe that's why my wife is in love with you, because you're the fool here."

310

Adrian sat on the edge of the bed, shaking with fury. He glanced at James and gave him the signal. James withdrew the gun from his coat and put it to Eugene's head. He pulled the trigger.

"Get him in the car. We'll dispose of him on the way back to Charlotte."

Adrian made his way to his study and pulled down the wedding portrait of Charlotte and himself. Opening the safe behind, he reached all the way to the back and pulled out the package wrapped in newspaper. Ripping it open, he stared down at the cardboard box filled with small stones from the driveway. Throwing it across, the room he screamed out Ester's name.

Ester scurried up the stairs to his study. "Ester, I will pay you triple to clean up the house right now. I want everything returned to order before I get home tomorrow. Do you understand?" Ester nodded quickly. "And pack up my wife's belongings, everything she owns. She will not be returning with me."

As Adrian reached the car, James motioned for him to come to the trunk. He opened it just enough for Adrian to see what was inside. Underneath Eugene's body lay Henry's.

"I caught him in the hallway on my way out, spying on us."

Adrian slammed the trunk closed. "Better grab a bigger shovel then, James."

***

In the back of the van, Elizabeth held Gerard's head in her lap as they made their way to the safe house. With Angelina kidnapped, no key, and no chest, Elizabeth found herself at the end of the road. She touched Kent's face, who lay beside her.

311

You never deserved this, either, she whispered, gently stroking his cheek. The van lurched to a stop before reversing slowly. The back doors swung open to reveal Mr. and Mrs. Cartwell with a stretcher ready to go.

"Looks like you've gotten yourself into a right state this time, Elizabeth. He's waiting for you upstairs, second door on the left."

Elizabeth knew this day was coming, and she only had herself to blame for it. She should never have accepted that assignment back in the marketplace in Paris, but how could she not? Her children's lives had been in danger, something Elizabeth had fought so hard to avoid. Undecided, she had made her way back to the apartment to tell Charlie they would need to move back to London for a while. When she'd arrived at the apartment, the door had been kicked in, the place trashed. Elizabeth hadn't even bothered going inside; she already knew what had happened. The decision had been made for her.

Feeling like a naughty school girl climbing the stairs to the headmaster, Elizabeth slowly turned the doorknob and entered the room. With his back toward her, it was hard to judge what the outcome was would be.

"Elizabeth, please sit down. Would you like a cup of tea?"

"Yes, I suppose," Elizabeth stammered.

Never turning to face her, he walked to the small kitchenette and filled the kettle. "Tell me, Elizabeth, why are we here? You said you had everything under control, but clearly that's untrue. You remember our deal, don't you?"

"Yes, I remember the deal. You only allowed me to leave MI6 duties here if I then became a double agent with the Habsburg Secret Intelligence. I gave you names and bodies of those who'd targeted our own. I became a nurse to gather information, I risked my life in Austria and Russia for this country. I had no idea Madame Lockridge was a mole. I know I entrusted her with too much, and now I'm paying for it in full."

Slowly pouring the water into the teapot, he continued, "And your children are now paying the price. Or, shall I correct myself? One already *has* paid the price for your foolishness. You dragged Gerard back in and almost had him killed. To top it off, you now have Lord Pentworth as we know him, head of the Habsburg Secret Intelligence, after you."

His movements over the kitchenette were slow and deliberate. "You must have known you were could never promise two intelligence agencies the same information and follow through, especially when its information I hear you do not have yourself. No key and no chest. What in the world are you going to do?" He turned toward her and brought her a china cup and saucer. "Here you are just the way you like it."

Elizabeth took it from him. "Thank you, brother."

***

Charlotte ran through Madame Lockridge's estate towards the lake. The full moon lit her way along the banks, keeping her from stumbling into the water. She'd hidden the chest here, thinking it would the last place anyone would ever look. As she made her way along the jetty, she counted the wooden boards. At twenty, she knelt and wiggled the board in front of her, having already loosened the nails months ago. Pulling it free, she rolled up her sleeves and felt around for the end of the rope. She pulled on it with all her strength until the box and rock weighing it down were almost on top of her.

She grabbed the box and returned to the driveway, stopped by the sight of sudden headlights coming towards her.

313

Ducking behind the shrubs, she heard Adrian's and James' voices. She had to creep along the hedge until she was almost opposite the car, watching the men retrieve two bodies from the trunk and drag them into the horse stables. They wasted little time there, getting quickly back into the car and speeding away from the estates again.

Charlotte hesitated. After all these years, she now had both the chest and the key. The options of delivering them to her boss, being done with it and living happily ever after as the wife of a barrister, or seeing what her husband truly plotted tore her apart. She resigned herself to just taking a peek before making her way back to town.

Careful not to scare the horses, Charlotte walked along the rows of stables, peering over the top of each gate as she passed. With four down and two to go, she braced herself for the unexpected. A wet nose greeted her in the dark from the next stall, and she stifled a scream. The silence was interrupted by a moan coming from the last stall. After a quick, reassuring breath, she opened the last gate to see Henry Parker, the lawyer who'd helped her husband with the estate paperwork, struggling with the ropes with which he'd been bound.

"Mr. Parker, what the devil are you doing here?" Removing his gag, she noticed the blood running down the side of his temple.

"Henry, please," he said, then fixed her with a blazing glare. "Charlotte, they've killed Eugene, and when they return they'll kill me as well."

***

"James, grab the girl. I'll get my wife." They pulled into the side lane of the hotel. The sun would be rising in a few hours, and Adrian wanted to take care of Eugene, Henry, and now his darling wife before the exchange. As he strode through the lobby, the bellhop cornered him before the stairs.

"Your wife has not returned from her outing," he explained.

"You mean, my wife is not here?"

"No, sir. She left a few hours ago."

"Ah, I see. Well, if you see her, be sure to tell her to stay in the room until I return. If possible, try to prevent her from leaving again. The poor thing's a little muddled in the head and sometimes forgets where she is." Adrian dug in his pocket and handed the boy two pounds. "I trust you will remember to do this."

***

Elizabeth stared into her teacup, unable to make eye contact with her brother. She'd always thought she was an only child, until one day at the market a man approached her, claiming to be her brother. Over tea and cake, he showed her photos of their Austrian parents and told her she'd been given up for adoption and taken in by the Heathburns in England. He was the one who recruited her into MI6 and taught her how to speak fluent German and Russian. He was the one who had helped broker her a deal so she could travel abroad to meet her real parents in Austria, leaving Angelina to grow up without fear. She'd never imagined she would meet someone there as cold and calculating as Lord Pentworth.

Her skin crawled just thinking of the way he used to touch her. Once Elizabeth realized he was in love with her, she would have done anything to get away, including promising him the information he wanted. He had followed her ever since, after discovering she had left him and disappeared. She could only hide for so long. She remembered his last, cruel note he'd left with the key only too clearly. '*Don't you know, you can't ever go home?*' She'd fallen for his trick, thinking he'd found the chest. But he never had it, and maybe that wasn't even the key.

A brisk knock at the door startled both Elizabeth and her brother. "Enter," he commanded.

Mr. Cartwell entered. "Sir, we've just received word from the agents stationed around Madame Lockridge's estate. A woman was seen entering the stables and carrying what could be a chest. They watched her remove it from the lake's jetty."

"Get the team assembled now. We need that chest before the sun rises and anyone else gets their hands on it. We're going to retrieve Angelina and finally take care of Lord Pentworth."

***

Nox Harrington had not moved from Delores' office chair. As he read the final page of the manuscript, he picked up the telephone.

"Chief of Police, please," he barked. "Yes, sir. Nox Harrington again. Remember when I delivered those Christmas hams to the precinct? Well, now I need a favor. What's the last known address you have for an Angelina Waters? I'll be there in an hour. Yes, of course I can get hams for this year."

On his way to meet with the police chief, Nox couldn't help but feel this original story may just be the real deal. What was Delores thinking? She obviously hadn't realized this herself, and it cost her her life. After a brief, terse greeting with the Chief of Police, he grabbed the address from the sergeant at the front desk and tracked down the house. The door was wide open when arrived.

As he glanced around the sitting room, it appeared a confrontation had taken place there. He searched the house, but no one was home. This was another dead end. Nox left the house and walked out to the street, lighting a cigarette. Then he had the sudden, distinct feeling someone was watching him.

Turning back around, he spied the neighbor's lace curtain twitching closed. He stubbed out his cigarette resolved to have a chat with the neighbor as well. "Good evening, Madam. Nox Harrington of the Daily Legal. I don't suppose you know the whereabouts of your neighbors. I'm currently helping the police with an investigation," he lied, showing his press identification.

The short, plump woman eyed him cautiously. "There was a hell of a commotion the other evening, and I saw a man carrying a limp woman away in his arms. She did not look to be in a very good way. He hailed a taxi and left. No one has returned since."

Nox thanked the woman and bid her farewell. *Off to the hospital, then*, he thought.

He used the same story on the receptionist at the hospital. His charming demeanor could win over even the most matronly woman, which she definitely was. She remembered a woman brought in by a lovely young man, and the nurse told him the woman may have died had he not gotten her there when he had.

The woman in question was dozing when Nox knocked on the door to her room. "I am so sorry to startle you, Madam. Nox Harrington of the Daily Legal. I believe you may know something about this." He pulled out the tatty manuscript and put in down on the bed beside her.

The woman started to cry, then reached for her notepad and pencil.

***

317

"Charlotte, you really need to untie me," Henry pleaded. "They could return any minute. Your husband and that mad henchman of his are killers. Adrian knows you have the chest. I have no doubt they'll kill you, too."

For once, Charlotte couldn't deny the truth she heard. She wondered if she could explain her side of things to Adrian; perhaps then he would see it differently. Or perhaps not. Untying Henry's hands and feet was enough proof of her decision. They ran from the stable and straight into the headlights of a car.

Adrian and James, with his gun pointed at them, stood beside the vehicle. "What do we have here?" said Adrian, walking towards them. In a swift move, he grabbed Charlotte by the hair and pulled Henry by the arm. Then he threw them both into the car, and they drove up to the house, James' gun trained on them all the while.

***

Angelina was inside the house already, the cloth bag still draped over her head. James sat Henry and Charlotte down with her, all back to back with their hands and feet tied. They'd been placed on the rug on which both Jonathan and Madame had so crudely met their fates. The chest rested on the sideboard, and James pointed his gun at all three.

"This is how it will go," Adrian began. "Henry, you're going to die. Sorry, ol' chap, but you know too much, and I'll not have my life ruined by you, of all people."

Bending down toward Charlotte, Adrian continued. "You, my dear wife, will also die. I have decided you're too much of a burden, but thank you so much for bringing the chest with you." He turned to Angelina. "And last but not least, Angelina. You

318

were the one who truly had the potential to ruin me. Due to your mother's—shall we say, shortsightedness—it seems Lord Pentworth has his own designs for you both."

They heard a car coming up the driveway. Adrian stepped outside to meet Lord Pentworth, leading the man and his goons into the living room.

"Even without Elizabeth here, I think you'll agree I have more than delivered for you."

Walking with his hands tucked neatly behind his back, Lord Pentworth moved around the living room, stopping in front of an oil painting of Madame and Jonathon. "I think I'll make that decision. It's what your mother and father would have wanted."

"I don't follow," Adrian said, the confidence in his voice fading.

"You don't remember me, do you? I don't suppose you would. You never had much time for the servants here. I used to watch you from the garden, and even then I wanted to strangle you." One of Lord Pentworth's men stepped behind Adrian, wrapped a length of rope around the man's throat, and pulled.

Charlotte screamed. "Stop. Don't hurt him. I have the key. I'll give you the key, just don't kill him. It's in my purse."

The man released the tension of his weapon and Adrian dropped at Charlotte's feet. Pentworth's man retrieved Charlotte's purse and handed it to Lord Pentworth.

Then the lights in the house went out. Lord Pentworth ran to the window and peered through the curtain. He instructed his men to search the house and kill anyone not in the living room.

Angelina struggled frantically to untie her hands, clawing with her nails at the rope. The sound of gunfire seemed to come from all around the outside of the house. Suddenly, she smelled her mother's perfume, and the bag was removed from her head.

Elizabeth untied her feet and hands, and they crawled out of the living room on their knees. In the dining room, they stop under the large mahogany table.

"Henry's still out there," Angelina whispered. "I have to get him."

"No," Elizabeth said softly, grabbing Angelina by the wrist. "I'll find him. You stay here." Angelina couldn't think about anything besides making sure Henry was safe, so she did as she was told and stayed put.

Elizabeth crawled back to the living room, hiding behind chairs and the few tables in the dark. The sun had almost risen, and she glimpsed Lord Pentworth's shadow beside the window. She reached into her coat, steadied her aim as she crouched on the floor, and fired a shot.

Blue flashing lights made their way up the driveway. Lord Pentworth's men bolted, deciding not to the bother with the woman clutching a gun, and headed into the fields with MI6 on their heels.

Angelina crawled out from under the table and rushed to the living room. Henry sat stone-still, his wrists still tied, and she quickly fumbled with the knots to get his hands free. He only looked at her blankly, still in shock, and she helped him slowly to his feet. When she turned to look for her mother, she found Lord Pentworth lying on the floor just beyond her, clutching his chest with one hand and a pistol in the other. Angelina froze, thinking that this couldn't possibly be the end.

She turned her head at the streak of movement in the dark, watching helplessly as Elizabeth jumped on top of the man, knocking the gun from his hand.

***

Angelina set down the copy of the Daily Legal beside her freshly squeezed orange juice. Thanks to Beth, Nox Harrington had alerted the police, who'd arrived just in time. Adrian was now behind bars for his part in the murders, his wife Charlotte now in a mental institution. The MI6 had done their best to help her, but the government felt her loyalty had swayed.

Henry had returned to work, and on his first day back had a special package waiting for him. Inside was one letter from Madame Lockridge, leaving the Lockridge estate and all its contents to one Angelina Waters. Henry had an inkling Beth, who had since disappeared, had something to do with it, but the uncanny resemblance in hand writing offered Henry all the chances he needed to push the document through legally.

"Madam, a parcel has arrived for you." Ruth handed over a small brown box wrapped in red and white string. Angelina took the box with her up to the study, passing the silver chest now resting on her mantelpiece in place of the ornamental bust.

From the postcode, she knew it was from her mother. Eagerly tearing open the package, she found a letter and a small, red velvet box, which contained the diamond and emerald ring.

My Darling Angelina,

Gerard and I are so very happy here in France. I found the letters and ring when I packed up the apartment. The letters you had yet to decode were about my true family in Austria. This I told you before I left. This ring belonged to my birth mother, who gave it to me as a token of good luck. I now wish to give it to you. May it stay with you always.

Love, Elizabeth

Angelina walked towards the window in the study and looked out at the lake, as Madame had so often done herself. She'd buried Rupert alongside Madame and Jonathon, knowing it was what they would have wanted. The silver chest gleamed in the morning sun, reflecting patterns of light that danced across the walls. The contents had been passed over to MI6—names, dates, and times, cataloguing all the spies Madame had double-crossed, including Elizabeth. And there was nothing more now to that story.

Angelina returned to the desk and sat in front of the typewriter. It was now time to tell her own.

The End

Noir Extra Dark

By

Jason Pere

His eyes were wide open, but his pupils had been reduced to this size of pinheads. *He must have been terrified when he died,* I thought. I had seen my fair share of dead men over the years, even helped to make a few on occasion. I had learned how to tell the ones who saw it coming from the ones who bought it in blissful ignorance. The eyes gave them away. Wide and glassy, like a deer unable to tell the bright light barreling towards it belonged to a speeding car. Being a detective, you learned to read the story told by the dead. Broken fingernails meant a struggle; body face-down meant they'd been taken by surprise; scuff marks on the ground meant someone had moved them afterwards.

I didn't know why the locals had called me in on this one. A man wearing a shopkeeper's apron laying behind an empty cash register and sporting a bullet wound in the chest, this crime solved itself. It was an open and shut robbery gone wrong. Some two-bit, first-time triggerman who knocked over the wrong grocery store.

"Poor fella. Not much to go on here," said the patrolmen watching the body and waiting for the detectives to finish questioning potential witnesses, who all stood gawking outside the shop. He must have been new to the department. I remembered what it was like in the early days on the force. I thought I could make a difference. I thought I was one of the good guys.

"Well, it's the usual mess. Nobody saw nothing," said Detective Daniels as he flipped to a fresh page in his notepad and made his way over to the body. The short, stocky man had only been a beat cop at the time I left to be a privet investigator. His charcoal pinstripes did not fit him as well as standard-issue navy blue, but I could tell he was proud of himself for landing a detective badge. "What do you think, Miller?" Daniels said to me, trying his best not to sound utterly without a clue.

I thought about giving the two other men a hard time with a lengthy run around of questions to which they should have known the answers but didn't. I decided against it; I had a bottle to get back to. "I think this is a waste of time. You don't need to bother looking for the guy who did this. He'll find you," I said, not wanting to completely spell it out for these two numbskulls off the bat.

"Huh, what?" they blurted in unison.

I took a deep breath before painting them a portrait of the punchline to a joke whose set-up nobody had heard yet. "In about a week, maybe two or three, the precinct is going to get a call about a dead body found washed up on the back of the Hudson and stuffed in a shipping crate. Your dead man is going to be missing all of his teeth and fitted with a very tight necktie made out of elevator cable. He's also going to be the poor sap who knocked over this store."

"Wait, wait. How can you be so sure of that, Miller?" Daniels said to me while he folded his arms across his chest. The patrolmen smirked and imitated Daniels' gesture, silently voicing his skepticism as well.

"This block is in the middle of Boss Antione Donnello's territory. All the shops around here are paying him for protection. Nobody connected would hit this place. No worthwhile crook would rob a place on a Tuesday. They would wait until Friday when the cash drawers are full with a weeks' worth of business." I looked down at the cold, pale body of the shopkeeper once more. "This was a job by some first-timer with real bad judgment. Donnello's guys are going to find him, if they haven't already, and show him what happens to people who step out of line around here." There were several quiet moments while my words precipitated through the layers of wax and stupid clogging the ears of Daniels and the greenhorn.

"I see you haven't lost your touch there, Miller," came an all-too-familiar voice. I knew it was Lieutenant O'Neill before I turned around. When I spun to look, I saw the Lieutenant making his way through the front door of the grocery, confirming with my eyes what my ears didn't want to believe. He wore a freshly pressed brown suit and dark red necktie. His shoes still had the sheen of new polish on them. O'Neill had always kept his appearance antagonistically tip-top. It was one of the many things I disliked about the man. One of the only reasons it had been so nice to be cut loose from the precinct was that I didn't have to suffer this lousy sack on the daily anymore.

O'Neill came up beside me and flashed that phony, fake smile of his that made me want to empty a bottle of Kentucky bourbon down my mouth and break the bottle over those oversized pearly whites of his.

"I should have figured you were the reason I got called down here to waste my time with this case," I said as politely as I could. The stench of O'Neill's heavy aftershave attacking my nostrils made diplomacy difficult.

"Just trying to do a favor for an old friend is all. I figured you could use some extra cabbage for that—what do you call it—consulting fee of yours," O'Neill said with a grin as wide as the tie he wore. "What with all the business you *aren't* doing out on your own and all."

"That's real swell of you to look out for my bankroll like that, but I'm doing just fine, O'Neill." I turned and headed out. "If this turns into a real case, give my office a call and I'll happily do some *consulting* for the department."

O'Neill caught up to me as I turned the knob to the front door of the grocery. "Hey, I don't mean to bust your chops about it. I just know it isn't easy to make it as a private investigator." He put his hand on my arm and it was all I could do to keep myself from slugging that little worm in his mug. "You're still a fine detective. I spoke to the Captain, and there's a badge waiting for you back with the department the second you dry out."

"Gee, thanks for that. I really mean it, from the bottom of my heart. You just reminded me that it's after five and I'm still sober. Goodbye, O'Neill." I turned and walked out. I could understand my wife had to leave me; I was a drunken train wreck who was scarcely ever home, and my mind had never been with her even in those rare moments when my body had been. It was the fact that she left me for that piece of garbage O'Neill that plunged the knife in deep.

Underneath the overcast Manhattan sky, I felt the first drops of rain falling. My pockets being filled with nothing but lint and desperation meant I was going to get wet on my way back to the office. I fumbled around in my coat pocket for my cigarette case. I figured I could at least smoke one before the rain took away any hope of enjoying that little vice. My case was empty. *Damn,* I thought.

Around the eighth block I trudged past, I felt the threadbare heel of my left sock voice its objections to my pride as it gave way and opened a proper hole. I was not about to take O'Neill's charity, or any charity for that matter, but I needed to do something fast. I ran the numbers in my head again, hoping somehow it would change things, but I knew the score. Unless I got something big and juicy passed my way, I would have to close my doors at the end of the month, and that was only ten days away. It looked more and more like I might just have to take up my brother-in-law's offer to move into their spare room.

As my foot chafed itself raw against the stiff leather of my shoe, I took comfort in the mantra that had seen me through the days of my failure as a private investigator. *Its tomorrow's problem tomorrow. Now's the time for a drink.*

I stomped up the steps to the sorry-looking building which housed my office. Normally, I would have tread with a lighter step, but lucky for me it was Tuesday. That meant my landlady was out at BINGO. I don't think I had it in me to withstand another one of her scoldings for the back-rent I owed her. I was glad to be out of the rain; it had toyed with me at first.

I was about halfway home when I could have sworn I saw sunlight break through the clouds and the sporadic drops of rain subside. In the end, I had been soaked. Less than three blocks from my front door and the sky opened up and dumped out like an egg crashing down onto a hot skillet.

The hallway smelled of mold, booze, and regret. Nobody chose to live in this building; we were here because our hands had been forced. None of the tenants had the money to live anyplace worth living. My office was on the top floor. No elevator meant I had five flights of stairs to greet me whenever I returned to this crumbing tower of plaster and dirt. The daily climb alone was reason enough to stay at the bar for another round. Five flights of stairs to walk up may have also been a contributing factor to my firm's inability to attract any worthwhile clients.

My soggy feet sang a sad duet as they pressed down on the creaky, tired floorboards of my hallway. Even though it was pouring rain, the sun was still out. I didn't care; today was over for me and a bottle and glass would soon send me on my way to tomorrow. I rooted in my back pocket for the key to my office. I was about to take down the sign I left hanging on my door that read "Out of Office", but I stopped myself. I was kidding myself if any new business was about to come knocking at my door, so I didn't want to advertise the fact that I was in. That would only invite nosy neighbors and an obnoxious landlady. I did not want to have to contend with either, not while I had a bad case of sobriety I was trying to remedy.

I withdrew the key from my pocket and slipped it into the lock. I went to turn it but I was thrown off guard when I felt the door was already unlocked. I knew I had locked it when I left earlier that morning—at least, I was pretty sure. I had only a small hangover from the night before and I always made it a point to lock the door behind me. Something was amiss. My first thought was that my landlady had let herself in to do some snooping and perhaps subsidize the rent I owed her with anything of value on which she could get her little rat claws. Then I thought of her boney little knees and hunched back. There was no way she would take on five flights of stairs for the prospect of coming up empty-handed, and she had to know that if I had anything worth hawking, I would have already done so.

Someone I didn't know had come to call, I was sure of it. It dawned on me that they might still be inside my office. I unsnapped the small piece of leather keeping my Smith and Wesson forty-four snugly secured in the holster on my left side. I had no idea who might want to waste their time on a drunk like me, but I wasn't about to be caught with my pants down. I tucked my revolver into my jacket pocket and kept my right hand on the trigger while I opened the door to my office with my left.

"I was beginning to think that perhaps you are too drunk to find your way back, Monsieur Miller."

I was blown away by the thick, silky French accent greeting me on the other side of the door. She was a brunet with dark, deadly eyes and vicious red lips. Both colors stood out like a priest in a brothel against the contrast of her milk-white skin. Delicate and sleek, she stood in a long black dress and a matching hat with a fishnet veil to cover her eyes. She took a nonchalant drag from the long cigarette holder in her left hand. It gave me time to see the smooth, supple legs peak out from the slit in her dress.

I was mesmerized. I had seen my fair share of pretty dames, but this one—she was something else. I couldn't say we'd ever met before, but something about her was like a dream from my past. She was the kind of woman who would get you killed. I knew that just by looking. I didn't care that she broke into my office, that I didn't know her name, or that she seemed to know more about me than any reasonable person would care to know. One look at her, and the only thing I wanted to do was sit her on my desk, hike that dress of hers up over the lacy garter belts I envisioned clinging to her thighs, and feel her wrap those long legs around my wait as she proceeded to show me the face of God. I was in big trouble.

I swallowed hard and forced myself to say something just

to break the silence and get the blood flowing someplace other than between my legs. "I'm like a bad penny, doll. I always turn up." I barely recognized the voice coming out of my own mouth. "I didn't mean to keep you waiting. I just had no idea I would have company."

"I do not wait too long. I try and find a drink to pass the time, but all your bottles are empty."

"That's because I hide the good stuff, sugar." I slid in behind my desk and reached up under it to find the bottle I had designs on polishing off. It was cheap booze, truthfully. By good stuff I had meant a bottle that still had something left in it, but she didn't need to know that. I placed two glasses on the desk and began to pour, but she stopped me.

"Wait. I have something special I was saving to, how you say, butter you up," she said as she pulled a polished silver flask from her clutch.

"Sweetheart, you show up looking the way you do and bearing gifts, I have to imagine you have one hell of a favor to ask," I said as I took the flask from her and poured two drinks. "First thing, though. You know who I am, but I never drink with a stranger. What's your name, doll?"

"You may call me Josephine, Monsieur Miller," she said with a flutter of her shadowed eyes.

"My pleasure, Josephine," I said as I raised my glass to her. I knocked back the drink. It tasted like a long summer night's stroll along the Atlantic City Boardwalk over ice. "Now, what brings you to my office?"

She smiled a lethal smile, her lips turned in a cruel and twisted sneer. "Oh, that is for me to know and you will find out very soon, I think," Josephine said as she put her drink down on my desk untouched. The fact that she didn't partake of the beverage might have set off alarms had everything else about this moment not reeked of unusual.

"I may be a private investigator, but that hardly means I like a mystery," I said. The drink burned in my belly and I loosened my collar at the newfound heat boiling inside me. "Kitten, I'm not the sort to be ungrateful when a beautiful woman decides to knock on my door, but I have to believe you didn't come here and wait for me just to share a drink."

"You are right, Monsieur Miller, but you see, I already have everything I need from you now." Josephine turned her back to me and shot me a look over her shoulder. "I think I say au revoir to you," she said. The woman glided towards my office door.

I was at a loss. Today had started with a case about as complicated as a box of rocks, and now I was scratching my head at a situation I could read about as well as I could read braille.

"Wait a second…" I started. I made to go after her, but I found myself on my knees. My heart raced like a Kentucky Derby champion and I had the Fourth of July blasting in my head.

Josephine stopped at my doorway and looked back at me. "My pardon, Monsieur Miller, but I think you do not drink what women you only just meet give you," she said. "You also should be careful who you call a, oh, what is word you used? Nutcase."

"Nutcase? I never called you a nutcase."

"Oh no, monsieur, you do not call me this. But you did call my sister Matilda this terrible name."

It hit me in the face right then—the memory I should not have forgotten. "Matilda," I said hoarsely. I had been on the force less than a year when I had given testimony that had seen the city lock up a sixteen-year-old girl and throw away the key for stabbing her parents to death with a carving knife. I had called the girl a nutcase in open court, along with a number of choice

331

names, all in front of her eleven-year-old sister—a girl named Josephine. "Your sister was crazy. She killed your parents."

"No, *we* killed our parents. *She* just got caught." Josephine let out a heavy breath and spoke again, but this time it seemed more directed at herself. "I think I will like killing in this city." And then she was gone.

I fell to the floor, and as I lay there, the last thing that passed through my mind before the blackness came was that I had been right about Josephine the second I had seen her standing in my office. She was the kind of woman who would get you killed.

ARK
Chapter 1

The two suns of Santelli Minor peeked over the horizon in perfect harmony to the east. Mearon, Santelli's only moon, faded from view in the west as the light of the suns effortlessly erased it from the mauve sky. Dirk Forrett walked across the coarse red sand, taking in the spectacle for the umpteenth time and still totally amazed.

It was another new planet, and while the *Ark* was his home, he took solace in sampling the breathable, untouched air for himself. He reached down and patted his Chihuahua's head, who was named after Dirk's favorite zoologist, Alfred Kuhn. "Well, Kuhn, time to get back. Another day, another specimen. Or fifty."

Unlike his idols Achille Valenciennes, Adison Verill, Alexandre Brongniart, and of course Alfred Kuhn, Earth's first zoologists in the eighteenth and nineteenth centuries, Dirk traveled the cosmos for his research. As a planetary zoologist, he spent his existence identifying, categorizing and studying the behaviors of creatures from dozens of planets.

333

The man looked more like a high school kid, much too thin to betray his twenty seven years. His pocket laden pants sagged with the weight of their cargo, and he belted them just above his navel to compensate. He readjusted the trifocal horn rimmed glasses, more than occasionally the butt of fashion jokes, underneath his jet black crew cut. He strode casually back to the parked ship, stark against the background of one of Santelli's mountain ranges. He reassured himself with a quick pat to the breast of his long-sleeved shirt. It was his favorite shirt, completed by two pocket protectors holding pens, tweezers, and an array of carefully wrapped instruments designed for probing, separating, and clipping for specimen analysis.

Kuhn scratched at Dirk's leg, hoping to be picked up and held tightly as was the routine whenever they boarded. Holding his only true friend, Dirk marveled at the sight of his creation. He couldn't believe that he had actually designed and overseen the building of that ship. He had dreamed of such a craft back in his early college days, when traveling to distant planets had barely become a reality. His single goal back then had been to create a ship that could be piloted to newly discovered planets, a home base traveling laboratory to temporarily store the new lifeforms they discovered and document them. He was blown away by the speed of those technological advancements, and how quickly his dream had been realized.

Kuhn clamored up Dirk's chest and buried his head in his owner's armpit. The huge door on the side of the ship lowered to the ground and out danced a monster of a man. Dirk struggled to get the dog back on the ground.

"You stay right there, Kuhn. Here comes foul-mouthed Franklin."

Franklin was nearly seven feet tall under a head of dirty blonde hair that curled down to the middle of his back. There wasn't an ounce of fat on his herculean body, and Dirk was certain he felt the ground tremble under the man's feet as he sprinted the forty yards toward them.

Breathing as if he had just awakened from a nap, Franklin said, "Hey, Dork Ferret, have I got some cool shit for you!"

"Why do you insist on calling me that?"

"What the hell do you want me to call you?"

"You could call me Doctor Forrett, or Dirk, or anything else fitting your superior. Not Dork Ferret." Dirk expected the exploration pod to already have returned by the time he and Kuhn finished their walk, but he could have done without Franklin's greeting.

"Well now, you're touchy today," Franklin mocked. "Hey, check this little fucker out. This'll blow your shit back a couple hundred feet."

Franklin tilted his head back and looked to the sky as he dug around in his shirt pocket. He fished out a four inch long, zebra striped worm with an enormous head, and presented it to Dirk. "Ain't he the cutest thing? And check this shit out." He grabbed a pebble from the ground and laid it before the worm in his hand. The worm swallowed the pebble, and the lump it created in the middle of the worm's body disappeared rapidly. The creature then excreted a small amount of a black, soil-like substance. "We threw him in a terrarium filled with pea gravel. This little fucker ate every last pebble and pooped out this dirt shit. Your hot little assistant Jenny, she says the stuff is just like peat moss. I bet this guy could shit a cubic yard of this stuff in the course of a day. Just think about it. You turn a couple hundred thousand of these guys loose in the Sahara and the next thing you know you got fucking farmland."

Yes, Dirk's dreams for an exploratory ship had come true, but that ship had unfortunately not been fully equipped with all the most brilliant minds.

"Franklin, you have to stop carrying specimens around in your pockets. You have no idea what it's capable of."

"Quit being such a pussy. There ain't no harm to him. He's cute. Eats rocks and shits soil." Franklin stroked the top of the worm's segmented body.

"Cuteness is not an excuse to keep specimens in your pocket." Dirk swallowed and adjusted his glasses once more.

Franklin's eyes lit up. "Hey, speaking of cute, I've got another surprise for you." He grabbed Dirk by the wrist and half dragged him with surprising speed back toward the *Ark*. Kuhn stood where he had been left and shook feverishly.

Dirk tried to pull free to turn back for a check on Kuhn. Franklin kept an iron grip on his wrist, but the zoologist managed to catch a last fleeting glimpse of his four-legged friend, curled up now in the sand. He called quickly to the dog, but Kuhn made no move to follow.

The *Ark's* cargo hold housed cages and specimen carriers, and served as a place for the pod to unload its findings after each excursion. They stopped in front of the first occupied cage and Dirk blinked at the reptilian specimen inside. Franklin eyed him for any sign of shared excitement, but Dirk only stared.

"C'mon, Dork. It's a fucking lizard! They apparently feed on the pebble-eatin' zebra worms. Hot Jenny cut one open and found a bunch of them in his gut." Again, Dirk had nothing to say. How many times did he have to tell the man that he would not respond to any information that was not properly documented in an initial report?

Franklin sneered and raised a thick eyebrow. "I got an even better thing to show you, Dork." He spun off down the walkway, lined with cages that increased in size the further they walked. They kept the larger specimens in the back of the cargo hold before transferring them to the *Ark's* research facilities closer to the bridge. Franklin skidded to a halt in front of a large wire enclosure and grinned. "Huh? Do these things qualify as cuter than shit or what?"

Dirk looked into the enclosure in horror. 'Cuter than shit' was not a phrase he would have chosen, but his mind was now too muddled with potential consequences to correct the description. ""Franklin! You've disregarded the first protocol directive. We don't take humanoid specimens, don't engage them at all unless the safety of the *Ark* or her crew is threatened. That is a 'no exceptions' mandate. What were you thinking bringing them aboard?"

With his standard amount of over-exuberance, Franklin defended his actions. "They didn't utter a sound. They didn't even move. We found them sitting cross-legged and silent just as they are now. They're so beautiful." He opened the door to the enclosure and stepped in. "Come on, touch one. They're so soft, like…I don't know. Does exquisite describe them? Hell, if you gave them a pole to dance around, you could probably hire them out at strip clubs. Fucking gorgeous!"

Despite his colleague's obtusely crude comment, Dirk couldn't argue with that observation, found something strangely alluring about the serenity of the sleeping humanoids. They may have been female under the wavering layer of what seemed to be scales *and* fur that looked so strangely soft. But he couldn't ignore the protocols, nor the gut instinct that something was wrong here.

"Get out of there," he yelled at Franklin, feeling his face flush hot. "Close the door. Lock it. And set the quarantine field!"

"Really? They don't even move, haven't moved once since we found them. They're perfectly harmless." Franklin reached out a hand in an effort to stroke one of the creatures.

337

"Do it."

Franklin froze, staring at the humanoid creatures, and gave them a weak wave. "Sorry about this," he whispered, then left the large wire cage and did as Dirk had ordered.

Dirk reached up and grabbed Franklin's shoulders, tried to exude more authority than panic as he stared up into the wide eyes of the security officer who was definitely not a scientist. "Where is everyone, Franklin? There are usually a lot of people here when the pod returns with specimens. Is there something you aren't telling me?"

Franklin looked up and down the corridor. "Maybe they're in the cafeteria. We had a helluva morning."

"Get up to the bridge and tell Johnson to sequence a pod for an unplanned excursion so we can return these creatures. What quadrant of Santelli did you find them in?"

"P13-04."

"Oh, you can remember *that* piece of information, you overzealous..." Dirk took a deep breath and briefly closed his eyes. "Just do it."

"Yes, sir," Franklin said, and ran off.

Dirk watched him round the corner of the hold, then slid the thick glasses back up his nose. He'd go to the lab and speak to Jenny, see what she could explain of the situation. As much as he wanted to entirely blame Franklin, he had a feeling the man wasn't alone in this dangerously careless blunder.

T h e *Ark's* hallways were unusually silent, unusually empty. He couldn't justify passing the lab to get to the cafeteria just to check Franklin's hypothesis. But he soon became quite aware of the fact that he hadn't passed a single person in the normally bustling corridor, had not been greeted by his usual team of scientists on the way out of the *Ark's* cargo hold. He felt his heart racing, and it was not from exertion of the walk he took

338

every day.

At his arrival, the lab's hydraulic door hissed open and Dirk stepped very slowly inside. The room's walls were lined with shelves and a few specimen carriers, and two stainless steel counters ran the length of the lab, leaving an open isle down the middle. There in that isle sat almost half the ship's personnel, positioned in a perfectly straight line one after the other. They sat cross-legged, their hands folded in their laps, unmoving. Their eyes focused on something ahead of them he could not see, glazed over and absent. They did not blink, did not look at him, and he thought of the humanoid specimens in the cargo hold.

Stepping around his closest associate, Dirk whispered a few names in wary greeting. There was no response, not even when he raised his voice in what was supposed to be a command. It sounded only like terror. He ran down the line, saw Jenny's brunette ponytail, and hovered over her. "Jenny? Jenny! Wake up!" He grabbed her by the shoulders and gave her a violent shake. She didn't move a muscle.

Dirk weaved through the line of sitting personnel, throwing his arms in the air and shaking clenched fists. He felt like he was going to explode and finally roared the first expletive of his life.

"Shit!"

ABOUT CW PUBLISHING HOUSE

CWPH was founded in 2015, dedicated to publishing CWC novels. Due to numerous requests, we have opened our doors to submissions from completed collaborative novels, and will work exclusively with collaborative novels written by two or more authors. CWPH has also arranged a number of Anthologies, with more to come. To learn more about our books and our authors please visit: www.cwpublishinghouse.com